A FRACTURF

MW01257053

THE BLI(

Scott Kaelen

2018

For Electa

Scott Kaelen writes primarily in the genre of epic fantasy. His debut novel, *The Blighted City*, achieved semi-finalist in the SPFBO4 contest in 2018 and finalist in the Independent Audiobook Awards in 2020, His follow-up novel, *The Nameless And The Fallen*, reached the quarter finals in the 7th Self-Published Fantasy Blog-Off. Scott's interests include etymology, prehistoric Earth, the universe, and reading and watching science fiction, fantasy and horror.

Amazon
Twitter
Goodreads
Facebook Profile
Facebook Page

"Death cures all diseases passed on by dead things."

CHAPTERS

THE FRACTURED TAPESTRY

Night Of The Taking (2015)
The Blighted City (2018)
The Nameless And The Fallen (2021)

OTHER LANGUAGES

Portuguese: *A Cidade Sinistra (2019)*
Italian: *La Città Di Sventura (2019)*
French: *La Cité Ravagée (2019)*
Dutch: *De Verwoeste Stad (2019)*

The land of Himaera has learned much since the Days of Kings, foremost being the price of greed and ambition. To challenge the gods is to invite their wrath. The ire of Morta'Valsana was brought to bear upon King Mallak Ammenfar of Lachyla, cursing the over-reaching monarch and his sworn subjects. For ever thereafter, Mallak's name was synonymous with avarice and excess, and the city of Lachyla became known as the Blighted City. It was a pockmark on the land of Himaera, an eternal remnant of the wrath of the goddess, and a place to be avoided at all costs...

From *A Codex Of The Ages, Vol. IV*

CHAPTER ONE
THE CHIDDARI CONTRACT

The battle's almost over. The thought filled Maros with a shameful sense of triumph as he glared at his final challenge. Across the clearing, the cottage's shuttered windows returned his gaze with prodigious disinterest.

"Just another hundred yards. Get on with it," he admonished himself. He stabbed his crutches into the dirt, and a jolt of pain lanced up his leg. Gritting his teeth, he lurched into the clearing. Slowly, the distance to the cottage shrank, with Maros grunting and cursing the whole way.

"Should'a sent a runner," he muttered. *A year ago, I could've run this in a quarter of the time and still been ready for a fight at the end. Now?* He barked a wry laugh. *Dripping like a spitted pig.*

With a loping stride, he reached his target and stifled a roar of jubilation. His face was a mask of sweat, beads dripping to the sun-drenched dirt to be consumed under the noon sun. Composing himself at the door, he cast a sideways glance to the far edge of the crescent-shaped hamlet where a middle-aged woman was busy pegging out her linen and eyeing him over the sheets. He switched his gaze to two young girls in the centre of the clearing. Sensing Maros's scrutiny, they ceased their game of hop-rings and stared at him with undisguised horror. He flashed them a wide grin, and they bolted away into the surrounding forest.

He shook his head. Folk in the hamlet of Balen rarely left their quaint little microcosm and weren't accustomed to seeing anything out of the ordinary. The woman no doubt regarded him as a freak of nature or, worse, a gods-cursed creature to be pitied. The gammy leg didn't help matters. If they had ever heard the name Maros the Mountain, they would not recognise the exhausted human-jotunn at the cottage door as the man from those whispered tales. His reputation belonged to the past. These days he was scarcely more than an oversized quill-scratcher.

He wiped a forearm across his brow and rapped his knuckles upon the door. The muffled sounds of dragging feet drifted from within and the door clicked open to reveal a gaunt, elderly woman. Her dewy eyes lifted to regard him, a mask of austerity plastered over her wrinkles. She looked him up and down, frowning at his crutches and sweat-soaked vest.

"I presume the commotion I heard out here was you?" she said. "One would presume an ox was being slaughtered. What on Verragos were you *doing*?"

"I…" Stifling a sigh, Maros waved a feeble gesture behind him to the woodland trail. *Well done. Show the frail old lady how you were traversing a flat, open area. That's sure to impress her.*

"Hmph," No matter. I must say, I haven't seen one of you in decades."

He frowned. "One of me *what*? A man? A cripple?"

"A halfblood." Her rheumy eyes narrowed to slits. "Well then, what do you want? I don't have all day."

"I, ah…" He cleared his throat. "A pleasure to make your acquaintance. The name's Maros, Official of the Alder's Folly Freeblades. Might I be speaking with Cela, ah…" Rummaging into his vest pocket, he withdrew a sweaty sheet of paper and brought it to his face. "Cela Chiddari?"

"You might at that. Official, you say? Not accustomed to memorising family titles though, are you? Hm. Well, since they've sent me the man at the top, I suppose I should feel honoured."

The man at the top sent himself, you aged fruitcake. Maros forced a congenial smile. "I'm sure the pleasure is all mine."

"Then allow me to thank you for responding to my summons. As you can see, I'm in no fit state to be traipsing all the way to the Folly."

Summons? His smile faltered. "I don't tend to do house calls in person, but when I read your note from the courier I was prepared to make an exception."

"I don't doubt it." Cela peered around the door at her neighbour across the crescent. "You had better step inside, young man," she muttered, shuffling into the gloomy cottage. "Our discussion is not for prying ears."

Maros leaned lower on his crutches and squeezed through the threshold. He heeled the door shut and squinted as the room was plunged into darkness. A few thin slivers of daylight knifed between closed shutters, and the musty stench of age wafted into his nostrils. He swallowed a cough and watched the old woman lower her skeletal frame into an armchair beside the empty hearth. As she shifted to sit upright, he imagined her toppling to the rug in a heap of dusty bones.

"Take a seat, freeblade." She waved a hand around the room. "Whichever is best for you."

Maros scanned the dark lumps of furniture for a suitable sturdy perch and limped across to a bench on the opposite side of the hearth. He eased himself down, stifling a sigh as the aches in his leg receded.

"I hear you've been keeping Alderby's tavern ticking over in his stead," Cela said conversationally.

"I have."

"Running a guild *and* a tavern. Quite the workload."

2

"Nothing I can't handle. Truth is, it was a boon when old Alderby passed so soon after my... accident." Maros rested his hand on his knee. "Sad, though. The place was never without one or other Alderby at the helm."

"So I gather. Well, enough chitter-chatter." Cela's eyes were glints in the shadows. A tight smile sliced her wizened features. "To business."

"To business indeed. The bounty you've offered is enough to raise even the Brancosi Bank's eyebrows a touch. No offence, lady, but I'm looking at this cottage and thinking I don't see five hundred silvers' worth of property here."

"I dare say you'd be right if I was offering my house. You'll be getting coin, freeblade, rest assured. My savings will do me little good now unless you acquire that which belongs in Chiddari hands."

"Yes," Maros said carefully. "How is it that you hold a family title when they fell into disuse centuries ago?"

Cela issued a reedy laugh and ticked a finger at him. "Questions, questions, halfblood. Shall we stick to the matter at hand?"

"Aside from the reward amount, your note was vague at best," he prompted.

"With good reason! You appreciate the sensitivity of information, I'm sure."

"Then, please, tell me what you need and I'll see if we can accommodate."

"My family's heirloom has been lost to us for many generations." Cela regarded him intently. "Lost, and yet I know of its precise location. It resides in a graveyard dating back to a time when the dead were still buried intact."

"Those places are all sunken beneath the wilderness. There's scarcely a trace of the old kingdoms left."

Cela's tight smile returned. "Except, that is, for *one* place."

"Now listen here. If you're implying what I think you're implying, then you're asking me to send freeblades into Death's Head territory."

"I'm not *asking*. I'm offering you a contract for a considerable reward. If you don't want the job, I can look to less reputable sellswords..." She shifted in her chair and eyed him askance.

This is likely a fool's errand, he thought. *But for a bounty of that size...* "I should warn you that the guild deals in real issues, *not* in legends. There's only one burial ground that was never purged. If that's where you're talking about, then let's stop bandying words. Where *exactly* is this heirloom?"

Cela sighed. "In a crypt within the Gardens of the Dead, in Lachyla, the Blighted City."

The last pretence of formality slipped from Maros as he roared a hearty laugh. "I knew it! Let me get this straight. You want my lads and lasses to cross a vast region that's been devoid of gods and men for centuries. You expect them to risk their lives scouring a cursed city's boneyard in search of some trinket your ancestors left behind to rust in a crypt?" He snorted. "Lady, either you've lost your mind, or..."

Cela glared at him in stony silence.

Or you're serious. He shook his head and cast the floorboards a bemused smile. "Alright, what exactly does this heirloom look like?"

"It's a gemstone."

"You'll have to give me more than that. Whoever takes the job needs to know what they're looking for."

"I've never seen it, have I? All I know is it's banded with burial runes, and larger than your average gemstone. They will find it at the tomb of my most ancient ancestor."

"And who might that be?"

"I have no idea," Cela said curtly. "Do you know *your* lineage, halfblood?"

"Fine," Maros sighed. "A stone of unknown description, at a tomb of unknown name. Do you realise how large that boneyard's reputed to be? They could search the place for days and still not find your stone. You'll have to give me something better or it's no deal."

"Oh, I will." Cela reached to the table beside her and picked up a folded square of vellum. "It's only a rough copy, but it's accurate enough."

"What is it?"

"A map of the Gardens of the Dead."

Maros repressed a chuckle. "Where on Verragos would you have gotten hold of that?"

"More irrelevant questions, freeblade. You have all the information I can give. Make your decision."

He looked at her levelly and considered the ramifications. What happened in Lachyla was the catalyst for the dead being burned nowadays. The city, and its graveyard, were more steeped in myth and superstition than anywhere else on Himaera. *But who really knows what's down there at the arse-end of the Deadlands? Maybe the legend's true, maybe not. Either way, securing such a bounty would be a great boon to someone. Plus, my own modest cut wouldn't go amiss. Not to mention the reputation that'd put the guild back on the map.* "Alright," he said. "Let's cut to it. Show me the dari."

Cela reached into the neckline of her blouse and withdrew a thin chain. She gave the rectangular pendant on the end several twists, then passed him the lower half; its interior had been fashioned into a key. She pointed to an ironwood stump in the corner of the room, upon which a squat coffer was securely bolted. "Open it," she said.

Maros heaved himself from the bench. He unlocked the coffer and loosed a whistle at the neatly piled silvers.

"Five hundred in total, as promised, and not a copper among them." The old woman issued a rattling sigh. "I fear there may be very little time to waste, so tell me now – *will you accept?*"

Maros licked his lips and glanced sidelong at her. "Lachyla, you say. Well. I guess it *is* only a legend…"

4

Cela Chiddari smiled. The murky light deepened the hollows of her face and, for a moment, she resembled the death's head symbol itself. "That's the spirit, freeblade," she crooned. "Such bravado. Congratulations, the job is yours. Now, *find me my heirloom.*"

———— • ————

Jalis glanced up from the cards in her hand with a distracted sigh. The stone walls of the common room buzzed with the chatter and clatter of the tavern's patrons. A serving girl hurried past, carrying empty plates to the kitchen. Behind the bar, Jecaiah busied himself with replacing an empty barrel in preparation for the evening's surge of customers.

She turned her attention back to her cards. The high card was the Arkhus, but it was useless beside the others. The best she could manage was a low flush of the Artisan suit. She glanced to her two companions. Dagra was waiting patiently, wiping a dirty kerchief over the froth of ale at his scraggly beard. Across the table, Oriken scratched idly at his stubbled cheek, his eyes glazed as he regarded her from beneath the brim of his hat.

"Orik," she said, getting his attention. "My face is up here."

"Huh? Oh." He cleared his throat. "Well, come on, then. Take your turn. You're only delaying Dag from winning, and you know how much he loves counting his coppers."

"Shit on you," Dagra said.

Jalis glanced to the minuteglass on the table and watched the last of the grains trickle through.

"Time's up," Oriken said.

She tossed her cards to the table. "I fold."

"Why?" Dagra frowned at the scattered cards. "You had a hand there."

"I'm not feeling it," she said. "Whether winning or losing, you have to know when to quit."

Oriken gathered the cards onto the stack. "How about a round of Five Seasons?"

"Not now, Orik."

"Okay, fine." He sighed and looked over to the saloon doors at the common room's entrance. "Might step outside for a roll of tobah."

Jalis cocked her head and regarded him. "You're supposed to be trying to give it up."

"Hmph. Yeah. What should we do, then?"

She shrugged. "Maybe we should take a contract."

Dagra snorted. "Have you *seen* the guildboard? The jobs are scarcely fit for a novice! The decent ones get snatched up straight away, and there hasn't been one of those for weeks. Believe me, if a good contract came along, I'd be the first to take it and get out of this tavern."

Jalis nodded. "I can think of a hundred things I'd rather be doing right now. It's bad enough we have to live here, but at least it beats the guildhouse." She glanced to the front of the common room. A wedge of sunlight streamed over the tops of the doors. The blue sky beyond was inviting. "We shouldn't be wasting our days waiting for a good job to turn up. We should be out there."

Oriken snorted. "Can't argue with that, but if we go wandering around outside, we miss our chance at snagging a decent contract."

She brought her cup to her lips and took a sip of water. "Don't get me wrong," she said. "I love being with the two of you, but we're freeblades – with the emphasis on *blades*."

"The problem is," Oriken said, "we're too good at what we do."

Dagra nodded in assent. "Between us and the rest of the branch, we've practically rid Caerheath of all bandits. Now the troubles in town are rarely more than petty disputes."

Jalis sighed. "That should be a good thing. We're maintaining the peace, but we're not doing *ourselves* any favours. Since when did the guild become the primary lawmakers in Himaera?"

"Primary?" Dagra's brow creased. "Try *only*. This isn't Vorinsia. We don't have a fancy Arkhus ruling the land, nor a military, not even a damned sheriff. Nothing since the Days of Kings. Freeblades are all this land's got."

"I've lived here for long enough," Jalis said, "but I still can't get used to the lack of a military or a ruling figurehead. It's a miracle how Himaera wasn't consumed by the Arkh centuries ago."

Dagra shrugged. "They tried to invade us during the Uprising, but even a broken Himaera managed to bloody their noses and send them packing with a few lessons learned. The Arkh's gone soft since them days. Nothing conquerable left." He gave Jalis an apologetic look. "No offence, lass."

"None taken."

Oriken leaned back against the wall. "Anyway," he said, "I wouldn't worry. Something good'll land on the job board soon enough. It always does." He flashed Jalis a chirpy smile.

"Ever the pissing optimist." Dagra jutted his beard towards the guildboard alcove at the end the bar. "Have you seen the rewards for those job offers? The best is for eight coppers. It's an insult."

"Maybe it's time we took a vacation," Oriken said.

"That's not a bad idea," Jalis said. "I haven't visited my homeland for a while."

"Not really what I had in mind."

"I'm going for a piss," Dagra announced, pushing himself to his feet.

Oriken watched him wander away. "We do need to get out of town for a while. Maybe Middlemire needs some extra hands. Or Brancosi Bay. We should ask Maros to check for us."

A shadow cleaved through the sunlight on the floorboards. Jalis glanced across to see Maros's bulky frame hobbling through the saloon doors. He noticed her gaze and limped across to join them.

"The wanderer returns," Oriken said. "Can't keep you in your own tavern these days."

Maros barked a tired laugh and gathered his crutches into one hand. "Balen's the farthest I've been since I took over this place. Remind me never to go back."

Jalis tilted her head to meet his gaze. "You've been in Balen? All afternoon?"

"Hardly! Most of it was me struggling there and back."

"Why didn't you ask Ravlin to drive you in his wagon? He wouldn't have minded."

"I tried. The merchant's in Brancosi, replenishing his stock."

"What's so important in Balen you couldn't send a novice?" Oriken asked.

"On any other day, absolutely bugger all." Maros glanced at Jalis. "Listen, I've got a bit of business to attend to. I'll catch up with you shortly."

Jalis watched him limp to the guildboard. After a moment, he hobbled out of the recess and headed down the adjoining corridor to his private office. "He's up to something," she said to herself.

At a table near the opposite wall of the common room, several freeblades were engaged in a game of knucklebones. Alari, a veteran blade with a few more years in the guild than Jalis, peered towards the guildboard and muttered to her nearest companion.

"I'll be back in a minute." Jalis rose from her chair and crossed quickly to the alcove. She scanned the guildboard's contents until she spotted a new slip of paper and unpinned it from the cork. Seeing the reward offer, her eyes widened.

"Girl, you're as quick as flint over firesteel," Alari said from behind her.

Palming the note, Jalis turned to her colleague. "You weren't far behind me."

Alari's smile tugged at the pale scar beside her mouth. "What's the boss put up there this time? Another that ain't worth the paper it's written on?"

Jalis shrugged. "Looks a little better than the usual. Why don't you take some of the smaller offers? They'll do for the novice you're looking after. We all had to start somewhere."

Alari's brow furrowed in thought. "You're not wrong. Kirran could most likely do 'em on his own. I'll tell him to pick one." She gave Jalis an amiable wink. "You and the lads go earn yourselves some crust, love."

As Alari headed back to her table, another freeblade strode past her for the guildboard. Jalis eyed the man coldly as he closed the distance.

"What's that you got?" Fenn said as he stepped into the alcove, positioning himself before Jalis to block her from leaving.

"Back off, Fenn."

"Let's have a look." He snatched for the paper, but Jalis whipped her hand behind her back.

"First come, first served," she said. "You know the rules. You want a job, there are plenty on the board that'll suit you."

Fenn's beady eyes glared at her. "At least I can do my work alone. We all know that you and your two bodyguards get preferential treatment around here." He grabbed Jalis's shoulder.

She rammed her hand between his legs and squeezed. "Those are my companions and my friends. I'll tell you what, how about you take your hand from me, and I'll do the same. Then you go back to your seat like a good boy."

Fenn's lip curled in a silent snarl. Jalis increased the pressure and, reluctantly, he took his hand away. "You've got a problem."

"If I have any problems, you're not among them." She clutched harder. "Just so we're clear. Are we clear, Fenn?"

"Get your fucking hand off me!"

"Oh, I will. But first I want to give you fair warning that next time you touch me, it won't be my hand but my dagger at your groin. By all means test me, and I'll do the world a favour." With a final twist, she released her hold.

As Fenn staggered backwards, he threw a punch at Jalis's face. She ducked and jabbed a fist into his ribs, then launched an uppercut that smashed into his nose and sent him careening from the alcove and sprawling to the floor. A scattered applause trickled from the tavern's patrons, cut short as Maros hobbled out of the corridor.

"What in the Pit is going on in my tavern?" he boomed.

Fenn rose to his feet, blood trickling from his nose. "You wanna keep a leash on that bitch. Everyone knows she's your favourite." He flicked a glance at Jalis's gossamer chemise. "Not hard to see why."

"Is that so?" Maros limped across to loom over him. "You ought'a show a bladesmistress a little respect – no, a *lot* of respect – especially after she's put you on your arse. Step out of line one more time, Fenn, and the Grenmoor branch can have you back. Get yourself to the guildhouse. Now. You've had your fill for the day."

Fenn's face glowed with anger, but he said nothing. After a moment, he turned and strode for the doors.

"Oh, and Fenn," Maros called after him, "if you ever speak to *me* like that again, you won't be walking out of here, you'll be flying out."

"What did I miss?" Dagra asked from beside Jalis.

She shook her head. "Nothing."

Maros limped around to look at her. "I take it you were first to the new job I posted?"

"I was. Your time in Balen wasn't wasted."

"I'm not sure I want you taking this one, Jalis."

"Why? I'd be a fool not to."

Maros grunted. "Just promise me you won't do it alone." He nodded to Dagra. "If the lads don't agree, the job's going back on the board. I'd sooner let Fenn have this one, and good riddance to him."

Jalis frowned. "What's getting you concerned, old friend? If there's another bandit group taking hold somewhere—"

"Not bandits." Maros glanced briefly around the room and said in a low voice, "Speak with Dagra and Oriken. See what they say. If you all agree, then it's yours. But I won't be happy about it. You and I spent too many years together, lass. Don't underestimate what this job entails."

She studied his face. "I've never heard you talking like this."

"We've never had a contract like this."

As Jalis returned to her seat with Dagra in tow, Oriken raised an eyebrow. "Well, that was the most entertainment I've had all week. You missed it, Dag. Jalis ripped the local arsehole a new one."

"I did no such thing." Jalis waved away Dagra's questioning look. She folded her arms upon the table and beckoned her friends to lean closer. "I've snagged us a contract, and you won't believe the bounty."

"I'm not sure I want to hear," Dagra said, "not after Maros's reaction. But go on."

The chatter of the common room had resumed, but still she glanced around to ensure no one was eavesdropping. "Five hundred silver dari."

Oriken blew a low whistle. "Stars above. You're joking."

"I'm not."

Dagra's eyes were shadowed with scepticism. "What are the details?"

"I don't know. I didn't exactly have time to check."

"You didn't have time? Jalis, you don't go blindly accepting jobs. You know that better than me and Orik."

"I know! But five hundred silvers. What job wouldn't you take for that?"

"I can think of a few I wouldn't do," Oriken said with a smirk. "Dagra, though, probably not so many."

Dagra ignored the jibe. "Come on, then," he said to Jalis. "Let's have a look."

She uncrumpled the note and spread it upon the table, frowning in confusion as she scanned the details. "Er, where's Lachyla? What's the Blighted City?"

"Oh, suffering gods." Dagra wiped a hand over his face.

"What?"

Oriken laughed. "Maros put that on the board? He's playing with us. He has to be."

Jalis shook her head. "He wouldn't. Wait, isn't that a Himaeran folk tale? The Blighted City was one of the Taleweaver's stories a few years back, no?"

"Keep your voice down," Dagra said. "Look, whether this is just a dragon chase or for real, forget it. We're not going there. It's marked with a death's head for good reason."

Oriken scoffed. "Come on. Just because you were brought up believing every story under the sun. There's no reason to think this'll be anything but a long stroll in the countryside."

"You can't believe that," Dagra said. "Since when did *you* ever enter the Deadlands? Never, that's when. Stroll in the countryside? More like a walk to the gallows."

"I don't know much about your legends," Jalis said, "but the ten percent alone for non-retrieval would keep us good for a few months. If we fulfil the objective, it will be a more lucrative catch than Maros and I ever managed in our golden days. This is a big one. If we let it pass, Alari or Fenn or Henwyn or any of the others will snatch it up."

"No need to convince *me*," Oriken said. "I'm in."

"You're in for everything." Dagra glowered at him. "Always running into every dark hole you find. Even when we were boys. Won't you ever learn?"

Oriken shrugged. "You're the superstitious one. Show me proof that Lachyla is anything but a scary story told by the Taleweavers. Give me some evidence that we shouldn't take the job."

"You know I can't. But we shouldn't go angering the Dyad by wandering into a dead goddess's domain. The whole region is unhallowed ground."

"The Dyad are *your* gods," Oriken said. "Not mine. And not Jalis's. For the stars' sake, Dag, we're freeblades."

"Even if we found the place, the chances of locating... What was it?" Dagra glanced over the note. "A crypt? Oh, no. No way. I am not going into a crypt." He looked to Jalis. "Do you know they used to bury their dead without burning them? It's barbaric, I tell you. Sacrilege."

Oriken gave him a bemused grin. "Sacrilege? You're talking about a time before the Dyad came to Himaera. How can you accuse the ancestors of sacrilege when they existed *before* your gods?"

Dagra blanched. "You're going too far, Oriken."

"It happened everywhere," Jalis said, "not just here on Himaera. It was the same in the Arkh."

Dagra drained the last of his ale. "Jecaiah!" He signalled to the barman for another drink, then looked pointedly at Jalis. "At best, we'll be wasting a month or more wandering the wilderness before heading home empty-handed."

With an inward sigh, she decided to try another tactic. "You do realise that if we complete this contract, Maros will probably put the two of you forward for your bladesmaster tests."

"Imagine that, Dag. Third-tier freeblades after only five years." Oriken raised an eyebrow. "We'll be the talk of the guild."

"Hmph." Dagra pushed his chair back and stomped across to the bar.

"He'll come around," Oriken said.

Dagra glanced over his shoulder. "I heard that. I'm still waiting to be convinced."

"You don't sound as unconvinced as you were," Jalis said as he returned to his seat. "Look, if you don't want to come along, it'll only mean more for Oriken and I. It would be a shame to not have you with us, but if that's your choice…"

"Don't try that with me, lass. You heard Maros. He said it's all of us or none."

"He did. But ultimately it's not up to him. I've seen the details. If he tried to stop me, he'd be doing it as a friend, not as the Official."

"Think of all the good it'd bring," Oriken pressed. "You and me getting our bladesmasters. The recognition it'd bring us and the branch, not to mention the whole guild. It's not just about the money. Stars, I don't even know what I'd do with my cut. Imagine it, Dag. Once word circulates that we've braved the blight, conquered a legend and returned victorious…"

"I don't intend to risk angering the gods, not for any amount of dari."

"Stars!" Oriken sighed in exasperation. "All we have to do is walk into a crypt and find some rusty trinket. Can't you lighten up just this once? You could even wait outside while me and Jalis do all the brave stuff."

Dagra glared at the contract offer in stony silence.

"Okay," Jalis said. "I doubt the Dyad would be happy if you let Oriken and I walk to our fates without you, but if that's your choice, then I will respect it."

Dagra glared at her. "That was a low blow."

She shrugged and rose to her feet. "I'm accepting the contract, and Maros *will* allow it. In or out, it's up to you."

He sighed. "I'm not happy about this. Not happy at all."

Jalis smiled. "You're in, then?"

Dagra hunched his shoulders in defeat. "I'd hate myself if something happened to the two of you. What choice do I have?" His lips pressed together and he cast Oriken a hooded look. "Aye, you'll have my blade at your side. As always."

CHAPTER TWO
INTO THE DEADLANDS

Jalis lay on her front, propped on her elbows by the riverbank as Dagra and Oriken refilled the waterskins. A map of the region was opened out before her. As she studied it, she shook her head. "None of the settlements we've seen in the last three days are marked on here, just the old ringfort we passed a while back."

"I'm not surprised," Oriken called from beside the stream. "Wouldn't even call them settlements, just clusters of run-down old cabins. The looks we got as we walked by, you'd think we were bandits or worse."

"They're a simple folk down here," Dagra said as he left the waterside and sat close to Jalis. "Living within the fringes of the Deadlands, they've a right to be suspicious of strangers when they probably never see any. And the weapons we're carrying aren't likely to incite friendliness." He patted the old gladius at his hip. "To them who don't know the difference between a freeblade – or even a regular sellsword – and a bandit, one looks much the same as the other."

Oriken wandered over to join them and tossed Jalis her waterskin. "We don't need to know where we are yet," he told her. "As far as the stories of this area are concerned, we'll reach the city as long as we follow the road." He removed his hat and lay upon the grass, folding his hands behind his head.

"There's hardly anything left of the road," Dagra muttered with a glance to the overgrown remnants of the Kingdom Road a short distance away. "Imagine what state we'll find it in tomorrow, or the next day."

"Road or not," Oriken said, gazing into the afternoon sky, "according to the Taleweavers, we can't go wrong if we head south and west. We'll get there. And then we'll likely turn around and come all the way back empty-handed. It's almost tempting to camp for a few weeks then return for the ten percent."

Jalis glanced from the map. "And risk losing the other ninety percent? Do you have so little faith in us finding the jewel?"

Oriken shrugged. "I have faith in nothing. I'll honour the contract, you know that. But from what Maros said about Cela, it sounds to me like the crows have drunk what's left of her brain. Using a family title! Who even does that now?" Catching Jalis's glance, he said, "Okay, maybe *you* do, and a few others who came here from the mainland, but our client's Himaeran." He gave a derisive snort. "Claiming she's descended from Lachyla. Ha!"

Jalis quirked an eyebrow. "Who's to say she isn't?"

Oriken grunted and closed his eyes.

"There were allegedly some survivors of the blight," Dagra pointed out.

"Whether Cela's crazy or *we* are," Jalis said, "we'll cross Scapa Fell and find this so-called Blighted City and give it our best shot at searching for the heirloom." She glanced at Dagra. "Something troubling you?"

He gave her a hooded look and waited a moment before answering. "Aye, something's troubling me. First off"—he leaned forward and stabbed a finger onto the map, where the Death's Head symbol ringed the centre of Scapa Fell—"*that* bothers the shit out of me. There's a good reason why no one comes down here."

"Yeah, it's because the whole of Himaera has gone gods-soft," Oriken said drowsily. "We got rid of the rule of kings, but it was only one side of the coin."

"Secondly," Dagra continued, casting him a scathing glance, "presuming for a moment that this whole region is the tamest stretch of wilderness we've ever seen, what happens if we do find Lachyla?"

Jalis stashed the map into her backpack. "What do you mean?"

"Dag's worried about the graveyard," Oriken said.

"Damned right I am! It ain't proper, folk being left to rot like that. And we're expected to wander into some hole in the ground filled with all manner of ancient, unsanctified corpses? I mean, who in their right mind—"

"I'll tell you who." Jalis sat up and looked him square in the eye. "Three freeblades who can barely scrape together enough coin from meagre jobs to pay our keep. Money's short, and we'd definitely not be in our right minds if we'd turned our noses up at this one. We're lucky Maros tipped us off about it. He didn't have to do that."

"Our rooms in the tavern come courtesy of Maros," Oriken pointed out. "And the food courtesy of the guild itself."

"My point remains. Work has been dismal lately." Jalis climbed nimbly to her feet. "We won't get anywhere sitting here discussing it. It's still a few hours before nightfall, so let's press on."

Dagra grunted and climbed to his feet, grabbed his pack and slung it onto his shoulder. As he made for the road, Jalis walked at his side and cast a glance back to see Oriken lean up onto his elbows.

"Just when I was getting comfortable," he called.

She winked and turned to Dagra. "Five years and he hasn't changed a bit."

Dagra snorted. "Five? Try *twenty*-five. The man's as lazy as the boy was, but if I had to descend into the Pit itself I'd choose none other than Orik at my side. And yourself, of course."

13

Jalis smiled. "Same for me, my friend." And then an unwelcome thought came to her. *Descend into the Pit. I hope to whatever's listening that we're not heading to do just that.*

As the evening deepened, they spotted a collection of four stone-and-wood cottages and a scattering of barns and outhouses set a ways off the road, nestled against the edge of a large copse of trees. The buildings were intact but covered in moss, the roofs festooned with grass and flowering plants. Signs of disuse permeated the area. If the place was still home to someone, they hadn't looked after it in years.

"Looks like we'll have shelter tonight," Oriken said.

Jalis was doubtful. "If the houses are as untended on the inside as the out, we might be just as well sleeping under the stars again."

Dagra grunted. "We'll soon find out." He quickened his pace, his short legs striding for the nearest of the small cottages. With a sound knock on the door, he called out, "Hello?"

As Oriken reached Dagra, he laughed and slapped a hand onto his friend's shoulder. "Dag, if anyone's alive in there, they must be well-stocked with provisions. This door hasn't been opened in years." He pointed to the dandelions growing in thick clumps at the door's edges, and the unbroken ivy that trailed its way along the frame and across the front of the door. He reached for the handle and pushed; it creaked inward an inch and a musty stench drifted out. Dagra wrinkled his nose in disgust.

"It just needs an airing out," Oriken said. "It'll be fine." He slammed his shoulder into the door. The vines snapped and the door scraped across the floorboards, its hinges groaning until it touched the adjacent wall. A shaded interior greeted them, permeated by a dank, pungent stench that caused Oriken to take a step back. "Or maybe not," he added with a shrug.

To the right-hand side of the sparse and dusty living area, an open doorway led into a second room. Oriken strolled across and peered inside. "Hm."

Jalis paused in the centre of the first room. "What do you see?"

Oriken squinted into the darkness. A disconcerted expression made its way onto his face. "Oh."

"What in the Pit does *that* mean?" Dagra growled as he hung back behind Jalis. "What's in there?"

"Spider webs." Oriken turned to a set of shutters behind him and pulled the left one open, allowing the evening light to wash into the room.

Most of what Oriken could see was blocked from Jalis's view, but his narrow-eyed glance into the room before stepping out and shaking his head told her they wouldn't be sleeping there tonight.

"We should try another house," Oriken suggested, with a pointed look at Dagra.

"Don't be such a wimp." Dagra pushed past him.

"Ah, Dag, I wouldn't—"

As Dagra stepped into the room and glanced to the side, a look of horror spread onto his face and he backed up against the door frame. "Gods above and below!" He staggered away and barged between Oriken and Jalis to disappear through the front door. "Damn you!" he called. "You could have warned me!"

"I tried!"

"Warned him of what?" Jalis asked.

Oriken shrugged. "Like I said, there are webs everywhere. Couldn't tell until I opened the shutter. The damned things are all over the corpse, covering it like a shroud."

"Oriken! You know how Dagra gets about that sort of thing!"

"Never mind him! What about me? There was a huge, fat spider crawling over the fellow's face." With a shudder, he strode away. "I *hate* spiders!"

"And I hate surprises!" Dagra shouted from outside.

Grinning to herself, Jalis glanced into the adjoining room. The grin faltered as she spotted a sheet of parchment upon the arm of the chair where the corpse was slumped. She stepped across and brushed the clinging threads away, picked the paper up and blew the dust from it. After reading the faded note, she replaced it beside the corpse and glanced at its wizened features with a touch of sympathy.

"We'll leave you in peace," she said softly. "Sorry to disturb you." She left the building and regarded her companions as they stood bickering. "You know," she mused, "it sometimes feels like I'm a nursemaid in an orphanage rather than a bladesmistress in the Freeblades Guild." As the men mumbled their protests, she hitched her thumb towards the open doorway. "The fellow in there stayed behind when the last of his neighbours packed up and left. He refused to join them. Instead, he remained here alone and died with what he thought was dignity. It's so sad that someone would care more about a small area of land than a better chance at survival elsewhere."

The men looked at her blankly before resuming their argument. With a sigh, Jalis strolled past them. "I'll check the next house. Spiders or corpses, you boys stay right behind me. Mamma will protect you."

"You're a big idiot," she heard Dagra tell Oriken as she strode to the farthest dwelling.

"I did try to warn you," came Oriken's reply. "But you had to storm in there all brave. Thought it was just spiders, didn't you? Thought you'd make me look like a tail-tucker. Stupid little dwarf."

"Dwarf? I can put you on your arse any day of the week, you gangly bastard."

"Yeah? Well how about right now?"

"Children!" Jalis shouted back as she reached the next dwelling. "Start behaving right now, or I swear I'll put you both over my knee." She glanced back at their stunned expressions, then turned to the cottage door and slammed her heel beneath the handle. Hinges splintered as the door flew inwards. With her hands close to her daggers, she stepped into the gloom and waited for her eyes to adjust. The grey outlines of sparse furniture dotted the single room; there was a hearth on the opposite wall, a large pallet to one side and a larder to the other. A quick check confirmed there were no dead things lay around – except for the skeleton of a rat in the fireplace – and very few spider webs.

Dagra and Oriken sheepishly entered.

She cast them a flat look. "The coast is clear. You're safe."

Some minutes later, with Oriken busy building a fire in the hearth, Jalis lowered herself into a rickety chair and regarded Dagra. The bearded man was stood in the middle of the room, looking down at the dirt-strewn floor. It was clear to her that he was still unsettled.

He looked across and met her gaze. "Doesn't anything bother you?" he asked. "Even the toughest of men or women have a weakness, but we've known you for five years and I've yet to see yours."

"There is one thing I'm afraid of," she admitted. "Losing."

"Losing what?"

She cast him a level look. "People I care about."

He snorted, though his beard cracked into forced but warm smile. "Well, you aren't likely to lose either of us any time soon. Not unless a great monster spider climbs down the chimney and gobbles Orik up."

"Or," Oriken said as he struck flint against firesteel, "maybe that dead guy in the house yonder'll get up in the night and come scratching at the door for Dag."

Dagra whirled on him. "You had to say that, didn't you?"

"I'm serious," Jalis told them. "We're heading into the unknown, and I don't like not knowing. We nearly lost Maros last year. The unstoppable team of four became three, and we're lucky he pulled through."

"Aye." Dagra nodded. "That we are."

"It's a dangerous profession." Jalis stood up, unclipped her bedroll from the pack and rolled it onto the pallet. "True enough, eleven years in the guild and I've known only a handful of blades die during contracts. Most of those were journeymen or lower." Tossing a blanket onto the bedroll, she turned to raise an eyebrow pointedly at both men. "Statistically, the chances of dying as a freeblade are lower the higher you climb the ranks; both of you should be up for your bladesmasters in the next year or two, but you're not there yet, so don't get cocky. And, for the stars' sake, try to control your reactions. Dag, in a different scenario, you might have panicked and ran blindly from a dead thing right into the jaws of a living creature. How would you explain that to the Dyad in the afterlife?"

Dagra puffed his cheeks and blew out. "Point taken."

"And Oriken, there are few spiders in Himaera that can hurt you. You ought to see some of them in Sardaya. Big bloated bodies with red and white stripes. A bite from one of those and you'll be swollen like a ripe cadaver." Oriken and Dagra groaned in unison, and in the dim light of late evening Jalis fancied she saw both their expressions turn pasty. "See how easy it is?"

"Easy and unnecessary." Oriken scowled at the tools in his hand and resumed striking the firesteel into the kindling.

"Not to mention the Stone Dancers that infest the Ghalendi Flatlands," Jalis continued, with a nod to Oriken. "The adults are half your height. They could pop any other spider with a touch of their blade-like legs. If you weren't covered in armour and brandishing something heavy to smash them apart, one of those arachnids would make fast work of you."

Oriken turned his back to her. "You're making it up."

"Are you going to get that fire lit or not?"

With a grumble, he bashed the flint faster against the steel. "Damned wood's not the driest. So, you seen one of those things, have you?"

"No, But I've known people who did. There may be a little embellishment, but I don't doubt that Stone Dancers exist. My point is that your fear is unnatural; the little spiders here can't harm you."

"That's not what gets to me, It's the way they— There!" A small flame caught in the kindling. Oriken blew softly and the fire began to spread, easing an amber glow into the greyness of the room. "What bothers me about spiders is how they look and move. Disgusting creatures." He hugged himself and rubbed his arms. "Can we change the subject?"

"Shush!" Dagra held a hand out for silence.

"What?" Oriken said after a moment. "I don't hear anything but wood crackling."

"There it was again." Dagra kept his voice low. "While you were talking."

Jalis reached for the swordbelt on the table beside her. "I heard it." It had been faint, but the pack-call was unmistakable. "Cravants. Dag, close the door. Orik, help me push that cabinet behind it." She buckled her belt around her hips and stepped to the large piece of furniture. As Oriken took position beside her, Dagra eased the cottage door shut and hastily closed the shutters. Jalis and Oriken crouched low behind the cabinet and set their shoulders against it. They pushed, but it barely moved. Setting her feet firmly, Jalis put all her weight into the task and felt Oriken doing the same. The cabinet scraped and groaned across the dusty boards, its contents rattling with each shove. Soon enough, they had it wedged tightly behind the door.

"We need to get something behind the shutters!" Dagra cast his eyes about the contents of the room.

Jalis shook her head. "There *is* nothing."

Oriken twisted the brim of his hat. "Cravants usually leave humans alone, but down here past the last of the settlements…"

"This is *their* domain," Dagra said grimly. The creatures' calls were rapidly growing nearer as he drew his gladius "They've broken out of the woods."

"They heard us and now they have our scent." Jalis reached into a pack for their mini crossbow. "If we're quiet, they might wander away after a time."

With the shutters unable to be barricaded, they were the cottage's weakest point of defence. Jalis loaded and nocked the crossbow, then stood ready behind the men as they took position before the shutters. They waited in silence, listening as the cravants bounded across the clearing, their guttural calls only vaguely reminiscent of the monkeys indigenous to the far south of the Arkh. Jalis could picture them outside, their jutting jaws with chaotic clusters of fangs, and that second, smaller set of eyes like spheres of obsidian at the sides of their heads. The countenance of a cravant was hideous, but, despite their appearance, Oriken was right that the primate pack-hunters tended to steer clear of humans, keeping themselves unseen and mostly unheard within the depths of woodlands. But here on the edge of Scapa Fell it was possible that they had rarely laid eyes on humans, with the last populated settlement being half a day's trek to the north.

Something crashed outside, and Jalis visualised the creatures charging into the first house, following the scent of her and the men but finding only the long-dead corpse. The muted thump of feet and fists upon the ground drew close to the cottage and, despite herself, Jalis flinched as fists smashed against the door, wood splintering as it jarred against the cabinet. The cravants roared, sensing the freeblades' proximity.

The cabinet shifted an inch. Beyond the threshold, the attacking creature grunted in frustration and thumped harder against the door. A hinge popped from its fixture and a narrow gap appeared; through it, Jalis saw a mass of black hair on a thick-set body. The cravant was Dagra's height, slightly shorter than Jalis. A black, round eye peered within, and the cravant roared.

Jalis fired the bolt. Her aim was true; the projectile shot through the gap and straight into the creature's mouth. It screeched in pain and staggered away. Another took its place as Jalis reloaded the crossbow.

A glance from Oriken told her to hold as he strode across and thrust his sabre between the door and the frame, sending a series of quick jabs into the cravant's bulk. The creature roared and smashed a grey-haired fist against the door frame. Its thick, taloned fingers flexed open and reached through the gap. Oriken swept the sabre down, cutting deep into the creature's fingers and taking one of them off. The incensed cravant withdrew its hand and loosed a furious roar. Oriken sprang backwards, and Jalis released her bolt. The primate grunted and fell back. In the clearing outside, dark flashes of movement told her that the rest of the pack were converging on the cottage.

Fists slammed into the shutters. Dust shook from the cracks between the boards. Dagra stepped back and raised his gladius as the shutters crashed

18

inwards. The dark shape of a cravant filled the gap, its muscle-laden chest rippling as it raised its arms and roared.

Jalis grabbed another bolt and slid it onto the crossbow, watching the creature raise its thick arm to take a swing at Dagra. Hastily nocking the crossbow, she squeezed the trigger and the bolt punched into one of the cravant's four eyes. Dagra swerved aside and hacked into the reaching arm. The cravant snatched at its face, wrenching the bolt from its eye.

There was little Jalis could do but keep loading the crossbow, but there were only so many bolts. Nor was there enough room at the shutters for the men to hold position without risking injury to one another. They needed a new tactic.

"Fire!" Jalis called. "There's an old torch on the wall."

Oriken sprang to the task. He pulled the torch down and thrust the head into the now roaring hearth. The flames took and he ran to Dagra's side as the injured cravant loomed in for the attack. With its attention on Dagra, Oriken stabbed the burning torch into its face. It let out an ear-piercing shriek and threw itself in the dirt in an attempt to douse the flames. As it scrambled back to its feet, Jalis shot a bolt into its face. The cravant howled and staggered away, took several loping paces across the clearing, then pitching to the ground. The howls faded and the creature's movements ceased, allowing the flames to spread.

The remaining cravants cowered into the evening murk, their black eyes glinting in the firelight. One dared to approach, and Oriken swiped the torch as it reached in. The flames licked at its arm and the cravant swiped the torch away, knocking the top off and sending the ball of pitch flying into the room to roll beneath the hay-stuffed pallet.

As the stench of singed hair and roasting flesh wafted in through the opening, Dagra stabbed his gladius into the creature's shoulder. It staggered backwards onto its fallen packmate; the fires that consumed the first caught the second, and with an agonised shriek it scrambled to its feet and bounded towards the rest of the pack, sending them scattering back towards the trees. The blazing cravant loped around the side of the cottage and the cries of the pack faded as they disappeared into the woodland.

The pallet was smouldering, smoke billowing into the room. Oriken had saved her pack and bedding in time and was busy stashing their gear away.

"Through the shutters," Dagra shouted, glaring from Jalis to Oriken. "Now!"

They grabbed their gear and Jalis climbed through the shutters behind Dagra. There was no sign of the pack-hunters, save for the one on the ground which no longer moved, small puddles of flames dotting its seared back. Oriken hauled himself through the open shutters, gasping in pain as he slung his sabre back into its scabbard.

"You're bleeding," Jalis said.

19

He glanced briefly at the torn shirt over his forearm. Grabbing the sleeve, he tore it from the shoulder and wrapped the cloth around the wound. "I can deal with it later. Distance first."

As the three ran towards the Kingdom Road, Jalis thought grimly, *A walk in the countryside, indeed.* Above them, the sky was painted in swathes of stars, while behind them, growing ever distant as they fled across the open heathland, the inferno of the cottage roared into the night.

CHAPTER THREE
MINE, ALL MINE

"That's right," Wayland said as he crouched alongside Demelza. "Steady your breathing. Track the rabbit with the bow. Hold, draw, and target. Once you're certain, release."

From a short distance to the side of the Warder and the girl, Eriqwyn crossed her arms and watched both Demelza and the rabbit. *She will miss,* she thought with annoyance. *Her body is tense, and her focus isn't fully on the task.* Stifling a sigh, she shook her head. *I'm First Warder, I shouldn't be wasting time with this one; getting through to that thick head of hers requires too much patience.*

Fifty yards away, the half-obscured rabbit moved out from behind the shrub into the open. It paused, twitched its nose and turned to look directly at Demelza and Wayland. The girl loosed the arrow; it flashed before the morning sun and thudded into the grass several yards short of its target. The rabbit burst into movement. Demelza's petulant scowl traced it as it darted across the heathland. Taking her bow from the ground, Eriqwyn started towards the pair.

Wayland's eyes widened and he rose to his feet. "Ha! Would you look at that? You missed with the arrow, but it seems you frightened the poor animal to death instead!"

Eriqwyn turned. The rabbit had cleared a good distance in seconds but now lay stock still, its white belly nestled amid the short grass. She strode over to the fallen creature and nudged it with her boot. Kneeling, she placed a hand to its chest. Its heart had stopped, and its brown eye stared sightlessly up at her. Wayland was right; it appeared the creature had died from fright.

She took it by its tail and strode across to Demelza. "The kill is yours," she told the girl, handing her the rabbit. "However, it doesn't count towards your tally. You need better focus. Where was your attention? On the kill, or elsewhere? It seemed to me that half your mind was not on the task." She looked at Wayland. "Demelza needs more practice with non-moving targets until she can learn to give her undivided attention."

Wayland gave a brief shrug and a nod. "As you say."

21

"Well, girl?" Eriqwyn tilted her head at Demelza. "Aren't you going to retrieve the arrow Wayland was generous enough to let you use?"

Demelza's eyes looked as doleful as the rabbit's had in life, and almost as empty as they were in death as she nodded. Handing the longbow to Wayland, she ran off to retrieve the arrow.

As Eriqwyn sighed, Wayland softy said, "Ah, Queenie. You're too hard on the girl. It's true she's not the brightest sunfish in the rock pool, but she's not without skill."

"A skill it is beneath the First Warder of Minnow's Beck to waste time in finding."

"And what of me? Linisa and I are second only to you as protectors of the village. Is it beneath a Warder to help a young'un become a hunter? Of course it isn't. That's how the cycle continues and the village remains strong."

Eriqwyn sucked air through her teeth. "There's no need to lecture me, old friend. I know all of this. But that girl…" She glared at the returning Demelza. "Cursed on the day she was born, that one. There's something about her I neither like nor trust. And how often do rabbits just keel over dead from fright?"

"It does happen."

"But twice in two weeks? To the same girl?" She turned and glared intently at Wayland, but softened as she met his calm gaze. "Continue with her training, but, please, be sparing with your progress reports; I have no desire to know how poorly she is doing, nor how many creatures she's managed to scowl to death."

Wayland smiled and turned to the girl as she stopped before them, the arrow in her hand. "What have you learned so far today?" he asked her.

Demelza's wide eyes glanced from Wayland to Eriqwyn and back again. Her mouth worked soundlessly before she answered. "I learnt…"

Eriqwyn frowned. "Yes, girl?"

"I learnt that…"

Oh, for the love of the goddess, Eriqwyn thought.

"Consider the question," Wayland said, his voice full of patience.

Demelza stared at the rabbit in Wayland's hand, and after a long moment she nodded and said, "I learnt that the rabbit ain't so smart as the Melza." Eriqwyn stifled a sigh and turned on her heel. As she stalked away, she heard Demelza add, "It's still dead, though."

———— · · ————

"A marsh," Oriken grumbled as he pulled his boot from the bog with a wet suck. He glanced over the vista ahead, at the open flatland, the sparse, crooked trees, the tufts of reeds and marshgrasses that dotted the whole landscape. "That's just what we need."

Clouds had gathered and the air was becoming hazy with fine rain. The marsh was impassable unless they wanted to risk wading through, which, to Oriken's mind, wasn't going to happen. *Our sixth day on the road and we're not even half-way to our destination,* he thought, frowning down at his mud-covered boot. *Still, first obstacle so far, if you don't include those fucking primates.* Beneath the bandage on his forearm the scratch from the cravant's claw was beginning to itch.

"We'll have to detour," Jalis said, lowering herself to the overgrown remnants of the ancient highway and pulling her shoes off. "You said south and west, right?"

"Uhuh." Oriken rubbed a knuckle against his stubbled chin to keep from scratching at his healing arm. "The coast is a lot closer to the west than the east. From here I reckon twenty miles, give or take."

Dagra huffed. "And what good does that do us?"

Oriken shrugged, grasped the crown of his hat and took it off. "If we head east we could end up adding days or a full week to our journey. Besides, I'd rather cross rocky coastline or beaches than wade through a bog."

"West it is, then," Jalis said, taking her boots from her pack and pulling them on. "There's no sense in guessing how much distance the marsh covers. We'll follow its edge as close as we can." She reached a hand up to Oriken and he helped her to her feet.

"What if it leads right into the ocean?" Dagra asked. "Fat load of good that'll do us."

Oriken ran a hand through his mop of hair and replaced his hat, giving the brim a brief twist. "In that case, we turn back and head east. Why do you have to presume the negative, Dag? None of us are happy about this. You need to lighten up a little."

Dagra muttered under his breath and glared across the bog-riddled heathland.

"What's that you say?"

"Nothing. Forget it." Dagra's face was a brooding mask as he stormed off westwards beside the marsh.

As they followed behind, Oriken glanced down at Jalis. "He's too tense. If there were any damned shrines to the Dyad around here, we'd have him in a better mood in no time."

Jalis nodded. "I'm beginning to see how much we asked of him in joining us. I didn't appreciate his concern back in the tavern."

"He'll come around. His faith is stronger than anyone's I know, much to my lifelong annoyance. It'll get him through."

"I hope you're right," Jalis said, "though it sounds to me like you're putting faith in Dagra's faith."

Oriken snorted a quiet laugh. "You got me there."

The afternoon stretched on. The rain continued, light but relentless. Jalis and Dagra wore their half-mantles with the hoods pulled up, and Oriken had shrugged on his nargut-hide jacket. He was warm, but dry. Dagra rejoined them and walked to the other side of Jalis as the three wandered along the edge of the marsh. Conversation was sparse and Oriken found himself wondering what was truly ahead of them. They were just a couple of days beyond civilisation, but, despite the familiar Himaeran landscape, Scapa Fell had an atmosphere all of its own. The openness of the region made him feel unconfined but also uneasy, as if the land itself was aware of their presence and regarded them as interlopers. Which, of course, was nonsense.

Perhaps Dag's mood is rubbing off on me, he thought, then shook his head. None of them were strangers to travelling and seeing only wilderness from one day to the next, but knowing that they headed deeper and deeper into a vast, unpopulated region – a region avoided by the living and abandoned to the past – he couldn't shake the apprehension that was beginning to creep in. Was there really a city on the other side of the Deadlands? If so, then surely it was a shell of a place, crumbling into the ground and consumed by vegetation.

As he trudged along, the rain increased and began to drum down upon the brim of his hat, With Jalis and Dagra walking beside him in their own silent thoughts, Oriken considered the legend of Lachyla. The city was shrouded in vague history and embellished stories, but four years ago Oriken had heard it told best by a Taleweaver passing through Alder's Folly. The man had stopped for a night at the Lonely Peddler back when Oriken and Dagra were fledglings to the guild and new residents to Alder's Folly, living in the guildhouse with Maros and Jalis and the rest of the freeblades while the Peddler was still owned by Alderby.

At the turn of midnight, the tavern's common room was heavy with the smells of woodsmoke, ale and hard labour. The freeblades gathered on their tables near the single front door. Maros always had to duck and squeeze through that door, even before the lyakyn attack had crippled his leg, Oriken recalled with a stab of pity for his halfblood mentor and friend. The babble of conversation quieted in the common room as a stranger entered and glanced around. The middle-aged man was every bit as tall as Oriken. He strode to the bar, flicked the tails of his blue and tan greatcoat aside and sprang deftly to perch upon the service counter.

The enigmatic Taleweaver smiled within his closely-trimmed, salt-and-pepper beard. His gaze drifted across the rapt faces of the silent patrons. His eyes were vital. His chin jutted only slightly in quiet confidence. As the hearthfire crackled, he smoothed the folds of his longcoat and began to weave his tale…

At the height of the Days of Kings, Lachyla was a vibrant and bustling fortress city, with more might and influence than any other in Himaera. Its people celebrated death with elaborate ceremonies in the lavish burial gardens. The towering walls of the graveyard were the city's first line of defence, as had been proven decades before when an invading army had breached the gates – or so they thought – only to find themselves surrounded on all sides by archers. The warring days were on the wane, but the fleeting mortality of men can turn the great game of kingdoms in a single generation, as a new liege rises while the blood of the old lays slick upon the gameboard. The golden age of monarchs was destined for a calamitous end, thanks, in large part, to the actions of one man.

The last king of Lachyla was Mallak Ammenfar. In defiance of the tyrannical sovereigns of the era, Mallak was a just and fair ruler and quickly succeeded in forming alliances with his northern neighbours. In the early days of his reign, an uneasy peace prevailed across Himaera, but, as his tenure wore on, his diplomacy gave way to a rising paranoia. Intent on making Lachyla a self-sufficient city-state, he began to close the trade routes with the northernmost kingdoms, and restricted the travel of his citizens. Mallak neglected the Lachylan Kingdom's farthest settlements and focused only on the sprawling, fortified city.

After the death of his mother, he became reclusive and spent much of his time in the castle's lower sanctum. None knew what he did there, not even the queen.

Without the trade of Lachyla's metals, gemstones and other valued resources, the northern kingdoms fell into decline and tensions grew across the whole land.

Finally, hopeful merchants and envoys attempting to visit Lachyla from its allied neighbours returned home with reports that the city gates were closed and unmanned. Beyond those gates, they said, Lachyla's burial gardens and the grand Litchway – once a constant babble of quiet activity – stretched empty all the way to the city proper, with not a mourner nor a groundsman in sight. Entry was barred to all outsiders, even those Lachylan subjects from the outlying settlements and fortresses. Of the cityfolk within, none were allowed to leave.

The kings of Himaera left Lachyla to its own fate, deciding against war as they heeded the advice of their returning ambassadors. An unnaturalness had settled over the city. Even the birds altered their course to avoid flying beyond the walls, perhaps sensing the wrongness in the graveyard – the withered shrubs and grasses, the disturbed soil of the graves...

The king's secret activities beneath the castle were witnessed by no mortal, but Himaera's ancient deity, Valsana, had no such restrictions. The goddess of life and death reigned separate and supreme above all the gods of the Bound and the Unbound, long before the enlightened days of the Dyad.

Valsana saw the king's actions as a lust for rule beyond his station, and she judged him guilty of reaching for godhood. Her vengeance fell on the shoulders of not only Mallak, but all who dwelt within the city walls.

She summoned the denizens of the burial gardens from their resting places. The ancestors swarmed into the city and tore into their descendants, who were too terrified to fight back. Soon, every man, woman and child within the city had joined their ghastly ranks.

When the king saw his city fall into chaos, he ordered the last of his guards to bar the castle doors from within. On that first night, as the moans of the dead surrounded the castle, an elderly serving lady's heart gave in to the horror. She passed quietly into death, and rose just as quietly. One by one, each of the king's servants succumbed to the inevitable, followed by his family, and finally his guardsmen until only Mallak remained. For the living, the castle was their final sanctuary. For the restless dead, it was an eternal tomb.

Mallak locked himself in the throne room and sat upon the jewelled seat, listening to his dead subjects and family as they scratched upon the doors. After a time, they wandered away and he was left alone. There was a table with a modest feast within the throne room, but the food was spoiled and the wine turned to vinegar, and the king knew despair as he realised the depths of the goddess's curse.

Days passed, and with neither edible food nor water to sustain him, Mallak grew weak. He turned to eating the rotten fruit and drinking the spoiled wine, but his stomach could take neither and he vomited them back out.

Time lost meaning in the windowless throne room, marked only by restless sleep upon the cold stone floor. Parched and starving, Mallak vilified the name of the goddess for what she had wrought upon him.

Sinking deeper into delirium, the king understood the error of his ways. All he had wanted was to protect his city and his people from the poison of the other kingdoms, but that protection had suffocated them all. The Himaeran Kingdoms were not rife with enemies of Lachyla. The creatures roaming the streets and the castle corridors were not the true monsters. The real monster, he knew, had locked itself in the throne room.

"Valsana have mercy," Mallak whispered, his voice little more than a dry croak. But no mercy came. He brooded upon the throne, drained even of despair. As the murmurs of the dead tormented him, King Mallak Ammenfar slipped from this life into the next.

The goddess had granted that which the king so craved. Her gift to him was the complete domination of Lachyla, with not even the finality of death to usurp him – because the only true ruler of eternity… is death itself.

"We need shelter," Jalis said from beneath her hood, drawing Oriken back to the present. "The clouds are darkening, and the rain is getting worse."

26

"If my eyes don't deceive me," Dagra said, "that shelter may be just on the horizon." He pointed into the hazy landscape.

Oriken could just see the shapes of several small structures amid the blanket of rain. "Well, I'll be damned."

"Aye," Dagra huffed. "Probably."

As they picked up the pace, Jalis said, "At least, with no woodland around, there'll be no cravants this time,"

Dagra grunted his assent. "Let's not get complacent, though. There's no telling what other surprises the Deadlands might have in store for us."

Oriken's stomach growled. *A roof and rest for a while would be fine right now, but I'd prefer a roasted rabbit. Haven't spotted a potential lunch the whole day.* As they neared the buildings, his hopes for either dissolved. The three wooden cabins were in advanced stages of collapse, and several smaller structures were scarcely more than piles of rotting timber. Roofs had partially fallen, doors were missing or lying half-sunken into the ground, and the interiors were overgrown and water-logged.

Oriken drew his sabre and strode for the farthest cabin, leaving Dagra and Jalis to inspect the closer buildings. A brief search confirmed it was no shelter at all, nor was there anything worth salvaging from the remains of the worm-eaten furniture within. He stepped around to the collapsed side of the cabin, meandering between the mossy debris. Behind the building, several short, prickly trees nestled in the lee of a hillock; behind them, the warped timbers of a man-made opening stood askance in the side of the hill.

"There's a mine back here!" he called over his shoulder.

Jalis stepped into view a moment later. "Be careful."

Oriken jogged to the mine entrance and peered in, With a shrug, he stepped over the threshold. The first set of supporting beams were visible a short distance along; beyond that, the rest of the tunnel stretched away into blackness. He took several paces further in and stooped to brush his fingers through the dirt. Satisfied it was dry, he tossed his pack to the ground and lay his swordbelt over it, then sat against the tunnel wall.

Jalis hurried into the entrance and pushed her hood back with a sigh. A moment later Dagra stepped in behind her, shaking the water from his cloak. Out on the heath, the wind gusted and the rain pelted down with a fresh fervour.

Once free of her gear, Jalis sat cross-legged beside Oriken. "As soon as it eases off, we'll head back out."

"Wherever there's a mine, there's usually a settlement close by," Oriken said.

Dagra issued a non-committal grunt. "Any settlement will only be in as bad condition as those workers cabins out there. The houses back at the outskirts weren't empty for more than a few decades, but this mine has been abandoned for at least a hundred years."

"He's right," Jalis said. "No sense getting our hopes up. Besides, the woodland around here is much sparser; if it stays that way, we won't be bumping into any more cravants."

"Aye, well," Dagra muttered as he stepped past. "No more surprises. That'll be fine with me." He dropped his gear against the wall and hunkered beside it, laying his gladius over his lap.

Oriken looked past Jalis to gaze out at the broken buildings. He wondered what the miners had been like back then, and if they'd been anything like his father. Puffing his cheeks, he glanced in the opposite direction into the deep gloom of the tunnel. "Hey, hold on," he muttered. "Is that... Dag, look out!"

A shape rushed right at Dagra. He was on his feet in a flash to meet the attack head-on, swiping his sword into the dark shape. With a grunt, the attacker wrapped its hands around Dagra's neck, and he stabbed the wide-bladed gladius up through his assailant's belly, thrusting it higher into the chest. The hands around Dagra's neck slackened and his attacker slumped over him. He wrenched the blade free from the body, and it fell to the ground. It had all happened in seconds, but Oriken and Jalis had their weapons out and ready for more to rush them from the tunnel. The moment drew long, but nothing came. Oriken looked to Dagra, whose eyes were set on the body at his feet.

Oriken looked down. "Shit," he said, as he regarded the dirty, sore-covered skin, the long, matted hair and scraggly beard of a naked man.

Dagra groaned, walked over to the entrance and stood staring out into the rain.

"A hermit?" Jalis pondered. "Or are there more, deeper within the mine?"

"An idiot, either way," Oriken said. "What was he thinking?"

"We invaded his home." Dagra kept his back to them. "He was only protecting himself."

Jalis shook her head. "We posed him no threat," she told Dagra.

"We should burn him."

Oriken threw his hands up. "Great idea. I'll just go and get some dry wood for a fire. There are so many trees around here, and it's not pissing down at all."

"Okay, fine!" Dagra turned to face them. "Let's at least drag him further in, if we're staying a while."

"That, I can do," Oriken said, trying unsuccessfully to keep the hard edge from his voice.

Dagra looked at him, and after a moment gave a brief nod.

Oriken grabbed the hermit's wrists and dragged the body into the tunnel, keeping his senses alert for further danger. The blackness was pitch, but he knew mine entrances well. Fifty feet further in, the tunnel angled away and he dropped the corpse into the corner. For a full minute he stood and stared into the darkness while unformed thoughts pushed at the edge of his emotions.

"Orik!" Jalis's voice rang down the tunnel. "Are you alright?"

"Sure," he called. He gave the darkness a sombre glance, then turned to rejoin his friends.

"You didn't have to go so far inside," Dagra said as Oriken approached the entrance.

"I didn't go far. I was just thinking."

"You do choose your spots for introspection," Jalis said. "In an abandoned mine, in the dark, next to a corpse."

"A little respect please, lass," Dagra said. "That was a living person a few minutes ago."

"*He* attacked *us*," Jalis said, "not the other way around. You defended yourself. You have nothing to feel bad about."

"I didn't have to kill him."

"No, but you had no way of knowing how dangerous he was, nor that he was even a man until it was too late. Don't beat yourself up over it. We've got a long way to go yet, and we all need to keep our wits as sharp as our blades."

Dagra rumbled a wordless acknowledgement. "I wish that fucking rain would ease off so we can get moving."

Jalis smiled. "That's the spirit."

Oriken slumped down to sit against the wall.

Jalis sat cross-legged beside him. "Something up?"

"No."

She studied his face. "Remember it's me you're talking to. I can see your soul."

He snorted. "I don't have one of those."

Dagra came to join them. "You don't need to follow the Dyad to have a soul," he said. "Everyone has one. Even you."

"Yeah, right." Oriken turned his eyes to the darkness.

"*Yes*, right," Dagra insisted.

"I don't believe in any of your gods, Dag. You know that. Not the Dyad. Not the Bound. None of them."

"Well, maybe they believe in you."

"For fuck's sake!" Oriken climbed to his feet and glowered at his friend. "Can't you leave it alone, just for once?"

Jalis rose and stood between them. "I don't know how the two of you managed to stay friends all these years," she said, passing a stern look from one to the other.

Dagra waved a hand dismissively. "Neither do I."

"I do," Oriken said. "I owe—" He bit back the rest of the words and pressed his lips firmly together.

Dagra slowly turned his head. His eyes raised to fix Oriken with a baleful glare. "Don't stop there," he said calmly. "You still think you owe me? What I did for you, I did too late. I had a chance earlier, and I didn't take it. You owe me nothing."

29

Idiot! Oriken admonished himself. *You couldn't keep your mouth shut.* "Dag, look, I'm sorry. I didn't mean—"

"You didn't mean," Dagra sneered. "You didn't *think*. That's your problem, Oriken. You *never* think." With a sigh, he sat back down.

Oriken stared at him, but Dagra said nothing more and kept his eyes on the opposite wall, his fingers upon the pendant around his neck. When Oriken turned to Jalis, she was regarding him serenely. Restraining the urge to light a roll of tobah, he shook his head and wandered into the darkness. Things hadn't been this bad between him and Dagra for a long time. The place was affecting them both.

CHAPTER FOUR
STONES OF TIMES PAST

"What will you girls be getting up to today?"

Eriqwyn stifled a sigh and spooned the last of her broth into her mouth to avoid giving her mother a flippant reply.

Across the table, her sister shared a glance with Eriqwyn. "I expect it will be a day like any other," Adri said. "We're happy to have you join us at breakfast, Mother. Did you sleep well?"

Their mother gave Adri the briefest of nods, then her eyes glazed over and she looked down at her food.

"Back into her own world," Eriqwyn muttered.

Adri cleared her throat. "How are the young hunters getting along with their training?"

"Most are showing promise, but they still have a long way to go, and won't be hunters until I accept them as such."

Adri cast her a flat look. "That, sister, is an understanding which doesn't fly above me as the leader of this community."

Eriqwyn inclined her head in deference. "Of course. Tell me one thing though, Adri. As First Warder, accepting the trainees is my responsibility, but why on the goddess's green heath did you insist on putting Demelza forward?"

"Ah, yes. Demelza." Adri gave a tight smile. "Your dislike of the girl is quite apparent, and I know you would never have accepted her otherwise. I admit there's something about her which unsettles me also, but she's harmless and I believe she has potential."

"You and Wayland see something in her that I do not," Eriqwyn said. "Her progress is slow, and her attentiveness is almost non-existent."

Adri placed her spoon in her empty bowl. "It doesn't mean she can't learn. She lives alone, Eri. She's proven herself to be self-sufficient since old Ina died. I've seen her return to the village with rabbits, pheasants, baskets of crabs. One time I saw her dragging an adult nargut back to her shack."

"Well, I don't know how she managed to catch them without nets or traps or a well-aimed arrow. What she appears to be capable of doesn't match her observed skills. I don't believe she has what it takes." Eriqwyn shrugged. "No matter. Wayland has charge of the girl. If anyone can turn her into a hunter, it's him. He's fond of Demelza, and his patience is unparalleled."

"Wayland is a strong Warder. As is Linisa." Adri rose from her chair and reached across the table for Eriqwyn's bowl. "The three of you might be the most capable team of Warders this village has ever known. Minnow's Beck is indeed well protected."

"It's good of you to say so, sister." *But protected against what?* As Adri left the room, Eriqwyn rose from her seat and glanced down at their mother. "I'm going out to gather flowers now, Mamma," she said, hating herself a little for knowing her words were spoken less in kindness and more in mockery.

Her mother looked up and met her gaze. Despite the passing of years locked inside her memories, for just a moment her eyes showed the ghost of the woman she had once been. "All right, dear," she said, with a faint smile. "Have fun."

Fun. Eriqwyn pondered the word as she walked from the room. *As if life is still about playing skip-rope and gathering flowers. I grew up, Mother. As did Adri. We scarcely remember what fun is any more.*

A babble of voices drifted from open doorways as Eriqwyn strode down Fallen-Shrine Row, her unstrung bow in hand. Heat and the smell of steel filled the air as she passed by the open front of the smithy. Tan, the younger of the two blacksmiths, glanced from his work and raised a hand in greeting. Without breaking stride, Eriqwyn acknowledged the gesture with a brief nod, and continued down the street.

As she reached the village's southern edge, a figure stepped out from behind the last house. Eriqwyn gritted her teeth as she recognised Shade. The woman's dark, lustrous hair fell about her shoulders, and the sheer material of her long skirt and sashes that crossed over her breasts clung to her figure in the warm breeze.

Shade paused beside a wooden beam and lifted her hand to caress the smooth wood. "Hello, Eri," she purred. Her brown eyes glinted in the morning sun.

Eriqwyn made to move past her, but stopped when Shade touched her shoulder. "What do you want?" Eriqwyn snapped.

Shade smiled. "Such hostility. You know I like that in a woman. I haven't seen you for quite a while, Eri. Have you been hiding from me?"

"I have no need to hide from you," Eriqwyn said acidly. "And don't call me Eri. You and I are not close."

"More's the pity." Shade's voice exuded sensuality every bit as much as her appearance. "What would you have me call you instead? First Warder?"

"That would be acceptable."

"Such formalities," Shade chided. "I thought we were long past that. With the places you and I have been, I would say we are more... intimately connected than most in Minnow's Beck." Her eyes traced Eriqwyn's body.

Eriqwyn glanced along the street to ensure there were no eavesdroppers. "There is no intimacy between you and I," she said forcefully. "If there ever was, it is long gone. I know you for what you are, Shade. You are a gemstone – beautiful, but cold."

Shade took a step closer, seeming to glide the short distance between them. Her fingers traced their way down Eriqwyn's bare shoulder to her arm. "Do I feel cold?" She moved closer still. "Or do I feel *warm*? Do you remember that warmth, Eri? You should come visit me some time, I would remind you how pleasing I am to the eye *and* the touch."

With a gasp of frustration, Eriqwyn glowered and shrugged Shade's hand from her arm. "You will address me with the respect of my position."

"Oh," Shade purred with a tantalising smile, "but I do respect your position." The tip of her tongue snaked between her teeth. "Every one of them."

Eriqwyn pushed past and stormed away.

"See you soon!" Shade called after her.

———— • ————

Dagra grasped his Avato pendant and whispered a prayer to the Dyad and their prophets as he trudged through the low grass, still damp from the previous day's downpour. To the west, a range of hills swept along the horizon, the faintest sigh of the ocean drifting over their peaks. To the east, reeds and marshgrasses jutted from the fog-laden wetland like steeples of tiny temples, while ghostly globes of fae-fire floated serenely above the white shroud.

They had followed the marsh through the rest of the previous day, and when the wetland finally gave way to firmer land to the south, Jalis called a halt for the night and they slept beneath the stars. Since daybreak they had kept a steady pace, hoping for the vast marsh to finally end so they could turn inland and head back towards the Kingdom Road. As the first hour of morning stretched into the second and the third, Dagra felt more and more as if a crushing presence filled the heathland.

It wasn't the open space that unnerved him, nor was it the potential of any physical danger; he was a freeblade, after all, and if the going got too tough they could always turn back. What troubled him was the godless atmosphere that began when they entered the Deadlands, and which had only worsened since. He could scarcely feel the presence of the Dyad this deep inside Scapa Fell. His only hope was that Aveia still heard his prayers, and that her counterpart Svey'Drommelach also listened from the Spirit Realm; it was

33

disconcerting, and – Dagra grudgingly admitted – ironic that his hopes almost outweighed his prayers in this place where the Dyad had never reigned, this place that was the domain of a primitive and long-since unworshipped goddess.

"Before the Uprising," Dagra said, more to himself than the others, "they didn't burn their dead. Just buried them and left them in the ground to fester and rot." He shuddered. "Ungodly practice."

"It was the same in the Arkh before the emergence of the Dyad," Jalis said. "Some places bury their dead without cremation – in the remote areas where they still worship the Bound and Unbound over the Dyad."

"I never much cared either way," Oriken commented. "What does it matter what happens to you when you're gone?"

"The dead should be burned and their ashes spread to the winds," Dagra insisted. "Leave the bones to sink into the mud, but let the spirit fly free." Mouthing a silent addition to his prayer, he released his pendant and glanced past Jalis to the western highland. At that moment the upper corner of a square stone structure came into view between the distant hills.

Jalis had spotted it too. She paused and shrugged out of her pack. "Is that a castle?"

"I doubt it," Oriken said. "Too small."

"It's bigger than that ringfort on the outskirts." Dagra frowned at the ugly grey block that was as tall as it was wide. "No windows on the lower floor. Who'd want to live in such a place?"

"I don't think it was built for comfort," Oriken said. "More than likely it's an old garrison."

"Hm." Jalis had the map in her hand and stabbed a finger down onto it. "It's here. Caer Valekha." She glanced around the map. "That means we're a little under halfway to Lachyla."

"Almost past the point of no return," Dagra muttered. "When the destination's closer, the sensible route is onward."

Oriken quirked a brow. "Do I hear a surge of enthusiasm?"

Dagra snorted. "More like resolve."

"Wait." Jalis stared at the stronghold as she replaced the map and slung her pack over her shoulder. "I thought I saw movement."

"You did," Dagra said as he strode off along the edge of the marsh. "It's the dust-trail behind me as I hurry to leave this place."

"Dag's right," Oriken said as they hurried to catch up. "There's no telling what's over there, but it's not our objective and I ain't curious enough after the cravants and the hermit."

Jalis nodded. "Agreed."

After putting distance between them and the fortress, Dagra cast a wary glance over his shoulder at the building. *Caer Valekha. Why did places have to have such grim names back then?* As they continued on, the stronghold shrank behind the hills, beyond which a shimmering strip topped the horizon – the morning sun glinting from the coastline. "It's a long time since I last saw the Echilan Ocean," he said wistfully.

"Yeah." Oriken sighed, then barked a laugh. "Remember when we went all the way to Mount Sentinel?"

Dagra nodded. "Clambering over its foothills to see as far as we could across the water."

"We couldn't climb any higher."

"And there was fuck all out there except frothing waves."

Oriken laughed. "True. It was quite the underwhelming end to an otherwise fun adventure. Your grandparents were sick with worry."

"They didn't let me out of their sight for weeks. Yes, I remember."

"Gentlemen, I hate to interrupt the nostalgia, but it looks like we're running out of dry land again."

Dagra looked ahead and saw that she was right. His resolve wavered. Although the marsh-fog was clearing, the telltale signs of bog-infested ground spread out not only to their left but now also before them, blocking the way. A half-mile distant, a dark-green strip of conifers marked the return of solid ground. "If we keep heading west, the wetlands might thin out closer to the coast."

"That's the spirit." Oriken clapped a hand to Dagra's shoulder. "We'll find a way across. We always do. Right?"

"Aye," Dagra rumbled. "We always do."

Their break came long before reaching the coastline. Five hundred yards along the edge of the marsh, a crude crossing of partially sunken tree trunks had been slung across the marsh in rows of three.

"Well, there you go." Oriken grinned. "That was helpful of someone."

"Thank the gods," Dagra said. "But I'm not sticking around to meet whoever built it." He placed a foot onto the first half-submerged trunk, testing his weight upon it. "Seems firm enough." He stepped up onto the wood, found his balance and moved across to the next trunk.

Jalis sprang lightly onto the timber. "This walkway looks decades old, maybe a century, and probably laid upon the remnants of a previous crossing. Whoever constructed it should be long dead."

"A hundred years or a day, the gods see the future and set the pieces in place," Dagra said. "They send things to test us, but they send things to aid us, too."

"Hey, Dag," Oriken called from behind. "I don't care if it's gods or goat-herders. Whatever gets you to the other side."

Dagra shook his head. "The gods have been using you to test me for years, Orik. Mock all you like, my friend. One of these days I'll convince you I'm right." Smiling to himself, he added, *Even if it takes until the afterlife.*

Eriqwyn wandered along the gently rising coastline several feet from the rocky shore. The hushed lapping of the tide was the only sound other than the distant cries of gulls behind her. Ahead there were no birds as the green grasses yellowed and thinned to lifeless earth. The steady incline of coast rose to a cliff that jutted into the ocean and circled the distant promontory of land. With scarcely a shrub or sickly-looking tree in sight, the arid earth sloped towards a looming, jagged wall that stretched all the way into the heath. Another wall topped the southern outcrop, and beyond its battlements the hazy tops of towers and spires faded against the blue sky.

Her bow was strung, but Eriqwyn did not expect to have to use it. The closer she walked towards the perimeter of the Forbidden Place, the chances of seeing wildlife of any kind became increasingly unlikely; as with the grasses, the creatures shied from the high and ancient wall. Here, only one reason existed for which she might need a weapon, and she prayed to the goddess that such an event never come to light.

There was no need to head all the way up to the wall, she could see enough detail from a distance to be sure that nothing lurked near its base nor between the battlements above. Veering inland, she took a parallel course to the long wall, following a route walked by Warders or hunters of the village each day for generations. Far to the east, the angular lines of Minnow's Beck's southernmost buildings peeked from behind the foot of the tree-covered Dreaming Dragon Brae, the village's natural hide from the north and west. Increasing her pace, she kept her eyes alert and cast continuous glances all around, especially towards the Forbidden Place's implacable barrier.

Half an hour later, Eriqwyn reached the north-east corner of the wall and the vast heathland opened up ahead of her in swathes of green and gold, the high sun streaming down onto the rolling landscape. Glancing along the northern wall, she traced its length until it tapered into the horizon. It was not her turn to check on the entrance today; that job fell on Linisa, who would be taking a hunter-in-training to look through the iron bars of the Forbidden Place's entrance for the first time, just as one of the previous Warders had done with Eriqwyn when she was a girl, and just as Wayland would soon be doing with Demelza.

Satisfied that the coast was clear, she turned onto the third and final leg of her circuit, following the trail that led back to the village. After some minutes, she saw a lone figure up ahead.

Demelza, she thought. *Out on her own again. Off to get a peek through the bars, is she?*

No sooner had she spotted the girl, than Demelza darted off the trail and disappeared into the tree-line. Frowning, Eriqwyn's hunter instincts kicked in and she entered the wood, stepping lightly through the undergrowth between the trees. Catching a glimpse of movement as Demelza flitted up the shallow foot of Dreaming Dragon Brae, Eriqwyn lowered to a half-crouch and gave pursuit. At the flat crest of the hill was the natural clearing of Dragoneye Glade. Eriqwyn hid within the trees and bushes and watched the girl enter the glade. Demelza crossed to an ivy-covered stone block at the glade's centre – the offering stone after which the clearing was named, its only attendant the ivy as none had worshipped the primordial gods since long before Valsana changed the world.

Eriqwyn waited as one minute stretched into the next, and Demelza remained hidden behind the altar. Across the clearing, the underbrush rustled. Eriqwyn's senses pricked. Her eyes quickly found the area of disturbance. Within the bushes a pair of wide-set yellow eyes glinted in the sunlight low to the ground. The creature poked its head into the clearing, and Eriqwyn immediately reached for an arrow. *Sarbek*, she thought, nocking the shaft as the wolf-like creature crept from the undergrowth, its sword-like ridge of bone arcing over its back, pale against its dark fur.

Wolves were uncommon this close to Minnow's Beck, but Sarbeks were much rarer. Such creatures tended to keep to the hilly woodland far to the north-east, but if one were to come across a lone, unarmed human...

The sarbek's attention was on the altar stone, behind which Demelza was still hiding. The creature took several tentative steps forward, then crouched, ready to spring.

Eriqwyn drew and released the arrow, and it punched into the sarbek's side. With a high-pitched whine, the creature toppled and Demelza was out of her hiding place in an instant and running to its side. Crouching, she held a hand to its flank and with her other gently stroked the sarbek's head. Eriqwyn stepped from the trees and the girl stared at her, her eyes glistening with moisture.

What in the name of Valsana is she crying for?

"Why'd you have to do that?" Demelza sobbed.

Eriqwyn was taken aback. That was not the reaction she'd expected from the girl. "You shouldn't be out here alone."

Demelza blinked and tears spilled down her cheeks. She turned her attention to the sarbek, and after a moment the creature blinked and closed its eyes, huffed one last breath, then died. Still kneeling, she turned on Eriqwyn. "What's she ever done to you?" she yelled.

"I..." Eriqwyn faltered, then checked herself. "You were in danger, girl! Clearly you can't fend for yourself. You should be thanking me, you ungrateful child! If I hadn't been here, you'd currently be getting mauled to death in that creature's jaws."

Demelza hung her head, tears spilling to the dead sarbek's fur. "I were in no danger. She was my friend. Couldn't you see that?" She rose to her feet and squared on Eriqwyn. "I got no friends in the village, do I?" she said accusingly. "Ain't none there who likes me."

Eriqwyn drew a breath. "That's not true, Demelza."

"Aye, it's true. And you know it, cos you're one of 'em what don't like me. I see it, you know? I ain't daft."

There was nothing for Eriqwyn to say. It was true, she really didn't like the girl, not that she could say exactly why. And that was the truth for many of the villagers. But this was a different side to Demelza she hadn't witnessed before. The death of the sarbek had animated the girl more than Eriqwyn had ever seen.

"You can't make friends with the predators of the wild," she said. But, somehow, despite her years of training, the statement felt weak. Had the sarbek really been about to attack? Eriqwyn was no longer so sure.

"Maybe *you* can't," Demelza sobbed. "I only kill to eat, not cos I think everything wants to kill me or cos I enjoy it."

Eriqwyn stifled a gasp. "I don't enjoy—"

Demelza cast her a venomous glare, then ran off into the woods.

Leaning her bow against the altar stone, Eriqwyn blew out a long breath. She turned to the sarbek, grasped the arrow jutting from its side, and pulled it free, Taking a rag from a pouch at her waist, she wiped the arrowhead and replaced it into her quiver, then paused to regard the dead creature. No matter the reason, the sarbek was dead, and, in the wilds of Scapa Fell, nothing useful should ever be left to waste. With a shrug, she unsheathed her hunting dagger, knelt, and began to work.

CHAPTER FIVE
CONTRACTUAL COMPLICATIONS

Maros winced as he leaned down to the barrel of Saltcoast Tan, transferring his weight to his good leg while giving the ruined one some slack. He grabbed the iron rim of the ale barrel, tensed his muscles and heaved upwards. With a grip as strong as the metal in his grasp, he brought the barrel to his chest and locked his elbows, holding it firm. Transferring a little weight to his bad leg, he took a step forwards. Agony lanced up the side of his leg and he spat a curse as a breeze blew through the back yard of the tavern, cooling the sheen of sweat upon his brow.

"Damned leg," he growled. *Time was, I could've carried this barrel across the way with no effort. Now I'm straining and sweating like a rutting pig, not to mention having to use this accursed cart.*

He felt a sudden urge to kick the wheel of the barrel-cart, but restrained himself; it would be foolish to lose his temper while hefting twenty gallons of his most popular ale. Another precarious step forwards brought him to the rear of the cart. He lowered his burden to the planks beside a smaller barrel of Carradosi Pale and an even smaller cask of Vorinsian Redanchor.

Rubbing at his rounded belly, he sighed and shook his head. "It's Maros the Mountain more than ever these days," he mumbled. "Curse that krig of a critter getting its damned needle teeth in my knee." He limped around to the front of the cart and paused to massage the side of his throbbing leg.

If I could kill that lyakyn all over again I'd do it here and now; smash its teeth in and tear its jaws right off its face. And it'd be as satisfying as the first time. He sighed and shook his head. *Aye, but no amount of daydreaming'll get me walking proper again.*

Hefting the cart's long handle, he limped and grunted his way across the evening-dark yard to the tavern's rear door. Once there, he began the task of dragging the barrels off the cart and into the Lonely Peddler.

The tavern was quiet. Other than a handful of freeblades at one of their regular tables in the front corner, just a few townsfolk were peppered throughout the common room. Maros had allowed the young barman, Jecaiah, to leave early and go home to his wife, and he'd sent a couple of the serving girls home, too. With the unopened barrels secured beneath the bar beside those currently in use, Maros set the cask of Redanchor atop the rear counter, ready for tomorrow or the following day for the patrons with more expensive tastes.

He snatched up his barstool and limped out from behind the counter, hobbled over to the freeblades and sat with his back against the wall.

"What were they thinking?" Alari was saying. "The ten percent divided between the three of them"—she nodded to indicate Maros—"and the boss's and headquarters' cuts; it's good, but it ain't gonna get them far."

Beside Alari, the novice under her charge snorted. "They could've gotten a bunch o' menial jobs instead, in the month or more they'll be gone, like you told me to do."

Maros frowned at the young man. "Kirran, that's the right attitude for a novice, but not if you want to stay one for the rest of your freeblading days."

"Uh, sorry, boss."

"Don't be sorry. Those menial jobs have to be taken by somebody, and right now that person is you."

Kirran pressed his lips together and said nothing more.

Across from him, Henwyn gave a hearty chuckle. "The boss has you there, lad." He took a sip of his wine. "Seriously though, boss, you think this contract will prove to be worth it?"

Maros grunted. "Your guess is as good as mine, Hen. Truth is, I've been wondering about the Chiddari woman's agenda. That's some serious money she's handed over, but something ain't sittin' right with me. You ever known someone to care so much about a trinket they've never seen? And at her age?"

Henwyn shrugged and glanced at Alari. "Me, I'd have taken the contract just for the ten percent. It's still a sizeable amount. Truth be told, I'm a little miffed that I wasn't here when you posted it on the board. I would've snatched it up. A month alone out in the wilderness? Aye, I'd take that."

"Alone?" The girl beside Henwyn fixed him with a disheartened look. "What happened to you showing me the ropes?"

"Bah." Henwyn grinned through his close-shorn beard. "Don't take this the wrong way, lass, but you don't know your tits from your toes out there yet. You ain't ready for being one with the land for that amount of time."

The girl eyed him coolly. "I know the wilderness," she said, then turned away.

Alari cleared her throat. "Do you put any stock in the legend?" she asked. "I mean, I just hope our friends are fully prepared, is all."

"I don't know," Maros admitted, shifting his weight on the stool. "I know some who disagree, but I reckon stories is all they are. If I were able, I'd be out there with them instead of cooped up in the Folly. I ain't never been inclined to venture into the Deadlands, and I ain't been too curious about the Blighted City, but—" A phlegmy cough issued from the table beside them. Maros glanced across at Jerrick, a regular at the Peddler, sitting alone as usual and spluttering into his cup. "That cough's getting worse, old feller," Maros said. "You oughta get a tincture for it."

"Heh." Jerrick looked up, his rheumy eyes darting to Maros. "It don't help when I hears what you young'uns are flapping your lips about."

"This is freeblade business," Maros chided. "Not for you to be listening in on."

"Aye, well, when a man hears what he hears, he has to speak up, don't he? I had a friend in the blades once, you know? Hard to fathom that an old codger like me might'a had friends, ain't it? Well, I did. All dead now, an' Lijah was the first to go. He were a good man." Jerrick sighed and frowned in thought. "Let me see now… Must be fifty years gone when Lijah and me were sat in this very tavern an' he said he was off on a mission. Aye, they called 'em missions back then."

Maros glanced at Alari and gave her a discreet shrug.

Jerrick coughed, then cackled into his hand before wiping it on his trousers and raising a bushy, white eyebrow. "Said he'd be gone awhile, that he were going down south to find a stone for a lass. You know, the usual questy nonsense you freeblades get up to. I asks him where south, an' he says to the Blighted City, of all places. Well, off he went. Never did come back. Consensus were that he'd got himself lost, beset by monsters or such, fell into a swamp, somethin' like that. Me, I'm not so sure. Lijah were a wily one."

Alari shifted her stool around and waited as Jerrick noisily cleared his throat against his gnarled hand. When he was finished, she leaned closer and said, "Who was the lass?"

"Buggered if I know."

Maros shook his head. "This is news to me."

"No reason you'd have heard," Henwyn put in. "One contract among thousands, from half a century ago?"

"Check the records," Alari suggested.

"Won't find anything in there," Maros said. "The archives here only go back ten years. The headquarters at Brancosi has all the older contracts and member records."

Jerrick spluttered another bout of coughing, then drew a wooden pipe and pouch of what Maros knew to be nepenthe-laced tobah from his coat. Despite his gnarled knuckles, he deftly stuffed the moist leaves into the pipe, then took a sip of ale. "Live by the blade, die by the blade, you young'uns say, don'tcha? Aye, well, I reckon these are my blades." He brandished his pipe and cup, drained the last of his ale, then rose from his chair. "It were good chatting with you lads." He nodded to Alari. "And you, lass."

"Hey, Jerrick," Maros called after him.

A puzzled expression crossed the old man's face. "Ah, what were we talking about?"

41

Maros smiled sadly. "Life and death, I believe."

"Ah, yes." The old man gave a toothy grin. "Two topics I know enough about. Well, then." He raised a liver-spotted hand to his head as if tipping a hat, then shuffled across the common room and out into the evening.

As the saloon doors swished shut, Maros sat in thought. Jerrick's revelation bothered him. It bothered him a lot.

Henwyn was looking at him. "When the courier next arrives, send him back with a request for the files from fifty years ago."

"The courier won't be back for a fortnight," Maros said. "Then he'll have rounds to finish before heading back to the Bay. And it'll likely be several more weeks till he returns again. That's too long."

"Too long for what, boss?" the girl beside Henwyn asked.

Maros frowned at her. "I'm sorry, lass, I've forgotten your name."

"Leaf," she said.

"Hm. Well then, Leaf. How would you like a little courier contract of your own? Show Henwyn what you're capable of."

Leaf's eyes widened. "A job on my own? Sure."

"Right, then. Meet me here at noon tomorrow. I'll have the request form drafted up by then."

"Where am I going?"

"Guild HQ at Brancosi Bay."

Leaf's jaw dropped. "I never been to the capital before."

"Well, now's your chance. But don't dally, because I want those papers as quick as possible."

"What's the rush?" Kirran asked, keeping his tone careful.

Maros eyed the novice. "The rush, boy, is that I would tend to agree with Jerrick, that his friend didn't just die on the road. If one freeblade gets sent on a mission"—he shook his head as he caught himself using Jerrick's antiquated word—"then the likelihood is that he or she is a veteran – journeyman or journeywoman at least, if not a bladesmaster or bladesmistress."

"What are you saying?" Henwyn asked.

"What I'm saying, Hen, is that I think this Lijah did find the Blighted City. More to the point, I think Jalis and the lads'll find it, too, and I'll be damned if I'll let them meet the same fate."

The last of the night's patrons disappear through the saloon doors into the darkness, leaving Maros alone while a pair of serving girls mopped the boards and wiped the tables clean. The clattering of pots and pans drifted through from the kitchen where Luthan the chef was busy performing his own end-of-shift duties.

After a few minutes, Maros heard a *swish-swish*, and he glanced down the walkway behind the bar. Luthan had exited the kitchen and was heading towards Maros. His bleached apron and bandanna were as pristine as always when he entered the public area, even if the place was devoid of customers. More than just a chef, Luthan's famous whitesand meal had given him something of a name in these parts and he had an image to maintain, something he managed with quiet, yet confident, decorum.

"How'd you like a bite to eat?" The chef said. "I'm fixing something for myself before I head home. Why don't you join me? Boss?"

"Hm?" Maros caught Luthan's gaze and puffed his cheeks. "No, not for me. It's too late."

The clean-shaven chef pulled up a barstool and propped himself upon it. His blue eyes studied Maros's face. "Something's troubling you." It wasn't a question; with Luthan, it never was.

"I'm worried about Jalis and the lads. I was getting to think I'd sent them chasing dragons, but now I reckon it might be worse."

"That's always a chance for a freeblade," Luthan said.

"True." Maros clenched his fist and rubbed the knuckles with his other hand. "Something's starting to feel off-kilter about this one, though."

At the far end of the common room, the saloon doors swung open. A man entered, pausing in the doorway to smooth his overcoat and remove his plaid cap. He eyed Maros across the distance as he made his way purposefully towards the bar.

Luthan cleared his throat and hopped down from his stool to head briskly back into the kitchen.

"We're closed for the night," Maros told the newcomer. "Unless it's a room you're after?"

The man sighed as he reached the bar and laid his cap on the oaken counter. "I'm not here as a customer, good tavernmaster."

Maros sized him up. The stranger's flaccid face was clean-shaven, his attire ruffled but finely-cut, and he certainly wasn't the sort who liked getting his hands dirty. Maros guessed him to be in his late forties. "Can't say I've seen you around these parts, friend. You here to offer a contract?"

"Not quite." The man sounded weary. "I'm here *about* a contract, but one that is unfortunately already agreed upon."

"I see." A trickle of annoyance crept in as Maros wished the man would get to the point. "Then please, state your business."

"I left the hamlet of Balen five hours ago," the man said, reaching into his cloak and bringing forth a tied roll of parchment which he placed upon the polished counter beside his cap. "I'm too tired for extended formalities, and I might just take you up on that offer of a room. It's been a long and decidedly rare day."

"Eleven coppers for a room," Maros rumbled. "Fifteen if you want a hot breakfast in the morning."

The man pressed his lips together and held Maros's gaze. "Good tavernmaster, I rather think that after you've read and fully digested the

43

contents of this document"—he tapped the roll of parchment before him—"you may consider extending me the use of a room as a gesture of good will."

Maros clenched his teeth, glanced at the parchment, then fixed a scowl on the newcomer, his patience waning. To give the man his due, he didn't seem aware of Maros's reputation, nor did he seem in the least bit intimidated by his half-jotunn size; Maros could have reached over the bar and crushed the man's face in one hairy fist if he had the mind to. Even slouched on the high-stool he still towered over the man by more than a foot.

"I'll accept the breakfast as a courtesy, as well," the man added.

Maros's scowl deepened that bit further as he eased himself up from the stool, planted his large hands upon the counter and loomed over. "And why," he rumbled, "would I extend you these generosities, friend?"

The stranger drew in a breath before answering. "It appears that in my fatigue I neglected to introduce myself. My name," he said, seeming completely unperturbed as his eyes lifted to meet Maros's, "is Randallen Chiddari."

"Ah." Maros glared at him. "Then I'm glad you're here. Some years ago – *quite* some years ago – it seems that one of our 'blades was hired to head into the same territory as three of mine are in now, fulfilling your mother's contract. That man never returned, and it's my strong suspicion that he was hired by your mother, or perhaps one of her parents. I need to speak with her."

Randallen snorted. "I never knew her parents. Her mother has been dead for fifty years, buried in the family plot in Eihazwood. As to my dear mother, I'm afraid she can't answer any of your questions."

"Oh?" Maros pursed his lips. "And why would that be?"

"Because, good tavernmaster, in the early hours of this morning she lost all interest in your little agreement. She is, to put it bluntly, dead."

CHAPTER SIX
TWO ENDS OF THE ROAD

Maros left his quarters above the tavern's common room and made his way downstairs, gripping the sturdy banister as he limped down the stairs one at a time.

Why in the Pit do I still have the private wing upstairs? He made a mental note to swap the freeblades wing, which included his own rooms and those of his three absent friends, with one of the downstairs guest wings.

Half a dozen steps from the bottom, he paused and stifled a yawn behind his hand as he studied the public area. Only three patrons were in the common room at this early hour. All were overnight guests, taking solitary breakfasts at separate tables.

Maros's boot scraped across the stone as he dragged his ruined leg down the remaining steps. His eyes fixed on one particular guest, who glanced up from his breakfast and nodded a sombre greeting. Randallen Chiddari held one of Luthan's famous whitesands over a plate, a dribble of sauce oozing from a thick slice of meat that protruded between the crusty slabs of bread. Maros whispered a tired curse as he made his way over.

The kitchen door swished open as he passed and he was greeted with a gap-toothed smile from the emerging serving girl. "Morning, Diela," he said, returning the smile.

"Mornin', boss. Coffee?"

He nodded.

"I'll bring it right out."

Maros reached Randallen's table and peered down at his guest. "Master Chiddari, May I sit?"

Randallen dropped his whitesand to the plate and glanced up. "Please do," he said flatly.

Maros could sense the man's ill humour. *Gods*, he thought, *how I hate the diplomacy that comes with being Guild Official.* "My thanks," he said. He lowered himself onto a stool opposite, suppressing a wince as he shifted his foot to a more comfortable position. *I should put a Maros-sized seat at each table to avoid moments like this.* Squirming on the low seat, he cleared his throat. "Master Chiddari—"

Randallen rolled his eyes. "I haven't the patience for that nonsense. I'm a village man. In Balen, everyone calls me Ral, even those with whom I hold a mutual dislike. I'd ask you to do the same."

So, he wants to be a straight-talker this morning. I can live with that. "Very well, *Ral.*" Maros gestured to the partially consumed food on the man's plate. "How do you like your breakfast?"

Randallen cast him a flat look. "Have you had time to consider our problem?"

"I've done little else all night," Maros said. "*Including* sleep."

"That I can empathise with."

Maros reached into his vest pocket and produced a parchment, unfolded it and placed it upon the table. "The contract between your mother and the Freeblades Guild is for the discovery and retrieval of one burial jewel belonging to the Chiddari family."

"Yes, yes. And there are five hundred silver dari of my mother's sitting in your coffers."

Maros nodded. "Set aside for the freeblades who have undertaken the contract."

"Which brings us to the problem." Randallen stifled a sigh as Diela arrived at the table.

"Here you go, boss." Diela set a steaming tankard of coffee before Maros. He gulped a mouthful of the hot drink and sighed in satisfaction, nodding his thanks.

As the serving girl went about her business, Randallen raised an eyebrow. "The problem?"

"As I explained to you last night, a contract doesn't expire in the event of the client's death." Maros paused to take another mouthful of coffee. "I'm truly sorry to hear about your mother. She seemed like a—"

"I've been in this tavern for far too long already," Randallen said sharply. "So, please, spare me the platitudes and let's thrash this business to a conclusion. You have in your possession a sum of money which just happens to be the vast majority of my mother's life savings. Do you understand what that means?"

"I'm beginning to."

"It means that I, as dear Mother's son and only heir, suddenly find myself with no inheritance. That won't do. I have a wife and two daughters. I took care of my mother for as long as I was able. When I die, my wife and my girls will get whatever I manage to amass in my life, as I in turn deserve with my mother's savings."

Maros pursed his lips, considering the point. "Following the terms of guild contracts and policies," he said carefully, "payments can only be returned if a

46

contract is left unfulfilled. In which case, a full ninety percent would be returned to the beneficiary."

"Oh."

"Indeed. But I must advise you, and I'm afraid this is the part you may not like…" Maros took the contract from the table and brought it to his face, squinting at his own handwriting until he found the section he wanted. Turning the paper around, he placed it before Randallen and tapped a finger on the relevant paragraph. "See here? You'll notice your mother named no beneficiary. Technically, that means I'm not obligated to accept you as such. However—"

"What? Didn't you even *prompt* her for a name?"

Maros gave a stony smile. "If a client wishes to name a beneficiary, they may do so, but it isn't an essential part of the agreement. If your mother had you in mind, she had every chance to mention you."

"Why, the ungrateful…" Randallen's cheeks glowed with anger as he stared at the parchment.

"It's a predicament," Maros said. "That much I agree with. We've talked about your problem, but you must realise the coin has two sides." He leaned forward and lowered his voice. "I've got three good people risking their lives venturing to a place that no one's been in centuries, one of very few in the whole of Himaera to bear the Death's Head symbol. My freeblades – my *family* – have travelled to the Blighted City to find your mother's heirloom. The potential dangers, I'm sure you'll agree, are unimaginable." He prodded a finger against the parchment. "This contract is insurance against my freeblades losing their lives during its undertaking. You lost your mother. That's regrettable. But if my freeblades don't return from the Deadlands—"

"That *isn't* my concern! Nobody forced them to take the contract."

"*Master* Chiddari." Maros eased himself to his feet and loomed over the table. "You have a tendency of interrupting me. If you hadn't done so, you would already have heard me say that I'm considering accepting you as beneficiary in lieu of your mother. Please note I said *considering*. Whether I do or not depends on you. The way I see it, you have one option. If my people return with the heirloom – which they will if it exists, or they'll die trying – I'd advise you to graciously accept it from them. If they don't return—"

"That's unacceptable!" Randallen's face quivered with repressed rage. "I demand that you—"

Maros's knuckles cracked as he clenched his fists and leaned them upon the table. The wood creaking beneath his weight was the only sound in the common room. "You *demand* nothing of the Freeblades Guild, little man. One more unsavoury nugget of attitude from you, and I'll not only forget about adding you to the contract, I'll also launch you through the saloon doors. *Don't* test me further."

Maros took a breath to compose himself, satisfied to see Randallen swallow the lump in his throat. The message seemed to have gone through.

"Think on this," Maros said, lowering his voice once more. "The jewel will be yours. I can't say if it's worth less or more than your mother's savings, but I'd wager it likely comes close. If you want the money so badly, do yourself a favour and sell the damned thing. I'm sure you'd find a buyer in Brancosi Bay. I could even put you in touch with a few potentials, for a small fee, of course."

Despite Randallen's abating anger, the defeat was in his eyes as he lowered them to the table. "I'm afraid selling the jewel will be out of the question."

"Why so?"

"Because"—Randallen drew a shaky breath—"Mother was emphatic that it be with her when she died. That was her sole purpose in wanting the bloody thing in the first place. I had hoped that with her passing…"

"So you're trying to get the money back because you think the contract's nullified, is that it?"

"Perhaps." Randallen's face was a stony mask.

"Well"—Maros shrugged—"I'm sorry to say that's not the case. Your mother may have missed that particular boat, but the contract stands. The jewel will be yours to do with as you wish."

Randallen shook his head. "Not so. She didn't merely wish for it to be in her possession *before* she died."

"Are you saying she wanted it burned with her?" Maros barked a laugh. "If you're willing to throw something of that value onto the funeral pyre, then that's your business."

"Oh, it's worse than that. Much worse. You see, my dear, dead mother wants the damned jewel tossed into the ground. For what? To be dug up in a hundred years by some lucky prospector? *She* won't benefit from it, and *I* certainly won't!" Randallen drew a deep breath. "It's a damned, pointless waste."

Maros shrugged. "It's not an unreasonable request. People get their possessions buried with their ashes all the time."

Randallen sucked air through his teeth. "Have I said *anything* about cremation?"

Maros frowned. "Well, I… Oh."

"Yes." Randallen smiled coldly and reached into his overcoat. He withdrew the roll of parchment from the previous evening and brandished it at Maros. "It's all in here. Mother's last wishes. She's not getting cremated, she's getting *buried*."

———— • ————

Renfrey swayed on his stool at his usual table along the side wall of the Lonely Peddler's common room. It was not yet noon and he'd already lost count of how many cups of Redanchor he'd consumed. On his days off from the mill, he drank early to avoid the crowds. By the time the evening patrons poured in, he'd be home and sleeping it off until two hours before dawn. Then it was off to work, hauling and hitching grain sacks, hefting sacks onto farmers' wagons, relieving the gears that turned the mill of clumps of flour and dirt, and clearing shit from the dam and pond. By the gods, it was wretched work, but it paid for the ale.

Renfrey enjoyed his privacy. A man could sit alone and banter from a distance if he wanted. Not that there was any bantering to be had from the dozen or so patrons in the Peddler. The pretentious merchant twat in the corner had a pair of burly bodyguards keeping him company. The two woodsmen quietly eating a meal at the far side of the common room looked no fun at all. And then there were the freeblades.

Wouldn't piss on 'em if they needed dousing. He frowned at his cup of Redanchor, then took a mouthful of the strong ale and set the cup back down with a *thunk*. Liquid arced over the rim before sloshing back inside. "Aye," Renfrey slurred, "get where ye belong, ye rotten…"

His gaze roved around the room, over the freeblades who were deep in quiet conversation, onto the huge oaf of a barman, and finally landing on the serving girl cleaning a table in the centre of the room. *Nice legs on that one. Creamy. Soft. Nice tits, too.* Pert little things, they were, pushed up by her outfit, small but still managing to spill over her dress. *Face ain't much to look at, though.* Renfrey leered at the softness around the girl's waist.

The serving girl glanced up from her work and caught him eyeing her. He grinned, and she smiled back.

Oh, aye, I'd rut that one like a pig, he thought, watching her soft arse wobble as she walked away. He licked his lips and tongued a gap between his teeth.

Conversation from the freeblades' table drifted over, and Renfrey muttered a curse. Freeblades could rot in the Pit for all he cared, every last self-important one of the women-stealing braggarts. They were a scourge on the town. If there was another tavern in Alder's Folly, he'd be drinking there instead of at the Peddler. He took a pull of ale and listened to their words.

"…that amount of dari…"

"…wouldn't have taken it, myself…"

"Maros says…"

"What if there's truth to it?"

"Fucking freeblades," Renfrey drawled. "Good for fucking nothing."

One of them, a bearded fellow a little younger than Renfrey, glanced over but continued to talk with his companions.

"Aye, go on," Renfrey said, his voice rising. "Talking nothing but shit is what ye're doing!" That got their attention.

"Begging your pardon, Ren," the one with the beard said. "Are we offending you somehow?"

Renfrey didn't know the bastard's name. Didn't like that the prick knew *his*, though. "Offending me?" He smacked his cup onto the table, teetered on his stool and steadied himself. "Aye, I'd say y'are."

"How are we doing that, Master Renfrey?" the young girl beside beardy-face said.

Master? Fucking Master now, am I? Ain't seen that ripe little bitch around before. "Well now, girl, I reckon we could start with ye not calling me *Master*." He glanced to the bearded one beside her. "Or *Ren*, for that matter. How's that sound?"

As the freeblades exchanged glances, a rumbling voice echoed from behind the bar. "You keep your voice down now, Renfrey. You know the rules."

He turned his attention to the ugly brute that loomed like an oak behind the service counter. "Ain't no business o' yours, barkeep. Let me and this lot talk it out, why don't ye?"

"Ah." The halfblood folded his arms. "So it'd be *barkeep* now, would it? Demoted me, have you?"

"You what?" Renfrey frowned as the idiot's grin split his scarred face wide open. *Maros*, he thought. *Aye, that's his name. Never much cared as long as he kept pouring the ale.*

"I'll tell you what," Maros said, and Renfrey realised that the babble of conversation in the room had hushed, "I'll let you call me tavernmaster, just once. How about it, big feller?"

Renfrey burst into laughter, spittle flicking from his mouth. "How about I stick to calling ye barkeep? How's that sound, *barkeep*? Heard they once called ye the Mountain. Don't look so mighty now, do ye? Reckon ye toppled, is what I reckon."

Maros narrowed his eyes. Slowly, deliberately, he rose to his full height. "Aye, the Mountain's toppled," he said in a controlled voice, "but I ain't finished falling yet."

Renfrey sneered. "Heard it was a critter what felled ye, like the ox what raped your ma." He reached for his cup, but his knuckles caught the rim. The bronze receptacle tipped, spilling its contents into a frothy pool on the table. He watched as the cup rolled from the edge and clattered upon the floor.

BOOM. Scrape. BOOM. Scrape…

He looked up to find the source of the commotion. The barkeep lifted the hatch at the end of the service counter, limped out into the common room and headed straight towards Renfrey.

"Shit."

50

"Do you know what happens to soft, squishy little gobshites who get in the way of a falling Mountain?" *Scrape. BOOM.* Maros towered over Renfrey. "They break."

Two huge hands lifted him into the air. He dug his fingers into the tree-trunk forearms. His head swam and the monster beneath him blurred into two. "Fucking ogre!" he squawked. "Help!" The contents of his stomach threatened to evacuate as he was swung one way, then the other.

"You're out!" the ogre boomed in his ear.

He was flying. He was actually flying. Bright light burst into his vision, and he dimly realised he was staring up at the sun.

"Sweet, blessed Aveia!" he cried. Then he struck the dirt, gurgled a spume of ale, and fell into unconsciousness.

———— • ————

Frustration welled in Maros with each passing minute. The Peddler had been cleared of the remaining patrons and he'd pulled the latch over the saloon doors to stop any further intrusions. The only people in the common room were Henwyn and Leaf, both of whom had suffered Renfrey's abuse, sat with Luthan on one of his rare breaks from the kitchen.

He grabbed his stool and limped across to join them. "Finish this phrase," he said to Leaf. "When a freeblade's got a hunch…"

With a smile, Leaf flicked a glance across the four men. "She's usually right."

Henwyn chuckled. To Maros, he said, "You're talking about Jalis and the others again."

Maros nodded. "

"Look," Henwyn said, "I've got no open jobs, and I'll be without Leaf while she's off to Brancosi Bay. If it'll put you at ease, I can go find them. Cost you a small cut, of course."

Luthan leaned his elbows on the table. "If you hired a wagon, you'd catch them up in just a few days."

Maros mulled it over. "I put them into this by accepting the contract in the first place. If bringing them back is on anyone's shoulders, it's mine. I made it to Balen and back, I can damn well venture into the Deadlands." He caught Henwyn exchange glances with Luthan, while Leaf turned nonchalantly to gaze across the room. "Oh, I know what the three of you are thinking. You're thinking there's not a chance in the Pit I could catch them up."

"If you'll allow me to be blunt," Luthan said, "I think it'll be good for you to, ah, stretch your legs, as it were. I'd rather that than watch you sit around here and stress about our friends until you put a man in the ground."

"What's that supposed to mean?"

51

"Come on, boss. You know you could have handled Renfrey with a little more decorum. The man might be a streak of verbal diarrhoea and a waste of good ale, but he's a regular customer and his pockets are deep."

"Hmph. That arsehole's lot was long overdue."

"Maybe so, but the likelihood remains – you won't rest until you know Jalis and the others are safe, and a tavern's not the place to be hanging around with a hot head. I'm telling you this as a friend. When you requested me to join you as your chef, I came here all the way from Aster because I had faith in you as a tavernmaster, even though you'd never turned your hand to the task before. Likewise, I've got faith in you now."

Maros grunted. "I appreciate the vote of confidence."

Henwyn raised his hand. "At least let me join you. I'd rather be on the road than hanging around here waiting for a job to turn up."

"Ha! Hen, you're the longest-serving of all of us. I'd be glad to have you tag along. Besides, I reckon I do need a bowman if I stand any chance of putting meat on the fire. Best I can offer you though is one tenth of the ten percent non-retrieval."

Henwyn shrugged. "That's a more than fair cut. If it were Fenn instead of Jalis though, I'd insist on a lot more."

Maros grinned tightly. "If it were Fenn, we wouldn't be having this discussion."

"If that's settled," Luthan said, "then I don't want you worrying about the tavern while you're gone. I'll look after her in your stead – aye, even on top of my kitchen duties."

Henwyn sipped the last of his wine and stood up. "I'll ask around town for a wagon. If none o' those what's got one are willing to help, I'll pick the one I like the least and make it happen. Leaf here's got your request form for headquarters. She'll be setting off soon enough. Right, lass?"

Leaf rose to stand beside him. "My bag's already packed. Just need to grab it from the guildhouse."

"Good luck," Maros told her. "And don't tarry."

Leaf grinned. "I never do." With a wink to Henwyn, she strode across the room and slipped through the saloon doors.

"She's got more potential than most novices, that one," Maros said. "And a fine teacher in you, Henwyn. I couldn't ask for a better bunch. That includes you, Luthan."

"Hey, now." The chef pushed his chair back and straightened his apron. "Don't go getting soft on me, not when I've got pots to clean."

Jalis crouched, aimed and squeezed the trigger of the crossbow. A moment later, the distant balukha let out a pained squawk and took several faltering steps to the side, then slumped over.

She gave the men a satisfied grin. "Got it!"

"Good shot, lass," Dagra said.

Jalis grinned. "I live for your praise, Bearded One." She rose and affected a curtsy, fully aware that the gesture was out of place with her weapons and travel-worn gear.

As she jogged to claim the flightless bird, Oriken called after her, "That'll fill us tonight. Makes a change from scrawny rabbits and bogberries. May as well take a break here. What do you say?"

Jalis's stomach growled in agreement. "Do it," she called over her shoulder as she reached the dying balukha. "I made the kill, you men can argue over who builds the fire and who prepares the carcass." She took Silverspire from its scabbard at her thigh and slid the thin blade into the creature's heart. Hefting it by its legs, she returned to the men and dropped it to the ground.

Stepping to a grassy mound, she slouched down against it and placed Silverspire in the grass beside her. She rummaged inside her backpack in search of a rag and a leather strop, watching as Oriken unsheathed his hunting knife and knelt before the carcass, and Dagra wandered away to gather firewood from the edge of a nearby thicket. There were still many hours before nightfall, but now was as good a time to eat as any.

With a frustrated sigh, she called across to the men, "I can't find my strop. Have either of you borrowed it?"

"The strop's yours." Oriken paused in his work to pat the sabre at his hip. "You know I never polish this pitted old thing."

"The whetstone's in Oriken's pack," Dagra called as he stooped to gather wood.

"I'd get it for you," Oriken said, "but I'm wrist-deep in guts right now."

"Forget it. It'll turn up." Balling the rag, Jalis wiped it over the dagger and gazed idly along the Kingdom Road they'd rejoined after traversing the marsh. The wetlands were far behind them now, though small patches of swamp still dotted the unfarmable landscape. Why anyone would choose to live here was a mystery, unless the area had once been a gentler habitat for farms and pastures. It was obvious the colossal swamp hadn't always covered the road, and Jalis wondered if somebody had created it, perhaps trenching the land from the coast inwards, a deliberate attempt to dissuade travellers from continuing south. If so, it was an impressive deterrent.

She finished cleaning Silverspire and sheathed the blade, then rested her head against the grass. She quickly dozed off, stirring some time later to the crackle of the fire and the aroma of roasting meat.

"Ah, the princess awakens," Oriken said with a wink as Jalis stretched against the mound. "Good timing. Dag's nearly done with the bird."

The fire burned to embers as they tucked into the sizzling white flesh of the balukha. With full stomachs, they repacked their gear and resumed their journey, following the remnants of the road. The hours stretched by, the golden orb of Banael coursing across the blue sky.

As they walked, Jalis hoisted the weight of the pack at her back, then pinched her chemise and pulled the material from her clammy skin. "I should be used to this warmth," she muttered. "I've been in Himaera for too long. I spent over twenty years in the Arkh, most of those in Sardaya. Compared to there, the temperature here is nothing."

"Bah." Ahead of her, Oriken shared a glance with Dagra and grinned over his shoulder. "There's no such thing as spending too much time in Himaera."

Jalis scoffed. "This coming from a man who's never set foot outside of his birthland? Forgive me if I don't take your word for it."

"Hey, we all took the ferry to the Isle of Carrados, remember?"

"How could we forget?" Dagra said. "You threw up all over the deckhand."

"That wasn't my fault! No one warned me. You won't get me on a boat again, that's for sure."

Jalis shook her head. "Carrados doesn't count. It's still part of Himaera. Nice try, though, Hat Boy."

Oriken clasped the crown of his hat and lifted it to wipe his brow. "Truth is, I enjoyed our time with the monks on that island. If it wasn't for the ocean, I wouldn't mind leaving Himaera one day for a bit of recreation. Jalis makes Sardaya sound kind of sexy."

"Sexy?" Jalis burst out laughing. "I wouldn't go that far. The scenery is beautiful. The men and women are attractive, for the most part. The culture is rich. But there's also the constant presence of reivers, and Ashcloak troops passing from town to town collecting taxes. Plus, although the wildlife is much more varied in the Arkh, so are the monsters. And then there's the—Hey!" She stumbled into Dagra as he stopped in his tracks. "Dag, watch yourself! Don't tell me you need another break already?"

Dagra touched her shoulder and pointed ahead. In a sombre voice, he said, "I think we've reached our destination."

They had topped a low rise in the land, and before them a shallow valley opened the view in all directions, its far rim climbing into the distance. To the right, the almost indiscernible hush of the ocean drifted in on the warm easterly breeze, and ahead of them...

Oriken blew a whistle. "Now *that's* a wall."

A dark line dissected the heathland above the valley, stretching almost from the western coast to disappear behind rolling hills far to the east. The sun-bleached tops of the battlements, like crooked teeth jutting from the jawbone of an impossible giant, reminded Jalis of Cherak, the ancient god of stone. "Okay," she said, her voice hushed in awe, "I admit it; that wall is longer and altogether uglier than any in my homeland. You boys have me beat on that score."

Dagra clenched his pendant. "Never mind the wall," he said, hoarsely. "Look further back. It's the city." He turned a pale face from the view to glance back the way they had come.

Jalis shielded her eyes from the sun. Her gaze drifted beyond the wall into the extreme distance, roving across the nebulous vista. "Oh," she whispered.

Above and far beyond the jagged ramparts, the grim buttresses of the last vestige of civilization from the Days of Kings sprawled, barely visible amid the hazy horizon.

"The legendary city of Lachyla. Impressive." Oriken tore his eyes from the view to glance at Jalis. "Sort of puts things into perspective, doesn't it?"

"What do you mean?" She kept her eyes on the towers and spires, the rounded roofs that pockmarked the landscape like swollen blisters. The city of Lachyla *was* impressive, but knowing that the place had been dead and empty for centuries sent a chill through her.

"What I mean," Oriken said, "is that our contract for a little trinket pales in comparison to…" He stretched his arm to gesture at the distant city. "To *that*."

Dagra turned back around to face them. "I was convinced that the place must be a myth," he said. "Just a fable for the old'uns to scare the kids with."

"And for Taleweavers to scare *everyone* with," Oriken said.

"Well, it worked. The legend of Lachyla scared the wits out of me whenever Grandma told it when we were boys." Dagra drew a shaky breath.

"You okay?" Oriken asked.

Jalis caught Dagra's gaze. "Hey," she said softly.

"I know. I'll keep it in check." He cleared his throat. His expression set into a resolute mask. He glanced from Jalis to Oriken and gave a tight smile. "Well? Are we going to retrieve that rutting heirloom or not? Yes? Let's go then!"

Dagra strode away along the Kingdom Road. Oriken shared a serious glance with Jalis before following him. He always hid his emotions beneath an outward casual demeanour, but Jalis knew that Oriken was battling something inside almost as much as Dagra, and it wasn't merely that they'd come face-to-face with a ghost story. From the nuggets of information she'd gleaned during their journey, the legend of Lachyla was so fanciful that neither Oriken nor Dagra could be certain whether the place truly existed. The thing about people was that they tended to lack the imagination to conjure a legend from nothing. *Every* legend had a source, no matter how small or, in this case, how large. The sprawling city before her came as no surprise, but time had a way of exaggerating history's finer details.

Jalis glanced back to the north, and for a moment an undercurrent of loneliness washed over her. Being so far from civilisation, and in the presence of such antiquity, stirred an unexpected longing to revisit her own past. But that desire was dulled by the melancholic atmosphere emanating from Lachyla. With a sigh, she followed her friends towards the Blighted City.

———— • ————

The hard-packed dirt of the roads and pathways was already beginning to dry after the recent shower, with the warm orb of Banael half-way through its downward journey. Maros stood outside the Lonely Peddler, his hands atop the timber fence. He brooded as he looked out at the familiar scene of stone and wooden houses and shops, all haphazardly positioned with no thought for symmetry. Such was the way of flockers and settlers.

He looked between the buildings to the hills and woodland. His thoughts returned to Jalis, Oriken and Dagra, his companions before he was forced to hang up his blades. Maros's certainty that something wasn't right had grown considerably since hearing Jerrick's story. And then there was the added complication of Cela Chiddari curling her toes up…

"Boss."

"Gah!" Maros swung about to see Henwyn standing beside him. "Banael's burning balls, man! Are you trying to send me to an early afterlife?"

The veteran freeblade repressed a grin, but inclined his head apologetically. "Good news," he said. "Leaf is well on her way to the headquarters, and I've secured us a wagon and a driver. Can't say as two mules will get us anywhere fast, but I'd rather that than me carrying you on my back if you get tired. No offence, boss, but you're likely a touch heavy even for my legendary strength."

"Ha!" Maros clapped a hand to Henwyn's shoulder, dropping the man down an inch as Henwyn's knees buckled. "Fewer truer words were ever said, Hen. Who did you hire?"

"Mill owner. Wymar."

Maros grumbled.

"Aye, I know. I tried others before him, but none wanted to risk getting stranded past the fringes of the Fell with nowt but backwater hamlets thereabouts. Wymar was the first not to overly object. With greed as a motivator, no doubt."

"How easy the folk around here forget about the freeblades who do 'em a good service just by existing in this town. When it comes to returning the favour a little—"

"That's not all, boss."

Maros issued a low growl. "What else?"

"Wymar's somewhat pissed that his workload's been thinned out between the rest of his staff for what'll likely be a good few weeks."

"What on Verragos is he dribbling about?"

"Renfrey," Henwyn said, by way of explanation.

"Bah, that little weasel? I barely touched him. What's the problem?"

"Well, it seems he got home right enough after I poured that bucket of dirty water over his head to wake him. But, when he'd slept the ale off, he found that his finger was bust."

"His *finger*?"

"So, he's off work for a bit."

"Aye, and Wymar's taking full advantage of it. I see how it goes. What's the damage?"

"He wants ten silvers for the work loss."

"Ten! That drunken shit Renfrey can't be earning more than one silver a week!"

Henwyn shrugged. "True, but mill owner claims that redistribution of work's making added costs, plus covering damages for loss of skilled labour, reducing production levels, as it were."

"Skilled labour. I'll give him skilled labour. Fine, ten silvers to the thieving bastard. And what about the wagon?"

"Aye, well, Wymar'll be driving us himself, plus he's talking about food for the mules, wear and tear of the wagon wheels—"

"Cherak's furry cock!" Maros gripped the fence. The muscles in his arm bunched as he squeezed the timber.

"Easy, boss," Henwyn warned as the fence began to splinter.

"Right. Right. Cut to the end, Hen. I'll stay calm."

"Fifty silvers."

The timber ripped from the fence. Maros tossed it aside. An unamused smile split his face. "Violence makes me calmer." He raised his eyebrows for emphasis.

"Aye," Henwyn sighed. "I'm just glad you had something other than me in snapping distance."

"Fifty silvers is a full ten percent of this job. That's the whole lot going to Wymar if they don't find the jewel, or it's half my cut if they do. Gods, man, it would've been cheaper to buy a pair of mules for you to drive and a cart for me to ride in."

"Tried that, too." Henwyn shrugged. "You know how few mules are around town. No one was willing to sell. Turn the tables around and I can't say I blame 'em. Can't even blame Wymar for wanting to keep an eye on his beasts rather than trust 'em in our hands."

Maros sighed. "Ah well, anything for friends, right? You go tell that thief of a mill owner that for the price he's asking we'll be setting off before sundown this evening. He's got four hours to get his shit together and we're on the road. I didn't get this far in life by not trusting my guts, and my guts are saying that Jalis and the lads are in danger."

CHAPTER SEVEN
PATIENCE AND PRAYERS

The early evening sun drew ever closer to the distant horizon as Dagra and his friends descended into the valley. The phantom spires and towers of the distant city sank from view, followed by the wall itself and its portcullis. It would take another hour to reach the wall, but night would be upon them shortly after. Dagra looked to the east, narrowing his eyes as he regarded a lone gawek tree nestled at the base of the rising land. Its twin trunks were curled around each other, the high boughs casting a long shadow onto the valley's side.

"We're not stepping inside that gods-neglected place till morning," he said. Seeing Oriken's expression, he added, "No, it's not up for dispute. I'm not setting foot in there unless we've got plenty of hours of daylight ahead of us. It's bad enough we have to wander into some crypt, but I'm not spending ages trying to find it within a huge, dark graveyard when there's no need."

Oriken shrugged. "It's deserted, Dag. I don't see the problem."

"Dagra's right," Jalis said. "We don't know what's in there. There could be a lyakyn nest for all we know. Or cravants that have adapted to living in ruins rather than among the trees. Or there could be ancient traps laid about that we wouldn't see in the dark."

"That," Dagra said hoarsely, "and the spirits of all those heathen dead that are probably haunting the place. Forget it. I call for making camp till tomorrow. We've come this far; what's the rush?"

"We'll crest the valley and find a spot to camp," Jalis said.

"We may as well shelter under that tree." Dagra nodded towards the gawek. "It's as good as anywhere in this accursed region."

Oriken shook his head. "We're almost there, and you're getting cold feet."

Dagra cast him a hooded glance.

"It's a sensible call," Jalis said, altering course for the tree. As Dagra followed her, she glanced back to Oriken. "Come on, let's call it a day and tackle it with fresh energy in the morning."

"Fine, fine." Oriken twisted the brim of his hat and trudged after them. As they neared the gawek tree, he said, "At least let me scout the entrance before nightfall. I promise I won't go inside alone."

"No. None of us go off alone. Not this time. Besides, the entrance is barred. We'll have to use the grappler to climb over." Seeing Oriken's disappointed expression, Jalis cast him a pointed look. "There's a saying in Vorinsia: Eagerness ended the Edel."

"I have no idea what that means."

"It's a phrase coined by the Prime Ascendant of the time when Vorinsia conquered the southern lands of the Arkh, first Sardaya, then Khalevali. The nobles – or *Edel* in the Vorinsian tongue – of Khalevali and my homeland were too sure of their countries' strengths and mounted a revolt against the stranglehold of the Vorinsian forces. The higher nobility was crushed, but the Arkhus called for leniency, allowing their surviving family members to leave their estates and fortunes with their lives." Reaching the shade of the wide-reaching gawek branches, she added, "No heroics, Oriken."

He shrugged. "You're the boss, boss."

"Less of that."

"As you say, boss."

Jalis flashed him a finger. "*Malan-gamir!*"

Oriken smirked. "I'd be happy to accommodate you with that, siosa, but can it wait till we're settled for the night?"

Jalis reached up and swatted the hat from his head.

"Hey!"

As he stooped to retrieve it, she cast him a warning look. "The divine rod, dear Orik, points to treasure and trap alike. Be careful where you point yours. Now, take a bowl and see if you can find us some fresh berries."

"I'll use my hat." By his tone, it was clear she'd hurt his feelings.

"We're not eating from that battered old thing," Dagra said. "Bogberries taste bad enough without adding your stale sweat and hair into the mix."

Oriken shrugged and took a bowl from his pack..

"Pass me the crossbow, lass," Dagra said. "I'll go with him."

Oriken glanced at him as he retied the pack. "That's a bit excessive."

Dagra chuckled as he took the crossbow from Jalis. "Don't worry, I wouldn't shoot you just for disobeying our leader."

"Don't you start," Jalis warned.

Dagra inclined his head and gave her a discreet wink before turning to follow Oriken. Though he'd joined in the levity, it had done nothing to quell his inner turmoil.

Dagra leaned against the intertwined trunks of the gawek tree and looked across the silver-dusted nightscape. Wispy clouds dulled the rising orb of Haleth to a wan glow in the star-studded sky. Beyond the stones of the highway, pockets of marsh were signposted by tiny dots of fae-fire that glimmered upon the heath. All was quiet except for the subdued chirp and chirr of heath-hoppers, the distant croak of a frog, and Oriken's soft snores.

Dagra rested his elbows on his knees and, for what seemed the thousandth time since entering the Deadlands, he willed his thoughts to reach the gods. *Blessed Aveia and Svey'Drommelach. Prophet Avato. Wise Ederron. Hear your devoted in his time of need. Shield him beneath your wings as he steps toward the darkness, and let your divine goodness extinguish the evil amid the shadows. Give him the strength to go where you are not, and from there to return to your domain. If it be your will, guide him home that he can serve you still, or, if it be your will, guide his soul to Kambesh to be reborn.*

As Dagra finished the prayer, Oriken snorted in his sleep and smacked his lips. Dagra glanced towards him and froze, his heart jumping into his throat. A squat, bipedal pale figure was leaning over Oriken, its featureless head pressed to the blanket over his torso, its handless blobs of arms padding at the wool. Dagra stared, transfixed by the featureless oddity

Shaking himself from the trance, he whispered Oriken's name. Although the creature showed no obvious aggression, he didn't want to spur it into action by shouting. A basic rule of the wilderness was to never underestimate unfamiliar fauna or flora. Oriken mumbled and began to snore softly.

Dagra took up his gladius and moved into a crouch. He crept forwards, but the creature was intent on nuzzling its face into the blanket. Drawing close enough, he thrust the sword. The blade sank deep into the creature, but it scarcely jerked. He withdrew the blade and stared open-mouthed at the lack of blood on its white skin, his jaw dropped further as he watched the wound seal itself.

"Right, you little bastard," he muttered, and launched a sideways swipe into its head. The gladius sank into the soft flesh with little resistance, but as the blade passed through, the tissue formed instantly back together. The creature raised its head and stood upright. It stepped away from the blanket, turned its faceless head towards Dagra, then plodded away.

"Orik! Wake up!" Dagra rose to his feet, his eyes on the creature as it faded into the night.

Jalis stirred and sat upright. A throwing dagger appeared in her hand as she scanned the darkness.

Dagra grabbed Oriken's shoulders and shook him roughly. "Wake up, damn you!"

"Ugh..." Sluggishly, Oriken rubbed at his face and cracked his eyes open. "Did someone slip some mandrake into my tea?"

"You didn't drink any tea," Jalis muttered, returning the throwing dagger to its pocket.

Oriken lifted his head from the bedroll and glanced around. "What gives, Dag?" he said groggily. "Something out there?"

"Yes! No. I don't know. There was a..." But the strange creature was gone.

Jalis gave him a wilting look. "Did you doze off and have a dream?"

"No! I swear there was something..."

"Hey!" Oriken pushed himself to a sitting position and stared at his blanket. "What's this white stuff all over me? Dag? I'm not joking, you better not have—"

"There was a creature!" Dagra protested as Oriken snatched the covers away. "It was a... Ah, I don't know!" He gasped in exasperation.

"Disgusting." Oriken pinched at his shirt. "It's gone through."

"Let me see." Jalis leaned over and raised his shirt to expose his torso. Three blobs of the sticky substance matted the hair at his abdomen, with red circles showing through the slime.

"What in the..." Oriken grabbed the blanket and wiped the ichor away. "It feels numb."

Dagra's eyes were drawn to the blanket. The parts of the wool where the creature's head and arms had touched were beginning to disintegrate.

Jalis had spotted it too. Hastily she drew a waterskin and a pouch from her pack and poured the water over Oriken's middle. With the corner of the blanket, she dabbed as much of the sticky residue away from the sores as she could. From the pouch she took a moist leaf and placed it over the larger of the three wounds. "Nepenthe is the best treatment we have right now. With luck, the creature wasn't venomous."

Oriken nodded his gratitude and glanced at Dagra. "What did it look like?"

Dagra shrugged. He described the strange creature as best he could, but neither Oriken nor Jalis had an idea what it could have been.

"We'll have to be extra vigilant." As Jalis took two more leaves from the pouch, to Dagra she said, "Well done for spotting it in time. There's no telling what damage it might have done to Oriken while he slept. I'm guessing whatever it secreted contains an anaesthetic."

Oriken blanched as Jalis pressed the nepenthe leaves to his sores. "I owe you one, Dag. Look, I'm sorry for yelling."

Dagra grunted. "Forget it. Go back to sleep. I'll take a longer watch and wake you in two hours. I want to do a quick walk-around anyway. If I catch sight of that thing without you in the way, I'll cut it to pieces."

"Thanks," Oriken said. "I doubt I'll get back to sleep now, though."

"Then don't," Jalis said. "Just rest. If you feel strange, tell Dag or wake me up." She glanced at his arm. "How's the wound from the cravant?"

Oriken clenched and unclenched his fist. "Much better." He rummaged into the bottom of his pack and took out his fleece-lined, nargut-hide jacket and pulled it on. As he secured the row of clips along the front of the jacket, he glanced from Dagra to Jalis. "Hey, I ain't taking any chances." He lay back and placed his hat over his middle.

Jalis returned to her blanket, and within a minute had drifted back to sleep. Oriken clasped his hands behind his head and gave Dagra a brief nod. Sheathing his gladius and checking the loaded crossbow, Dagra set off to begin a patrol.

Corpses, cravants, wildmen and weird white blobs, he thought. *And, come morning, very likely the spirits of the ancient dead.* He sent another quick prayer to the gods and their prophets that tomorrow would not be another test. It was now a waiting game to see if – and how – they would answer.

CHAPTER EIGHT
WATCHERS AT THE EDGE OF THE WORLD

Oriken chewed half-heartedly on a tough strip of jerky as he traced a finger across the tender sores on his belly. The nepenthe had done its job; the skin was raw but healing to the beginnings of scabs, and the numbness had faded by the time his watch was over. He took one of three boiled quail eggs from the cup beside the fire and cracked it open. He regarded the tiny egg sullenly. They were all he'd managed to find the previous evening, despite following the call of the elusive quail. Along with the last of their salted rations, a tiny egg each and a bowl of bogberries was their entire breakfast. He popped the egg into his mouth and swallowed it in seconds.

"I'm telling you," he said, "if we do find any cravants in the city, I'm eating one."

Dagra screwed his face up.

"Hey, there's no telling when we'll have our next decent meal. I'm just thinking forward."

"I wouldn't do that if I were you," Jalis said.

"What, think forward?"

She gave him a withering look. "Cravant flesh is tougher than leather, unless you let it simmer for a full day."

Dagra wiped his hands on his trousers and stood up. "Don't tell us that's something you learned first-hand."

"Actually, it is." For a moment, Jalis's expression turned distant. "It's something of a rare delicacy in Sardaya, or at least it was when I was a girl. The winged cravants could be a nuisance if they ever came down from the mountains. My father often took part in a monthly hunt, and sometimes he would bring home a shank of cravant meat for the maids to stew." She looked at Oriken. "But we won't find any in the city because we're not going in there. There's no need. During my shift, I checked the map Cela gave Maros. The Gardens of the Dead are directly inside the gate, so we've no need to go into Lachyla itself."

"Hm." Oriken snatched his swordbelt from the ground and stood up. "That's a real shame. I was looking forward to having a wander around in there."

Dagra sighed. "Of course you were."

"We'll discuss it later." Jalis sprang to her feet and clasped her hands together. "First, boys, I believe we have ourselves a jewel to find."

The perimeter wall towered overhead, as solid as the ages but for the occasional crumbled merlon and broken pieces of finion on the ground below. Oriken felt small and insignificant compared to the ancient, implacable stones.

"If there were archers on those battlements," he said, "there'd be no getting inside, not even for an army, let alone a trio of freeblades."

"Good thing we've got the grappler," Jalis said.

"And a good thing we've got the place to ourselves," Oriken replied. "Eh, Dag?"

"You hope," Dagra said quietly.

Oriken glanced along the wall to the rotten remains of a rope that dangled from the crenellated ramparts. "Something here look out of place to either of you?"

Jalis frowned at the threadbare rope.

"Been there for a long time," Dagra said.

Oriken nodded. "But I don't reckon it's as old as the blight. And if *that's* a fact, it means we're not the first to venture here since the death's head was stamped onto maps."

He turned his attention to the lowered portcullis, its spikes biting into the dirt between the crumbled flagstones. The rusted iron bars were each as thick as his wrist. He stepped up to peer between them, and stared open-mouthed at the sight beyond.

"The word *dead* seems a little superficial right now," he muttered.

Jalis was at his side. "Oh, my," she whispered, then took a step back. "Well then, Orik. Care to do the honours?"

With a grin, he shrugged out of his pack. He fished into his pack and produced a long coil of thin rope tied at one end to a hefty grappling iron.

"Step back." He coiled the rope around his arm and stepped to the wall. Treading on the loose end of the rope, he sized up the battlements and began to swing the hook. He released it and it sailed upwards, clipped the edge of the wall and continued on before arcing down and snagging onto the walkway above. He tugged on the rope to ensure the grappler was firmly stuck, then hoisted his pack back onto his shoulders.

"Ladies first?" he said to Jalis.

"Why, thank you, sios. So kind of you to offer." She took the rope, sprang nimbly onto it, then made her way up the wall.

Oriken watched her ascend until she scrambled over the top. He turned to Dagra. "After you."

Dagra didn't reply. His face was set as he stared up at the wall. He took hold of his Avato pendant and pressed it to his lips before grabbing hold of the rope.

64

He began to hoist himself up, the fronts of his boots finding purchase in the ruts between the stones. Oriken could hear him grunting with exertion by the time Dagra hauled himself onto the battlements.

The wall had the slightest of slopes as it tapered towards the top, but it scarcely made the climb any easier. With Oriken's long limbs and the weight of the pack on his back, his shoulder muscles were begging for mercy by the time he reached the top. Sweat trickled down his face as he hoisted himself through the crenellations. Without pausing to rest, he pulled the rope up and began winding it into a coil.

Dagra squatted beside him, a troubled look on his face.

"Hey," Oriken said, "we'll get the job done. We're freeblades. It's what we do."

With the rope and hook stashed in the pack, Oriken stood straight and took his first clear look over the Gardens of the Dead and the city of Lachyla far beyond, and he understood Dagra's concern. He rubbed a hand over his stubble as he looked at the countless rows of headstones within the graveyard's vast expanse. Cracked clay vases stood or lay near their grave markers. Partially-collapsed stone statues dotted the bleak vista, the arms and heads of some gathered at the bases of their plinths. Rarer were the larger statues of bronze, standing as sentries beside ornate crypt entrances. Leafless husks of trees that should have been in full bloom at this time of year cast shadows like reaching fingers across the ground. The stain of centuries blanketed everything.

"Lost for words?" Jalis asked.

"For once," he admitted.

The rise and fall of the grave-studded terrain led all the way to far-distant walls encasing the dead in a rectangle of tall stone. The distant battlements were tiny from here, but the wide, central Litchway bisecting the graveyard stretched all the way to a second portcullis in the centre of the far wall.

The Litchgate. Oriken recalled its mention in the stories.

As dismal as the Gardens of the Dead were, the city beyond was something else entirely. Heavily fortified walls surrounded the cityscape. The nearest buildings were hidden from view behind the graveyard's perimeter wall, but as the ground gently rose beyond the portcullis, a main thoroughfare snaked between rows of domed, slanted and crenellated structures towards a grim fortress. The castle's bulk dominated the cityscape, crouching atop a low hill like a colossal, implacable sentinel, ready to lurch into action at the first sign of intruders.

"And here we are," Oriken muttered. "Hello, Lachyla Castle."

"Not the most welcoming of sights, is it?" Jalis said.

"Hard to believe it ain't among Himaera's top recreation spots." Oriken glanced at Dagra. "And you thought Caer Valekha was bad."

"It was." Dagra's face was a stoic mask..

The base of the hill upon which the castle nestled was dotted with myriad buildings, smaller than the castle but still formidable, gathered like high-born worshippers around a shrine. As the trickle of buildings spread further from the city's heart, they became shorter and less regal-looking. The spires and domed roofs might once have looked beautiful in a city that teemed with life, but now they were ghosts of forgotten grandeur; pockmarks of blight, swelling from the land itself. Oriken had to admit, Lachyla could be the bleakest place he'd ever set his eyes on.

From his vantage point, misty blankets of golden-tinged ocean to the east and west showed that Lachyla sat upon a tapering peninsula. He could imagine sheer cliffs dropping away beyond the defensive walls into the frothy depths of the uncharted Echilan Ocean.

The edge of the world, he thought, once again recalling how he and Dagra had clung to the steep sides of Mount Sentinel and gazed out at the same ocean.

He turned at the crunch of footfalls to see Jalis and Dagra heading along the battlements towards a winch tower. Gathering his gear, he jogged to catch them up. The tower's slanted oaken roof had warped with age and weathering, but was mostly intact. Beneath it was a winch mechanism with a long, iron handle on one side. The end of the coiled chain disappeared through a gap in the stone floor above the side of the portcullis.

"It doesn't look too rusty," Jalis observed. "We'll give it a try on our way out, save us from scaling back down and having to leave the grappler behind if it gets stuck.

Oriken grasped the handle in both hands, tensed, and heaved. It shifted, turning the chain around the spool with a dull *chink-chink-chink* as the chain scraped against itself, and a creaking groan from the portcullis as it protested to being awoken from its long sleep.

"I reckon we'll manage to get it open," he said, dusting his hands onto his trousers.

From the winch tower, a set of stone steps led down into the graveyard. Oriken followed Jalis down to the arid ground, with Dagra dragging his heels behind. They crossed to the crumbled Litchway and stood before the portcullis. Oriken cast a sidelong glance through the iron bars to the open heath beyond, and for a moment felt as if he were a prisoner, trapped inside the words of the Taleweaver, transported to a time that perhaps should have stayed locked within the words of the old stories. Nudging the sensation aside, he watched Jalis as she produced an age-yellowed parchment from the pocket of her leggings and began to study it.

"Look here," she said. The men gathered around. She touched a fingernail to the map and traced a line north, to a point three-quarters of the way up. "It should be straightforward enough. We follow the main path to this point." She dragged her finger across to the right and tapped at the X marked by their client. "Then a short jaunt to the side, and we're there."

"If we didn't have that map," Dagra said, a stony expression on his face, "we'd have to comb our way through the entire graveyard."

"You can thank Cela for that when we return." Jalis motioned ahead. "For now, our prize beckons."

Oriken gently squeezed her shoulder, then set off along the central pathway. Jalis and Dagra fell in at either side. As they walked, a notion slowly crept up on him and he opened his senses to his surroundings.

I'm right, he thought. A seed of concern nested itself in the pit of his stomach. Not only were the trees dead and blackened, they were covered in fungal pustules. There were also no shrubs in sight other than the occasional brittle tumbleweed.

Can't hear any creatures scuttling around. Should be able to hear them even if we can't see them. Whatever this place once was, it should have long ago been claimed by the animals and grasses, not be devoid of them. No hoppers, no flies, no birds. Dead trees and no grasses whatsoever. What the fuck?

"There's not a sign of life in the whole blighted place, Dagra said. "Except for the three of us."

Oriken frowned. "Yeah, I was about to—"

"There's a scent on the air," Jalis said, her gaze shifting across the rows of tilted grave-markers.

Oriken could smell it now, too. It wasn't just the musty scent of long, desolate years, nor merely the hint of saltiness from the nearby ocean; it was something else, something almost unnoticeable but nonetheless there. He sniffed, narrowed his eyes.

Sweet, like a perfume that lingers long after the girl who wore it has left the room.

"This feels wrong," Dagra said. "Nothing's alive here. Just mould covering everything, and even that's all dried up."

"You know the legend," Oriken said. "Maybe there's a seed of truth to the Blighted City after all."

Dagra snorted. "A fitting name for a place, if ever there was one."

Oriken barked a laugh. "Yeah, and these so-called Gardens of the Dead, they're a…" He rubbed a thumb over his stubble and glanced at Jalis. "What's that word you use? None-secateur? Yeah, that's it. This whole place couldn't be any deader. They got that right. But *Gardens*? Stupid name for somewhere that ain't got one blade of grass."

Jalis gave him a bemused look. "It's great that you've once again paid attention to my home tongue, but I think you're looking for *non sequitur*. Secateurs are garden shears. In a sense, though, you're right. These Gardens definitely don't need their shrubs pruned."

"Well, blight or not, it was a long time ago." Oriken looked across to the rooftops of the sprawling city. "Now that we're this close, it's still a little tempting to take a look around."

Dagra huffed. "Even you can feel the wrongness here, Orik. Don't tempt fate more than we already have. I'm no coward and you know it, but I remember the fear I felt as a boy towards this place, and I don't need to enter the city for that fear to come flooding back. Being surrounded by these heathen crypts and gravestones and statues is already enough."

"I'm just saying, is all. Hey, Dag, you don't have to clutch your pendant so tightly. You don't need the Dyad when you've got us." Oriken winked at Jalis. Her lips twitched in a brief smile.

"I'll take the Dyad *and* the two of you," Dagra said. "Strength in numbers."

"Yeah— Whoa." Oriken stopped as his eyes landed on something protruding from the dirt a few yards off the Litchway. He stepped across and stooped for a closer look. A collection of small bones was half-encased in the cracked earth, unmistakeably a human hand. "I guess they didn't bury them too deep around here."

"What is it?" Dagra's voice had a hard edge.

"Remember that house where we bumped into those cravants?"

"Yes."

"Well, when I say let's just keep walking, do yourself a favour and listen, this time. You're already on edge enough, we don't need you going into a full-blown panic attack."

Dagra scowled and turned away. "Noted."

They continued down the Litchway until the wall dividing the graveyard from the city came into view in the distance, its portcullis lowered like the gate at the entrance had been. Oriken glanced over his shoulder at the towers and battlements of the heathland wall, barely visible behind the raised crypt entrances, larger-than-life statues and skeletal trees.

"We must be nearing the Chiddari crypt," he said.

Jalis folded the map and slipped it into her pocket. "There are quite a few crypts around here. I suggest we split up and check them separately."

Dagra shook his head vehemently. "Forget it. There's no way I'm going into one of those places alone."

Jalis stifled a sigh. "I don't mean for us to go into them, Dagra. I'm saying we should check the names above the entrances and on the statues of those that have them."

"Oh." Dagra cleared his throat. "All right. Fine."

Oriken regarded their bearded friend. Truth was, Dagra's bravado had waned more and more the deeper into Scapa Fell they'd come, and now, here in the graveyard, it was all but gone. That wouldn't do. It wouldn't do at all. He clicked his fingers before Dagra's face and fixed him with a stern look. "Hey. Come on. Snap out of it. I get you're having god-issues right now, but

68

do your friends a favour and try to pack them away. Let's get those name-plates checked, like Jalis says."

"Fuck off," Dagra muttered. He lifted his eyes to meet Oriken's gaze and gave a sharp nod, then turned on his heel and wandered away towards the nearest crypt.

Oriken shared a look with Jalis before striding away to check the dozen or so crypt entrances in the immediate area. Reaching the first, he stretched to inspect the stone carvings above the entrance. A crack ran vertically through the stone, right through the centre of the name Hauverydh. The crypt's accompanying statue lay on the ground near the entrance, its stone face pitted and worn, its hands clasped at the breast; whatever it had been holding had eroded or fallen away long ago.

Oriken passed between headstones as he strode for the second crypt. Some of the grave markers had fallen, some were sunken or leaning at angles, while others remained fully upright. The engravings on several contained the name Chiddari, or what seemed to be a variation of it.

"Getting close over here!" he called.

Reaching the crypt, he stood before its statue and checked the faded name on the plinth. *Cunaxa Tjiddarei.* The weathered features were those of a proud woman, clasping what appeared to be a small hammer and chisel to her breast. The bronze statue stood askance, leaning forwards as if about to take a bow in congratulation of Oriken discovering her resting place.

"Yep," he called. "This is it!"

"Well done," Jalis said from behind him, making him nearly jump out of his skin.

"Stars and fucking moons, Jalis!" Oriken hissed. "Don't do that!"

She grinned. "Sorry."

As Dagra approached, Jalis took the oil lamp and tinderbox from her pack and set to work striking sparks to a swatch of char cloth. Once the material caught, she touched a sulphur stick to the flame and used it to ignited the lamp.

When the lamp was lit, Dagra said, "Give it here." His expression was haggard, but he looked more determined.

Jalis eyed him. "You sure?"

"No. But do it anyway." He took the lamp and led the way to the Chiddari crypt's black entrance.

69

CHAPTER NINE
NOTHING WITHOUT FEAR

"Let's get this business finished." Dagra raised the lamp and peered into the stairwell. The flames cast a flickering glow onto rough-hewn walls and stone steps. Beyond the light's reach, the pit of the burial vault yawned an ominous invitation.

Steeling his nerves, he pressed his Avato pendant to his lips and stepped into the gloom, taking up a slow, deliberate pace. One step, two... His boots crunched softly in the dirt upon the worn stone. The hushed breathing and scuff of footfalls from his friends followed him into the depths.

"Don't worry, Jalis," Oriken said. "Anything gets past Dag, I'll keep you safe."

Jalis laughed. "You're a brave journeyman saying that to a bladesmistress when she's behind you in a tight space."

"How does the saying go? Keep your blade sharp, but your wit sharper." The amusement was rich in Oriken's voice, but Dagra knew he was masking his own uneasiness.

As he reached the next turn in the stairs, Dagra froze. "Suffering gods." The lamplight illuminated the right-angled walls, causing shadows to dance across the stone. With his free hand, he grasped the handle of his gladius.

"What is it?" Oriken asked.

"Nothing. I just... It's okay."

"You should put the legend out of your mind," Jalis said.

"That's not what bothers me." *No*, he thought. *It's the dark. That, and the crushing weight of the earth overhead. And the fact that we're descending into a place that's more bereft of the gods than the whole of the Deadlands.*

He peered anxiously around the corner and down into the darkness. As far as he could tell, the stairwell was empty.

"I'm acting like a little girl imagining ghosts," he muttered, forcing himself to continue the descent. *Except if anywhere has ghosts, it's this heathen crypt.*

Beyond the next turn, the steps touched onto level ground that stretched into a narrow, low-ceilinged corridor. Wooden supports ran the length of the walls between squares of hewn stone. Bunches of dusty cobwebs dangled from the corners of the crossbeams. The dank, penetrating darkness, coupled with the musty odour that drifted from the corridor's black throat, sent a chill down Dagra's spine.

"Curse the Dyad," Oriken said as he was forced to stoop into the cramped space.

Dagra scowled. "Please *don't* curse while I'm praying."

Oriken inclined his head further, dipping his features into shadow except for his smirk.

"Seriously, I've heard the same ridicule from you since we were kids, and it's never worth the debate. Now is especially not the time to make me defend the forces upon, beneath and above Verragos that I know are real, which you deny more and—"

"All I said was 'curse the Dyad.'"

"Bah." Dagra glanced up. "I hope you're not too busy cursing to keep an eye on the spider webs."

Oriken paused, then moaned. "Stars. There *had* to be spiders down here, didn't there? I could've placed a wager on it."

Dagra pressed onwards, with Oriken following close behind. Before long, an archway came into view, a portal into whatever heathen horrors lay beyond. With all his senses fixed on the black arch, he almost jumped out of his skin and nearly dropped the lamp when Oriken's yell pealed through the corridor. Dagra's heart pounded as he spun around to see Oriken prancing around and flapping his arms wildly, swatting at the brim of his hat and shuffling backwards into a bemused Jalis.

She grabbed him by the waist, no doubt to stop him barrelling into her rather than to steady the blundering fool. Despite her petite frame, she easily stopped their lanky friend in his tracks.

Oriken's movements had kicked up a blanket of dust, and a fine haze hung throughout the corridor, dimming visibility that much more. His hair sweaty and dishevelled as he pulled the hat off, Oriken stared aghast at the cobwebs that clung to the brim and indented crown. With a cringe, he began to swat them away.

Jalis placed her hands on her hips, cocked her head and fixed him with a disappointed look.

Noticing her scrutiny, Oriken shrugged apologetically and replaced the hat onto his head. "They make my skin crawl!"

Dagra sighed. "We know!"

Jalis couldn't keep her smirk away as she said, "You've missed a bit." She reached up and pulled a strand of web from his stubble, then wiped it onto the wall. "There. It's over." She pursed her lips, then added, "Will you try to be a brave freeblade now?"

"I *said* we should've brought a few torches instead of that stupid lamp," Oriken muttered. "We could have fired up the whole damned ceiling as we went."

Dagra shook his head and turned to stare at the black archway. He moved forward slowly, trepidation weighing on his every step. His focus was once again on his own fears.

I'm in no rush to find out what's beyond there, he thought. *No one's been in a burial vault in centuries. It's unnatural! We've come this far though, and I guess we'll be bringing home a good story if nothing else. Pull yourself together. We're almost there.*

He reached the arch and steeled himself. "In for a copper, in for a silver," he growled. Taking a deep breath, he stepped through the portal into the darkness of a high-ceilinged hallway, considerably wider than the cramped corridor. All was silent and still. Too quiet. Too still. He peered into the gloom for a long moment. The hairs pricked on his scalp as he stepped aside for the others to enter.

Oriken ducked beneath the arch with a grin and stretched to his full height. "Ah, that's *much* better!"

"I'm glad you think so," Dagra said, "but do you think you could express your pleasure with a *little* less noise?"

"Ah, come on, Dag. That cave incident was years ago."

"Aye, it was! Seven, to be precise. And I don't need you reminding me about it yet again, thank you very much."

Oriken scoffed. "Never mind collapsed ceilings and blocked entrances, you carry on shouting and you'll be waking the dead."

Dagra shivered, clenched his teeth and cast Oriken a seething glare.

"All right, children," Jalis said sternly. "Save the games till we're back out on the heath. You can play the whole way home if it pleases you, but let's pretend just a modicum of decorum while we're here, like professional freeblades." She looked at Dagra. "Lead on."

He set a wary pace into the hall. The lamp guttered as he swung it from side to side to peer into recesses set within the walls at periodic intervals. Shadows quivered everywhere like spectres shrinking from the light's reach. Assorted chunks of gemstones caught the lamplight within the alcoves and upon podiums set along the centre of the walkway; he recognised obsidian, starstone, lapis, cat's eye, thunderglass, and various other pretty but not so precious pebbles. A crimson-streaked sunstone caught his attention at the rear of one of the alcoves. He ventured inside for a closer look. The gem was set waist-high into the centre of a granite slab that reached from Dagra's knees to his chest, twice as wide as it was tall, its sides wedged tight against the pillared corners. He took hold of the sunstone to twist it free, but it was firmly embedded into the granite.

Words and dates circled the gem. Dagra leaned closer, but the chiselled lettering was in Old Himaeran and barely legible. With a shake of his head, he returned to the walkway.

As he passed a central podium, the lamp-light fell upon scuff marks in the dust several paces ahead. He approached and squatted to peer at the marks in the dust-laden floor. Oriken and Jalis hunkered down to either side. "Looks like we're not the first ones down here," he said.

"Probably just rats," Oriken said, receiving a raised eyebrow from Jalis. "Really *large* rats?" Dagra cast him a withering look. "All right!" He shrugged. "A nargut then. Likely has a warren down here some place."

"Not rats." There was a note of concern to Jalis's voice. "And not a nargut, Orik, but thanks for the suggestions. Whatever it is, it has to be two-legged. Maybe a cravant. But I think we all agree that's unlikely since the graveyard is closed off."

"Less likely than a nargut?"

Jalis closed her eyes. "Forget about your nargut. I'll catch you one later if you like. You can tie a rope around its neck and keep it as a pet for the journey home." Pursing her lips, she added, "It's probably worth mentioning that these prints are far from fresh."

"How old do you reckon?" Oriken asked.

"Considering this crypt isn't likely to have been cleaned since your Great Uprising… When was that? Early four-hundreds?"

"Close enough," Dagra said, keeping an eye on the darkness all around them.

Jalis rose to her feet, and Dagra and Oriken followed suit. "In that case," she said, "we're looking at two or three centuries of dust down here."

"Huh," Oriken said. "Wouldn't the dust have covered the prints after so long?"

"Not necessarily. The layer in this crypt isn't particularly thick like you would find in an uncleaned house after so many years. The footprints could be decades old." The corners of her lips curled in a mirthless smile. "Dagra, by all means start praying that the so-called burial jewel is still here. Orik, you can wish upon the stars and the moons if it pleases you. For my part, after our long trip into this grim end of nowhere I'm looking forward to securing us a bounty. But if someone's beaten us to it…"

"Let's not jump to conclusions," Dagra said. *And I was just starting to get used to the idea that maybe we'd find the jewel after all.*

The silvers from the contract would ensure hot meals and full cups for a whole year, for all three of them. Even Maros's cut as Guild Official would pull him a tidy profit. It was a job none of them could afford to pass up.

They resumed progress deeper into the hallway. Dagra once again took point with the lamp, following the faded dust-trails, checking the alcoves as they passed. He gave each a quick search for signs of the burial jewel, but they contained nothing but similar slabs of granite and gems of little value.

"You know," Oriken said, giving his stubble an idle scratch, "I've noticed one thing about this vault. Since that corridor back there, I've scarcely seen hide nor hair of a cobweb. Unless the ceiling up yonder is filled with them; thankfully we can barely see it to find out."

Dagra looked at Jalis. "The man's got a point."

"It's almost as if..." Oriken's face fixed with inner concentration.

Dagra shifted his weight. "Yes?"

Oriken raised his hands in defeat. "I don't know what it's almost as if. Something, anyway."

"Thanks for that insight," Jalis said. "Who needs an oracle when we've got an Oriken?"

"Forget it." He pulled the brim of his hat down a fraction, falling into silence as they continued into the crypt.

For Dagra, the oppressive gloom steadily became even more stifling the further they went. He wiped the back of a sleeve across the sweat that sheened his brow, and gave a tug on his already loosened shirt-collar. The ceiling was barely visible here; just a few grey lines and smudges that suggested rough-cut stone and crossbeams high overhead, but the open space crushed in on him more than the cramped corridor had. The last thing he wanted was to be trapped on the wrong side of a rock-fall, nowhere to run as phantoms of the long-deceased seeped from the walls, their ghost-lights drifting ever closer...

"Unholy place," he grumbled, suppressing a shudder.

Still, he was glad to be the one holding the lamp. He imagined Jalis taking up position at the rear, and he silently admired her bravery. Trusting in him to be her eyes, that took something uncanny, that did.

You've got more guts than me, lass. I'll give you that.

His eyes were on the dust-sprinkled flagstones when something moved at the upper edge of his vision. He froze, a gasp lodging in his throat. The reach of the lamp-light fell on a cluster of shadowy, twitching shapes that crept onto the walkway from an alcove to the left. He fumbled for his sword, his fingers forgetting their years of training, but the gladius was half out of its scabbard before he recognised the shapes for what they really were, and he let out a rattling sigh of relief.

Gods, I didn't need that. It was only debris, a shattered slab of granite fallen from its niche, neither crouching nor lurking. *Just a trick of light and shadows. And imagination*, he added in reproof. The shapes weren't moving in the slightest.

As he neared the rubble, he noted with concern that the scuff marks they'd followed led right up to the smashed stone and gathered in a cluster. He glanced back to Jalis. She nodded in acquiescence to the unspoken question. Bolstered by her quiet courage, Dagra stepped into the alcove, the scattered fragments of granite crunching beneath his boots. His eyes scanned the small area, drawn to the niche at the rear, from which the slab had fallen. In its absence was a thick wall of cobwebs. Spiders could have lurked deeper within, but it was impossible to tell; the densely-bunched threads seemed to absorb the lamp's glow, sucking it in, giving no secrets away.

His attention was drawn to the upper right corner of the oblong cavity. A dark patch of brittle-looking fungus clung to the stone, just like the stuff that covered the trees in the graveyard. A cluster of pale cysts with thin, crimson veins nestled atop the mildewy stain. Dagra leaned closer to inspect the curious growths. Lifting a finger to the largest cyst, he gently touched it. With a muted *pop*, the dried membrane burst in a puff of dust. He flinched back as a pungent odour filled his nostrils, but the cloud had already faded. He sneezed and hastily rose to his feet. Stepping backwards, he scowled at the wall of webs, the fungal growths, the scattered debris and disturbed dust.

It's no way to spend the afterlife, he thought, nauseated at the prospect of being left in a hole to rot rather than first being burnt to the bones. They were savages during the Days of Kings, they truly were. Bodies should be burnt, *had* to be burnt to free the spirits for their journey to Kambesh.

Spirits…

A faint, musty odour drifted from the web-filled cavity. He shuddered and rejoined his companions.

"Anything interesting?" Oriken asked.

Dagra cast him a pointed glance. "Nothing you want to know about."

"Spiders." Oriken grimaced. "If it's spiders, just say it's spiders. I'd rather know than not."

"I didn't see any spiders."

Oriken looked reserved. "Fair enough."

"But…"

"But *what*?"

"You know how there are no cobwebs in here?"

Oriken narrowed his eyes in anticipation of Dagra's next words.

"I think I found them." Dagra poked a thumb over his shoulder. "They're all gathered in that hole. Seems so, anyway." Oriken groaned, and Dagra shrugged innocently. "Hey, you asked."

"Yeah, but there's information and there's *too much* information. You couldn't resist adding the *but*, could you?" Oriken jabbed a finger at him. "My turn next time."

Dagra forced a tight smile. The banter helped a little to combat his current state of mind.

A pebble of bloodstone caught his eye in the strewn rubble. He bent and picked it up, rubbed it on his trousers. A smooth, dark-green oval, covered in bright scarlet flecks.

No value, but a nice-looking piece. It's not part of a tomb any more, Dagra reasoned, justifying the morality of taking it. *Maybe I could get the smithy to set it into the old gladius's pommel. Something to remember the trip by*, he thought sourly, stuffing the bloodstone into his trouser pocket.

"These baubles are next to worthless," he said quietly, "but what sort of common thieves would leave so many behind? Have either of you seen signs of tampering other than this slab?"

Oriken frowned. "Now that you mention it, no. But if someone was down here, they could've been after the same thing we are. Might even have been freeblades. You never know."

Jalis shook her head. "Except no one's crossed the Deadlands in centuries."

"Allegedly," Dagra said.

Oriken shrugged. "Maybe our client hired someone else before us, and this grave is where they found the jewel."

Jalis kicked at a piece of rubble. "The slab housed a gem the same size as the others around here." She cast Dagra a quick, knowing glance. "None that we've seen so far are large enough to be the jewel we're looking for."

Oriken nodded sidelong to the alcove. "Maybe it was buried with the body instead of being fixed to the granite."

Jalis looked doubtful. "These people went out of their way to cover this place in gemstones. What would be the point of sealing the jewel away where no one can see it?"

Dagra shook his head and said to Oriken. "Even if the jewel were in there, you haven't taken a look at that web. It's undisturbed. And thick. Whoever removed the slab didn't bother going any further. Or, if they did, it all happened plenty long ago, like Jalis said."

Oriken's eyes were pits of shadow beneath the brim of his hat as he risked a glance into the recess. "I can hardly blame them for not going in there. That web would be a deal-breaker for me as well. You just try getting me to crawl into a hole full of spider webs. Not going to happen. Not even for a sackful of *golden* dari." He tucked a thumb behind his swordbelt. "Not for all the dari in Himaera. No chance."

"Gods!" Dagra blanched. "I hope the jewel isn't stashed at the back of one of these holes, with some poor sod whose corpse has been left to rot and whose soul is trapped in limbo, and we have to clamber inside and rummage around..."

Jalis clicked her fingers in Dagra's face. "Snap out of it. Carry on with that nonsense and I'll help you expedite a cure for your phobia."

"Huh?" Dagra frowned in confusion, then followed her gaze to the web-filled hole. He glanced sidelong at her, and she nodded as he stepped further away from the recess. "You wouldn't."

She held a finger to her lips. "Then shush, Dag. Both of you." Glancing from Dagra to Oriken, she lowered her gaze to the scuff-marks in the dust. "I hate to mention it, but I'm realising something else about these footprints."

Dagra sighed, "Is there a chance this could be good news for a change?"

Jalis cast him the expected sardonic look.

"Go on then, spit it out."

"You were on to something when you said we haven't seen signs of looting. That got me thinking. If someone had been here, there ought to be at least two sets of footprints. One leading in, one going back out. But other than ours, I've seen only one set of prints."

Oriken looked sceptical. "You think whoever was down here didn't leave? That they... what, died down here? Oh! You mean there must be another way out!"

"That was my first guess. But if there's another entrance to this place, it's not indicated on the map. That's beside the point though. Look." She pointed along to the far side of the debris, and Dagra swung the lamp across to illuminate the area. "The tracks stop here," Jalis said, sombrely.

It was true, Dagra saw. The dust beyond lay undisturbed. He rubbed a thumb into his beard as a grim suggestion began to plant itself into his mind. He regarded Jalis with a cautionary glare and a shake of the head. "Don't say it."

"This wasn't somebody coming down here," she said. "It was something *leaving*."

"You had to say it, didn't you?"

Oriken crossed his arms. "This just gets better and better."

Jalis gave an apologetic shrug.

"For the gods' sake," Dagra growled. "We'll be scaring ourselves witless before we even find the damned jewel. Let's just keep looking." He pressed his lips together and regarded his companions as he drew his gladius from its scabbard.

Oriken inclined his head and unsheathed his sabre.

Jalis checked the daggers at her thigh and hip, though she left them in their sheaths. "Agreed," she said. "But knowing what we might be facing can only give us an advantage."

Dagra grunted. "You won't be saying that when the advantage is me shitting my pants."

They continued deeper into the burial chamber, giving each alcove a cursory check as they passed, until finally they came to the end of the crypt. Before them a tall rectangle of granite was set into the centre of the wall, reaching from the floor to higher than the crown of Oriken's hat. A line of waist-high pedestals ran to either side along the wall; on each rested a collection of dusty gemstones.

His jaw dropped as he saw the central feature. Set within the granite at Dagra's eye level was an exquisitely-cut jewel, twice the size of his fist. *By the Dyad, old Cela wasn't fooling us. And she wasn't exaggerating, neither.*

A silver band encircled the circumference of the jewel, holding it fast inside its stone casing. Soft pinks and greens flitted across the jewel's many-faceted surface; reflections of the flickering oil lamp.

"Sweet Khariali," he whispered, invoking the name of the primal goddess of gems and metals.

"Sweet Khariali, indeed," Oriken echoed. "There's our baby!"

"It's beautiful," Jalis whispered.

Dagra set the lamp on the nearest pedestal, pushing aside the gemstones it held, then stood back. It might have been his imagination, or it could have been how the light gleamed from the jewel's myriad faces, but it seemed to emanate a warmth that was in no way physical, more a calmness that touched not the skin but the soul. It may have been used as a burial stone, but it didn't belong in this crypt any more than Dagra himself belonged here. He'd be happy to take it with him.

"I was expecting something like a diamond," Jalis said reverentially. She stepped forward to trace her fingertip across its angular surface. "But this is no mere diamond, or I'm a fishwife."

She has the right of it, Dagra thought. The jewel made the few small diamonds he'd ever seen look as plain as glass.

In heavy, ornate script above the jewel, the words *Lajdie Cunaxa Tjiddarei* were engraved, along with the dates *152* and *225*. Ancient symbols were mixed with Old Himaeran and Middle Sosarran text surrounding the jewel in concentric circles. Dagra guessed the words might be a prayer or possibly a recitation of the lady's achievements.

"She died a long time before the blight," Oriken remarked.

"Probably the first of her line," Jalis said. "Or the first to rise to prominence, at any rate. Her position at the farthest reach of the crypt suggests she was the first to be buried here."

"How did the builders know how many Chiddaris there'd be?" Oriken asked. "All the niches seem to have graves in them. That's pretty good guesswork."

"I expect only the important individuals got a spot in the family vaults. The rest were likely buried aboveground. Plus, if we scrutinised the first few niches, I imagine we'd find they weren't taken as such, but merely reserved."

Dagra grunted. "It's a shame old Cunaxa here wasn't the last to be buried instead. Could've saved ourselves walking the length of this accursed hallway."

"I guess if she *had* been nearest the entrance," Oriken said, "then she wouldn't be the one looking after the family jewel, would she?"

Dagra cast him a cold glance before turning his attention back to their prize. He pointed to a group of carved symbols in the script surrounding the jewel.

"Here's some of those runes you get excited about, Jalis. Like the ones on my sword." He held the wide blade of the gladius into the light, indicating the darkened inscriptions that ran down its length. "Attic something-or-other, right?"

"*Antik rukhir.*" Jalis's Sardayan accent lent the old words a mystic edge, emphasising the *k* at the end of *antik* with a sharp click of the tongue, and rolling the *r* at the end of *rukhir*. She leaned closer to inspect the runes. "The language of the Umbral Era never ceases to amaze me. So many regional variations that seem to have evolved entirely separately from one another, and yet maintained recognisable common elements. We're talking thousands of years ago, before the first longboats crossed the Burning Channel, and yet antik rukhir was as prevalent on Himaera as on the Sosarran mainland. And it pre-dates *all* of the old tribes."

Oriken shrugged. "Who cares? I said it when you first saw the runes on Dagra's sword. Sure, it's an interesting weapon, but why get all excited about a dead language?"

"I don't know which is the greater treasure," Jalis sighed, with a wry smile. "The jewel, or your uncharacteristic insight."

"All I'm saying is we've got the jewel and it's worth a lot more than what Cela Chiddari is giving us. Even I can see that."

"We all agree we've found a small fortune," Dagra said, "but who's got the coin to pay us what it's really worth? Certainly no one I know. Five hundred silvers ain't to be scoffed at."

Jalis nodded in agreement and glanced at Oriken. "Besides, we're bound by the code. Even Orik wouldn't disregard the guild's rules."

Oriken gave his hat a brief twist. "Course not. Perish the thought. But do those rules cover how to remove a valuable jewel that's embedded in a solid chunk of granite? I'd prefer to deliver the thing in one piece, if possible." Dagra shrugged and glanced at Jalis, who shook her head. "I mean," Oriken went on, "it's not as if we've got a hammer and a chisel, is it?"

Jalis muttered a curse. "In retrospect, something of an oversight."

"So how do we get it out?"

"We use our blades." Dagra pointed to the weapons at Jalis's waist. "Yours would be best for the task, lass."

Jalis laughed. "You're making a joke, yes? I wouldn't ruin my blades on that jewel, no matter what it's worth." She patted the long, black-bladed dagger at her hip, and the slender, silver dagger on her thigh. "Dusklight and Silverspire are more than just weapons or tools. They're works of art, and irreplaceable."

Dagra sighed and sheathed his gladius. "All right. Leave this to me." He motioned for Oriken to turn around. Oriken did so, and Dagra untied the side-pouch of his backpack and rummaged inside, pulling out the short-bladed hunting knife.

"This ain't no fancy blade with a name," Dagra told Jalis, quirking an eyebrow. "Good old solid piece of steel Orik's had since we were kids."

"Actually, I *did* name it," Oriken said, a glint in his eye. "Called it Akantu after the patron of lesser creatures."

"No," Dagra said. "You did not. And you shouldn't mock the gods, least of all in this crypt."

Oriken scoffed. "Patrons aren't gods. They're men and women, no different from... well, no different from me and Jalis." He gave Dagra a wide grin.

"Fuck yourself," Dagra suggested.

He placed the knife's curved tip into the gap between granite and silver and began to lever it back and forth, working his way carefully around the jewel's circumference.

"Don't slip," Oriken said.

"I doubt your knife could harm the jewel," Jalis said. "That's why I won't tarnish my blades on it. It looks stronger than a diamond."

Dagra's heart raced as the hunting knife slipped over the silver band. Its sharp tip jittered across the jewel, emitting a high-pitched screech.

"Cherak's stones, Dag!" Oriken said. "Are you *trying* to lose us our bounty?"

Dagra puffed his cheeks and blew out as his nerves began to calm. He thought he'd ruined their prize, but there wasn't the faintest scratch on any of the jewel's angular surfaces.

Jalis sighed. "Thanks for testing my supposition, Dagra," she said flatly. "I think we can consider the point proven."

There was a slight shake in Dagra's hand as he inserted the knife's tip back into the groove. He twisted the blade, and the grind of steel on stone whispered down the black hall.

"Do you think it's magic?" he asked.

Oriken barked a laugh. "Don't be ridiculous."

"Maybe it's got incantations woven into it. Remember that girl in where-was-it?" Dagra frowned as he brought up the hazy memory. "The one Maros rescued?"

"I'd hardly say he came to her rescue," Oriken said. "She was chased by bees after disturbing a nest."

"Dag's got a point," Jalis said. "That girl magicked an oak back into a sapling."

"So we were told."

Dagra bristled. "Well, they carted her off to the Arkh after that, so there must've been truth to it." The jewel was beginning to loosen.

Oriken snorted. "If I saw it with my own eyes, I'd believe it. I don't take everything I hear for true."

"I know." Dagra sighed.

"She was a feyborn, Orik," Jalis said softly. Dagra could feel her warm breath on his neck as she watched him work. "Say what you like about some other things, but I can assure you that feyborn do exist."

Oriken gave no reply and the conversation ceased. As Dagra worked, so did his imagination. In his mind he again saw the exposed burial hole full of webs. Somewhere behind the silken wall lay a twisted, withered relative of their client. And behind the slab he worked on now lay the bones of Cela's most ancient ancestor, Cunaxa.

A skeleton by now, he assured himself. *Just bones. Nothing to be afraid of.* He levered the blade back and forth, and with a final twist the burial jewel slid from the stone...

Web-filled eye sockets stared at him. In mute horror, he stared back. The jewel's housing now framed the sunken features of Lady Cunaxa Chiddari, covered in silken threads and peeking through the gap. The skin stretched over her skull like boiled leather, with clumps of hair fused to the mummified flesh. The brow and cheekbones were festooned with scabrous growths, and the terrible, lipless rictus grinned at him as if delighted to have company after the long centuries of solitude. Her blackened teeth shifted and parted. Horrified, Dagra watched as the webs tore and the jaw stretched wide, then the jawbone slipped behind the slab and struck the floor with a muted *thunk*.

"Gah!" Dagra sprang backwards, uttering the names of the Dyad in the hope that they would whisk him from the heathen hallway and back onto the heath. Bile rose in his throat as he tore his gaze from the wizened skull.

"It's just a corpse, Dag," Jalis said softly.

"It moved!"

"You disturbed its position, that's all."

Saliva swam in his mouth. He swallowed it. "Aye. Just a corpse. Of course. A corpse, of course!" He issued a brief but manic giggle. Catching the bemused looks of his friends, he cleared his throat and composed himself.

The jewel was in Oriken's hands. He held it aloft and peered at it, undaunted by the grisly cadaver that watched them. Jalis took the lamp from the podium and held it by Oriken's shoulder. The light glinted from the jewel's multi-faceted surface. Its front was circular, the silver band clasped tightly around the circumference, seemingly forged into place. From side-on, the jewel was flatter but bulged in the centre around a shadowed core that broke into prisms in the lamplight. The dark spot put Dagra in mind of the black-yolked eggs of the dusk balukha, or a blot of ink trapped within a solid glass sculpture. He was beginning to amend his assessment of the jewel's aesthetic value.

Oriken brushed his hand over the rear of the jewel. His face scrunched in distaste. "We'll have to give it a scrub later. Got some of her face stuck to it."

Dagra's stomach lurched and his knees buckled. He clutched onto the podium beside him for support.

Jalis opened her backpack and passed Oriken a blanket. She held the pack open while he wrapped the jewel and stuffed it inside. She pulled the cord tight and knotted it, fastened the pack's straps and slung it onto her shoulder.

"That better be your bedding and not mine," Dagra told her. As he released the podium, his glance landed on the eyeless, noseless, and now jawless head of Cunaxa. As he glared blackly at the Chiddari matron, the head shifted again.

"Sweet mother of the prophets! Don't tell me *that* didn't happen!" The head was tilted askance, like an attentive child curious to know what the commotion was about.

"You can let go of my arm now, Dag," Jalis said.

He mumbled an apology and staggered to the wall, leaned upon the stones and vomited. When he was finished, he wiped a sleeve over his beard and turned to see Jalis and Oriken regarding him sombrely, their faces awash in the glow of the lamp.

Dagra forced a laugh. "Don't know where that came from." He waved away Jalis's proffered handkerchief. "No. I'm fine, really. Just a…" He could feel the corpse staring at him, but kept his attention firmly on Jalis. "We've got what we came for. Let's get out of here. No sense lingering, right?"

Jalis nodded and turned to leave, but Oriken placed a hand on her shoulder. "Why don't we treat ourselves to a few extras on the way out?" He gestured to the gems atop the pedestals, and into the recesses where gemstones winked from the shadows. As Jalis considered his words, he pressed the point. "We should at least take the ones on these pedestals for our client, since they obviously come as a package with the jewel. Right? If she doesn't want them…" He shrugged.

Jalis didn't look convinced.

"Walk and talk," Dagra said. He took the lamp from Jalis and set off down the hallway, his friends falling in behind to follow their only source of light.

"The contract mentions nothing except for the jewel itself," Jalis said. "If we take more, our actions might be deemed sacrilegious."

Dagra spat a curse. "This whole place is irreverent."

Oriken scoffed. "How can it be fine to steal the greatest treasure, but wrong to take the minor ones?"

"Hey," Jalis said, "I don't make the rules."

Oriken sighed."It's not like Dag hasn't pocketed a stone."

"Oh, you child!" Dagra whirled around. "Seriously? It's a worthless bauble! A pretty pebble from a ransacked grave!"

Jalis grunted under her breath. "Is that what you think, Dag, or is it what you *hope*?"

"Don't start with that again. Not now. Let's just head home, back to wealth and a warm bath."

"You'll get no argument from me there," she said. "Orik, the graves in this crypt belong to our client's ancestors. If we disturb any of them by removing

82

their gems – most of which seem to be comparatively worthless anyway, as Dagra says – we'll effectively be stealing from Cela herself, regardless of our intentions, however *ostensible* they might be." She eyed Oriken keenly. "Dagra found his gem in the broken rubble; he can keep it, but we leave the rest."

"You're the boss," Oriken said with a sigh. "But what about the city?"

Jalis sucked air through her teeth and glared at him side-long. "We'll talk about that after we've left the graveyard. We've wasted more than half of the day already."

Oriken looked at her a moment but said nothing more, and the conversation lapsed into silence as they retraced their steps through the long hallway.

Dagra couldn't have cared less about the bloodstone he'd picked up. His thoughts were on the burial jewel, set to bring them a lucrative windfall indeed. But, more-so, his thoughts were on the matron of the crypt, her eyeless gaze intent on their departure from her resting place.

Soon, the desecrated burial hole came back into view. The scuff-marks, now covered by the footprints of Dagra and his companions, led from the broken slab to the stairwell...

To distract his wandering imagination, Dagra said, "Orik's got a point, though. It's questionable ethics that we can desecrate a grave if it's part of our contract, but otherwise it's frowned upon." He barked a terse laugh and fished around in his pocket for the bloodstone. "You know what? I don't even want this piece of trash. Thought it might look good on the gladius, but with the coin we'll be earning I could buy one of Khariali's glittering teats if I fancied."

"Better Khariali's teats than Cherak's stones," Oriken quipped.

With a flick of his wrist, Dagra skimmed the bloodstone into the shadows and listened to its clatter echo down the hallway.

"Dag." At his side, Jalis's eyes flashed a smile. "I didn't say the other crypts in the graveyard aren't viable targets, just the Chiddari crypt. This whole place has already been blighted by a goddess and abandoned for centuries. A few little mortals can't desecrate it much more than has already been done."

Dagra returned the smile with a weak one of his own. "True. But I'm not sure I'm interested. It's not like we brought a mule with us; anything we found, we'd have to lug across the whole of Scapa Fell and part of Caerheath. Thanks, lass, but no. I just want to get out of this damned, dead and dusty place and breathe some fresh air, blighted or otherwise."

Oriken mumbled under his breath as he trudged along behind them, though whether in assent or disagreement, Dagra couldn't tell and didn't much care. He forced his thoughts to the journey home, and to spending the rest of the year in and around Alder's Folly with no long, arduous contracts, no dark and dismal underground places, and no more corpses.

Gods, he thought. *Please, no more corpses.*

83

CHAPTER TEN
INTERLOPERS

Dagra blew into the oil lamp's flute to extinguish the flame, then passed it to Jalis. With a sigh of relief, he stepped from the Chiddari crypt into the cheerless vista of the graveyard. The red orb of Banael was diffused behind a full cloud-cover, its underbelly dipping closer to the horizon than Dagra was comfortable with. He cast a hooded glance at the statue of Cunaxa.

Well, lady, he thought. *I could say you were once quite the beauty, except I've just watched your jaw fall off.*

Wispy rivulets of mist were trickling through the cracks in the barren soil. Tendrils of the stuff licked and caressed the mildewed bases of headstones and crawled against the crumbled pathways. Even as he watched, the mist was spreading.

"How long were we in there?" Oriken asked, his eyes in soft shadow beneath his hat as he glanced at the low sun.

"Hours," Jalis said.

"It didn't feel that long."

"Maybe not for you," Dagra said.

Oriken turned his attention to the city, puffed his cheeks and let out a low whistle. "There must be a heap of treasure over there. The castle alone has to hold a fortune. We could take shelter in one of the buildings for the night. The place has been derelict for centuries; I doubt any of the owners would mind."

"Come on, Orik," Jalis said. "Are you a man or a magpie? Don't forget we've got a long trek back to the nearest bog-rotten pocket of civilisation, plus another couple of days travel till we're back in Alder's Folly. I don't fancy lugging treasure across a hundred miles and more of countryside infested with marshes and monsters and very likely more that we didn't encounter on the way here."

"I'm not talking about filling our pockets and packs, just a handful of keepsakes. It wouldn't hurt."

For a moment, Dagra found himself considering the point. He'd meant what he'd said to Jalis about not being interested in looting for second-rate gems, but as he looked towards the sprawling city it was difficult not to imagine a greater wealth than mere chunks of pretty stones. Coins likely littered the place. And jewellery with precious diamonds and sapphires, emeralds and rubies. Or weapons, like his own ancient gladius; the wide-bladed short swords were rarely forged since the end of the Great Uprising, and Lachyla would be the best place to find another.

I'd like a second gladius, he thought, *but not that badly. Still as harrowing as it's been, it wasn't quite as bad as I imagined. Maybe tomorrow, during full daylight…*

He shook his head to purge the temptation, and frowned at the gathering mist. "We should get moving before this stuff becomes a problem."

"But, listen—"

Jalis cast Oriken a cautionary look. "I said we'd discuss it later, and we will. For now, Dagra's right. Back to the portcullis." Catching Oriken's glance at the distant Litchgate that separated the graveyard from the city, she thrust a finger northwards to the heathland. "*That* portcullis."

They set off down the narrow path connecting the Chiddari crypt to the central Litchway. As they walked, Oriken maintained a monologue concerning the types of treasures they might discover in the castle. He was in mid-flow when Jalis halted abruptly and raised a hand to signal for a stop.

"What is it?" Oriken asked.

"Tell me something," she said. "How confident should we be that the city is deserted? Can we assume that every Lachylan citizen died during the blight?"

"Huh? Of course. Even the ones that escaped are long-dead by now. Why do you ask?"

Jalis gazed past Dagra's shoulder into the mist-hazed graveyard. "So, you're saying that we three fearless freeblades are the only people here?"

Dagra frowned. "I know that tone, lass, and it's never a good sign. If you've got something to say, just say it. If not—"

Jalis's distant look turned stony. "I was just wondering why it suddenly seems to be grieving hour in *li Gardine dessa Mortas*."

"I have no idea what you—" Silenced by Jalis's expression, Dagra followed her pointed finger. *Oh, gods*, he thought. *No…*

Frail-looking figures were emerging from the mist and moving listlessly among the gravestones. More were materialising in the distance among the ground mist, difficult to discern from the blackened trees and the more ornate grave markers. One was closer than the rest – Dagra had already looked right at it and mistaken it for a short, twisted tree. It swayed in the breeze, its skeletal limbs held before it like reaching branches and twigs.

"Please tell me," Oriken whispered as he stared at the shambling figures, "that somebody ordered a guided tour of the graveyard and forgot to mention it."

Steel hissed as Jalis drew her daggers. "I'm afraid not."

"What are they?" Oriken asked.

As Dagra stared at the wraith-like forms, Jalis's observation in the Chiddari crypt came back to him, that the footprints only headed in one direction. He'd assumed someone else had been in the crypt, but what if...

"We go," he said. "Now."

He broke into a run along the centre of the Litchway, with Jalis and Oriken hot on his heels. The mist was quickly thickening to a rising, heavy fog, the clouds above bunching in mimicry, darkening the early evening to a fake dusk. More figures were approaching from the far edges of the graveyard, heading slowly, but surely, for the Litchway.

Up ahead beside the pathway, a withered hand grasped the rear edge of a crypt and a grotesque form stepped into view. What remained of its clothing had become one with its blight-ridden body, the age-darkened flesh flapping alongside the fabric. The sunken face turned towards Dagra. Its shrivelled lips and blackened gums with broken shards of teeth hung open in a silent scream.

He slowed as the creature took halting steps towards him. The rays of Banael broke through the clouds for just a moment, falling on the decayed face and deepening its shadowed cavities. The corpse lifted a hand to shield its face. It faltered in the sunlight, but continued its slow advance.

"Dear, sweet Aveia," Dagra breathed. "It's dead. They're *all* dead. Merciful gods, Cunaxa Chiddari *did* move! I knew it! She *moved*, and we just stood there chatting!"

As Oriken came alongside, he grabbed Dagra's arm and gave it a rough squeeze. "Snap out of it, Dag! Don't gawp. And use your energy on running rather than blabbing." He ran on, his long legs taking him quickly along the wide Litchway.

The prospect of falling behind was enough to jolt Dagra from his rising panic and spur him onward. He pulled his eyes from the leering corpse and pumped his short legs faster. Jalis caught up and matched pace at his side.

"The dead of Lachyla," he gasped between breaths, "are supposed to stay in Lachyla."

"The dead everywhere are supposed to stay dead," Jalis said. "But if you're right, we'll find out soon enough."

In every direction, the place was filling with the creatures. A guttural moaning began from the nearest; a wet, crackly whisper like thick liquid pouring over crisp leaves. The noise intensified as more of the dead lent their voices to the ghastly chorus. Within moments, the graveyard rang with the sibilant murmur of its denizens.

Oriken's bounding run took him quickly along the tumbledown pathway, directly towards a crowd of corpses. As he leaped over a raised flagstone, his hat flew from his head. He snatched it from the air, hit the ground running and fixed it firmly back where it belonged, without even the slightest pause.

Despite the surrounding horror, Dagra barked a laugh at Oriken caring about his hat even while the Pit itself broke out around them.

As Oriken reached the horde, he swept his sabre in a high back-slash across the front line of corpses, the curved blade biting into their faces and throats. Unbalanced by the force of the blow, they staggered backwards and a couple toppled over. One wasted head toppled from a parchment-thin neck and thudded to the stones. Oriken smashed the sabre's hand-guard into the face of the nearest corpse, then slammed his boot into another's chest. Within moments, the way was cleared for Dagra and Jalis to run through. Dagra's palm sweated as he clenched the gladius's leather grip. He shared a grim glance with Jalis, and they pushed onwards.

The pathway and the barren soil to either side was lost beneath a rising blanket of fog, forcing Dagra to slow his pace as he stumbled over loose debris and sunken stones. The fog had consumed the shorter headstones, and the upper portions of crypt entrances protruded like the bows of sinking ships, their statues of stone or metal serving as grim figureheads. Skeletal horrors and mouldering abominations flailed between it all like drowning passengers.

Oriken was a blur of motion in the thickening haze as more creatures wandered towards the Litchway. He hacked and slashed, punched and kicked his way into them. He shouted over his shoulder, but the words were lost to Dagra amid the clamour of the dead. Dodging a corpse's grasp, Oriken struck it with a glancing left punch, almost pitching it over, but it took a faltering step in Dagra's direction and paused. Hunched over, its ruined features seemed to sniff the air, sensing him.

Then Dagra was upon it, swiping the gladius in a brutal upward arc. The blade sang through the fog and bit deep into the corpse's raised forearm, shattering the bone. The almost-severed appendage dangled uselessly, the fingers twitching into the curls of fog as the creature made to follow him, but Dagra pushed on, his terror muted by raging adrenaline. Visibility was all but gone now. The mist forced him to slow to scarcely more than a jog as he navigated hidden obstacles of uneven paving stones and other detritus. His eyes darted from side to side as he stumbled through the gloom. The dead lumbered on, moaning their unholy lament.

"There!" Oriken shouted from somewhere ahead. "The gate!"

Thank the gods! Dagra thought. *Almost there.*

A corpse loomed before him. He loosed a yell, but swallowed his fear and slammed a shoulder into it. The corpse flailed backwards but righted itself. It stood firm, blocking his way.

Dagra's chest heaved as he stared in revulsion. The once-elegant dress and vaguely feminine shape marked the corpse as a woman. Its eyes were messes of crusted gore over sunken cheeks. Swollen pustules covered the cavity of the missing jaw. A cyst popped as it gurgled through its throat-hole. Dagra retched, and the corpse jerked into motion.

He lunged and drove the gladius into its chest. As he pulled the blade clear, the head lurched forwards and exploded, spraying him with foul ichor. He flung his arms up to protect his face, and staggered backwards.

Oh, blessed gods, I've got its head all over me. Aveia, how did I deserve this?

The headless corpse pitched over into the mist, replaced by the unmistakable profile of Oriken.

"Ha! Straight through the face!" Oriken grinned and raised the haft of his sabre to his shoulder in mock salute, the blade dripping with gore. With a wink at Dagra, he pinched the brim of his hat with a filth-streaked finger and thumb.

Too horrified for words, Dagra nodded his gratitude.

Another corpse emerged from the fog behind Oriken. Dagra began to issue a warning, but Oriken had already caught the look on his face; he spun and lashed out. The sabre sliced deep into its throat. He slammed his boot between its thighs with a sickening crunch. The corpse crumpled, swallowed by the mist..

From somewhere behind, the sound of soft and brittle things being rapidly and repeatedly sliced grew until it was right behind Dagra. A final rending swipe and a triumphant grunt, and Jalis emerged, brandishing her daggers. Silverspire's slender blade was now as dark as Dusklight, its partner in carnage. Jalis's face was set in a mask of concentration, at one with her craft. She remained by Dagra's side, and on they ploughed behind Oriken through the nightmare madness.

Dagra couldn't be sure they were still heading in the right direction, but he trusted in Oriken's lead as his friend carved a route through the onslaught of corpses. Time lost meaning; it had become one long moment that hung suspended, and it seemed an age since Oriken announced he'd spotted the gate.

But the portcullis is closed, he recalled as he stabbed a corpse in the face and kicked it away. *If only we'd operated that damned winch. But how were we supposed to foresee this?* There was no way to pre-empt such madness, and the guild's handbook didn't cover how to deal with the undead, of that he was certain.

Gnarled hands continued to reach for him, and he continued to hack at them, but as the shapes fell away, they were replaced by more. Oriken had disappeared into the murk. Jalis, too, was nowhere to be seen. He was alone again. The ungodly moaning of the blighted dead was swallowed in the haze. The muted sounds of fighting ricocheted in the mist, seeming to come from all directions. He waded through the nightmare dreamscape, plunging blindly onward. He called out for Oriken and Jalis, but his shouts fell flat and were not answered.

Yet another monstrosity burst from the mist and bore down on him. Cataracted eyes stared from its lacerated face, the flesh hanging from its cheeks like curls of jerky. Mildewed teeth gnashed as it lunged towards him. Its fingers grasped his shirt. He floundered, teetering backwards as the thing clung on to him. He pitched over. The backpack struck the ground, padding his fall.

Within the grey-green fog, the corpse's features clouded to a shadow. Its pungent reek assailed Dagra's senses. Its weight pressed onto him like an insistent lover.

He struggled against it, trying to shift his sword-arm but it was pinned across his chest. All he could do was push against it, grappling with his free arm as it crushed down on him. A foul stench assailed him. His throat clenched as he breathed a lungful of the stuff. For a moment, the fog thinned to reveal the snapping maw inches from his face. His muscles strained as he pushed against the mindless onslaught.

The gnashing teeth paused. The corpse gripped him and locked its eyes with his. "*Lie...*" it hissed.

Gods please get it off me get off sweet Aveia help me!

Its broken nails raked at his shirt, snagging in the drawstring neck, scraping, gouging at his flesh. He fought with all the strength he could muster, punching wildly. His fist mashed into its neck.

Moans and shuffling feet of more of the undead drew closer. In his periphery, their shadows shifted like ghosts in the mist. His heart hammered loud in his ears. Stars swam in his eyes, a cry trapped in his throat.

"*Lie,*" the corpse repeated, the word a bubbling gurgle.

In desperation he struck it again and again, mashing his fists into its flesh in quick repetition. A final, crushing blow and its head pitched to the side with a gristly snap. It was the break Dagra needed. He pushed it away and cast it to the ground. Scrambling to his feet, he caught movement at the edge of his vision as hands touched his shoulders.

He whirled around, grabbed the nearest corpse and heaved it into the others, planted his fists on two of their chests and shoved hard.

As he stepped backwards, taloned fingers wrapped around his ankle. He stabbed the gladius down into the curling fog, and the blade found its target. He kicked at the unseen corpse's hand, but it clung on. He stamped down, his boot scraping across the gripping fingers, and felt them crunch beneath his heel. Shifting his aim, he slammed his boot onto the dark haze of its head and put his weight into it. Bone cracked and his foot sank in, lodging and sticking fast. The fog swirled, dissipating enough for him to see his heel wedged into the side of the corpse's head. He recoiled, and his boot wrenched free with a slurp.

Sweat dripped down his face. Exhaustion engulfed him. The crowd of corpses were closing in, their liquidy hisses rising with intent. He gripped the sword and spun about, but all he could see through the fog were lurching shadows.

The corpse on the ground struggled into a sitting position and turned its broken head towards him. "*Liar!*" it rasped.

"Fuck off!" He staggered away and broke into a stumbling run. He screamed the names of his friends, but no answer came. Muted, unrecognisable noises were everywhere and nowhere. *Blood of the Pit! Where's the gate? Where are Jalis and Orik? I'm lost!* "Aveia, help me!" he wailed.

"Dagra?"

"Avei— Orik? Orik! I'm here! Can you hear me?" Dagra strained to listen as he hurried forward. It *was* Oriken, he was sure of it. He sounded close, but *how* close? And in which direction? "Here!" he called again, reaching blindly and stumbling through the gloom. "Where are y— *Gah!*"

Something snatched at the wrist of his sword-arm and gripped tight. A shadow loomed before him, filling his vision. He threw a sweeping punch...

"Whoa, there!" Oriken cried as he rocked out of reach, releasing his grip on Dagra.

Relief flooded Dagra like a deluge. "I thought," he gasped.

Oriken nodded in understanding. He was a gore-streaked sight, carnage splattered indiscriminately all over him. A dark smear streaked his stubbled cheek, and a questionable lump perched upon the brim of his hat.

"Where's that gate, you great, lanky bastard? You said we were close to it ages ago."

"I said I could see it. I didn't say it was near."

Dagra's nerves were shot, but he desperately wanted out of the gods-forsaken place. "Well?" he snapped. "What are we waiting for? Let's go!"

Oriken gave a single nod and stepped into the fog. "Stay close."

"Wait!" *I forgot about the lass. How could I do that?* "We lost Jalis! We have to find her!"

"She's okay." Oriken grabbed Dagra's arm and pulled him onwards.

"How do you know? We can't just—"

"Dag!" Oriken swung his sabre into an emerging corpse. "She's already ahead. Come on!"

Dagra followed him into the gloom, fearing the worst for Jalis. But he trusted Oriken, had done forever despite the occasional mishap and disagreement. Still, a tightness clutched his chest at the thought of losing Jalis, especially like this.

The sky had darkened to a bruised purple with the deepening evening. Fewer of the blighted creatures approached now, though their wraith-like shadows were everywhere. Dagra's courage bolstered anew by Oriken's presence, and together they pushed onward.

His ears pricked at a faint shout. It must have been Jalis, but it could have come from anywhere. *Gods*, he thought, *let her be alive.*

The fog was thinning. He could dimly see the cracked ground at his feet, and prayed it was the Litchway and not one of the many side-paths that criss-crossed the graveyard. Up ahead, a dense mass of darkness writhed in the retreating mist.

Dagra grabbed Oriken's sleeve and brought him skidding to a halt. He pointed at the gathering and leaned close to Oriken. "They're facing away," he whispered. "They haven't spotted us." *Their attention is on something else*, he thought. *But what?*

His hopes returned as he spotted the top of the perimeter wall through the fading fog, just beyond the corpses. And poking above the stone...

Is that the portcullis? How in the fiery Pit... Ah, Jalis, you brave, beautiful lass. Dagra wanted to shout her name, to be sure she was there, to let her know he and Oriken were close, but he didn't want to gain the attention of the creatures that blocked their escape.

"She managed it," Oriken said. "Partly. Let's hope it's enough."

"You knew? How could you—"

"Stash a codpiece in it, for fuck's sake, Dag." Oriken slid his sabre into its scabbard and cast Dagra a determined glance. "Ready?"

Shit. No. Understanding Oriken's intention, he knew that the swords would be of little use in such close quarters. With a nod, Dagra sheathed his gladius.

Oriken loosed a battle-cry and sprinted for the corpses.

In for a silver, indeed, Dagra thought. He broke into a run behind his tall friend. Oriken squared his shoulders and ploughed headlong into the mass, shoving the creatures aside as he pressed through. His momentum slowed. Ragged fingers found purchase on his shirt and backpack. And then Dagra was upon the horde and barrelling into them, his short legs pushing him on as he struck out. Nails raked his face and shoulders. Fingers curled around his arms, but slipped away from the slick coating of sweat and gore that covered him.

Through the ghastly mass he glimpsed the heathland and the overgrown Kingdom Road and the latticework of the portcullis; the open vista of Scapa Fell beckoned him to reach its sanctuary. The gate wasn't fully raised, but he reckoned he could crouch beneath it. He was almost there, almost out. Desperation had pushed him this far, but renewed determination stretched his reserves still further.

He shoved through the last of the creatures and ducked beneath the partially-raised gate. Hands grabbed him and knocked him to his side, clutching at his legs, his waist, pinning him to the ground. He stared up at the rusted spikes hanging inches over his face, at the leering death-masks and desiccated limbs that filled his vision. Hands grasped him roughly by the straps of his pack and dragged him backwards, and suddenly he was out and staring up at a purple evening sky. A few wisps of fog followed him through the gate, but faded quickly. The blighted corpses made no attempt to crawl beneath the portcullis. Dagra's heart was hammering with relief and fading terror as Oriken leaned over him and gave a tight smile as he pinched the brim of his hat.

Dagra lay there. He stared up at his friend, scarcely believing he'd made it out alive. *We should've paid more attention to the legend.*

Oriken reached down and helped him to his feet.

"About time you two showed up. Talk about making a girl wait."

Jalis! Dagra spun around to see her standing not ten paces away. Her hair was stuck to the sides of her face in wet, grimy strands. Her chemise was so torn it clung to her only because the sodden fabric was plastered to her corselette and skin. She was a mess, but she was alive.

"Thank the gods!" he said as he walked towards her. "I thought you were done for." He was suddenly aware of the clamminess of his own clothing against his body, and the gods-awful stench that permeated from him. "I could hug you." He looked down at himself with a shrug and glanced to Oriken. "Both of you. But I'll not."

"Wise choice," Jalis said. She gestured to the gate. "Looks like you were right about the dead, Dag. They're not following."

He glanced over his shoulder to see the creatures shifting around beyond the iron bars, swaying listlessly and not even reaching through. Many faced into the graveyard and were beginning to shamble off into the gloom, wandering away from the threshold of the blight as if no longer interested.

The dead can't leave their Gardens. Something's *holding them here, making them stay where they belong.*

Beyond the hanging spikes, only a few ravaged forms lingered. Dagra turned away in disgust as the adrenaline suddenly wore off and the reality of the situation slapped him in the face. He stuffed his hands into his pockets to mask the shakes that coursed through his body.

"Waiting at the gate and keeping their attention was a big risk to yourself," he told Jalis, unable to keep the tremor from his voice. "But it worked. Thank you."

She nodded. "I only wish we'd raised the gate earlier."

"Good thing you got the winch working," Oriken said, squatting to rub his hands on a clump of yellowed grass.

"Not an easy task, trying to turn a rusted chain and kick corpses back down the steps. I might be nimble but I'm not built for raising a portcullis on my own."

"You raised it enough, and we're grateful." Oriken's expression was earnest as he climbed to his feet and met her gaze.

Jalis's lip twitched. "Yes, well, we all made it in one piece, and the jewel's safe and sound." She reached a hand behind her and patted her backpack.

"Good." Dagra drew a breath and blew it out. "Right then. If no one has any objections, let's get the rotten fuck away from this cankerous shit-hole."

Oriken gave a tight smile. "How does the saying go, Jalis? The stupid fisherman fishes in shark-infested waters?"

"Something like that." She reached for Dagra and Oriken's shoulders and turned them around. Together they set off along the Kingdom Road.

Dagra's eyes tracked the dirt-covered flagstones that stretched ahead, disappearing around a low hill. *We must be the stupidest people in Himaera,* he thought. *The only ones to ignore the legend. Against my better judgement I let myself be talked into it.* He cursed under his breath. *No, that's not fair; it was the silver that convinced me to take this foolhardy contract.*

As they walked, the clouds began to dissipate and the last rays of sun washed the heathland in a dark red, casting the sparse clusters of trees that dotted the landscape into shadow. Although ancient and gnarled, those trees were covered in leaves as it should be in the Vur season, the warmest of the year. Dagra doubted he would ever feel so relieved at the sight of greenery as he did right now. The heath was far from verdant, but it was alive.

"I don't know whether those things wanted to kill us or only cast us out." Jalis glanced over her shoulder as she walked. "But we *are* out, whether that was their intention or not. I want to err on the side of caution and put some good distance between us and that krig of a city before setting camp."

Dagra rubbed a shaking hand over his face, pushing back the fatigue that crept up on him now that their ordeal was over. "The stream we stopped at before you caught the balukha," he said to Jalis. "The one that forded over the road? There was a wooded hill further east along its course. If we hurry and head there directly, we can reach it by sundown."

Jalis nodded as they broke away from the road. "The soap will be coming out as soon as we've made camp." She rubbed a palm against the thigh of her leggings. "These I can soak. But this top"—she plucked at the shredded chemise—"is getting thrown. It's beyond salvageable."

"I'll hold you to that." Oriken flashed her a weak grin. "I knew the trip had to be worth something."

Jalis huffed. "Dream on. Some of us know how to pack for a trip and bring spare clothing."

"I packed spares," Oriken said defensively. "You know what I don't get? How does the corruption stop right at the wall? Nature and blight look like they've been at an impasse since it started, but which is keeping which at bay?"

Jalis shrugged. "Impossible to guess. But nature does tend to abhor an aberration."

Oriken grunted. "I reckon the feeling was mutual back there. They sure as shit didn't like our presence."

Jalis nodded, then lifted her gaze to his hat and wrinkled her nose. "You might want to check that."

"What?" Oriken grasped the crown of his hat and took it off. "Oh, for the love of—" The shrivelled clump of gore still clung to the top of the brim. "What *is* that?"

Jalis pursed her lips. "I think it might be a piece of brain."

Oriken unsheathed his sabre and flicked the lump away. It landed softly atop a small shrub.

Jalis unfastened Oriken's side-pouch and pulled out a waterskin, took a swig and passed the skin to Dagra. He swilled his mouth out, then took a long drink.

The water did nothing to quell the taste of corruption, not when he remembered the putrid stuff that had sprayed him as he cut through the blighted dead, not to mention the contents of the head that splattered him as Oriken lopped it off.

And I probably swallowed some. His stomach heaved at the thought.

He longed for a tankard of Redanchor, but he guessed that no amount of alcohol would shift the acrid taste or erase the memory of the corpse pressing down on him as he lay trapped beneath it. He could still see its lipless jaws snapping so close to his face, its blackened teeth jutting from its leathery gums. The shrivelled curl of muscle that lay within its mouth like a dried slug…

The beginnings of a headache pulsed behind his eyes as bile rose in his throat. He gulped it down and turned his face away from his companions. As he did so, he caught sight of the long perimeter wall, more ominous now than when they'd arrived under the blue sky of late morning. He paused, and his gaze drifted to the partially-opened entrance. Beyond the portcullis, the fog lingered; a pervading pall enshrouding the dead within their gardens.

A lone figure remained at the gate, its visage pressed between the rusted bars. The corpse's head was broken on one side from where Dagra's boot had crushed it. Its dead gaze locked onto him, and in that moment something passed between them.

Spoke to me. Dagra suppressed a shudder. *The damned thing spoke to me.*

As the corpse shuffled into its gods-neglected home, Dagra jogged to catch up with his friends. He touched the raised, stinging welts on his chest, shoulders and neck. The cuts would need cleaning and padding with nepenthe as a substitute poultice, but there would be time for that after making camp.

A good wash is what we need. A steaming bath. But that'll have to wait until we're home. One thing was certain. The hardest part of the contract was over, and it had been the greatest test the gods had ever given him. What mattered was that Cela Chiddari's burial jewel was secured, and Dagra and his friends were alive.

No, he thought, *what really matters is that the dead of Lachyla are staying in Lachyla. Right where they belong.*

94

CHAPTER ELEVEN
SOJOURN AT DULÈTH

The wagon rattled across the flagstones of the Kingdom Road, all but drowning out the sound of the mules' hooves and the crack of Wymar's whip. Maros slouched upon a pathetically scant pile of hay against the forward boards of the wagon, looking out at the cloud-dulled landscape as it shook past and shrank into the distance. His leg, mercifully, had gone numb, which was marginally preferable to pain pulsing from his knee to his thigh.

Shitting gods, he thought. *I could strangle that fucking mill owner. A paltry bundle of hay for fifty silver dari. When we get back to the Folly, I swear—*

Wymar shouted something, the words lost beneath the racket of the shuddering wagon.

"What's he say?" Maros called.

"He says to keep yourself still!" Henwyn said through the slit beside Maros's head. "You're rocking the wagon!"

Maros grumbled to himself as he tried to keep calm. They'd been on the road for more than half a day, Wymar driving the mules through the night by the light of Haleth, stopping only briefly to give the beasts a little hay and a rest. *Give* them *a rest? It's me who needs a rest! Never knew keeping still could be so exerting.*

"Farmland up ahead!" Henwyn announced. "A few dwellings. Likely the last ones before we head into the Deadlands. Looks like a downpour's on its way, too, boss!"

"Fine!" Maros shifted his weight. "Get us over there!"

The wagon rolled on for another minute before lurching to a stop. Maros grunted in relief and pushed himself along the floor of the wagon, inching towards the lowered rear hatch. He heard Henwyn jump down from his seat beside Wymar, his footsteps fading as he crossed to the nearest farmhouse. As Maros's legs bent over the back of the wagon, his gammy knee made a pop and fire lanced through his leg.

"Gah!" Gritting his teeth against the pain, he pushed himself to a sitting position. As the toes of his boots touched the ground, he glanced across at the modest stone dwelling they had stopped beside. A young boy was standing upon the grass, his eyes wide as he gaped at Maros's fierce expression.

Here we damn well go again, he thought. Glaring at the boy, he hitched a thumb towards Henwyn. "Would you like my man there to paint a rutting portrait for you?"

The boy blurred into motion, screaming as he ran for the house. "Monster! A giant monster! It's gonna eat me!"

Maros spat a curse. He grabbed his crutches and heaved himself from the wagon. As the fire in his leg flared anew, he raised his face to the sky and loosed a roar. When the pain subsided, he glanced across to see the boy had reached the farmhouse door. A young woman stepped out and squatted to wrap her arms about him defensively, the fear as plain on her face as on her son's. A man raced from the dwelling and skidded to a halt as he took in the scene. He backed away to stand before his family and raise the kitchen knife in his hand.

"Boss!" Henwyn called. "Let me deal with it."

"Please!" the man shouted in a shaky voice as he clutched the knife. "We have nothing! We're just simple folk."

"What?" Maros hobbled forwards a step. "Do we look like bandits to you, lad?"

"N-no…" The man turned to his wife. "Go inside. Now!" She ushered the boy inside and rushed in behind him. Her husband pulled the door shut and planted himself before it, trying to look brave as he brought the knife to bear.

"Suffering gods," Maros sighed. "Simple is right."

The man glanced nervously to Henwyn. The veteran was slowly closing the distance, his hands held open for the man to see he held no weapon.

"We're freeblades," Henwyn told the man and nodded towards Maros. "This is the Official of Caerheath. We're only seeking shelter from the rain a while. That's all."

The man's weapon lowered an inch. "I don't know nothing about freeblades. Please, whatever your business is"—he drew in a deep breath—"we want none of it."

Maros took another step forward. "Look, man. Surely you've got a barn we can stay in for a few hours? A little hay to feed the mules?" He gestured to the wagon, where the mill owner watched the scene from the comfort of his seat. "I'd make it worth your while. Ten coppers for your trouble."

The man hesitated as if considering the offer, then looked to Henwyn. "No," he said vehemently. "Please, you've already scared my boy. We don't want no trouble."

Henwyn gave a placating smile. "We'd be no trouble," he said. "You'd hardly know we were here."

"No. Just go."

"Oh, for the love of the rutting gods," Maros growled. "Fine." He brandished a crutch towards the man. "But I tell you this, you good-for-nothing peasant: If you're ever in need of some freeblade assistance – bandits, critters, whatever – *don't* come calling on me or mine! You hear?"

The man gawped, then gave a curt nod.

"Right then." Henwyn's smile dropped within his close-shorn beard. "I believe our business here is done. Thanks for your time."

As the man grabbed the door-handle, Maros called out, "Just a moment! Since *you* won't help a fellow, maybe you can tell us where we might find shelter around these parts. Any of the other houses over yonder likely to let a giant monster wait out a storm in their hay barn?"

The man paused, clearly glad to be getting rid of them and keeping his family alive. "The ringfort of Dulèth's down the road a ways. It's gone to ruin, but it's a shelter."

"How far?" Maros asked.

"Few hours."

"A few hours? It'll be night by the time we get there!"

Henwyn crossed to the peasant and passed him a copper piece, which he looked at warily before snatching it from Henwyn's hand. "Thank you for the information."

The man paused only an instant before scurrying through the door and slamming it tight behind him.

Maros leaned on his crutches and frowned at the crumbling circular wall of the ringfort, framed by the late evening sky. "Dulèth. Huh. I didn't know this place was still standing."

"Such as it is," Henwyn remarked.

"If you think I'm sleeping in *that*," Wymar spat as he busied himself with unbuckling the mules from the wagon, "then you can think again."

Maros shrugged. "You've been paid good money. You can sleep where you like."

"Good Wymar," Henwyn said, "I did explain that there would be several overnight stops."

"Overnight, perhaps." Wymar tugged frustratedly at a strap. "But you said nothing about roughing it in a bloody tumbledown ruin. The place is probably crawling with rats."

Maros barked a laugh. "And your mill isn't?"

Wymar whirled around. "Now listen here, tavernmaster—"

Henwyn raised his hands placatingly. "I'm sure we can find some amenable middle-ground here. How about we go inside and see what we're dealing with?"

"Hmph." Wymar frowned. "Easy for you to say. You're accustomed to sleeping in shit pits."

"I'm accustomed to sleeping under the stars," Henwyn said. "And, if it doesn't rain tonight, I might just do so. You're welcome to join me."

"Not fucking likely."

"Don't say I didn't offer." Henwyn strolled through the wide gap in the ringfort's wall where the doors had once stood. "Boss," he called from within, "I'd be careful if I were you. You've a strong competitor here for an inn. Furnishings are second only to the Peddler."

"Competition is healthy!" Maros called, casting a thunderous glare at the mill owner's back. Setting the crutches firmly under his arms, he swung himself into the shaded interior of the ringfort. *Furnishings indeed*, he thought. The floor was all rubble, dirt, rodent droppings, and puddles of rainwater from the recent shower. *Should've brought a few extra blankets. And maybe a broom.*

From the entrance, Wymar said, "I'm sleeping in the wagon."

"Suit yourself. I can see a nice spot that's not too damp or covered in mouse shit. How about letting me bring that hay in for a bed?"

"That's food for the mules."

"Okay. How about not letting me and just watching me do it anyway."

"You can have half," Wymar said begrudgingly. "But only as a borrow for the night."

Maros narrowed his eyes at the man. "Mighty generous of you. Wait till you see what I charge you for a cup of ale next time you're in my tavern."

"Right," Henwyn said. "Anything you need me to do before I head out to catch us a meal?"

"Some firewood wouldn't go amiss, Hen. And a few goats to skin for blankets. And a couple hundred birds for feathers to stuff 'em with."

"I'll gather some sticks," Henwyn said flatly, and stepped out of the ringfort.

"Don't be gone too long," Maros called after him. "Wymar promised us a juggling act."

Henwyn cast an amused glance at the red-faced mill owner. "Ah, shame," he sighed. "But duty comes first!" He grabbed his bow from beside the wagon and strode away.

I'd rather be gathering sticks than sitting around here with a pair of old mules and a crotchety skinflint for company, Maros thought. He swatted his crutch at a broken stone in the rubble, disturbing a scattering of rodent droppings as it skidded across the fort. *Aye, it's gonna be a long trip, and a long night for starters.*

CHAPTER TWELVE
UNDER A PALE MOON

Oriken squatted before the campfire and poked a stick into the flames, stirring new life into them. The firewood crackled and spat ephemeral motes into the night. Frogs and heath-hoppers hid amongst the grasses, keeping their distance from the clearing as they chirred their languid night songs. The Vur season was on the wane, but the night was comfortable even with the treacherous southern coast a mere handful of miles away.

Coast? He scoffed at the thought. *Some coast it is, this headland on the hairy arse of Himaera, with the Gardens of the Dead and the Blighted City at its warty pinnacle. A far stretch from the Saltcoast.*

Scapa Fell was a region no one with an ounce of good sense would venture into. Though the corruption of Lachyla did not continue beyond the edge of the graveyard, the mere knowledge that it harboured a legion of undead negated any enjoyment over the notion of lazing around among the grasses or taking a noon-time stroll along the stony coastline and its scant beaches. The rest of Himaera was a verdant contrast with these uninhabited wilds. Here in the Deadlands, the trees were few and far between, small swatches of fir, copses of birch and aspen like those they camped beside tonight. The loneliest sight in the south of Scapa Fell was the solitary oak or gawek tree, its boughs reaching like the arms of lost wanderers who came searching for their own story but found only despair, rooted in place by their own loss of hope.

There was nothing good here, nothing worth the journey unless you came with the express purpose of carving your way through a horde of pissed-off dead things. They'd found what they were sent here for – the burial jewel – so good riddance to the rest of it. Lachyla could rot for another few centuries for all he cared. There was one thing to say for this desolate heathland, that it did a great job of keeping the blight from the rest of Himaera. For that, he was grateful. It was a place for fools and risk-takers, Oriken knew in hindsight. And yet, despite all that, the desire to enter the city and search out its untold treasures was still strong.

They were going hungry tonight. No rabbits, no fish in the nearby stream except for a whiskery brookbug that darted away as soon as Oriken spotted it.

The animals likely smelled the unnatural corruption on him and his friends, wisely deciding to stay quiet and give the camp a wide berth. *Nature bores a... what did Jalis call it?* He shrugged.

Rocking back on his heels, he lowered himself to the blanket, removed his hat and placed it on the grass, scowling at the state of the material; it would be getting as good a scrub as his own body when it was his turn to venture down to the water. Dagra had gone first, given how his cuts required more urgent attention than either Oriken's or Jalis's minor scratches. Dagra sat now in sullen silence upon his bedroll by the fire, while on the other side of the copse of trees, down where the stream meandered around the foot of the flat-topped hill they were camped on for the night, the faint splashing of water drifted to him as Jalis bathed herself and her apparel.

Oriken laced his fingers behind his head and gazed up at the sky. Only a few stars were visible, but the large moon of Haleth hung bright above the horizon, its light beaming through the thin clouds and bathing the heath in a lambent lustre. The second largest moon – the dark-green Larindis – peered down through a break in the clouds high above its brighter, larger sibling. Of the ever-present Grey Watcher there was no sign, though Oriken knew its faint smudge was hidden somewhere up there, in the same place it always was.

The gentle sound of trickling water melted with the crackle of the fire and the distant chorus of night bugs. He glanced along the ground to where it sloped down through the tree-line. The camp's higher elevation offered a view through the trees to the black stream, moonlight glistening in its ripples. He could just see Jalis, silver-edged and dark, partially obscured by low-hanging branches. The shallow stream scarcely reached her knees as she crouched and scooped water into her hands and poured it over her hair. She repeated the process several times before taking a bar of soap from the bank to scrub the grime from her body. She was a fine sight to behold, here under the pale light of Haleth, or anywhere. Scarcely an inch or two taller than Dagra, on any other woman her slight figure might speak of frailty, but Jalis exuded vitality and elegance with or without her blades in her hands.

He turned his eyes away, sat up and shuffled closer to the fire; not that he was cold – far from it – but the heat of the flames felt good on his skin. It was optimistic to build a fire tonight since there was nothing to cook, and he'd argued that making it was a waste of time, that the moon and the stars gave enough light to see by. But, when Dagra returned from the stream, he insisted a chill was in the air, that the ocean breeze was blowing cold from the west. So, as Jalis had started down the embankment to the stream, Oriken and Dagra gathered wood. With the fire built, he helped Dagra apply a poultice prepared by Jalis to his cuts, pressing nepenthe leaves over the worst of them.

Dagra was sat with his back to the flames, his bearded face in shadow. He coughed, then groaned. He hadn't been right since leaving the graveyard, complaining of a headache and tender guts. The hour following their departure

100

from the Gardens of the Dead had mostly been spent in tired speculation as they approached the campsite. Dagra became more irritable and sullen as the minutes stretched by, at times ignoring Oriken and Jalis completely.

Fair enough, Oriken thought. *He took a fright back there, but it was a waking nightmare for all of us.*

He preferred not to think too hard about things that made no sense. The dead don't get up and walk around, especially bodies that had supposedly stopped being alive centuries before. And yet, it seemed they *did* get up and walk around in Lachyla. What troubled Oriken, though, was that the worst moment for him had been the spider webs in the tunnel, not the vicious horde of undead. By the stars, those webs were embarrassing, especially in light of everything that came after.

Still, what's life without a little fear, right? A crippling phobia reminded a man he was alive. No matter how much embarrassment it caused, it kept you on edge. He sighed inwardly. *Yeah, or it makes you panic. And panic leads to mistakes. A mistake in the wrong place and your life's over, gone to the under-side of the world to be reborn, if you believe that nonsense, and embarrassment be damned because dead men don't feel emotions. No,* he added, *nor do they attack innocent freeblades, or so I believed, except that belief is a load of old cowshit now, isn't it?*

A cough from nearby brought him from his ruminations and he looked across to see Dagra holding a hand to his forehead.

"How are you holding up?" Oriken asked.

Dagra reached for the tin cup of boiled nepenthe tea beside him and brought it to his mouth for a sip. The fire's glow lit the side of his face, deepening the shadows on the other. "Bloody headache's worse," he said. "Throat's burning, too." His voice was raspy, and a little slurred, likely from the herbs coursing through him.

"Give the nepenthe time," Oriken told him. "You'll be good by sun-up."

"*I* believe you, but my head doesn't. Gods, I could sleep for a week." He took another sip, then set the cup beside the fire.

Oriken turned at a soft sound behind him to see Jalis approaching, barefoot but dressed in her freshly-washed leggings, a clean corselette of thick cotton, and a fine lace chemise that reached almost to her hips, its diaphanous sleeves hanging to her elbows. Her wash gear and shoes dangled from one hand, while the other clasped a bowl filled with white and brown berries to her breast. Several superficial scratches lined her cheek, scarcely more than grazes, with several more across her arms and hands.

She gave Oriken a cool glance as she passed, then squatted beside Dagra and offered him the bowl. "Here," she said. "Eat. It's the best we've got tonight besides the jerky."

101

"Fuck the jerky," Dagra drawled. "You want more, you can have mine." He took a handful of berries, muttering something that didn't sound particularly grateful, something about meat.

Oriken could guess. And he agreed. He scarcely had an appetite either, and the lack of a fresh, roasted rabbit was not a huge loss for one night, given the abundance of bogberries in the region.

"You're welcome," Jalis said to Dagra. With a rueful smile, she dropped her shoes and wash-gear and sat cross-legged before Oriken. She reached for the backpack containing the Chiddari jewel, took it out and unwrapped it. "I was thinking about these runes while I bathed," she said, stroking a finger across the silver band.

"Of course you were," Oriken said. "Of all things."

She gave a small shrug. "I recognise a few of them. Many antik rukhir have never been fully translated, their meanings only guessed at. But symbols like those for the old gods are quite common if you know what you're looking for. These here"—she pointed to a section of the band—"they represent the Supreme God, differing slightly depending on whichever of the gods held that title at the time or place. Back in the Umbral Era, most of the tribes seemed to worship Banael as the supreme god, but the sun rune is missing here."

"This is Himaera, lass," Dagra said from behind her. "They never worshipped the sun here like your ancestors did. At least not as the ruling deity."

"He's right," Oriken said. "They were all about the Bound and the Unbound in equal measure back then, Banael and all the others. Then they worshipped the Dyad after the apostles came preaching from across the Channel. But Himaera's goddess was always Valsana. Morta'Valsana, if you prefer her scriptured name. There are still some people who say that the duality of the Dyad are just a fancy modern interpretation of the old goddess."

Jalis raised an eyebrow. "That would explain it. Of course. *Morta*. Surely it cognates with the Sardayan word, *Mortas*." She checked the runes and pointed to several. "Yes, here are the symbols for fertility, birth, life, death, and... what's this one? Hm. If I had to guess, I'd say this represents *un*death. Interesting. This jewel pre-dates the blight by a couple of centuries, no?"

Oriken yawned. Whatever nonsense was scrawled on the band was of no interest to him. Besides, their reward was for the jewel, not for the silver surrounding it.

Jalis traced her finger over another rune. "This one represents Drilos, though how his rune came to be on an ancient Himaeran artefact, I couldn't begin to guess."

"Who's Drilos?" Oriken took a handful of berries from the bowl and popped one into his mouth. He knew the names of most of the gods, but he'd never heard of a Drilos. "Is he one of those, what do you call them, patrons or something?"

102

Jalis made a noise of exasperation. "Patrons are people, remember?"

He rolled his eyes. "I know that!"

Rummaging in her pack and withdrawing a pair of short woollen socks, she said, "Drilos is a god from a land beyond the city of Midhallow."

Oriken barked a laugh. "Well, I know *that's* nonsense. They say there's nothing past Midhallow, that it stands guard against the edge of the world."

"Oh, Orik." Jalis's expression turned to one of pity as she pulled her socks onto her feet. "Do you really believe that? Have you no grasp of the concept of size? You do realise the difference between, say, somewhere like Brancosi Bay – you know the town, you've been there often enough – and the whole world of Verragos? Do you suppose the people of Midhallow hear stories that the world ends on the western coasts of the Arkh? If that were true, there'd be no Himaera, and yet here we are."

"Huh. I know you've been a lot of places, but are you saying you've been to Midhallow, too?"

"No, but I've seen it from a distance, sprawled across what used to be called the Ÿttrian Pass. It wouldn't be called a pass if it didn't connect two places, would it?"

"All right, okay," he mumbled. "I get the point."

He didn't like being made to look stupid. He'd been the object of Jalis's ridicule many times, but he knew he often deserved it. A moment of feeling foolish was worth it if he could see the look on her face, the one she got when she spoke about faraway places or ancient things. He considered himself a creature of logic, but Jalis possessed a worldly knowledge that went beyond his grasp. She spoke to him like a teacher to a student, but little did she know that he saw her more as a priestess. In his mind, he played the role of the eager acolyte, ever wanting her to properly notice him, but never daring to voice how much he revered her.

As she sat cross-legged before him, the fire and the moonlight enhanced the glow that she naturally exuded. After so many years of working together, of tightening the bonds of friendship, he guessed he'd become as addicted to her as he had to the tobah. And yet, despite their closeness, she still remained exotic, and his sense of wonder for her had not dulled but strengthened. Watching and listening to her was almost enough to chase away the nightmarish images of undead things that clawed at the back of his mind; almost, but not quite.

"Snap out of it, Oriken."

"Huh?"

"You're staring."

"Oh."

A low growl resonated from Dagra's direction. As one, Oriken and Jalis turned to look at him. He held his hand to his belly and cast them a sullen glance. "Ignore it. I'm not hungry."

103

"Have you finished your tea?" Jalis asked as she pulled her shoes on.

"Not yet," he muttered.

"Drink it up, Dag. We need you fit for the road."

By way of an answer, he belched loudly, turned to face the fire, then hawked and spat into the flames.

Jalis suppressed a sigh as she returned her attention to the runes. "What I can't figure out is how knowledge of a god from a thousand miles away reached Himaera long before anyone in the Arkh had even heard of Drilos. It's a mystery."

"That's all well and good," Oriken said, "but it's a mystery that's worth less than the bounty on that fancy lump of rock. Why don't you give Cela a visit after we've passed the jewel on to Maros? Maybe she knows something she never told the guild."

"I might just do that."

The conversation lapsed into silence. Dagra closed his eyes and hung his head to his chest. Jalis continued to inspect the runes around the jewel. Oriken gazed past her into the treeline, his thoughts drifting past their escape and back into the Chiddari crypt, grunting softly at the memory of the thickly-bunched cobwebs.

"Hey!" he exclaimed as a sudden thought came to him.

Jalis dropped the jewel to her blanket, Dusklight instantly appearing in her hand. She sprang to a crouch and pivoted, scanning the clearing and the trees beyond. The moment grew, and the chirping of the heath-hoppers resumed. She glanced over her shoulder and shot Oriken an exasperated look. "What did you see?"

"Hm? Oh, nothing. I just realised—"

"Oriken, you fucking dolt." Sheathing her daggers, she sat back down with a sigh. "You realised what?"

"Ah… Yeah, so, er…"

"Oh, for the love of the gods." Jalis pressed her lips together.

"Sorry."

Dagra gave a mirthless chuckle.

Oriken cleared his throat and cast Jalis an apologetic glance. "Do you remember when we entered the main chamber of the crypt? What I said about the spider webs?"

Dagra nodded wearily. "Sure. I vaguely recall you making a tit out of yourself."

Jalis cast Oriken an incredulous look. "You're still thinking about spiders?"

"No." He pulled a sour face. "Not really. It's just that I realised what I was trying to think of back there."

"Go on," Dagra said flatly. "Don't keep us in suspense."

"It almost seemed," Oriken said, brushing aside the sarcasm, "as if the place used to be looked after and the webs cleaned away, say till the Great Uprising.

But they only maintained the crypt area. We ran into cobwebs all the way down the stairwell and through the adjoining corridor. Don't know why they'd only do half a job, but there you go. My point is, I reckon the webs used to gather in there all the time, right up till they didn't." He nodded at Dagra. "The burial hole you checked is testament to it. The way I see it is, at some point, two things happened. The main hallway was no longer cared for, and the spiders stopped spinning their webs. Why do you suppose that would happen?"

Dagra cast him a disinterested look. "That's great, but I scarcely have a clue what you're talking about."

"Fascinating," Jalis breathed, seeming to genuinely mean it. "I see what you're saying." Her eyes glinted and her lips curled into the trace of a smile. "Well spotted. It makes sense. Something did happen that stopped the natural course of everything in that place; not the Uprising, but the blight. Whatever transpired in Lachyla didn't just affect its human inhabitants."

Dagra closed his eyes and puffed his cheeks. "If you're suggesting that there are little undead spiders scuttling around in the graveyard, too brain-dead to make webs any more, you're wrong; there wasn't a single insect or bird or cute little mouse – alive *or* dead – in the whole blighted place."

Oriken grabbed his hat from the ground and pushed it onto his head. "It was just an observation."

"What it tells us," Jalis said, "is that the crypt entrance might not have been used by whoever cleaned the place, which would explain the presence of the webs."

"Right." Oriken gave her a brief nod. "So wouldn't that suggest there might be another entrance after all?"

Jalis raised an eyebrow. "It does seem possible."

"Or," Dagra said, "only the main hallway is clean because it's the only part that's sanctified." With a wheezing sigh, he turned an intent stare first on Oriken, then on Jalis.

"What is it?" she asked.

"One of those corpses spoke to me, you know?"

Oriken snorted. "Come off it."

"I'm not fucking around!" Dagra snapped. "The cursed thing called me a liar. A liar!"

"That's not possible, Dag," Oriken said. "Get some sleep."

"It's just your imagination fuelled by fear," Jalis said.

"Oh?" Dagra fixed them with a fevered glare. "And the dead walking around *is* possible? Thanks, both of you. First a corpse calls me a liar, and then my friends do too." He burst into another cough, and this time it went on for a full minute, culminating in a hacking bark that made Oriken wince, punctuated by a long belch. Climbing unsteadily to his feet, Dagra headed for the trees at the edge of camp. The lower trunks and boughs were silhouetted against the moon-washed backdrop of empty heathland. He wandered around the side of the copse, a black shape crunching through a carpet of brittle twigs, and disappeared behind a birch.

The quiet night grew quieter still as the chirring and clicking of far-away heath-hoppers faded to a whisper. From behind the undergrowth, Dagra retched loudly, followed by a wheezing intake of breath, then a series of wet slapping sounds. Oriken pursed his lips in concern.

"I'm worried about him." Jalis squatted to take a bogberry from the bowl. "There's something he's not telling us."

"You think?"

"That's my instinct. You've known him longer than I have. You tell me."

"He's definitely out of sorts." He shrugged. "But that business back in the graveyard would mess anyone up. I mean, no one ever believed all that shit about Valsana being the goddess of undeath. Adults tell stories to children about gods and monsters and dead things to scare them, or they tell the kids about other gods and friendly, fluffy creatures and all the cowshit about Kambesh to make them feel safe. Then those children grow up believing all the pleasant things they were told, like about going to the Underland when they die."

Realising he'd been getting heated, he lowered his voice. "Dagra's grandparents believe in the whole bloody lot. Valsana, the Dyad, all of the Bound and Unbound, and then some. Dagra was—" He paused as there came another strangled bout of vomiting from behind the trees. "Stars, is he ever going to finish? Dagra was the recipient of every single story you could think of, good or bad. If there was one thing old Grandma Ilhdra could do, it was tell stories. I should know; I listened to most of them after... well, for our last couple of years before leaving home. But Dag got it all since birth, I reckon. That sort of stuff buries itself deep in your head. That's where he is now, more than likely – got the stories back in his head. I love him like my own blood, but he's always been a sucker for superstition."

"None of that explains him being ill," Jalis said as more strained groaning drifted from the trees. "Certainly not *that* ill."

Oriken bent to the pile of kindling and threw several branches onto the fire; their sap popped as they set ablaze. "No," he said, "though it might explain why he's hallucinating talking corpses. We all got our share of scratches and scares back there, and I know I got some acrid shit in my mouth. Dag's probably just puking up bits of corpse brain. Nothing a little water and miremint hasn't sorted out. I'll be honest, the whole thing makes me shudder just thinking about it now it's over, but what's done is done, right? We lick our wounds and move on."

Jalis glanced at the scratches and scabs on Oriken's hands, which were more numerous than her own, given how he'd punched his way through their undead assailants as much as using his sabre. "If you want to lick those wounds," she said, "be my guest, but *my* tongue is going nowhere near the rest of my body until I've had ten hot baths with salts and scented oils."

Oriken puffed his cheeks in embarrassment as he forced a series of half-formed thoughts away. "Yeah, bad choice of words." *For both of us*, he added silently.

"Don't ever change, Oriken," Jalis said with a smile, seemingly oblivious to his emotional turmoil.

"Hm."

A small frown creased her brow. "You know, considering the festering sked-hole we almost didn't escape from, only the stars know how many infections must have gathered in that graveyard over the centuries. The surprise isn't that Dag is vomiting his insides out, it's that we're not. And there's another question. If those creatures have been dead for so long, how is it that they still haven't fully decomposed? Some of them only looked months dead."

Oriken cast her a sharp glance. Her words rang an alarm in his mind. She was right; he'd seen dead bodies often enough, and he knew how they rotted. The corpses in the graveyard should all be skeletons by now, if not crumbled into dust. But, as Dagra observed, there were no animals – not even spiders, thank the stars, except for their abandoned webs. No creatures meant nothing to feed on flesh. The only thing with a semblance of life, other than the dead that didn't realise they were dead, was the fungus that covered everything.

"When did the Chiddari matron die?" he asked Jalis. "The dates on her slab, do you remember them?"

She pursed her lips, her eyes glazing over in thought. "225 is when she died."

"More than four centuries ago."

"Closer to five."

"It makes no sense that they've still got meat on their bones. Admittedly there's not much on most of them, but some were *very* meaty. They're wandering around, exposed to the elements. Walking with *what*? Working muscles and tendons?" Oriken shook his head. "Withered and useless, or they should be. And as for brains, okay, some of those skulls were filled with head-soup, but I'll bet most just have a dried little fig-like thing rattling around—"

Dagra stepped into the edge of the firelight. He mumbled a curse, bent over and retched. When he was finished, he cast Oriken a venomous glare as he wandered to his bedroll. He sat cross-legged near to the fire and pulled a blanket over his shoulders.

"Feeling better?" Jalis asked.

"Cold," he muttered, though a sheen of sweat covered his brow. "And I'd appreciate it if you stopped talking about dead things." He lowered his head to his chest, his breath coming in shallow gasps.

"I hate to say it," Oriken told him, "but you do look like shit." Dagra grunted, and Oriken leaned back on his elbows. "Let's discuss whether we're gonna have a look in the city."

Jalis gave him a flat look and raised an eyebrow.

"I vote no," Dagra said. "As if that should be a surprise. We'd be tempting fate stepping back into that accursed place. I can't believe you still want to."

"Yeah, okay. I get it. You're out. It's obvious Jalis is, too." Oriken sighed. "Understood." He glanced sideways at Dagra. "You know, we'd probably be put forward for our bladesmasters if we secured a fortune from the Blighted City."

Dagra tossed a twig onto the fire. "A promotion can wait, preferably for when I'm not feeling like shit."

"All right," Jalis said. "Let's drop it. As much as the place intrigues me, and that there are probably tons of historical artefacts to be found in there, it's not like we're going home empty-handed."

Jalis's expression changed. Her smile faltered and her eyes became focused. It lasted only a second, and Oriken almost missed it. Then the smile returned as her hand moved stealthily to a slit in her leggings, from which she palmed a throwing dagger.

"Why don't you tell me some more of the legend?" she said to Oriken, a touch louder than necessary.

Taking her cue, he reached casually into the backpack at his feet. "Okay. Let me think how it goes..." He took out the mini crossbow and a case of bolts, keeping them low to the ground. Clearing his throat to disguise the noise, he pulled the string taut and nocked it onto the catch. "Ah, yes," he said. "Er, far across Himaera over many a wild heath and moor, in the farthest corner of the land lies Lachyla, the Blighted City." He loaded the bolt onto the crossbow deck as Jalis palmed a second throwing blade. He could feel his heart thudding as he flicked glances into the darkness. "Um... Lachyla looms over the southern cliffs like a calloused hand, held out to the waters as if warning the creatures of the deeps to stay away." His heart thudded as he scanned the darkened heath, but beyond the fire's glow, the grey clumps of foliage stretched into blackness.

He shared a glance with Jalis. Her nod was brief. She flicked her eyes to the edge of the clearing, where a swathe of ferns covered the descending hillside. She drew a breath. Oriken pointed the crossbow and sprang to his feet.

"You can show yourself now!" Jalis called in a clear voice. "I'd advise doing it slowly, though; my friend here has something of a twitchy finger."

There was silence, then Jalis rose nimbly to her feet. The small blades appeared in her hands, held between thumb and forefinger. Oriken glanced at her eyes and adjusted his aim to where she was looking.

"You should be aware," Jalis said, her tone casual, "that even a small crossbow bolt can slip through the branches of a bogberry bush. We don't want

108

to hurt you." Still nothing. After a long moment, she sighed. "All right. You leave us no choice. Orik—"

"No!" The shout came from within the foliage. "Please! I'll stand, just don't hurt me." It sounded like a girl. "I'm getting up now. Here I come." A slim figure rose amid the bushes, as nicely and slowly as Jalis suggested, and lifted her hands in surrender.

"Are you alone?" Jalis called.

"Aye. I mean, I am. Please don't shoot me."

"I promised we wouldn't," Jalis said. "Step forwards."

The girl edged around the bushes and approached the camp, entering the reach of the fire's glow. She was in her mid-teens, Oriken guessed. She was dressed in leggings of soft hide, a simple tunic vest and shoes, all of varying shades of tan, and all of which had seen much better days. Her light brown hair was swept across her forehead in a side parting, and hung past her shoulders. She stepped closer, and the firelight revealed faint smudges of dirt on her face and neck, arms and ankles.

Oriken eased the string off the crossbow and clipped it to his belt as Jalis returned her daggers to the folds of her leggings.

"What are you gonna do with me?" the girl asked, a tremor in her voice. Slowly, she lowered her arms. "If you ain't gonna kill me, what then?"

She looked at Oriken with fear in her eyes, her gaze taking in all of him from boots to hat. He supposed he must strike an imposing figure, being head and shoulders above the delicate waif, and still stained in graveyard gore. She probably wouldn't have looked so scared if it had been Dagra standing before her instead, since she was about the same height as their bearded friend. Not that Dagra had even risen or uttered a word during the exchange, though his feverish gaze was glued to their unexpected visitor.

"Here," the girl said, "you're not gonna have your way with me, are you? Please, mister—"

Oriken stepped forwards. "For the love of the gods," he growled. "No, I am not going to do anything to you. None of us are. Not me, not that hairy-faced midget over there, and not even this lovely lady with the daggers. What do we look like? Bandits?" The girl nodded, her eyes wide. Oriken shook his head. "Stars… Girl, we're freeblades."

"Feeble whats?"

Jalis beckoned her over. "Come and sit down. Tell us why you were spying on us."

"Aye," Dagra said. All eyes turned to him as he fixed the girl with a scowl. "And while you're at it, since this whole region is supposed to be uninhabited, you might want to mention where in the cursed Pit you came from."

The girl stared at him blankly.

Oriken sighed. "A little quicker, if you don't mind." He gestured with both hands down his grime-splattered clothing. "The sooner we figure out what to do with you, the sooner I can scrub off this fucking corpse juice."

CHAPTER THIRTEEN
DEMELZA

They gathered a short distance from the fire. Jalis bade the girl sit, though she herself remained standing. Oriken slouched onto a boulder, keeping close to Dagra who sat with his back against a tree trunk. Although the night was cool and pleasant with scarcely a breeze, Dagra's drawn face and tangled hair were laced with sweat.

Oriken lowered his head and regarded their visitor from beneath the brim of his hat. She curled her legs and tucked them beneath her, leaning a hand upon the grass. To Oriken it seemed she tried to give the pretence of relaxation, but her eyes told a different tale; she was uneasy, and well she might be. Dagra's question hung unanswered between the four of them. Where *had* the girl come from? No map Oriken had seen showed any settlements this deep into Scapa Fell, just Lachyla itself, the locations of several forts in the mid and northern areas, and the Death's Head symbol right in the centre. *'Nothing here but death'* was the grim and obvious meaning.

The cartographers nailed that one on the head, Oriken thought as flashes of their escape flitted through his mind.

"Are you hungry?" Jalis asked the girl. "You look hungry." She placed the bowl of berries on the ground in reach of them all. "Help yourself."

The girl eyed the bowl sceptically, then she eyed Jalis. "You've been in the Forbidden Place, ain'tcha? I seen yous going in there. Didn't think to see yous come back out again. Here y'are, though."

"Is that why you were watching us?" Jalis asked. "What do you know about Lachyla?"

The girl glanced from her to Oriken, then to Dagra. Her gaze lingered on him a moment, catching his fevered eyes scrutinising her in return. To Jalis, she said, "None has gone in the Keeler since long afore me mam's mam were born, not an' what come back out. It's forbidden. Anyways, it's common sense, ain't it? Why'd you wanna go in there for? Full o' death, an' nowt else."

Oriken removed his hat and tossed it across to his bedroll, folded his arms and slouched further down onto the boulder. The stench from his own body was beyond irritating. Not only did his clothes reek of dead people, but they

111

also itched to the high Void, from sweat, and grit, and the stars knew what else had found its way beneath his trousers and shirt, not to mention his hat. He could almost hear the song of sirens in the nearby stream, softly calling his name. *Come to us, Oriken*, they sang in their sweet, dulcet tones. *Come, let us wash you clean…*

"What's your name?" he barked at the girl, then grimaced; it had come out much harsher than he'd intended, half-directed as it was to his imaginary sirens.

"Me?" The girl grinned. Still looked wary, though. Her teeth were surprisingly clean for someone so ragged-looking. "Me's the Melza."

"Huh?" Oriken shared a glance with Jalis. "Demelza, you say?"

"Aye." The girl nodded. "That's what they call me."

Jalis leaned in slightly. "They?"

Demelza pursed her lips and glanced sidelong at Oriken. "You don't smell so good, you know?"

"I'll ask you again, lass," Dagra growled. "Where are you from?"

Demelza cocked her head to the east. "Out yonder. From the Minnow's Beck."

Oriken gave her a bemused grin. "You live in the stream?"

Jalis shot him a look of disappointment. "Is Minnow's Beck your village?" she asked the girl.

Demelza nodded, drew her legs from beneath her and hugged them to her chest. "That's the beck, down there." She pointed between the trees to the quietly-trickling stream.

"The stream runs to where she lives," Jalis said. "So there *are* settlements out here, after all."

"No minnows, though," Dagra mumbled. "Another stupid name. Seems to be a trend in these parts."

Jalis lowered herself to her haunches, took a berry from the bowl and placed it into her mouth. "Demelza, we're leaving this area in the morning. You'll not see us again. You've got no reason to be afraid. We have what we came for, and believe me when I say we have no intention of returning after we've gone."

The girl frowned. "You took summat from there, didn'tcha?" She glanced up at Oriken. "You shouldn't have done that." Turning her gaze to Dagra, she said, "Ain't no good'll come of it. Mark me. No one goes in, an' nowt comes out. Mostly nowt an' no one, anyways. How it's always been. How it *should* be."

"Are you sure no one ever enters the graveyard?" Jalis asked.

"That's what I said, ain't it?" Demelza turned her eyes to the ground.

Jalis eyed the girl shrewdly. "You said *mostly*."

"You shouldn't have opened the gate," Demelza said.

"Near the entrance there's a rotten rope hanging from the ramparts," Jalis said. "That means someone entered the place, and either left the same way or didn't leave at all. Do you know anything about that, Demelza?"

Again, Demelza averted her gaze. "I do know someone else went in with a ladder a long time ago, back when me mam's mam's mam were alive. Not that I ever knew me mam. I seen the rope though; everyone has who's been to the gates, but I don't know nothin' about it. I ain't no Tail-whiffer."

"One riddle after another," Jalis said, looking deep in thought.

"It doesn't matter." Oriken scratched at his stubbled chin. "Come sundown tomorrow, the city will be so far south of us that no gates or runes or disgruntled dead folk will mean a jot."

"You're lucky to have come out, but you'll not stay lucky if you keep what you took. I ain't joking." Demelza shook her head vehemently, although the hint of a smile seemed to play at her lips. "You weren't the first; you're right wi' that. All I know is one went in there back in me mam's mam's mam's time. One from Minnow's Beck." To Jalis, she said, "Can I stand?" Jalis gestured for her to do so and Demelza rose, brushed the seat of her leggings, then folded her arms. "Feller who went in there, his boy had died, so they say."

Demelza's eyes flicked to each of them in turn. When she cast Oriken a sidelong glance, he shot her an equally sidelong scowl. Something was nagging at him and he didn't like the feel of it. "Go on," he told her.

"The feller went in the Forbidden Place at noon, safest time as it is an' all. Found himself a deadstone an' brought it home."

Dagra shifted against the stump, his attention snagged. "A deadstone?"

"Aye. Him an' his grievin' missus lay the deadstone wi' their dead bairn in the boy's room. Left it for ages; months, so they say—"

Jalis raised a finger. "I hesitate to ask this, but what's a deadstone?"

"Well, it's a stone, ain't it? Y'know, what the dead have."

Oriken smiled to himself as Jalis struggled to maintain her composure.

Demelza unfolded her arms and hitched a thumb into the top of her leggings. "Anyway, the bairn stayed in his room, decomposin' but not as much as he should'a done. Then one night, his mam – a woman named the Neira – she awoke to the sound o' summat eatin', all gristly and fleshy. She whispered her feller's name. He never answered, but the chewin' stopped. She reached out to him and touched summat wet and raw, and that's when she saw the glint o' starlight in the eyes o' the thing what squatted over him. She jumped from the bed and ran out the house, screamin' the place down. Their boy were back from the dead an' feastin' on his pa. After all that time, he'd got up when he were good an' ready and went lookin' for food. Must'a been starvin'. I reckon the Neira would'a been next if she hadn't woke. I'll take some o' them berries now." Demelza scooped a handful of the bogberries and popped them into her mouth, one by one.

113

Oriken regarded his friends. Jalis's expression was grave. Dagra's too, though that wasn't saying much, given his current condition.

"This deadstone," Dagra said to the girl. "Describe it."

Demelza shrugged. "I dunno, but they's in all the crips in the Forbidden Place. Them's what's shiny. I ain't never seen one. Thank the goddess for that, I suppose."

"She must be talking about the burial jewel." Jalis's voice was almost a whisper. "Good gods. The jewel is responsible for the dead walking around."

"Aye," Dagra rumbled. "And from the sounds of it, ours isn't the only one."

The distant chirps, beeps and clicks of night creatures were faint against the crackling of the flames as the moment hung suspended. Oriken regarded his companions and the quirky waif who looked at them with wide-eyed innocence and a hint of something else that plucked at Oriken's nerves. The revelation that there were more of the so-called deadstones in the graveyard called to his treasure-hunter senses despite the danger. It also acutely reminded him of his current hygiene issue. With a grunt, he pulled his shirt off and tossed it to the ground. Demelza stared at him, at the long cut on his forearm, the red welts on his abdomen, the assortment of old, pale scars from previous encounters mixed with the fresher scratches, and the dirt and gore that streaked over it all.

Oriken's lip twitched at the girl. "Pretty, ain't it? Welcome to my world." He looked at Jalis and Dagra. "So, what do we do with her? Let her go and we could have a heathland full of villagers heading our way within the hour, carrying pitchforks and brands."

"Are you suggesting we keep her prisoner?" Jalis said. "Look at her, Orik. What do you see?"

Demelza had inched closer to the fire which was now roaring quietly in full force. She hugged her arms against an errant breeze and met his gaze with her customary sideways glance.

What do I see? I see a girl, almost a woman, thin as they come and can't pronounce her own name. Petulant, whimsical, and, if I'm honest, a borderline imbecile. And yet...

And yet the nagging doubt remained. He didn't trust her. Didn't trust all she'd told them, either. He and his friends were too far from anything they could call sanctuary to take chances. Even if they kept hold of her until the morning and let her go before heading north, she could still alert her people.

"It's not that I'm overly worried about a bunch of peasants, Jalis," he said. "I just don't fancy watching my back for the entire journey home."

Jalis's brow creased in thought. "Maybe we should take a look at Demelza's village from a distance, see for ourselves how much of a threat they are."

"No, you mustn't!" Demelza blurted. "Deadstones are forbidden in the Beck since the Neira's feller got hisself eaten. You should take it to the Keeler, toss it over the wall so it's back where it belongs."

"Back where it belongs," Dagra mumbled.

114

"That's the real issue, isn't it?" Jalis glanced at Dagra, then at Oriken. "What do we do with the jewel now? Based on the words of someone we don't know and who doesn't owe us any allegiance, do we forego our bounty or complete the contract?"

"Those corpses didn't follow us," Oriken said. "They didn't care that we took the jewel. I don't know what got them rattled; I guess they just didn't like us." He shrugged. "Fair enough. I *was* hoping to head into the city, and I *did* have a plan to circumnavigate the whole graveyard, but the two of you have voted against me, so I can forget that. Besides, if going in there would attract an entire village of backwater peasants as well as the undead, it's not worth the hassle. I say we take the pretty rock home and claim our reward, and to the Underland with this nonsense." He waved a hand dismissively. "Not that they can say for certain that the jewels are responsible."

"It sounds legitimate enough to me," Dagra said. "And it only reinforces the legend."

"Huh. Yeah. The legend." Oriken shook his head. "And look what happens when people believe every story they hear. You'd have us put the jewel back with the Cunaxa woman, wouldn't you, Dag? Well, you took it out; do you fancy volunteering to put it back in? You want to go back down into that crypt to Miss Jolly-Joking Jawless?"

Dagra fixed him with a haggard glare.

"No," Oriken said, "I thought not."

Jalis grunted. "I'm not happy with the idea of losing the bounty. We know what's happening in the graveyard, and if that's what the blight looks like then it's been that way for centuries. Whatever we do isn't going to make any difference to Lachyla."

"Plus," Oriken said, "we're not planning on bringing anyone back to life."

"Let's hope our client also doesn't have that in mind," Dagra said. With a belch, he rose and wandered into the trees.

"Damn," Jalis muttered. "He's got a point. What if the old woman heard the same stories as Demelza?"

"They're just stories!" Oriken threw his hands up in exasperation. "And the one *she* came out with"—he thrust a nod towards Demelza—"is one *I've* never heard before. It's not part of the legend, that's for sure."

"Well, what *does* the legend say?"

"Not a lot," he admitted. "Mostly it's about the king – some fellow named Mallak Ammenfar, if I remember rightly."

Down behind the tree-line Dagra broke wind, loudly. It was only the precursor for what followed, which was enough to make Oriken grimace in embarrassment, not only for himself but also for Dagra. Jalis's expression showed she shared his sentiment.

"For the love of the goddess," Demelza whispered, her eyes wide. "I 'ope that's not from the bogberries."

Mercifully, the sounds quieted. *That was violent*, Oriken thought. *Let whatever was in his system be out now, for all our sakes.*

A thought occurred to him then, and he took a couple of steps closer to the girl, putting her within arms' reach. She wrinkled her nose and craned her neck to meet his gaze, looking like she trusted him as little as he trusted her. "Demelza," he said, "how do you know what you do about the Keeler? Er—" *Damn it.* He shook his head. "I mean Lachyla."

She frowned, as if the question was dumb and the answer obvious. "'Cause that's where the 'cestors are from, ain't it? We's the Keeler-kin in Minnow's Beck, from them what 'scaped."

Jalis raised her eyebrows. "Survivors of the blight?"

The girl nodded. "From them what 'scaped," she repeated, as if they hadn't understood it the first time.

"Interesting," Jalis said. "How many people are living in your village?" As Demelza's frown deepened and her face scrunched in thought, Jalis glanced at Oriken and said in a low voice, "When did the blight happen?"

"Right at the start of the 400s, as far as I recall."

Jalis pursed her lips. "Nearly three centuries ago. Depending on how many Lachylans escaped, there could be a bustling community tucked away among the hills and valleys."

"Three 'undred an' thirty-three," Demelza blurted, then shook her head. "No, thirty four with Jessa's bairn."

Oriken grinned. "Your reckoning of numbers is as sharp as Jalis's blades."

"Course it is." Demelza looked insulted. "I ain't stupid, you know?"

"Ah, no." He cleared his throat. "Of course not."

Twigs crunched underfoot as Dagra wandered into reach of the firelight. "Well," he growled, "have you come to a decision?"

"I think so." Jalis looked at Demelza. "It would be best if you don't mention us to your village. What they don't know won't hurt them. We're keeping what we've taken." She held up a hand as Demelza opened her mouth to protest. "The deadstone, as you call it, is going with us. You should forget we met, and we'll forget you were spying on us. We have no wish for trouble, but think about this: If we can withstand the attack of a massive horde of undead – many of which we tore apart, by the way – do you suppose we'd fare worse against a few hundred villagers? We're breaking camp with the dawn, then we're heading back home. Stay silent, Demelza, and you'll never see us again. Do we have a deal?"

The girl tilted her head petulantly.

"Do we have a deal?" Jalis pressed.

Demelza considered the question, then planted her hands on her hips. "All right. Deal."

"Swear it," Jalis said.

"Eh?"

116

"For the love of the gods," Oriken muttered.

"To swear means to make a promise," Jalis explained. "So, swear by the goddess that you'll not speak of us to your people. Go on."

"All right," she said carefully, still looking unsure. "I swear by the goddess. I'll not say nothin' to no one 'bout yous."

Jalis shared a glance with Oriken before fixing a stern look on Demelza. "You do understand what will happen if you tell, and your villagers come sniffing into our business?"

Demelza nodded. "I already said I sweared."

Jalis held her gaze. "All right. That's settled. You're free to leave."

"Whoa." Oriken stepped forward. "Just like that?"

"Just like that."

He barked a laugh and threw his hands up. "Fair enough."

Jalis looked at the third member of their group. "Dagra?"

"Couldn't care much either way."

Jalis glanced sideways at Demelza, as if imitating her. "Are you still here?"

The girl stood perfectly still, looking like a cornered rabbit as her eyes darted between them. She took several paces backwards, turned, and broke into a run.

Oriken smiled wryly as he watched her fade into the night. "Bloody peasants. I'm off for a wash."

Later, with a ragged towel around his waist, Oriken carried his freshly-washed clothing up the embankment from the stream, pausing at the top as he noticed Jalis was nowhere in sight. He crossed the clearing to the campfire, where Dagra snored softly beneath a blanket with his back to the flames.

Oriken shivered as an errant breeze curled around his drying body, causing goosebumps to prick his skin. The stream had been as cold as the Pit, but he felt better now that the dust and sweat and gore were scrubbed away. He could still detect a faint smell of death, but that came as no surprise; a quick wash in a shallow stream was a poor substitute for a hot, soapy, perfumed bath.

He dried off and dressed in his spare clothing before stretching his wet gear over sticks which he'd earlier plunged upright into the dirt, close enough to the campfire to catch the warmth from the flames.

As he pulled his boots on, a quiet rustling issued from the tall shrubs across the clearing. Snatching his sabre from the bedroll, he sighed as Jalis emerged into the firelight. Between the moonlight and the fire's glow, she was awash with soft blue and amber; a lithe, lambent shape against the dark heathland.

"I was beginning to worry about you," he told her. "Where were you? On a perimeter check?"

She cocked her head at him, a faint smile ghosting the fatigue on her face. "No, Oriken. I was taking a piss. Even women need to relieve themselves once in a while. We're not all just pretty statues; some of us are made of flesh and blood, just like you men."

Believe me, Oriken thought, *I know full well what you're made of. Flesh and blood, aye. Steel and starlight, too, among other things.* "Ah," he said, feeling his face flush. *You're a grown man*, he admonished himself. *For the stars' sake! Talk about inappropriate moments.*

Jalis crossed to their packs and busied herself with reorganising the equipment, all the while casting frequent glances into the shadowed heathland. Oriken regarded her casually as he took his nargut-hide jacket from the bedroll and pulled it over his shirt. The soft leather outer and the sheep-wool lining warmed him against the breeze coming in from the coast. Jalis looked his way, and they shared a momentary glance before she returned to her work.

The urge to leave right now was strong, despite it being the middle of the night. The Gardens of the Dead were an hour away; he had no doubt those creatures were still stalking the graveyard, but it wasn't them that worried him the most. Mindless creatures, he could handle, and his rational mind had now absorbed that the corpses in Lachyla could walk and attack. There was no explanation for it, only the bizarre story from the peasant girl about a jewel bringing a toddler back to life.

More like brought to undeath, he amended with a shrug.

The details didn't matter. The most you could expect from any creature was for it to hunt, eat, or fuck. Predictable. People, on the other hand, were wild cards; Demelza specifically felt very much like a problem. He doubted Jalis's judgement this time. Usually he deferred to her; after all, she was a bladesmistress and she'd been at the freeblading game for much longer than he and Dagra. But letting Demelza trot away like that had been foolish, in Oriken's opinion. Still, it was done now. In a few hours they'd be setting off, but first he had to take watch after Jalis, and he knew the shift would be a slow one.

Having finished the repacking, Jalis stood and checked her assortment of weapons – Dusklight at her hip, Silverspire strapped to her thigh, and the numerous throwing blades concealed within her apparel. "*Now* I'm going on patrol," she said. "Keep the fire up for Dag. He needs to break his fever."

"Sure." Oriken's voice sounded as drained as he felt. *Stars, I'll be asleep within minutes, and no mistake.* He reached for the pile of deadwood and half-heartedly tossed a few pieces onto the fire. "Shout if you need me," he called after Jalis.

She raised a hand in acknowledgement as she strolled across the clearing. At the top of the embankment, she paused and glanced back over her shoulder to flash him a smile, her eyes cool and serene, glinting with stars and flames.

There's another portrait worth painting, he thought. He returned the smile with a thin one of his own, and she disappeared down the hill.

He lay on his back, pulled a thin blanket over himself and placed the hat over his face. The quiet babble of the stream, the subdued song of the heath and the hiss of wood on the fire were hypnotic, but he lay awake despite his fatigue, unable to push away the images of decomposed hands that reached for him through the fog, desiccated faces glaring at him with empty or gore-filled sockets, and a young girl casting him a sidelong glance. *You're not gonna have your way with me, are ya, mister?*

It was a long time before he slipped into a restless sleep in which crimson shadows stalked him through ancient ruins as he crawled over a mountain of corpses while crows pulled at their eyeballs. The ivy-covered pillars of his nightmare pointed into a morning sky, drawing his attention to the scrutiny of the small smudge amid the clear blue – the perpetual Grey Watcher...

CHAPTER FOURTEEN
MEAT FOR THE BEAST

Wymar slapped his hands to his thighs and rose from the mound of blankets. "I need a shit," he said, then crunched his way across the ringfort's dirt-strewn floor.

"Fill your boots," Maros muttered from his own makeshift bed of hay. "And thanks for feeling the need to wake me and announce it. Where's Henwyn?"

Wymar shrugged. "Said he was off to catch something for the morning."

As the mill owner stepped out into the darkness, Maros glanced at the campfire in the centre of the voluminous ringfort. Extra firewood was piled by the wall. There wasn't much of a chill to the evening within the ancient stone structure, but if Henwyn snagged them a meal for the morning they'd need to cook it. It had been many years since Maros was last in a situation where eating raw meat was necessary to stay alive, and he was in no rush to do so again. As he considered trampling the flames to embers to conserve the wood, a cry pealed out from behind the fort.

"Weeping gods! Wymar?" He scrambled to get to his feet. The familiar pain tore up and down his leg, but he rose through it. Snatching up his greatsword and one of the crutches, he lurched out of the wide entrance and around the edge of the ringfort. The screaming drew closer and Maros stopped short as Wymar came half-running, half-hobbling around the circular wall, scrambling to pull his trousers up over his knees. The mill owner spotted Maros and promptly pitched over onto his face, his bare arse showing beneath his shirt.

"Have you lost your rutting mind?" Maros roared, brandishing the greatsword in one hand. "I could've split you in two!"

Wymar scurried on hands and knees across the grass until he got behind Maros, then rolled onto his back.

"Gah!" Maros turned his face from the sight. "For the love of the gods, man, put it away!"

"There's a monster!" Wymar wailed, pointing at Maros.

"I've had enough of that shit for one day," Maros warned, then froze at a sound behind him. He glanced back to see a shadow creeping around the edge of the circular wall. *Oh, aye? What have we here?* He gripped the greatsword as the figure slunk into view.

As tall as a human, the lyakyn's wiry frame was bunched with muscles, though the small breasts and the tuft of hair between its legs marked it as a female. The long, gaping mouth ran like a fissure from its nose to its sternum. Two columns of needle-like teeth slid between each other like a deadly curtain as the jaws clenched and flexed apart, reminding Maros of the repulsive, meat-eating fabellasyr plant.

"Here to grant me my wish, are you?" Maros growled, visions of his previous encounter with such a creature stark in his mind.

The lyakyn's black eyes stared at him with malevolence, sizing him up. It hissed and crouched. Its maw opened as wide as its shoulders, and it burst into motion towards him.

He slashed his sword in a wide arc. The freshly-sharpened blade sliced the tips off the monster's reaching, taloned fingers, but the momentum unbalanced him and he pitched to the grass. He rolled onto his back as the lyakyn sprang at him. It landed with its feet spread to either side of his hips, then lunged its head forward and screamed into his face. Its uninjured hand swiped down. The talons raked across Maros's chest. He relinquished his grip on the cumbersome greatsword and smashed his fist into the lyakyn's belly, and again into its shoulder. It reared, arching its back as its scream tore through the night.

Maros shoved it hard, and the creature staggered backwards. He grabbed his crutch and hauled himself to his feet, the pain in his leg distant and dull in the face of survival. He hammered a punch into the lyakyn's face, knocking it off balance. As it fell to its back, he took the moment to scan the ground for his sword, but the creature was quickly up and whirling to face him. Claws outstretched, it sprang forward. Maros jabbed the crutch into the monster's open mouth. Its teeth snapped shut around the hard wood, and it grasped hold of the makeshift weapon. He heaved the crutch into the air with the lyakyn attached, swung the monster high over his head, then slammed it to the grass. Pulling the crutch free, he gave it a quick flip and, as the upper prongs pointed downwards, snatched it from the air and thrust it down onto the lyakyn's face. One prong plunged between its gaping jaws, the other into its eye. Maros put his weight onto the crutch, and the lyakyn's face broke inward. It released a screeching, bubbling death-cry, twitched, and lay still.

"There's another!" Wymar cried.

Maros ripped the crutch free and spun about to peer into the heath and see a second lyakyn creeping around the edge of a night-darkened out-building. It was larger than the first, marking it as a male.

"Interrupt your play-time, did we?" Maros roared. He bent to retrieve his greatsword from the ground, and brandished it at the creature. "Come on, then! Let's have at it!"

The lyakyn sprang forwards. Maros prepared to meet its attack. Maros readied himself, but before the monster had taken half a dozen steps, an arrow punched into its chest. It slowed and paused, its jaws wide open as its black eyes switched to a point beyond Maros.

He beamed a wide grin. "Henwyn, you beautiful bastard."

A second arrow thrummed past him and sank into the creature's chest beside the first. It staggered to its knees, raised its hands and face to the sky, and loosed a screeching roar.

"Glad to be of service," Henwyn said as he strolled to join Maros.

Hefting the greatsword, Maros hefted it over his shoulder and hurled it forwards. The blade and handle spun over each other as the weapon whirred through the air. It plunged tip-first into the lyakyn's belly and sank in deep. The creature fell backwards.

Leaning his hands upon the crutch, Maros sucked in several deep breaths and glanced at Henwyn.

"You okay, boss?"

"Aye," he panted as his heart slowed to normal. "Aye, I'm all right. Just out of practice." His chest stung from the creature's claws. His leather vest was sliced and bloody. He turned a black gaze to the wall of the fort where Wymar cowered against the stones, his trembling fingers belting his trousers around his waist.

"You." Maros raised the crutch and stabbed the dripping prongs towards the mill owner. "From now on, you need a shit, you damn well make sure it's safe first. Seeing you with your trousers down once is more than enough for a lifetime."

Wymar's eyes were wide as he gulped and nodded. "What if there are more?" he stammered.

"I'll check," Henwyn said. As he set off to the out-building, Maros heard him mutter, "I should'a done it when I checked the perimeter."

Wymar looked like he was on the verge of crying. "The mules are round the other side! I can't hear—"

"One thing at a time, man!" Maros snapped. "Henwyn? Talk to me."

"No immediate danger," Henwyn called as he emerged from the darkness, carrying the greatsword. "But in a year or so there might be, if they're lucky." In answer to Maros's questioning look, he added, "Hatchlings."

"Oh, great. Wymar, how about you be a good fellow and fetch my other crutch from inside." Wymar stared at him without moving. "Whenever you're ready," Maros added flippantly.

The mill owner hurried away and within moments was back with the second crutch, his mouth moving in nervous anticipation as Maros took it from him.

"Pass him my sword, Hen. Let him be good for something while we check the mules."

Henwyn handed the greatsword to Wymar. "Don't cut yourself."

Wymar wrapped his hands around the long handle, and Henwyn let go. The blade's tip plunged and bit into the ground.

With a shake of his head, Maros hobbled away. "Let's have a look at these babies, shall we?"

Henwyn walked at his side as they crossed to the out-building. Its wood-and-thatch roof was overgrown with vegetation, and a rotten door stood warped in its fixtures within the crumbling wall.

"What about the mules?" Wymar called after them.

Maros ignored him and swung around to the rear of the structure. A sizeable chunk of the wall lay in a mossy heap. The faint scent of decay drifted from the dark interior, and he caught a glimpse of movement within. He took a cautious step closer and peered into the shadows. In the farthest corner a trickle of grey light filtered in through the warped door. A tiny squeak was answered by a second. A cadaver lay within the rubble, its ribs jutting out, a fly buzzing around its face. It was another male lyakyn.

Behind the corpse lay a nest of leaves and branches. Snuggled upon them, three small bodies squirmed against one another. The clefts of the baby lyakyns' jaws opened and closed, emitting pitiful squeaks and clicks. The tips of a few teeth showed through the gums on the nearest of the hatchlings, the strongest-looking of the trio.

They're just weeks old, Maros thought. *Their mother only attacked because she was defending the nest. Frankly, I would've done the same if that miller came shitting in my personal space.*

He regarded the dead male. "Guess this one lost the battle for supremacy, and now he's meat, possibly for his own children."

"What about the mules?" Wymar urged. He gripped onto the handle of the greatsword, its tip plunged into the dirt at his feet.

Maros suppressed a groan and nodded to Henwyn to go and check on their transport.

Wymar tentatively approached and peered at the hatchlings as they squirmed upon their nest. His lip curled in disgust. "Kill them."

"No need," Maros said. "They likely won't survive long, not now their mother's dead." He felt a tiny stab of guilt at killing the mother, but he pushed it aside. He considered the cluster of dwellings several hours north along the road, and knew he'd probably done the peasants there a favour by removing the adult lyakyns from the area.

He recalled the young boy who'd taken Maros to be a monster. "Funny how one feller's perception of monstrous can differ so greatly from another's," he said quietly. "Am I hideous to look at? Maybe to some. Am I dangerous? Undoubtedly, if you know which buttons to press. So what makes me different from these babies?"

The mill owner wisely ignored Maros's rhetory. Instead, he said, "Let me put them out of their misery."

"Why should I do that?"

"Because they're monsters!"

Maros scoffed. "Dangerous? You could put your finger in those jaws and at worst it might tickle. A fenhawk could make easy pickings of the lot of 'em. Or a fox, or wolf. They're no danger to you."

"But the mules—"

Maros pointed towards the wriggling forms in the nest. "Those things couldn't harm a mouse right now. As for you, worst case is you'd wake to find 'em suckling your teats. I can see how that might be harrowing for an upstanding feller like yourself, but let's be honest, Wymar. You've already exposed your complete lack of dignity, so a little more won't make a difference. Best advice I can give is that you sleep with your trousers on."

"But—"

"They'll die, but not by my hand." Maros glared a warning at the mill owner. "I don't murder defenceless creatures unless they *really* piss me off."

Wymar's mouth opened and closed as he tried to find the words to argue.

"Here's the deal," Maros growled. "You make your charges more realistic and I'll waive the temptation of telling all and sundry about your dignity."

Wymar blustered. "That's blackmail!"

Maros grinned. "Call it what you will, my fine friend. Dignity or dari, one's as good as the other to a dead miller."

Henwyn cleared his throat and stepped around the side of the building to join them. "That's as may be, boss, but I'm afraid we've a more pressing issue than dari right now." He turned to Wymar. "The mules are dead."

Twenty minutes later, Maros bit into a shank of mule meat as he considered their predicament. The loss of the mules meant he had to either return home on foot or continue deeper into the Deadlands on foot. *Quite honestly*, he thought, *that might not be so bad. Being in the back of the wagon for hours nearly killed me.* But it would extend their journey time, and he had no idea how many days of travel were still ahead. Henwyn, he knew, would stay at his side. As for the mill owner... "Hmph." He tore off another mouthful and tossed the bone into the fire.

Wymar, who had been subdued since the encounter with the lyakyns, pushed himself to his feet and wandered over to the gear stashed in the corner.

Henwyn regarded Maros from the other side of the flickering campfire. "What's the plan, boss?"

Maros swallowed the bland meat. "Onwards."

"Right. Well, since we're already packed, we can leave whenever. Still a few hours till first light, but I doubt I'll be wanting any sleep."

Maros grunted. "Me neither."

Henwyn looked around, but Wymar had slunk out of the ringfort. "What about him?" he asked quietly.

Maros shrugged. "We'll see." He grabbed a crutch from the floor and hauled himself to his feet.

"Leaf should be well on her way to the Bay by now," Henwyn remarked.

"Aye, she should be. If the headquarters send her home empty-handed, or as good as, I'll be taking a trip to Brancosi myself. A few of those quill-pushers at HQ owe me some favours."

As he limped towards the broken entrance, Wymar stepped inside and froze as he spotted Maros. In his hand was one of Henwyn's arrows.

Maros frowned at the arrowhead. Dashes of blood were on the tip. They could be remnants of one of Henwyn's previous kills, but Maros knew the veteran, and knew he was meticulous. "Oh, aye?" he said, turning an accusing scowl on the mill owner. "What have we here, then?"

Wymar said nothing, but the guilt was plastered all over his red-cheeked face.

"What in the rutting Pit have you been up to?" Maros pressed.

"I did what you wouldn't do."

"And that would be?"

"I killed the monsters."

Maros sighed. "They were babies."

"They were abominations!"

"Aren't we all?" Maros shook his head wearily. "I told you not to kill them, and you went right ahead and did it anyway."

Wymar thrust his chest out indignantly. "You're not in charge here."

"Actually, I am. But you're free to leave, which might be in your best interests; there's no telling how long before *I* develop the urge to go stabbing a puling little defenceless shit."

Henwyn paced across to join them, a ghost of a smile on his lips.

Wymar squared on him. "You can forget about trying that placating crap on me. I'm not—"

Henwyn jabbed a punch into Wymar's nose. Maros beamed a satisfied smile as the mill owner crumpled to the floor.

Wymar climbed groggily to hands and knees, then sat down, a stupefied expression on his blood-splattered face. He touched his fingertips to his nose, spat on the ground and glared at Henwyn. "You fucking cu—"

Maros slapped a hand onto Wymar's shoulder and leaned down to look hard into his eyes. "Now, now," he chided. "My man here has the patience of Ederron, but you found his limit and he was right to put you on your arse. It's tough that your mules are dead; tough for all of us. And yes, I do know how much those beasts are worth, and it's less than you were charging me for this foray into the wilderness."

"I've halved the cost of everything! You're only paying thirty silvers now. My mules are worth more than that. And as for my wagon—"

Maros squeezed his fingers into Wymar's shoulder, just enough to see him wince. "If you weren't such a dari-pincher, you might have brought a bodyguard or two to watch over your belongings at night. But hindsight's a rotten thing, ain't it? Now, the way I see it, you've got two options. One, you head back to the Folly on your lonesome. You could be there in a few days if you push on and watch out for monsters. Two – and I'll probably regret giving you this offer – you continue into Scapa Fell with me and Henwyn and we'll at least keep you alive, if a little bruised, unless your manners improve. What say you, miller? Fancy your chances alone? I'm almost hoping you say yes."

Wymar shrugged Maros's hand from his shoulder, or at least tried to. Maros removed it anyway and hauled the man to his feet.

"Look," Maros said. "You and I have got off to a bad start. While there's certainly no love lost between us, I'd rather the tavern and the guild stay on good terms with the mill. Me and Henwyn are continuing on. I have no choice, but it's up to you what you do."

"It doesn't look like I have a choice, either," Wymar muttered into his blood-caked hand.

Henwyn passed him a rag. "I didn't want to do that," he told Wymar. "But, like your worker, Renfrey, you should learn to not let your mouth run away with you when you're talking to veteran freeblades. The safety of Alder's Folly – and, by extension, your mill – is largely up to us. We don't ask for much except a little common decency. Show us that, and we've got your back. Understood?"

Wymar held the rag to his nose and nodded.

Maros shared a glance with Henwyn. "Good. Then we'll salvage whatever we can carry from the wagon." He locked his gaze with Wymar. "While me and Hen are doing that, you should get some sleep if you're able. It's a long and much harder road ahead now. And, Wymar…"

The mill owner peered up at Maros with watery eyes.

"*Don't* take any of my man's belongings in future, especially to do something I've expressly told you not to. You might have noticed I have anger issues. With that in mind, as long as you shoulder your share of the gear and take note of Henwyn's advice, I won't leave you out here as a feast for the crows."

CHAPTER FIFTEEN
AN EPHEMERAL FLAME

In her private wing on the ground floor of Albarandes Manor, far from her sister and mother whose quarters were upstairs, Eriqwyn awoke to a *tap-tap, tap-tap* on her bedroom door that led directly out to the garden.

"Come in," she called, rising from the pillow to rest on her elbows.

The door clicked open and Linisa stepped in, holding a flaming torch which she set into an empty sconce on the wall. A dark green blush prepared from crushed leaves shadowed her eyes tonight.

Eriqwyn gave her friend a warm smile. "Lini. Come to wake me for my patrol?"

Linisa's black-dyed lips twitched as she returned the smile. "I've just finished checking the village. Thought I'd give you a call on my way back to the guardhouse."

"I forgot you were on duty tonight." Eriqwyn pulled her quilt aside, sat up and swung her feet onto the doe-hide rug beside the bed. "Have you been getting presents from the miners again?"

"They'll never win me over with the pigments they find, and they know it."

"They'll never learn either," Eriqwyn said as she stood and stretched her muscles into wakefulness. "How goes the watch tonight?"

"Quiet, as usual." Linisa sank into a chair beside the dressing table. "I did see Demelza leaving the village again earlier."

Eriqwyn sighed as she slipped the straps down from her cotton shift. It slid to her feet and she stepped out of it, her skin prickling with the coolness of the night. "I don't know where that girl disappears to all the time. I caught her on Dreaming Dragon Brae." She recalled Demelza's curious reaction to Eriqwyn saving her from the sarbek.

Linisa leaned back in the chair. Her gaze lingered casually on Eriqwyn's nakedness. "Tan brought a stock of new arrowheads to the guardhouse earlier."

"About time," Eriqwyn said, taking a pair of leather Warder leggings from the dresser drawer. Her voice took on a mocking tone as she pulled them on, one leg at a time. "I suppose he tried to impress you with his manly blacksmith muscles."

Linisa chuckled. "Not me. He only falls for those who charm him into making them things their husbands lack the skill for. Tan doesn't know how to manipulate, and he doesn't know when he's *being* manipulated." As Eriqwyn selected a long-sleeved tunic and pulled it over her head, Linisa added, "I have a rest-day after my shift. Lani and I are going for a dip in the ocean. Care to join us?"

Eriqwyn smiled. "I appreciate the offer, but I'll let you and your sister enjoy some peace and quiet alone. Maybe next time."

Linisa nodded. "You know where to find us if you change your mind."

"I do." Leaning in, Eriqwyn placed a kiss on the Warder's cheek. "Thank you, Linisa."

Eriqwyn selected a pair of woollen socks and hardy boots. She crossed to the bed and began pulling them onto her feet.

With a sigh, Linisa clapped her hands to her thighs and rose from the chair. "Well then, First Warder, I'll get back to the guardhouse and leave you to your patrol. Which route are you taking tonight?"

"I think I'll circle north toward the Knots." Eriqwyn reached to her bedside table and picked up her hunting dagger. "It's Banaelag – best month for hunting blind pygmies. Maybe I'll be lucky and thin their numbers by one."

"You'll be lucky to spot one at all." Linisa ran a hand through her mop of yellow hair. "Last time I saw a pygmy was two years ago, and if I'd blinked I'd have missed it."

"I found the fresh remains of a young fawn last week, its innards turned to mush. The pygmies are about, but they're wily." Eriqwyn plucked a calloused finger against the tip of the dagger and gave Linisa a crooked smile. "I could do with killing another of those little bastards."

Linisa took the torch from the wall and winked at Eriqwyn. "Good hunting." She left the room and closed the door behind her, and Eriqwyn's gaze lingered on the oaken boards for a long moment.

With a sigh, she slid her dagger into its sheath. "Good hunting, indeed."

Eriqwyn strung her bow, and with a last glance around her bedchamber she stepped out into the calm night. Beyond the manor's garden, the village green was empty and dark, with a scattering of faint lights through shutter-slats on several of the surrounding houses. At this time of the night a hush permeated the village for several glorious hours.

Eriqwyn crossed the green and turned onto the trail that led to the edge of the village. The black shape of the Founding Oak loomed into focus, blotting out the star-dusted sky. She slowed as she neared the tree. Her gaze drifted up its trunk to the crook of the lowest bough. A faint touch of moonlight caught the object nestled between trunk and bough, an object which had been there since long before Eriqwyn was born. The skull's sockets sucked in the blackness of the night, seeming to gaze northwards from its tilted position as if seeking the moon, or in longing for its forsaken home so far over the horizon.

128

She continued down the trail and was soon beyond the village's perimeter. After several minutes, the trail branched off to the right up a gently rising tree-lined slope that led directly over Dreaming Dragon Brae. When she reached the clearing at the top of the hill, Eriqwyn stepped across to the ivy-coated Dragoneye, set her bow beside it and leaned her elbows on the stone's leafy top. For a minute she looked across the dark clearing, then closed her eyes and soaked in the peace of the heathland. There was no rush to complete the patrol. She'd been a hunter for twenty years, a Warder for the last twelve, and First Warder for seven. In all that time there had rarely been a need for urgency. Cravants, lyakyns, blind pygmies, sarbeks, all of the most dangerous creatures of the heath were thankfully few and far between. Whenever a villager was killed by such a creature, it could often be put down to stupidity, like when Eriqwyn had found Demelza on this very spot days earlier.

Of course she was in danger, Eriqwyn told herself. *Any creature can seem timid one moment, and the next it's ripping your throat out. It's all part of survival.*

The snapping of a distant twig pricked her senses, and Eriqwyn's eyes shot open and peered across the top of the ivy. Soft footfalls were approaching from the north-west, climbing through a less-trodden trail towards the glade. She ducked behind the stone block, rested her back against it, and waited.

The soft crunch of dried pine needles underfoot entered the glade, paused, then drew closer. A slim figure stepped alongside the Dragoneye stone, glanced down at Eriqwyn, and froze.

"Hello, Demelza."

"F-first Warder?"

"Yes indeed," Eriqwyn said flatly.

"Wh-what are—"

"What am I doing here?"

Demelza nodded, a dumb expression on her face.

"I could ask you the same thing."

"I… I was out on me wanders, is all."

"Were you, now. And where did your wanders take you on this pleasant night?"

"Been up on the Knots." Demelza was clearly feigning indifference. "I ain't done no wrong."

"I didn't say you had." Eriqwyn rose from her crouch. "Did you see anything interesting on your travels? Any more sarbeks, perhaps? Ghouls out from the Forbidden Place wandering the heath? Or, goddess forbid, any outlanders?" Demelza's eyes widened at that, and Eriqwyn's narrowed. "Do you have something to say, girl?"

Demelza shook her head vigorously. "I ain't seen nothin'. I, er, I sweared it."

Eriqwyn folded her arms and scrutinised the girl. Demelza's face was a wan grey in the darkness, but Eriqwyn could see enough to know she was hiding something. She stepped closer to the girl and sniffed the air around her. "You smell of woodsmoke. Did you make yourself a fire?"

"Aye. I mean, yes, that's what I done."

"Mm-hm. Show me your tinderbox."

"My what?"

"Your fire-making tools, child. You can't make fire out of thin air. Or did you rub sticks together?"

Demelza paused, then nodded. "Rubbed sticks."

Eriqwyn smiled coldly. "That's quite the skill to learn. It seems my sister and Wayland were right about you, after all. Go on, then."

"Go on, what, First Warder?"

"Start me a fire with your stick trick."

"Uh…"

"Step to it, girl! I don't have all night."

Demelza glanced around, then jogged across to the trees where she selected a handful of branches and twigs. She brought them back and dropped them near the Dragoneye stone. As she squatted over them, she looked up, and Eriqwyn raised an eyebrow.

Demelza bunched the twigs into a pile, picked up a pair of branches and rubbed them against each other.

Oh, dear, Eriqwyn thought. *Just as I anticipated.* Demelza clearly had no idea how to start a fire by friction. Eriqwyn waited, content to let the girl make a fool of herself until she admitted she was trying to deceive her.

A dim glow appeared at the base of the twigs, and a tiny flame caught, fluttering in the faint breeze. Demelza dropped the branches and rose to her feet. The flame guttered and died.

Eriqwyn stared at the fading ember, then turned a fierce gaze on the girl. "How did you do that?"

Demelza swallowed. "Stick trick."

"No. *Not* stick trick. I could have left you there for a year playing with those branches and you would not – *should* not – have been able to start a fire. Yet you did." Eriqwyn took her by the shoulders. "Where have you been tonight? What were you hiding when I asked if you'd seen anything interesting? *Did you?*"

Demelza gasped and looked at Eriqwyn's hand on her shoulder. "Please, I… I sweared I wouldn't tell. To the goddess," she added with an emphatic nod.

Eriqwyn gripped her tighter. "You swore *what*, and to *whom*? Tell me now or you'll be facing the Founding Laws. Do you understand?"

Demelza was shaking. "I seen them. An' they seen me. I told 'em, I said they shouldn't oughta have taken it. They said it were all right, that they'd be long gone at sun-up."

"Who? Taken what? Where were they?" Eriqwyn released the girl.

"Gr-grey Knot," Demelza said.

"Graegaredh Knot?"

Demelza nodded.

Eriqwyn drew a slow breath, forcing herself to calm. "Now, Demelza, tell me who you saw, and what they had in their possession. Think carefully."

"Out…" Demelza's features scrunched as if she would cry. "Outlanders," she whispered, lowering her gaze to the ground. "They went into the Forbidden Place. Took a deadstone."

Eriqwyn felt the world turn beneath her feet as the girl's words struck her.

"Show me," Eriqwyn said, her tone like ice.

"But—"

"If you're telling me the truth, this is why Warders have protected our village since the ancestors founded it. You and I are going to the Knots. Now."

Chapter Sixteen
Rude Awakening

Oriken awoke with a start, gasping into the blackness as hands clawed at his shoulders. He reached to fight them off but they withdrew. His hat was swatted from his face and he stared up at a rotten face that quickly morphed into Jalis.

"Suffering stars," he grumbled as Jalis tried to mask her amusement. "You nearly gave me a heart attack."

He drew a shuddering breath and lifted his gaze to the sky, where the fading forms of dream-ghosts flitted across Haleth's cloud-smeared surface. Blinking the confusion of sleep away, he pushed himself to his elbows and regarded Jalis as she crouched beside him.

"For a minute there, you refused to wake," Jalis told him in hushed tones. She picked up his fallen hat and shoved it onto his head. "It was a commendable display of resistance to which I'm glad you finally succumbed. Are you ready to take the shift?"

He glanced across to Dagra. Their bearded friend was sound asleep, curled in a ball close to the fire. Oriken sat up and rubbed a hand over his unshaven face. "Just give me a minute."

He reached from the bedroll and tossed a branch onto the fire. As the flames grew, the fresh wood gasped long and low. Oriken grabbed his swordbelt and climbed to his feet.

No sooner was he off the bedroll than Jalis settled down upon it, oblivious to his thankfully fading predicament. "You don't mind me taking your warm one, do you?" she asked, though there was no doubt it was a rhetorical question.

You know me too well, he thought.

She pulled the blanket up to her chin. "Watch out for pitchfork-wielding peasants," she said, then winked. "I hear they're savage at this time of the year."

He frowned in feigned annoyance, then smiled. "I'll be sure to shout for your help if I get accosted by any."

Jalis closed her eyes.

He clasped the swordbelt about his hips and clipped the mini crossbow to it slung his pack onto his shoulder and crossed to a boulder at the edge of the clearing. Dropping his back beside the stone, he stepped up to the trees and unbuttoned his trousers.

No rush for a perimeter check, he thought as he pissed. *Jalis will have done one not long ago.*

When he was finished, he returned to the boulder and sat with his back against it. For a long while, he did nothing but gaze around the clearing and into the black night beyond. High above, Haleth's light was diffused behind a passing cloud. Closer to the tops of the nearby trees, the dark-green moon of Larindis was difficult to discern in a clear patch of sky. Behind Oriken and down the embankment, the trickle of the stream was as soothing as a lullaby.

He removed his hat, placed it beside the crossbow and rested the back of his head against the cool stone.

Still tired. Would have had enough sleep if that girl hadn't come spying on us. At least I finally got clean.

He reached for the backpack, dragged it closer and took out the jewel.

He glanced only briefly at the runes upon the silver band. Those were Jalis's department. He was more interested in the jewel itself. Each angular face was the size of his thumbnail, flat and smooth, jutting out in low pyramids of four faces each. He traced a fingertip over the surface. The jewel was neither cold nor warm, and the darkened core was difficult to see in this light. Now, after all they'd witnessed and heard from the peasant girl, he thought he could sense the wrongness in the oversized gem.

Demelza had called it a deadstone. Somehow that sounded more menacing than burial jewel. Still, the notion was ridiculous that the jewel could be responsible for the dead rising and attacking people. He chuckled quietly.

Laugh it up all you like, he thought. *The dead aren't laid at peace like they should be – or, in the case of Cunaxa Chiddari, stood upright – and they might've feasted on us like the kid in Demelza's story if we hadn't escaped.*

Why the undead wandered the graveyard at all was something he couldn't fathom, but the how of it, according to Demelza, was the jewel.

Jewels, he corrected. *Just how many more of these things are there? No, forget it, at least for now.*

He felt a sudden need to be back in Alder's Folly, sat at their usual table near the tavern's bar.

I could share a barrel of Carradosi Pale with the others right now, or spend a bit more coin on a cask of Redanchor.

He placed the jewel in the pack and knotted the cord. For a while he sat there, listening to the stream, the fire, the frogs and heath-hoppers and the lonely call of a nightjar. Eventually, the eastern sky began to lighten to a deep purplish-red, streaks of trailing clouds visible above the rolling horizon. Somewhere in that direction was Demelza's village, nestled away in some hiding place. There was still a good hour or two until dawn proper, but the time for Demelza's villagers to launch a night attack was over, so it seemed that the girl had stayed good to her word. Not that he imagined she understood what she'd agreed to, but still.

A groan issued from near the fire as Dagra rolled over and sat up. He glanced at the flames, blinked, looked across at Jalis's sleeping form, then he spotted Oriken and grunted. Oriken lifted a hand in greeting, and Dagra climbed to his feet and wandered over, pausing half-way to place his hands on his knees and break wind.

Oriken grinned. "I see you're back to your usual self."

"Aye, not quite, but I'm on the mend."

"Good, because as far as I'm concerned we can be walking from dawn till dusk, get as far as we can from this dismal place." Oriken shifted his back across the boulder to give Dagra room to sit beside him. "I mean, I know those things aren't coming out into the heath, but that's not the point. This whole region is wrong."

Dagra nodded. "Wrong is the word. So, you're not still keen to head back in there?"

Oriken chuckled softly. "The temptation's always there to discover places and things that are lost to history. That'll never change. But, yeah, the urge to delve inside the city isn't so strong now, not since that girl showed up. I don't like the implications it carries."

Dagra coughed into his hand. "A girl has you more worried than a sprawling, god-neglected necropolis?"

Oriken shrugged. "Somehow, yes."

Dagra spat. "Good, because not on my life am I going back into those unholy burial grounds again. We've seen some horrors in our time as freeblades, but all the dead things tended not to move."

Oriken glanced at Dagra and studied him a moment. His cheeks had regained some colour, though his eyes were still puffy and sore-looking. He did seem to be perking up some, though. "You sure you'll be strong enough for a day's walk?"

For a moment Dagra looked sombre, his fingers toying with the emblem of Avato on the leather cord at his neck, then a smile spread within the beard. "I feel as lively as a lyre, Oriken. In fact, I'm as ready as you are to be leaving."

They talked for a while, not about the graveyard or the city, but about normal stuff like being back in the Folly in their rooms at the Lonely Peddler, comfortable beds with goose-down quilts, the communal bath filled with freshly-boiled water, and the finest meals in Caerheath courtesy of Luthan. They talked about simpler, understandable contracts – escorting people or items safely from one place to another, and getting rid of troublesome creatures or bandits.

"It's strange that what we miss the most are the every-day things," Oriken said. "The ones you don't realise you take for granted until you notice their absence."

Dagra huffed in agreement. "You know, there's still an hour or more till sun-up. I'm still a bit drained but I want to pull my weight. Let me handle the rest of the watch. Go and grab yourself some more sleep. I've got it covered."

"You sure?"

"Go ahead."

"Hm. I didn't sleep much earlier, truth be told." Oriken slapped a hand to Dagra's shoulder and pushed himself to his feet. "You want me to check the perimeter before I head off?"

Dagra waved his hand dismissively. "I'll do it."

"Fine. Wake me if you need anything, okay?"

"Fuck off. If I need a shit I'll go behind the boulder. And I reckon I can wipe my own arse. Thanks for the offer, though. Actually, now you mention it, I could do with a piss."

Oriken grinned and turned to walk away, then paused. "If you spot any rabbits on your patrol, do shoot one for us, won't you? A hot breakfast would be welcome. I'm starving."

"Oh, aye. I'm a lousy shot at the best of times, and you know it. Go on, let me have some peace and quiet."

Jalis was sound asleep on her back, breathing silently beneath his blanket. Only the slight rise and fall of her chest told him she was alive. He settled down on the empty bedroll beside her and pulled a blanket across himself. No sooner had he closed his eyes than fatigue hit him. It had been a long day. Truth was, it had been a long fortnight, but after their encounter with the corpses and learning that there was some sort of civilisation down here, the whole trek was catching up to him. This time he sank quickly into a deep, and dreamless, sleep.

"Oriken! Get up!"

He awoke with a start, pushed himself to a sitting position and peered around the clearing. Jalis was stuffing their belongings into packs.

"What is it," he asked as he rose to his feet.

"Dagra's gone."

"What do you mean he's gone?"

"How would you like me to explain it?" She didn't look up from her work. "I've been all around the hill. He's gone, and so is the jewel."

Oriken was having trouble processing the information. He glanced to the boulder where he'd left Dagra only an hour or so earlier. He almost expected to see him wander around from behind the rock, belching and buckling his belt. But he didn't. The boulder was alone. The pack he'd left with Dagra was there, its top opened. The mini crossbow and bolts lay on the ground as he'd left them. And then it hit him.

"Shit," he hissed.

"Shit, indeed."

"He's taken the jewel."

"Right."

"He's taken the bloody jewel!"

Jalis hoisted her pack onto her back and grabbed the one by Dagra's bedroll. "Are you going to sit there repeating yourself or get off your arse and help me?"

"Huh? Oh. Course." He pushed himself up and paced across to the boulder, bent down to retrieve the crossbow and bolts. As he stashed them into the open pack he checked quickly that the jewel definitely wasn't there. Spitting a curse, he tied the cord and slung it onto his back, then returned to the bedrolls to grab his gear.

"I don't understand it." He clasped his swordbelt around his waist. "Where could he have gone? That village the girl's from? Or maybe he's set off already so we can catch him up."

"He's taken the jewel back to the graveyard," Jalis said as she tightened the pack's straps around her shoulders. "Just that and his sword are gone. No pack, no provisions."

"Why would he?"

"Remember what Demelza said? How the man in her village was eaten by his own dead child?" Jalis eyed him impatiently. "Come on! Talk and move!" She turned on her heel and ran across the clearing, heading in the direction of the graveyard.

"What about my wet clothes and the bedding?" he called after her.

"Fuck the bedding! We'll come back for it."

He spat a curse and stooped to whisk his hat from the ground and planted it firmly on his head as he hurried to catch Jalis up.

She glanced at Oriken as he caught up to run alongside her. "You know what Dagra's like when it comes to superstition," she said. "I imagine he's thinking our bounty's not worth the risk of the jewel staying out of Lachyla."

"But we burn our dead now. Have done since the Uprising. They can't come back if they're only charred bones."

"Right," Jalis said as she bounded up the gentle incline. "And in some parts of the continent they throw their dead into ravines"—she paused to draw a deep breath—"so deep that you can't see the bottom, no matter how many corpses are cast into it. Maybe it's not the dead that Dagra cares about. Maybe it's the living."

"Huh?"

"What if everyone knew that something existed with the power to bring their loved ones back to life, or to stop them dying in the first place?"

Oriken huffed and shook his head as he ran.

"No matter what the truth is," Jalis said, her words coming in steady gasps, "the powers of need and belief can turn a nation into a mob. The deadstones would make that happen."

136

"I don't give a plate of cowshit about that. It's Dag I care about. He's not the sort to do something this sneaky."

"And yet he has."

I was stupid to let him take the watch, and now me and Jalis are paying the price for my stupidity.

He took the second pack from her and slung it over his shoulder. They wasted no more energy on discussion. The minutes stretched by, and eventually they reached the remnants of the Kingdom Road. Up ahead, a single oak stood in the centre of the road, a testament to the years that the ancient highway had remained in disuse. They were almost at the rim of the valley where they'd camped the previous night.

Oriken's chest heaved as he reached the crest of the rise and the expanse of Scapa Fell's south-western tip burst into view. The sunrise knifed across the heathland, burning red shadows into the creases of land. With Jalis a short distance behind him, he sped down the shallow descent to lower ground, leaping over a narrow tributary at the bottom. Spiky foliage and jutting reeds blurred by at the edge of his vision as he ran. A breeze buffeted beneath his hat, cooling the sweat that trickled from his forehead.

Typical, he thought with growing annoyance, *I finally get a half-decent wash, then Dag does a fucking runner on us.*

He looked across to the west, where the hazy heath met the golden-washed ocean. His eyes traced the line of the graveyard's perimeter wall, its battlements and towers jutting like a monstrous backbone, the bumpy surface shining white in the sun. For a moment, he imagined he could hear the moaning of the creatures within, but perhaps it was nothing more than the muted crash of the distant waves.

Though the portcullis was still a mile away, the route to it was a level run with few obstacles. Oriken's attention was caught by a tiny figure approaching the wall. "Look there!" he called to Jalis. "Do you see? Is that Dagra?"

"I see," she said as she picked up her pace to run alongside him. "It's too far away to tell if it's Dagra."

They shouted Dagra's name as they ran, but it seemed to Oriken that the figure neither slowed nor turned to acknowledge them.

"I'll give him a headache worth complaining about when we catch him," he huffed.

"You and me both. But let's give him a chance to explain himself first."

"Huh. You know, when I asked him how he felt, he told me he was lively as a lyre."

Jalis frowned. "Who says that nowadays?"

"Exactly." Oriken licked his dry lips. "He called me Oriken. He hardly ever does that, and it wasn't a moment for it. It's just something you know after so many years."

"What are you getting at?"

"It just feels off. I shouldn't have left him alone."

Jalis grunted. "Save your breath and we'll get there quicker."

Far ahead, the figure reached the portcullis and dipped beneath it. Oriken quickened his pace and ran as fast as his tiring legs could go. Dagra meant to return the jewel to Cunaxa's tomb, most likely. But how on Verragos would he find the courage to enter the Chiddari crypt alone? Oriken doubted their bearded friend would have the nerve.

Finally, they arrived at the portcullis. Oriken slowed to a stride as he approached the partially-raised entrance, dropped the packs and took his hat off. He gripped the iron latticework and rested his forehead against the cool metal as his breathing slowed to normal. Sweat dripped from his face. He pushed away from the bars, ran his sleeve across his brow and peered into the graveyard. The last wispy remnants of mist licked at the cracked earth and flagstones, caressing the face of a nearby fallen statue like the tongues of ghostly lovers. The wide Litchway shrank into the distance, empty. The graveyard was devoid of wandering corpses, but also devoid of Dagra. Oriken swore in frustration.

Jalis had shrugged out of her backpack and was kneeling before a cluster of sickly-looking shrubs, pushing their branches aside to stash her pack between them.

"We'll leave the gear here out of sight," she said. "Take only what we need." With the pack stashed in the bushes, she took the oil lamp and tinderbox from the ground and rose to her feet.

Oriken snatched up the two remaining packs and crossed to join her. From them he took the crossbow, two cases of bolts and the hunting knife, then stuffed the packs between the shrubs.

He and Jalis ducked beneath the portcullis. As they rose on the other side, they shared a momentary look of understanding. Their itinerary had long since gone to cowshit. The Deadlands had played dirty from the moment they entered it, and Oriken suspected it was only just getting warmed up.

As they broke into a run along the Litchway, he glanced at the lamp in Jalis's hand. Oriken tried to imagine Dagra venturing into the black stairwell without a light source, and utterly failed to match the action to their friend.

CHAPTER SEVENTEEN
BACK INTO THE BOWELS

Oriken's skin prickled as he and Jalis ran down the Litchway, and not just from the sweat that made his clothes cling to his body. The air itself seemed charged this morning. The sun was bright in a clear sky to the east, while the west was turning black with a storm crawling inland from the ocean.

It was a small mercy that no corpses were in sight; no upright ones, anyway. The cracked stones of the pathway and the parched soil to either side were littered with the occasional piece of discoloured meat, as well as fragments of bone, bits of internal organs, and dark smears of dried ichor. Among it all, Oriken identified quite a few fingers, a couple of hands and forearms, several heads, and a leg that came complete with the remnants of a funerary slipper attached. Some of the limbs still twitched, fingers clutched at the air, and jaws opened and closed as if following an unknown instinct. Still, progress was progress, and the going was much easier without a lake of fog and a horde of ticked-off corpses.

He spotted movement between the burial markers several rows up ahead – a corpse clawing its way through the dirt, or at least trying to. Its attempts were futile. It couldn't have progressed more than a couple dozen yards during the whole night. It was missing one hand, and its entire lower half was gone, leaving its spine dangling like the macabre imitation of a tail. A streak of gore led up to the corpse from the Litchway like a giant, diarrhoeic snail track. Oriken slowed to a stop and studied the creature as it attempted to crawl onwards.

Jalis drew up beside him. "What is it?"

"There." He nodded towards the struggling corpse.

Jalis frowned at it. "Pitiful. How these bodies quickly grow, and yet slowly die."

"Hm?"

"Never mind."

"I wonder if its legs wandered off without it?" Oriken turned to go. "I don't know why I stopped. It's just wasting—"

"Wait." Jalis pointed off to the side, far out into the graveyard. "Do you see where it's heading – or, I should say, where it's trying to reach? Look, all the way over there."

The sun's rays streamed over the rows of headstones onto a scattering of figures in the far distance. He scanned the grave-studded landscape and located more of them wandering listlessly between the stones, heading for a large, pillared structure with a low, domed ceiling nestled in the graveyard's corner. Enough daylight filtered between the pillars for him to see a ripple of movement throughout the entire shaded interior.

"By the gods," he groaned.

Jalis grunted. "Just one god, apparently."

"So that's where they were hiding. What ungodly thing is drawing them to it?"

"It looks like an ancient type of chapel. Could be they're just sheltering from the sun."

"Yeah, but why there? Why gather inside a chapel? Why not go back down into the crypts?"

"Good for us that they don't. Most are likely from the topside graves, not the crypts. As mindless as they are, perhaps they have no desire to return to the earth; would *you*, if you'd already spent so long down there?" Jalis pondered the point, then shook her head. "Or maybe the chapel was their sanctuary in life and they're merely following what remains of their instincts. Flocking to service, as it were."

Oriken shuddered. "Damn, that's grim. Even as a heathen I find that wrong on several levels."

Jalis forced a tight smile. "Come on. As long as they stay there they won't bother us."

They resumed their run down the Litchway, retracing their steps from the previous day until they turned onto a narrow pathway and arrived at the Chiddari crypt. Cunaxa's statue bowed in greeting, and Oriken touched his hat in return. While he kept a lookout for any stray corpses, Jalis set the oil lamp on a dais beside the entrance and set to work lighting it.

With the job done, she stood within the entrance and glanced at him over her shoulder. "There's something deadly about this whole place," she said, "and I don't just mean the legion of corpses. There's something more than the blight here. Something beyond evil."

She was right. It was only a feeling, and Oriken always did his best to push aside such things, but there was an indefinable presence in Lachyla that went beyond the restless dead.

"Ready?" Jalis said.

He drew his sabre. "You want me to take point?"

"No, I've got it." Steel sighed as she slid Dusklight from its sheath, held the lamp low and ventured into the stairwell.

140

With a last glance around, Oriken followed. *Here we go*, he thought. *Back into the bowels. Back down to the leering death-mask of the* real *Cunaxa Chiddari. And, hopefully, to Dagra.* They passed the first turn in the steps, then the second. *He has to be in here. We've cornered him. Returning the jewel to where we found it is the only logical thing he could do. Unless…* "Damn all the gods," he growled.

Jalis paused at the next turn. "What?"

"Dagra might not be down here after all." He kept his voice low. "Surely he'd realise we'd come after him, that we'd just take the jewel again and be on our way. He might not be the sharpest blade in the armoury, but he's not so dull he wouldn't consider that."

"If he isn't here," Jalis said tightly, "he could have taken the jewel to any burial vault in the graveyard. We can't possibly check them all; the Gardens of the Dead covers a square mile if not more. It would be an exercise in futility that could take us longer than we've got daylight hours."

"That's my point. Dag can be crafty when he wants to be. Though the stars know why he's doing this at all."

"Stars, gods, or the Bearded One himself," Jalis muttered as she continued down the steps. "It's our only lead right now."

Oriken ducked into the narrow corridor behind her. He clenched his teeth and ignored the cobwebs as best as he could until he stepped into the main section of the crypt. It was impossible to tell if Dagra had returned to the crypt, since their footprints from the previous day were everywhere.

They ventured warily but with haste along the dark hallway. Jalis approached the alcoves to left and right, holding the lamp into each, checking behind the pillars and glancing around each dais along the centre of the hall. The dust in the recesses which they hadn't previously entered remained undisturbed, yet still Jalis gave them a cursory but careful check to ensure Dagra wasn't hiding behind a pillar.

Oriken held his sabre poised, ready for anything that might be lurking in the deeper darkness. *Dead things. Not Dag. If he's here, he'd better not jump out on us. I may be pissed off with him but I don't want to gut him by mistake.*

Before long, they reached the fallen slab. The exposed burial hole was just as they'd last seen it, the thick webs unbroken. Oriken turned away in disgust, his skin crawling; passing under the threads in the narrow corridor was bad enough, but looking at that deep cavity filled with a giant cobweb made his head swim. He conjured an imaginary spider waiting behind the silken wall, its leg-span as wide as a human torso, with hairy limbs and hairy back, myriad eyes as black and shining as pebbles of obsidian, fangs dripping with poison, the sac at its rear swollen with eggs…

"Ah," he gasped with a shudder, then turned to follow Jalis. Her deceivingly delicate form padded along the hallway, and he knew she would spring into a deadly blur of action if anything ventured out of the dark.

141

As he retuned his vision to the murk, he felt eyes watching his back – spider eyes, or dead eyes, perhaps both – but he attributed it to his nerves.

Getting as bad as Dagra in the dark. Forget the spiders already.

The last time they'd been in the crypt, he was able to keep his phobia at bay by harassing Dagra, a tactic he'd mastered over the years. But Dagra wasn't here now – only the stars knew where the bearded bastard was – and Oriken was far from in the mood for giving Jalis mischievous banter. He knew she was in no mood for it, either.

They reached the next pair of alcoves and Jalis approached the one on the left. The lamp shone a wan glow into the interior, and something within the penumbral shadows behind the right-hand pillar caught Oriken's attention.

"Hey," he whispered. "Look there." As with all the alcoves, the section of wall behind the pillar consisted of several columns of stone blocks, but the block that was level with Oriken's face was recessed deeper than the rest. On the block beneath, a vertical brass lever jutted from the stone.

"Huh," Jalis muttered. "How did we miss this before?"

"Dagra did most of the checking last time, and I doubt he looked behind the pillars since we were only searching for that damned jewel." Oriken reached for the lever. "Shall I?"

"No, wait." Jalis bent and held the lamp to the floor, revealing bootprints scuffed into the dust. "He's been here."

"Those could be from yesterday."

"Perhaps." She rose and stepped to the rear wall to study the granite slab. After a moment she muttered something Oriken couldn't hear.

He stepped up behind her shoulder. "What is it?"

"At first glance this burial hole looks like any other, but there's no gem set into the granite, nor any engravings. And the slab is taller like the one that contained the jewel."

"So there's a corpse behind this one, too? Good to know. Thanks for the warning."

"No." Jalis turned her attention to the upper corner of the slab. Carefully, she said, "I don't think this is a burial hole."

"Cunaxa was behind the other one."

"Yes, but hers isn't a blank slab." She ran a hand along the granite's side. "The edge is smooth in places, as if worn from years of being touched, like the stairwell steps are worn from visitors coming and going before the blight." She crouched down, and Oriken noted how the slab reached all the way to the floor, unlike Cunaxa's.

"I knew it," Jalis whispered, setting the lamp in the dust. "No doubt about it; this is a second entrance, and it's been used recently."

Oriken frowned at the floor, and at the disturbed dust that arced from the bottom corner of the granite to a point half-way between the side walls.

"That settles it, then." He reached for the lever.

"Hold on."

"What now? If Dagra's been through here, we need to catch up with him."

"I know. But we haven't checked the tomb at the end yet. The jewel *could* be there for all we know."

Oriken swore under his breath. He held his hand out for the lamp, which Jalis passed him. "I'll go straight there. It'll only take a few minutes. No messing about this time."

"If the lamp goes out," she said, unsheathing her second dagger, "you had better not sneak up on me, because anything that does will be getting sliced apart."

Oriken left the alcove, his sabre ready on the off-chance that some of the undead had wandered into the crypt. But at this point he doubted it and didn't much care either way. Other than Jalis and himself, the place was as silent as before; deathly so. He strode down the centre of the walkway as quick as the light would allow, arriving before long at the far end where, as he fully expected, Cunaxa's blackened skull greeted him through the hole in her slab. Of the jewel, there was no sign.

No sense wasting time, he thought as he gave a curt nod to the age-ravaged head of the Chiddari matron. "Madam," he said in a flat greeting. "We must stop meeting like this. People will begin to talk."

Cunaxa Chiddari looked singularly unimpressed.

He stalked back along the hallway, his mood becoming more rotten than Cunaxa with each step. When he reached the alcove where Jalis waited, the flicker of the lamp illuminated her leaning against the wall, arms crossed over her middle with the daggers still in her hands, the flat of Silverspire's blade resting against her cheek. She raised her eyebrows questioningly. When he shook his head, she hissed a curse.

"...which leaves only one course of action," he said, nodding to the brass lever. "Care to do the honours?"

Jalis gave him a tight nod. "You're too kind," she said, positioning herself before the lever.

He unclipped the crossbow and loaded it, then aimed it at the door. If something waited on the other side – as long as it wasn't Dagra – it would get a bolt to the face before he ran in with the sabre. A tiny bolt wasn't likely to do much, but loosing a shot into a corpse's face should slow it for a moment, maybe knock it back long enough for them to coordinate an attack.

"Do it," he told her. With both hands, Jalis grasped the lever and put her weight into pulling the handle towards her. Metal scraped against metal, stone scraped against stone. With gasps of effort, she managed to shift the door inwards inch by inch until it ground to a half-open halt. The yawning darkness beyond was silent and still.

"That's as far as I can open it," she said.

"It's enough."

The dust beyond the door was unsettled. Oriken squatted for a closer look. A clear set of bootprints led into the murk, joined a short distance ahead by a second set.

"He's not alone," Oriken said.

"What?" Jalis peered over his head at the tracks in the dust. "Oh, great. By the fucking stars."

Oriken glanced up at her. "I don't know if this is the right time to mention it, but I'm really not in the mood for this shit."

"That makes two of us."

"If only it made three."

They set off into the passageway. For half an hour, they trudged tediously past an unchanging array of beams and rough-cut stone, following Dagra's footprints and those of his unknown companion. There were no side-passages or doors leading off the tunnel. Oriken could see evidence of mining activity, but he guessed that wasn't the tunnel's intended purpose. More likely it was a chance opportunity after the discovery of a few veins when the tunnel was freshly dug, and any minerals were long since depleted.

Oriken drew a breath. "If I didn't know better—"

"Which you don't."

"Which, admittedly, I don't," he conceded with a scowl. "But *if* I didn't, then I might believe that this passage leads all the way to the Underland. It's like we're wandering into the arsehole of the Pit itself."

Being on their guard had spiralled into tediousness. Oriken had long since given up on keeping his voice low, as had Jalis, and their weapons were back in their sheaths.

"It seems apparent," Jalis said, "that as long as we continue on a level gradient, we can't go any further than the cliffs that line the promontory."

"What if it does go deeper? What if it carries on into the ocean?"

Jalis shrugged. "Then it'll be under water. In which case, two things will be certain. Dagra will be dead, and we'll be turning back. The chances of someone building a long tunnel leading nowhere but into the ocean are extremely slim, not to mention a flagrant waste of time."

"What I don't get is why the tunnel's not on the map. Sure, it was hidden from obvious sight, but I wouldn't call it secret."

"My best guess," Jalis said, "is that its exclusion from the map suggests it probably wasn't used by the common citizens, but by the clergy, guardsmen, or nobility. I'd further guess that the other crypts have similar tunnels leading from them. I admit that I can't begin to guess what's going on here, and I don't like that one bit. It makes us vulnerable. It's obvious at this stage that this isn't just about Dagra. Whatever the case, the question isn't whether there's trouble up ahead, but how big is it and how close are we to reaching it?"

Oriken sighed. "Trouble ahead and trouble behind. What about the chapel? Was that on the map?"

144

Jalis slowed her pace as she pulled the parchment from her pocket and unfolded it. Oriken held the lamp closer, and for a long moment the only sound was the crunch of their footfalls on the gravelly floor, then Jalis gave a disgruntled murmur.

"That doesn't sound like a yes or a no."

"It's a yes," she said. "It's a yes times four."

Oriken frowned. "You mean there's a chapel in each corner of the graveyard?"

"Right."

"Each one filled with a congregation of corpses."

"Could be."

"Any *good* news?"

"I'll get back to you on that."

Oriken peered at the map. "I can't make arse nor elbow out of the lettering. It doesn't help that half of it's written in Old Himaeran."

"You really don't know your own land's native language?"

He shook his head. "A few of the old folk back in Eyndal spoke a little of it, but for some reason learning the language just never cropped up in life's lessons."

"Well," Jalis said, "I do know a smattering of Old Himaeran, not to mention Sardayan, Modern Sosarran, Middle Sosarran..."

Oriken barked a wry laugh. "Old Cela must have some connections, getting hold of a map like that."

There was a soft rustling of parchment as Jalis returned it to her pocket. "The map's not ancient. No more than a few decades, I'd guess. Might be a copy of an original. Either way, it only gives us the most basic information. It's as crude as a Khalevali sailor in a bath-house."

Oriken snorted. "You're mixing your definitions."

"It was a play on words. Gods, your grasp of Modern Sosarran is also crude at times."

"My apologies, siosa. I'll leave the word-play to you."

"Promises, promises."

"And you leave the sword-play to me."

"Really? You've got a nerve saying that to a bladesmistress. And I'd love to hear you mention your affinity with sword-play in the wrong wing of the Brancosi Brothels; the boys there would *adore* you talking that way to them."

Oriken gave a low growl. It was a touch of playful banter, but it was enough to lift his spirit ever so slightly from the mud it was otherwise wallowing in.

They settled into silence and continued along the unchanging tunnel. His thoughts drifted through everything they'd witnessed since scaling the perimeter wall. True enough, this had seemed a fool's contract, but what did they have to lose?

145

The contract should have been easy, he thought. *It almost was, except for one detail which Dagra anticipated but I didn't consider. There's more than a seed of truth buried within the legend. This time, I was wrong and Dagra was right to hold to his superstitions. I never saw it coming. My sense of reason made me blind to the possibility of far-fetched truth.*

Up ahead, something was different about the shadowy sameness of the tunnel. Oriken touched Jalis's arm.

"Steps," she said.

The ceiling angled down, parallel with the descending stairs. Oriken crouched beside Jalis at the top and peered ahead. There were only half a dozen steps before the ground levelled off, the ceiling supported by a thick length of timber. Ten feet further along, a second set of steps led upwards. Dagra's footprints were discernible in the dust and grit, along with those of his unknown companion.

Oriken shared a glance with Jalis. They made their way down the steps and across to the second set. At the top, they were met with more tunnel stretching into blackness.

"I guess you were right about other tunnels leading from the crypts," Oriken said. "I reckon we just passed one crossing overhead."

Jalis nodded. "I'm surprised there haven't been more. Maybe the Chiddari tunnel takes precedence in route."

"Any thoughts on where we're heading?"

"Unfortunately, yes."

"Me, too."

"Don't ask me which direction, though. I got lost with all the turns in the stairwell and the curvature of this tunnel. But I don't see a point in it connecting to another crypt."

"Which leaves the only option being Lachyla itself."

Jalis nodded gravely. "The Blighted City."

"Well, we were considering a treasure hunt."

"That was before the dead showed up and we made a majority vote against returning."

"Uh-huh. And yet, here we are."

Again, they lapsed into silence, marked only by their steady footfalls. Oriken's mind wandered to nothing in particular but listening to the sound of Jalis's gentle breathing. He flinched when she grabbed his arm and pointed ahead. He peered into the gloom, silently cursing himself for letting his attention wander. Jalis drew Dusklight from its sheath with a soft sigh of steel, the black blade glinting in the lamp-light. Fifteen paces along the tunnel, softer shadows interrupted the deeper darkness.

"What do you see?" he whispered.

Jalis held her hand up and motioned for them to advance slowly. After several paces, Oriken could distinguish the dim shape of a round stone table, what appeared to be a set of shelves against the right-hand wall, and a narrow black recess to the left. A collection of objects were scattered upon the tabletop, and more items filled the shadowed shelves. He couldn't see any bodies lying around, either living, dead or something in between.

Slowly, quietly, he drew his sabre and passed the lamp to Jalis. He inched forward, grimacing as grit crunched beneath his boots. Jalis stayed close behind, and when they reached the table the glow from the lamp revealed three vertical beams marking a dead-end a short way ahead.

Oriken shifted his attention to the narrow alcove; as he made to approach it, Jalis stopped him with a hand on his arm. He raised an eyebrow at her, and she pointed to the floor. The footprints led directly into the alcove. He nodded in understanding and resumed his approach, treading carefully into the opening. With Jalis behind him, the light played upon two ascending stone steps several feet into the alcove, above which stood a heavy-duty wooden door. Reaching it, Oriken placed his ear to the wood and listened.

"I don't hear anything."

"Let's take a look around," Jalis said. "There might be something here that can help us appraise the situation."

Oriken stifled a sigh. "All right. But quickly."

They returned to the stone table and Jalis placed the lamp on its pitted surface. While she searched the shelves, Oriken scanned the contents of the table. The lamp guttered, causing shadows to flicker across the items. There was a cracked clay bowl, filled with dust-laden ore samples; a crude copper goblet, brittle and lined with rust; a small knife; a few worthless gem shards; and a leather-bound book, the edges of its pages brown and furrowed, the cover grimy with dead fungus.

"This is all junk," he said as he flipped the cover open. The pages were brittle but stayed intact. After the first couple of blank pages he found the title, scrawled in meticulous but faded calligraphy: *On The Nayture Of Mynerales.* Underneath the title was the author's name: *Cleve Hauverydh.* Oriken closed the book.

"Nothing much here either," Jalis said, moving to his side with something in her hand. "Except this statue, which I'm guessing is an idol of the goddess Valsana."

He glanced at the onyx figurine. "Yeah, that's her. You can tell by the exaggerated breasts and labia, and those big, sunken eyes. Ugly bitch, if you ask me. Not a patch on the likes of Khariali or Pheranisa. Now *those* are two deities I'd like to—" The oil lamp guttered, dimmed and snuffed out completely, casting the tunnel into total darkness. "Fuck."

"Oh, great," Jalis said. "I didn't bring a spare oil flask."

"Only one thing for it." Oriken inched across to the alcove until his boots struck the first step. He reached into the darkness. His fingers touched the rough wood and he climbed the two steps to stand before the door. He found the doorknob and pulled it towards him, but it didn't budge. When he pushed inwards, the door shifted, luckily with scarcely a sound. "I'm going in," he said. "Hold onto me." By way of answer, Jalis gave his arm a squeeze.

He kept a tight grip on the loaded crossbow as he grasped the doorknob and eased the door open. It swung inwards with a quiet creak.

So far, so good, he thought.

He took a step over the threshold, then another. Jalis's grip on his arm was slack but she stayed with him. He inched forwards one careful step after another, making his way along the wall.

"If we're somewhere beneath the city," he whispered, "then this could be anything. A castle keep, a treasury…"

"An oubliette," Jalis offered.

"Huh?"

"Shh."

Another step along the wall and the back of his hand touched something hard. He felt along the smooth edge and guessed it must be a table. He ran his hand over the dusty surface, inching along until he reached the table's corner. He angled around it and stepped slowly until he reached a wall, then wandered along it with his fingers tracing the stone.

His hip knocked into another obstacle and he froze as it shifted an inch across the floor. Something upon its surface rattled and began to roll. Jalis squeezed his arm.

"Shit," he whispered.

A moment later, the rolling sound stopped and he knew the object had teetered over the edge. Time slowed and his heart thudded, then the silence was shattered as the object clanged against the floor, and the metallic echo rang into the darkness.

Jalis dug her fingertips into his arm. "Oriken, you dolt!"

The crash resounded, echoing from the walls as the metal object spun upon the ground. And then silence returned – except for the hammering of his heart as he released a shaky breath.

"Sorry," he said.

Jalis didn't respond.

There was nothing to be done but resume course. He was thankful, at least, that his finger hadn't squeezed the trigger and released the loaded bolt. They only had a limited supply. *I knew I should've let Jalis lead the way. But no; big Oriken had to prove his worth, didn't he? Blundering in like a bull in an apothecary store! No more groping around blindly.* He nudged forwards. One inch. Two…

Click.

Oriken's gaze shot in the direction of the sound. An amber glow appeared in the air some twenty yards across the way, casting its lustre into the room. Stone

148

steps led up to a door that opened slowly to reveal the figure of a man standing at the threshold, a flaming torch in his hand.

Oriken frowned at the gladius on the stranger's hip, then locked his gaze with the man. Perhaps it was the light and shadows playing over the clean-shaven face, but the man's eyes seemed to be outlined with thin, dark circles.

The man's expression was calm. Confident. "You—"

Oriken's hand flashed up and he squeezed the trigger.

The crossbow bolt thudded into the man's jacket near his collar-bone. He grunted and glanced down at the protruding bolt, grabbed it, and plucked it out.

Jalis gasped. "What under the stars…"

The stranger sighed and cast them a cold smile. "If that's how they greet people in Alder's Folly, I'm all the more grateful for remaining in Lachyla." An unsettling, liquidy undertone trickled beneath each syllable, reminding Oriken of old Jerrick, the Peddler's nepenthe-smoking regular; watery, crackly, but not frail like Jerrick.

Oriken slotted the crossbow over his belt and drew his sabre. "What are you?"

The man smiled. "*Who* I am is Gorven Althalus. As to *what* I am…" He gave a brief chuckle. "Well, that, my uninvited friends, is a question that remains wide open for debate. What is *not* for debate, however, is that you will both accompany me from this cellar immediately." He half-turned, then paused to add, "And, please, *do* try to refrain from attacking me any further; it may not kill me, but I can assure you it does indeed rankle."

149

CHAPTER EIGHTEEN
ANOTHER BRANCH OF THE TREE

Their enigmatic host led them from the cellar along a series of well-kept corridors, up two separate flights of stairs with lacquered, dust-free banisters. Many doors were closed, but those that were open showed ornately-decorated rooms with faded portraits hanging over antiquated furniture. Oriken glimpsed strange devices to which he could assign no obvious purpose, and in one room he spotted an alchemical desk filled with alembics, retorts, a mortar and pestle, and a clay crucible. Another room was filled with shelves stacked floor to ceiling with ore samples, coloured stones, and some interesting items that could have been unearthed while mining: a polished skull, similar to but flatter and wider than a human's; a worn stone pictograph carved with runic symbols and displaying a creature covered in teeth, eyes and limbs; a dented copper helm of simple design that he guessed pre-dated the Days of Kings.

The building was fancy and gilded, but Oriken's intrigue was overshadowed by his concern for Dagra and the desire to not be in the place at all. Though the adventurer in him buzzed at the sight of the plethora of treasures, he kept it on a tight leash. The temptation to stick his sabre through Gorven's back was strong. He considered lopping the man's head from his shoulders as he led them through the elaborate house, but although their guide, captor or whatever he truly was, looked like a man and seemed amiable enough with his brief comments, Gorven had plucked the bolt from his chest as if it were nothing more than a splinter, and that, for Oriken, was that. Those feeble husks out in the graveyard were overwhelming in their number, but he wasn't prepared to get down and dirty with someone who brushed aside a wound that would have felled most normal men, especially when that man – or *creature* – had a hefty gladius at his disposal. Jalis's shake of her head told Oriken that she fully agreed with his unspoken assessment of Gorven Althalus, at least until they learned more about him.

Gorven led them into a long, ornate room. Several large windows to left and right overlooked an expanse of flat and domed rooftops. Lining the walls were paintings, sconces with unlit torches, and bookshelves filled with tomes. The floor was dominated by an elegant but worn rug. The cityscape to the east stretched away, capped by a roiling mass of stormclouds crawling inland. Through the western windows, jutting above the roofs were the battlements of a defensive wall. Between the wall's raised merlons, Oriken could see the horizon of the Echinus Ocean beneath a bright and clear sky.

Gorven closed the door they'd entered through, locked it and stuffed the key into a pocket of his leather breeches. "Wait here, please," he said as he strode across the room. "Do make yourselves comfortable." He swept an arm to encompass the various darkly-varnished chairs and tables and padded benches beneath the windows. "There are some riveting reads on the shelves, and a decanter of water in the corner, but I'm afraid we're all out of any other... refreshments." He swung about and strode towards a set of double doors.

"Hold on a minute!" Jalis's voice rang through the room. "Why don't you tell us how you knew—"

"Your concerns," Gorven said over his shoulder, "will be addressed momentarily." That faint crackly, liquidy sound beneath his voice added a menacing note to his words despite the apparent civility. "Now, please, be so kind as to extend me a moment of patience as I have done for you." With that, he opened the doors, strode through and pulled them shut behind him.

The slide and click of tumblers told Oriken they'd been locked inside. He ran to the doors, snatched the brass doorknobs and gave them a sharp tug, then slammed his shoulder into the crack between the doors. Reinforced with iron slats, the thick-set wood scarcely budged.

"Hey!" He slammed the flat of his fist upon a door.

"Oriken." Jalis crossed the distance to him. "Leave it."

Oriken swung on her. "The other door, I'll try that." He made to pass Jalis but she grabbed his arm and fixed him with a warning look.

"Cool your furnace. We'll get nowhere if you're running around like a caged cravant."

"We'll get nowhere if we can't leave this damned room, or this whole fucking rabbit warren of a house, for that matter."

Jalis released his arm. "Gorven said he'd return shortly. Let's give him ten minutes. Then, if he's not returned, you can try your best to smash the doors in, or the windows, if you prefer."

"The windows! Jalis, you're a genius. We've got the grappling hook. We can scale down. Ha! Thought he outsmarted us, did he?"

Jalis's expression was flat as she raised an eyebrow at him.

"Shit," he muttered. "No, we don't have the grappler, do we? We left it in those sodding shrubs."

"Mm-hm."

"So, what then? We just wait for a horde of undead to be unleashed into the room? Offer them all a nourishing cup of water as they swarm through the doors?" Oriken strode past Jalis and across the length of the room, his footfalls

151

muted upon the rug. When he reached the single door, he gave it the same treatment as he'd given the others, but to no avail.

"It's your call," he said as he whirled around. "But the longer we wait, the colder Dagra's trail gets. Gah! I could've carved that Gorven fellow up when his back was turned."

"I know," Jalis called. "I saw it on your face. But you were wise not to. If he knows something about Dagra, we won't get the information by slicing it out of him, not when doing so would only get us on his *rankled* side. Let's just sit down and wait. Conserve your strength." She walked over to a chair. "You might very well need it."

With a growl of frustration, he slammed his fist against the door, then took a deep deep breath. "Fine," he said. He strode to the chair beside Jalis and thrust himself onto it.

"I know how you feel," Jalis said tightly. "I'm right there with you."

Oriken paused, then placed his hand on her thigh and gave it a gentle squeeze. "I know."

The minutes stretched by as he waited restlessly, staring out of the window at the approaching storm, and still Gorven didn't show up.

"I've had enough of this," he said eventually. "We've given him long enough. It's time to act."

Jalis sat pensively, an arm resting on her lap, the other hand toying with the criss-crossed lace of her chemise. "All right," she said. "But I can't stop wondering, if Gorven intended us harm, why didn't he attack us back in the cellar room? He could at least have incapacitated us if he had the mind to."

"Hmph. Maybe so, but I still feel like we've been herded like sheep to a slaughterhouse."

"I can assure you," said a muffled voice from behind the double doors, "that is not the case at all." The echo of a key being turned resounded within the room, and the doors were pushed inward to reveal Gorven standing at the threshold, a hand on each doorknob, the tails of an unbuttoned dark-blue overcoat hanging to his thighs. He smiled wanly, his eyes on Oriken who was on his feet and striding towards him.

"Thank you for waiting," Gorven said, flicking a glance toward the still-seated Jalis. "My apologies for the precautions, but one can never be too careful, no? As you can see, I had to change my shirt since the other sported a bloodstained hole. I shall have to ask Krea to darn it. I do hope—"

Oriken was on him. Gorven's smile faltered as Oriken grabbed fistfuls of the man's fresh shirt and pulled him into the room. The doors swung shut and clicked together. Oriken bared his teeth and wrenched Gorven close.

"Not so amiable now, hey, feller? I'll tear you another new hole if you pull any shit like that again."

Gorven turned his face aside and grasped Oriken's shoulders, pushing him away until he was at arm's length.

Oriken balked. "What in the—" *Damn! The strength of the man!* Gorven exhibited scant effort in forcing him away; Oriken was no pushover, and he'd bested his fair share of men in arm wrestles back in the Lonely Peddler, but his arm lock was easily broken by Gorven as if doing so were no more strenuous than lifting a tankard of ale.

"I advise you to not get too close," Gorven warned. His smile dropped completely. "Just being in this place, you're putting yourselves at unnecessary and foolish risk."

Jalis stepped up beside them. "We're here to find our friend. We know you have him. It would be in everybody's best interests if you hand him back to us."

"Yeah," Oriken said as Gorven released him. Reluctantly, he did likewise. "We don't care who you are or what you're doing in Lachyla. When we have Dagra we'll be gone, and you can forget we were ever here."

"I'm afraid it won't be quite that simple," Gorven said as he smoothed the creases in his shirt. "Ah, here he comes now." Footsteps sounded beyond the room, stopping outside the doors. Gorven – ever the host – pulled one of them open to reveal a discomfited but very much alive Dagra.

Oriken and Jalis blurted his name in unison, breathing sighs of relief at the sight of their friend as Gorven ushered him in with a hand upon Dagra's shoulder. When the door closed behind him, Dagra regarded his friends with a curiously solemn expression.

No jewel, Oriken noted with a frown. "What in the Pit's going on, Dag? We should be several hours north of here by now. You know that, right?" He clicked his fingers before Dagra's face. "Just nod if you can hear me, you little shit! I swear I've never been so pissed with you in all our years." The urge to grab him and shake some sort of reaction from him was almost overwhelming, but Oriken managed to resist it.

Dagra held his gaze, then shrugged. "I was at camp. The two of you were sleeping. Then I was here and…" His brow furrowed as he regarded Gorven. "And Gorven was there, telling me to follow him." He shrugged. "And now I'm here. I don't remember much else."

Oriken raised his eyebrows. "Uh huh? You seem to know your way around well enough." He edged his face closer to Dagra and looked him in the eye. "How's that?"

"I can't tell you. I sort of recall some bits from before, but it wasn't me."

Jalis held her hands out in confusion. "What does that even mean?"

"How can you stand there so casual?" Oriken demanded. "You had us worried sick, and here you are swanning around with some sort of gro…" He waved a hand dismissively towards Gorven.

"Grotesquerie?" Gorven offered.

"That's the one."

Gorven sighed. "It's been quite a while since I was last called one of those."

153

"Well, you better get used to it," Oriken snapped, stabbing a finger towards him. "You'll be—"

"Oriken," Jalis warned. "Remember that furnace?"

He shot her a stony look. "Fine, fine." Turning his attention back to Dagra, he said, "You took over my shift, then you buggered off without a word. Why would you do that?"

"Please," Gorven interjected. "Don't be so hard on your friend. He's still waking up."

"Huh?"

"That's right. He sleepwalked his way here." With a small shrug, he added, "With a little help from me, of course."

With a derisory sneer, Oriken folded his arms. "Sleepwalking now, you say?"

Gorven gave a curt nod. "He's not well."

Oriken barked a mirthless laugh. "You don't fucking say?" He glanced down at Dagra. "And where in the name of all that's fucking unholy is the jewel? Hm?"

Dagra's surprise looked genuine. "It was in your pack."

"Well, it's not there now."

"I'm telling you," Dagra insisted with a perplexed shake of his head, "I don't remember—"

"You've already said that!" Oriken snapped in Dagra's face. He bunched his fists, barely resisting the urge to lay his friend out before beating Gorven Althalus to death.

"Forgive me for putting another word in," Jalis said caustically as she fixed Dagra with a level look, "but you don't seem overly concerned about any of this. In fact, my bearded friend, sleepwalking or not, you don't seem quite *you* at all."

Dagra's confused gaze turned to Gorven, who regarded him attentively.

Gorven's black-rimmed gaze passed between the three of them. "So, not only did you steal something you had no right to, but now it seems you've also lost it. If only we had been aware earlier that you had removed it from the tomb. We assumed it was still in your possession, hence bringing your friend to us for you to follow."

"Hey." Oriken brandished an accusing finger, first at Gorven, then at Dagra. "What are the two of you playing at here? It's time we got some answers, and quickly. If Dagra doesn't have the jewel"—he squared on Gorven—"and *you* don't have it"—he flicked a hand at Jalis beside him—"and I'm sure as cowshit that *we* don't have it, then who the fuck does? And who in the rutting, fucking Underland is *we* and *us* you keep referring to?"

Soft footfalls padding down the corridor beyond the doors paused any further discussion. One of the doors opened and in stepped a young girl, scarcely in her teenage years.

"Must you all talk so loud?" she piped in a weary and irritated voice as she planted her hands on her hips. She fixed her glare onto Oriken. "What does a lady have to do around here to get her beauty sleep?"

"Ah, Krea," Gorven said. "My apologies for disturbing you. It seems our new arrival and his companions have brought us an unforeseen and somewhat disturbing complication."

"Hmph," Krea declared by way of answer. She circled around Dagra, eyeing his unkempt hair. "You're not as tall as you think you are, you know?" She seemed oblivious that her own dark hair, pulled tightly from her forehead and clasped into a tuft at the crown to fountain to her shoulders, scarcely reached the top of Dagra's head. With a scowl that encompassed all their dirt-streaked and dusty footwear, she added,"And do you *have* to trample this *filth* through my house?" With a haughty gasp, she turned her scrutiny on Oriken.

He stared incredulously back at the girl, if indeed that was what she was; he'd seen a few under-developed women, skin the colour of copper, apparently from somewhere over the southern sea, brought on boats to ply their high-priced services in the brothels and harbours of Brancosi Bay. But the skin of the girl before Oriken was not coppery but pallid. Like Gorven, thin lines of black were beneath her eyelids, and her voice had the same faint, crackly, watery undertone like a hushed echo from deep within her.

Krea's lips were full, her eyes the lightest of blues. A single silver ring adorned one toe on her bare feet. She was slim but toned, which added to the notion that she might be older than her voice and stature suggested. Her pleated dress had a pinched waist and a square neckline, low enough to sufficiently show that her buds were indeed in bloom.

"You, on the other hand, are quite the strapping one. Inquisitive, too." She tilted her head and pursed her lips. "Hmm. I like that."

"Uh…"

Gorven cleared his throat – which made those weird sub-vocal noises all the worse – and said, "Allow me to introduce you to my daughter… although, after a certain amount of time, such a term does become quite moot." He gestured toward the three of them. "Krea, this is Jalis Falconet and, ah, Oriken and Dagra."

"Yeah," Oriken nodded curtly at the girl, still taken aback by her forwardness. He pinched the brim of his hat in greeting, despite feeling not at all in the mood for introductions. "So, what's with all the eye-liner around here?"

Krea flashed him a snarling grin. Nonplussed, he frowned at the gums around her teeth; where most folk's would be pink, hers were as dark as the paint around her eyes. And it wasn't just the flesh immediately arching her teeth, like some townsfolk he could name who had the hygiene level of ditch rats; no, Krea's entire gums were black. Not withered, just black. Her teeth, though, were as white as Jalis's.

155

Jalis was staring, too, but not at Krea, at Gorven. "Again!" she exclaimed. "How do you know my family name? What sort of information have you been squeezing out of our friend?"

Krea thrust her chin up at Gorven. "You mentioned complications, but I don't see any. You predicted his friends would follow. Do you really need assistance to deal with them?"

Jalis's hands went to her daggers. "*Dealing* with us?"

"Now, look here," Oriken said to Gorven, whose eyes were fixed on Krea. "You too, little lady. I don't know what sort of sick set-up you've got going on in this house, but we came for two things – our friend and the jewel. We got one back. Now, where's the other?"

Krea nodded to her so-called father as if in response to unspoken words. "I see," she said, then turned a stony look on Oriken. "You mean to tell us that you do *not* have my family's burial stone?"

Jalis's eyes widened. "Your family? Oh, this is getting ridiculous. Are you trying to tell us—"

"I'm trying to tell you nothing, girl," Krea snapped. "I *am* telling you that your meddling in our affairs could have dire consequences, the likes of which you would not comprehend."

"Wait." Oriken was scarcely keeping up with the shifts in the conversation. To Krea, he said, "Am I understanding this right? You're…"

The girl pressed her lips together. "You catch on quickly, don't you? Handsome you might be, but thick as pigshit. Yes, I am Krea Chiddari."

Oriken's black disposition sank deeper. *Great. Just what we needed. Another bloody Chiddari.*

The moment hung in the air as he shared a look with Jalis. When she shook her head, he turned to Dagra, but the bearded one hardly seemed to realise he was awake – which, apparently, he wasn't, at least not fully.

"You took the stone," Krea said accusingly. "It belongs to us, so you can drop the attitude and tell us where it is."

Oriken shrugged. "Don't ask *me*. Your daddy here seems to be the font of all knowledge. Ask *him*."

Krea's lips pressed to a line as she glared at Oriken. Perhaps it was meant to look menacing, but it seemed that she was one step away from throwing a tantrum.

"For the stars' sake," Oriken sighed. "This is the Blighted City. You're not supposed to be here. How were we to know anyone was living in Lachyla?"

Gorven chuckled. "Living. Now *there's* another word that's an eternal subject of hot debate."

"What does that mean?" Jalis asked.

Gorven ignored the question. "We can at least rule Dagra out. The stone was still at your camp when he left."

"What?" Oriken glared at each occupant of the room as he considered Gorven's words. There was only one explanation. *Demelza*, he thought. *That double-crossing waif pulled the burlap right over our eyes, snuck into camp after Dagra wandered off and before Jalis woke.*

"All right." There was an edge to Jalis's voice as she looked hard at Gorven. "I've had enough of this. How in the Pit do you know what happened at our camp?"

"Because," Krea spat, nudging her head towards Dagra, "that's when Gorven became aware of your scraggly dwarf."

"Hey!" Dagra protested, though he still looked confused.

"Krea, please," Gorven chided. To Oriken, he said, "What I sensed was faint at first, but, while Dagra and you conversed, I discerned a little of your words and actions. Not enough, unfortunately. Of course, by that time Dagra was not entirely his usual self, entering the second stage of—"

"This is nonsense," Oriken sneered at both the father and the daughter. "If you can see so damned much, you can find the jewel yourselves."

Krea bared her teeth. "I'm getting tired of your insolence, you little upstart. You stole my ancestor's burial stone, you have the nerve to act as if it belongs to you, and now you seek to test us? How *dare* you enter our home and speak to us with disdain?"

"Upstart? *Little?* Listen, missy—"

Oriken wasn't entirely sure how he ended up there, but, the next moment, he was on his back. His cheek smarted like it had been struck by a hammer.

"What on shitting Verragos just happened?" he muttered to himself.

A hand swam into view above him through the fading stars; it was Jalis, offering to help him up. He clasped her wrist and groaned his way to his feet, glancing around in confusion and wincing at the pain that blossomed over his face.

"Next time," Krea said, planting her hands on her hips, "I'll have you over my knee."

Oriken's jaw dropped. "You *hit* me?"

She flashed him a black-gummed grin. "Did you enjoy it?"

I should put you *over* my *knee*, he thought. *Teach you some stars-be-damned manners.* But then he remembered Gorven and the crossbow bolt. *I'd never be knocked on my arse by a girl. Jalis, maybe, but not someone the size of Krea.* He flinched as her hand swept up to flick at her hair, a glint of amusement in her blue, dark-lined eyes.

Oriken snatched his hat from the rug and took a step backwards. Resting his palm upon the pommel of his sabre, he nodded knowingly at Krea.

"You're unnatural," he said. "Both of you. Like those corpses. This city had more survivors, didn't it? Not just those villagers out on the heath. Some of the infected didn't die, did they? And you're descended from them." He fixed the hat onto his head and squinted beneath the brim at Krea. "You're blighted."

She raised an eyebrow. "How astute, dear outlander. But you're only half-right."

"Go on," Jalis urged.

Krea shrugged. "We are, as you say, blighted. That much is true."

"But," Gorven added, "we are not descendants of the survivors from that bloody time."

Krea's amusement slipped to an emotionless mask. "We *are* those survivors."

Oriken stared at her. "That's not possible."

A roll of thunder resounded, followed by a flash of lightning. Dagra held a hand to his head and wandered to the nearest chair. As he sank onto it, the aged wood groaned in protest and he let out a shuddering sigh.

Jalis moved towards him. "Dagra?"

He waved her away with a feeble flap of his hand. "I'm all right, lass."

"Cowshit," Oriken said.

"Ahem." Gorven moved to stand beside Dagra. "Why don't we utilise this juncture to move the conversation elsewhere? The aesthetics in this room aren't quite as hospitable as they once were." He looked down at Dagra. "Besides, there is someone I'd like you to meet."

A louder crack of thunder punctuated Gorven's words. Oriken glanced through the windows at the darkening cityscape, acutely aware that Krea had drifted closer to him.

"Who?" Dagra asked. "Why?"

"A dear friend of mine," Gorven replied. "We believe he may better help you adjust than I or Krea are capable of."

Jalis frowned. "Help us to adjust?"

"Not you." Gorven's gaze encompassed Jalis and Oriken. "Not yet, at least; and, I hope, never. No, only Dagra needs to hear what Sabrian has to say."

"Why only him?" Oriken demanded. "You said we were putting ourselves at risk by being here. If that's true, then why did you bring Dagra here? You knew we'd follow. Your words and your actions don't exactly support each other."

Gorven loosed a small sigh as he plucked at a button on his coat. "Yes, I had hoped you would bring the burial stone. But, either way, I couldn't leave Dagra out there. That would have been entirely remiss of me."

"Really?" Oriken looked at him flatly. "Okay, so who's this Sabrian character? Because if he's going to prove as useful as either of you two jesters"—he glanced to Jalis—"then I say we cut our losses and get out of here, jewel or no jewel."

A shadow fell over Gorven's features. "You are, of course, free to leave if you please. But I'm afraid my words and my actions make perfect sense. You see, for the two of you"—his gaze flicked from Oriken to Jalis—"there is indeed risk in remaining in Lachyla. For Dagra, sadly, the risk is passed."

158

"Why?" Oriken looked at Dagra, but his friend just stared forlornly at the floor.

"Because," Krea said, "Dagra is going nowhere. He's one of us now." She flashed Oriken a mischievous smile. "And if *you* continue to test my patience, dear outlander, I'm sure I could find a place in Lachyla for you, too."

CHAPTER NINETEEN
BURDEN OF DECISION

Adri settled into her seat at the far end of the longhall's table and waited with mild irritation and growing concern for her sister to arrive. Minutes later, Eriqwyn strode through the open door.

"Why have you called a meeting of the council?" Adri asked, her voice travelling across the room. "You should have consulted me first."

"There was no time, sister," Eriqwyn said as she paced the length of the hall towards Adri.

"What is this about?"

Stopping behind the chair adjacent to Adri, Eriqwyn slung the pack from her shoulder and placed it on the table with a soft thud. Her face was lined with tension. "I'll show you before the others arrive. Adri, I apologise for calling a meeting without consulting you, but the urgency of the matter gave me no choice; what I'm about to show you warrants such a bypassing as decreed in the Founding Laws."

Adri pressed her lips together, but she felt the weight of her sister's words as Eriqwyn unbuckled the pack to reveal a wrapped bundle. Folding back the cloth, Adri's stomach clenched as she stared at the object within. In a tight voice, she said, "Is that what I think it is?"

"I believe so. It certainly matches the descriptions from the family archives, don't you think?"

With a glance to the door, Adri saw the first of the council members approaching. "Put it away!" she hissed. "And not a word until all are present."

Eriqwyn took her seat and lay the pack on the floor at her feet as Kerysa and Fahrein, the senior woodworker and metalsmith, entered the longhall and paused at the foot of the table.

"Lady." Fahrein dipped his head in respect to Adri. "Why have we been summoned with such short notice?"

Kerysa's voice was terse as she said, "This is most untimely. I was busy making shafts for the hunters. It will—"

"It will be handled quite capably by your workers, I don't doubt," Adri said. Behind the two, Caneli, the head physician, peered around the door and Adri motioned for her to enter. "Take your seats, please. And no questions until I and the First Warder have addressed the council."

Ten minutes passed. Adri sat in brooding silence, considering the implications of what she had seen in her sister's pack, her voice tense as she bade each council member to take a seat as they arrived. All but two were now present, their hushed whispers circulating around the table. As the rotund Blachord arrived and eased himself into one of the few vacant chairs, Adri's gaze swept across the gathered assemblage. Their expressions ranged from concern to annoyance on all except Amiryn and Shade; the Priestess Superior of Valsana sat across the table from Eriqwyn, a serene expression on her face, while the seamstress casually regarded her peers, her sensuality apparent even as she skilfully masked any other emotions.

"Where is Onwin?" Adri asked of the assemblage.

Kerysa snorted in derision. "I swear that hunter thinks he owns the village."

Adri silently agreed with the woodworker's assessment, but swept it aside. "Has anyone seen him?" Blank expressions and shakes of heads were the only responses. The image of the object in Eriqwyn's pack remained fixed in Adri's mind. *I need to get this underway*, she thought. "Then we will have to begin without—"

A shuffling of material and the scrunch of boots pulled her attention to the doorway to see Onwin sauntering into the room. Adri's eyes followed him as he made his way to a seat and dropped himself into it with a grunt.

"Lady," he said with an abrupt nod as he caught her gaze.

Adri's irritation at the man's indifferent attitude was overshadowed by the need to hear her sister's news. Without responding to his token acknowledgement, she sat straight in her high-backed chair and cleared her throat. A hush fell across the room as all heads turned her way. In a clear voice, she said, "This meeting was called by our First Warder, and, it seems, for good reason. Those of you who are upset about being summoned will forget those concerns with what you – and I – are about to hear. Without any of the usual preamble, I give the table to Eriqwyn to give us the details." Adri glanced sideways to her sister and gave a brief nod.

Eriqwyn drew the bundle from her pack and rose from her chair, her hard gaze flicking among the attendants and landing on Adri as she said, "There are outlanders in the area."

Outlanders! Adri stopped herself from blurting the word out, even as several of the council members did so. There had been no sightings of outlanders in the area for generations. Gasps and murmurs washed along the table amid utterances of consternation.

"Quiet!" she called. "Let the First Warder speak."

With the disturbance quelled, Eriqwyn continued. "They entered where only outlanders would have the heathen nerve to tread. They are inside Lachyla."

As another wave of disbelief issued from the assemblage, Onwin shot from his seat and planted his fists upon the table. "They must be dealt with! Let me take—"

"I will *let* you take your seat," Adri snapped. "And I will ask you to not interrupt while someone else addresses the table."

"My apologies, Lady." Onwin's tone was wholly unapologetic. With a growling sigh, he reluctantly returned to his seat.

Adri's eyes were back on Eriqwyn, and she didn't miss the venom in her sister's gaze as she pulled it away from the recalcitrant hunter.

"How many?" Kerysa asked from the end of the table.

Eriqwyn held her hand up to halt any further questions. "There are three. Yes, that is a number we of Minnow's Beck know well when we look to the Founding Oak in the colder seasons. Three then and three now. But, this time, it is worse. Our ancestors never gave those three the chance to enter the Forbidden Place, but these have. I only learned of this after the fact, while they camped on Graegaredh Knot. I watched one of the outlanders leave his watch and walk away; this gave me the opening to enter their camp and take what they removed from the graveyard. Reluctantly, I brought it back to the village, but not before waiting to witness the remaining two wake and follow their companion back towards Lachyla, likely for more treasures. I believe they will still be in there now." As Eriqwyn paused, the withheld reactions of the delegates erupted around the table.

"Let 'em rot in there, that's what I say!" Blachord declared from his seat opposite Kerysa.

"I'll take hunters to the entrance," Onwin growled. "Wait for them to leave and ambush them. We need to ensure that they don't get the chance—"

"*You* need to stop making decisions like a Lord of the Manor," Eriqwyn said. "Unless you would like me to strongly suggest to the *Lady* of the Manor that we assign a new hunters delegate?" Onwin bristled but stayed quiet, and Eriqwyn flashed him a tight smile. "No? Good." She turned to Adri. "You have heard all I know."

Adri's thoughts were racing, but she kept her equilibrium. "How did you learn of their presence?" she asked.

Eriqwyn stifled a mirthless laugh. "Demelza, of all things. I intercepted her on her night wanders and she told me she'd been in the outlanders' camp."

Another babble of murmurs crossed the table as the council members frowned at the news.

"Do you think she is in league with them?" Fahrein asked.

"Of course she's not!" Caneli exclaimed. "Why must everyone be so immediately untrusting around here?"

Onwin scoffed. "That's easy for you to say. You're not the one who has to deal with threats to the village."

"That may be true," Caneli spat back, her pale cheeks gaining a red glow. "I'm a physician, not a hunter; I'm the one who stitches up the fool who attacks a bear in its own den!"

Onwin glowered but looked away from the physician, his hand absently touching his chest.

"That's enough," Adri said. "It seems to me that time is of the essence, and while the council bickers among itself, we get nothing done." She flicked a grim glance across all eight council members. "The First Warder has more to share with us, which you may consider graver than the news of the outlanders. Eriqwyn?"

Eriqwyn placed the wrapped bundle upon the table and pulled the material aside. Stunned silence was the first reaction from the delegates as Adri kept her eyes on them, then jaws dropped as each began to realise what lay before them.

Kerysa turned a fearful gaze to Eriqwyn. "Is that a…"

"A deadstone," Eriqwyn said drily. "Yes."

The senior woodworker's face turned sickly. Loosing an involuntary gag, Kerysa rose from her chair and made her way unsteadily to the longhall's entrance.

Adri allowed her to step outside without request. *I know how she feels. The sight of the thing makes me sick to the stomach, as well.*

"How…" Blachord rubbed at his stubbled cheek, unable to finish the thought.

"This was foreseen in the stars," Amiryn remarked calmly.

Adri caught the priestess's gaze, but before she could respond, Eriqwyn cut in. "Foreseen, was it?" She cast Amiryn a venomous look. "By whom?"

"Why, by the mortal voice of the goddess, of course."

"You," Eriqwyn stated flatly.

Amiryn inclined her head. "Last time I checked, I was still the Priestess Superior."

"Yet you didn't consider sharing the information with, oh, I don't know, *the rest of us?*"

Amiryn smiled. "My child, the goddess imparts her knowledge in cryptic ways, which are not always able to be understood until after the fact."

Eriqwyn bristled. "Then it is no use to me. Do you have a point about being gifted with this incredible insight? Anything that could actually assist us in what we will have to do?"

The priestess closed her eyes and gave an almost imperceptible shake of her head. "Valsana watches and listens, First Hunter. I advise you to be mindful of how you speak to her chosen." Amiryn swept her gaze across the council members. "The goddess has spoken. She has issued Minnow's Beck with a test."

As Eriqwyn took her seat and glowered at the deadstone, Blachord said to the priestess. "What is this test?"

163

Amiryn's smile returned. "Did we appease Valsana's will when last the outlanders came this way, all those years ago? We did, and the Founding Oak is our reminder. Decades later, it was the goddess's will to allow a deadstone into the village, and it is her will once more. We appeased her then by returning the stone from whence it came. Today, Valsana visits both tasks upon us at once, asking us again to prove our loyalty. And so we must."

A gasp of annoyance escaped Eriqwyn's lips. "The unfortunate occurrence with the first deadstone was our ancestors' foolhardiness; it was not meant to happen, and I don't believe it was the will of Valsana, only the will of desperate and grieving parents."

"The goddess spoke through their actions," Amiryn said. "It is not for us to question her intentions."

Kerysa wandered back into the room and meekly took her seat, glancing at Adri with a haggard expression. Adri nodded to her, and the woodworker gave a silent sigh of relief.

Fahrein's brow furrowed and he looked to Adri. "What say you, Lady? What are we to do about the outlanders and that accursed object?"

"I want each of you to give their concise opinion before I make my own, as is the purpose of such a meeting." Adri turned to regard the priestess.

"The goddess has spoken," Amiryn said. "We must do as our ancestors did before us."

Adri's gaze drifted along to Onwin. "What say you for the hunters?"

"Hm." Onwin folded his arms. "I say the Priestess Superior has the right of it. The stone must be returned to its crypt, and the outlanders must be dealt with as it is written in the Founding Laws."

Adri nodded and shifted her eyes to the senior metalsmith.

Fahrein looked troubled as he slowly said, "My conscience is reminding me that these are people we're talking about. I'm not speaking against Valsana's will, but casting a vote to murder them does not sit well with me. As for that deadstone"—his lips turned down in distaste—"of course we can't keep it here. Not after what happened last time."

"What do you propose we do about the outlanders?" Adri asked.

Fahrein considered the question, then sighed. "We can't risk them leaving with the knowledge of our whereabouts. Perhaps we could, I don't know, imprison them?"

"Or make them live among us," Kerysa offered from beside him with a shrug. The colour was coming back to her face. "Somehow make it so they can't leave. Hobble them, maybe. I don't like the taste of killing anyone either, and we should consider that our laws are not theirs; how would they know that they are committing a crime punishable by death? If the Lord of the village had been aware when the first stone was brought here by one of ours, *that* one would have been hanged under the boughs until dead if events had unfolded differently. But outlanders are not folk of Minnow's Beck. And consider if the situation were reversed; what if we wandered into their domain? Would we expect to be shown leniency, or would we happily abide by their laws if such laws decreed our death? Somehow I doubt even the revered priestess would prefer to be hanged or have her severed head set into the boughs of a tree rather than her life be spared."

Hobble. Adri mulled the point over. *Would crippling someone and holding them captive for the rest of their mortal days be any better than sending them swiftly into the next life?* She turned her attention to the farmer delegate across from Kerysa. "Blachord? What say you?"

Blachord sniffed. "Aye. Well. I reckon we all know what needs to be done, whether we like it or not. And I don't doubt some folk *do* like the notion of a bit of violence, but I'm not one of 'em." He looked along the table to Eriqwyn. "Still, if you're needin' a fellow of fortitude to join you, you'd do a lot worse than my man Lingrey. He's as stout as they come, an' well-weathered with it. A farmhand he may be, but a finer man you'll not find by your side at such a time."

"On that note, I'd recommend Tan," Fahrein offered. "He's a hardy young lad and as strong as a bull." He caught Onwin's glance beside him, and shrugged. "I'm just saying."

"If you're recruiting for the task," Onwin said in a gruff voice, "you'd best take some o' the hunters. What skill have smithies and pig-pushers when it comes to dispatching dangerous creatures?"

"Ah," Eriqwyn said flatly. "And how much hands-on experience do the hunters have in killing anything more than the animals of the wild? No more than any other in this village. I want people who are sturdy and reliable. And, besides, Minnow's Beck needs its hunters should I and whoever accompanies me fail. I have two Warders at my disposal, and yet I will take only one. There are other considerations beyond throwing our full force into an uncertain situation with an unknowable outcome. The outlanders are not the only danger within those walls." She looked pointedly at Onwin. "You may appoint one hunter to accompany me."

"Then I choose myself."

Eriqwyn pressed her lips together and glanced to the door, clearly impatient to bring the discussion to an end.

Adri turned to the seamstress sat beside Blachord. "Shade, you haven't said a word yet. Do you have anything to add?"

The dark-haired woman pursed her lips, her brown eyes agleam as always, seemingly with some private joke. "I may have," she said after a moment as her eyes flashed past Caneli to Eriqwyn. "For now, I acquiesce to the desires of the First Warder."

"Very well," Adri said. "Caneli?"

The physician drew in a breath and let it out. "Does it matter what I think? You've got two over there who are all for murder without a second thought, and you've got three others who would rather not cast such a vote but will go along with it anyway." Caneli sneered in derision and looked pointedly at Adri. "Do what you must; you don't need a unanimous decision here, but I want it on record that I find this abhorrent. That you are even considering murder or mutilation as a means to sustain our village's paranoid and fearful survival…" She lowered her eyes and shook her head. "Go and do the goddess's work, but it won't be the goddess who patches you up afterwards." Resignedly, she added, "I will be here to tend the wounded as best I can, as always."

The assemblage remained silent. None offered their agreement nor voiced their disapproval, though Adri sensed shame from those at the far end of the table. She did not need to ask Eriqwyn for her thoughts, yet procedure insisted she must. She held her sister's gaze. "Eri?"

Eriqwyn's face was resolute. "The safety of Minnow's Beck is paramount. Thanks to Demelza, the outlanders know where to find us; yes, she admitted as much to me. They cannot return to their homes with such knowledge. Demelza should have withdrew as soon as she spotted them, but she did not; a good hunter knows that the longer you hide in the shadows observing an animal, the greater your chance of being noticed, and that's what happened." She sighed. "Perhaps I would have settled for retrieving the deadstone and returning it to the graveyard, but Demelza's ineptitude has exposed our presence and therefore sealed the outlanders' fates."

"Then it's settled." The knot of responsibility in Adri's stomach tightened. "Blachord, Fahrein, you may tell Lingrey and Tan"—she glanced at Eriqwyn, who gave a curt nod—"to prepare themselves and join the First Warder on the village green with due haste. Onwin, you also. The rest of you may return to your work. And, please, *no* rumour mongering! I don't want panic spreading through the village. Dismissed."

As the council members left their seats and filed toward the door, Shade stepped behind Eriqwyn and bent to whisper in her ear before drifting away to follow the others from the longhall. Glowering at the woman's back, Eriqwyn rose, crossed to the heavy door and pushed it closed.

"What did Shade say to you?" Adri asked.

Eriqwyn strode to the end of the oaken table, planted her hands on the lacquered surface and stared down its length at Adri. "The woman is always cryptic and irritating. She apparently has information she didn't want to voice in front of the council, and will wait to speak with me on the green." She flicked a hand towards the deadstone on its cloth wrapping. "As if I have the time to listen to her nonsense."

"Indeed. She weaves intimations like silk on a spinning wheel. See what she has to say, but don't let her waste your time. Which of the Warders will you take?"

Eriqwyn considered the question. "Linisa came off night duty this morning and will be tired. I will leave her here with her sister. I will take Wayland."

Adri nodded. "He's a fine Warder. I would also like Demelza to accompany you." She lifted a hand to silence her sister's imminent protest. "Please, Eri, give her this chance to redeem herself."

Eriqwyn's eyes locked sombrely with Adri's. "Why on the goddess's green heath would you ask this of me? The girl has the brains of a balukha." She gave a derisive snort. "And I do not trust her."

"Many may not like Demelza, but I do," Adri said, keeping her voice calm though she felt anything but. "Her weakness is her upbringing, which was no fault of her own. She could be a good hunter one day."

Eriqwyn began to pace the hall. "That day may never come for her," she snapped. "The potential danger she has brought upon us is a crime in itself, in accordance with the Founding Laws." She spun on her heel and pointed at Adri. "And you of all people must know what the laws say about committing such a profound error."

"Well I do."

Eriqwyn resumed her pacing.

With a gasp of irritation, Adri fixed her with a scowl. "Will you stand still? You forget yourself, little sister. There are punishments in the old laws fit for ones who show a lack of respect for the Lady of the Manor, too. You of all people must know this."

Eriqwyn held Adri's gaze, then sighed and gave a curt nod. "Of course. Forgive me. This entire situation stinks, and it has me on edge. Do you know how tempted I was to kill that girl while we were out on the heath? To stop myself, I sent her back to the village ahead of me."

"You showed wisdom in that, and exercised patience."

"As I would with any docile creature. The only difference is that the animals usually end up dead."

Adri gestured to Eriqwyn's chair and bade her sit, which Eriqwyn reluctantly did. "It is well that you didn't kill her," Adri said. "That would only have exacerbated the situation. Besides, Demelza's skills are undeveloped and may eventually prove to be an asset to our community."

Eriqwyn pursed her lips and seemed to be considering saying more, but didn't press the issue. Instead, she eyed the deadstone on the table between them. Her distaste was obvious.

"Only once since the curse of the goddess has one of these entered the village," Eriqwyn said. "There are still some elders alive who can attest to how the last occurrence turned out. I will not be remembered as the bringer of a second such tragedy to the people of Minnow's Beck."

Adri shook her head. She found her eyes drawn to the dark seed at the heart of the translucent, silver-banded jewel. A shiver touched her skin beneath the thin tunic and she rubbed her hands over her arms. "Bringing the deadstone here was the right decision, Eri. You could not return it to the graveyard while the outlanders are still at large." Leaning forward to scrutinise the silver band, she added, "The inscriptions tell us which family's vault it was taken from. You can return it to its rightful place when the outlanders are gone." As her eyes found the family name etched into the silver, she said in a low voice, "The goddess indeed shows her wit today."

"Adri," Eriqwyn said levelly, "you know I love you and respect your position, but time is of the essence, in both cases. I should take the stone and deal with the outlanders simultaneously." She sighed impatiently. "The outlander who left their camp first was in no state for a fight; I could have taken him easily at any time and returned to slit the throats of the others, then gone directly to the graveyard with the stone. I could have kept the knowledge to myself, save for Demelza. Perhaps I should have done so. I have a feeling it would have saved us all a lot of hardship."

Adri raised an eyebrow. "And how would you have entered the Forbidden Place?"

Eriqwyn paused before answering. "Demelza says the outlanders have raised the portcullis."

"Damn," Adri hissed.

Eriqwyn nodded grimly. "Three tasks. Return the stone, dispatch the outlanders, and lower the gate."

"I can't help but agree with Caneli that we're not in the habit of mercilessly butchering people. I wish there were another way, but Kerysa and Fahrein's suggestions are little better."

"I won't take any pleasure in what has to be done, Adri. You know that. The success of Minnow's Beck lies in its peace, but also in its ruthlessness. As your First Warder, my charge is the protection of the village, and maintaining its preservation."

"As it is my charge. But these are the first outlanders we've encountered in generations. If it wasn't for the tales and archives—"

"And the skulls that adorn the oak."

Adri inclined her head. "My point is, it's been over a hundred years. For all we know, few people remain across all of Himaera."

Eriqwyn scoffed. "You don't believe that. The goddess's curse stops at the graveyard's limits. We are testament to that fact. If we live, then the curse surely began and ended with King Mallak. There is likely a thriving civilisation up north. Would you have an army of thousands descend on us, come for all the deadstones in Lachyla? They would take them back and disperse them throughout the land. Can you imagine the chaos that would reign unchecked?"

Adri furrowed her brow. Eriqwyn's words struck some troubling chords. "No, I would not want that." She absently turned to the multi-faceted gemstone and gazed into its depths, again finding the fragmented black core, and at once felt both a sense of repulsion and a sense of attraction towards the shadowed nucleus.

Cursed thing, she thought, disgusted at herself for the ambivalent sensations the deadstone evoked in her. *Eri is right; this abomination cannot stay here a moment longer than necessary.* She pulled her gaze away and found her sister regarding her.

"Things must be returned to normal, for the safety of our people," Adri said. She could not show lenience. To keep the outlanders as prisoners would be a waste of resources, but they could not be allowed to return north. She drew a breath and slowly released it. "Return the stone to its vault. As for any potential outside threat to Minnow's Beck, deal with it as you see fit."

CHAPTER TWENTY
OUTSIDER WITHIN

"Sit," Krea ordered from across the small room.

Oriken obeyed. The luxurious couch enveloped him, knocking his hat forward onto his face. He eased himself from the deep cushions and perched upon the front of the seat, twisting the hat back into place.

Why in the world did I agree to stay here and let the others go swanning off to see this Sabrian fellow? He had a vain hope that Krea might offer them a burial jewel that wasn't the one belonging to her family; if not, then all they'd be getting for their efforts was the ten percent for non-retrieval.

"You said you had something important to show me," he prompted.

"Mmm." Krea padded across the doe-hide rug to stand before him. She gave a disappointed sigh and took the hat from his head. "Look at you," she chided, scrunching her nose. "You are a dishevelled mess, and in serious need of a bath."

"Hey!" He snatched for his hat, but Krea deftly tucked it behind her.

"It's impolite to wear your headdress indoors. Don't you know that? What sort of backwater community dragged you up, Oriken of Eyndal? Hm?"

Perplexed, he watched as she tossed his hat across the room. It arced through the air and landed neatly on the peg of an empty coat-stand, circled around it, then settled into place.

"I, uh—"

"Exactly," Krea agreed as she placed her hands over his shirt. Her fingertips found the crook between chest and shoulder and she pushed him back, forcing him to drop into the voluminous couch. "Don't fret, my dear outlander, I will draw you a bath afterwards."

Oriken balked. *Gods in the Void! Afterwards what?*

She leaned in to him, a huskiness entering her voice as she added, "Complete with scented oils."

Oh, stars. At this proximity, he caught the faint scent of lavender on her skin, but the crackly, oily undertones in her voice were also more prominent; that, coupled with his still-throbbing cheek, reminded him that this was not a girl to be trifled with. *This is not a girl at all*, he amended. "Er, should you be so close? I mean, what your, ah, father said..." His hand touched the curved scabbard of the sabre as it pressed uncomfortably into his side. Almost subconsciously, his fingers traced its length to the pommel.

"Now, now," Krea purred. "You've no need for that weapon." She held his gaze as she reached down and unbuckled his swordbelt and pulled it free from beneath him, tossing it to the end of the long couch. He looked from her dark-rimmed eyes to her full lips as she smiled a dangerous smile. Her fingers touched lightly against his chest, his arms, his shoulders. "Oh, my," she breathed.

"Er..."

Krea gave a brief, lilting laugh, sounding oh-so-sweet yet disturbingly wrong. Her smile widened to show her white teeth and black gums. Her grip tightened upon his shoulders and she jumped up to straddle him, her pleated dress draping over their legs.

"You had nothing to show me at all, did you?" Oriken said. "It was just a ruse to keep me here, alone."

Krea arched her back and pressed her scant weight onto him. "You do catch on quickly."

"Ah, please don't do that. It, er..."

Her lips parted and Oriken balked as he glimpsed the tip of her tongue, as disturbingly dark as her gums and the lines at her eyelashes. "Don't pretend, outlander," she said. "I can't tell you how pleasing it is to be completely closed off from somebody." Her eyes glinted mischievously. "Well, not *entirely* closed."

He took hold of her wrists to wrangle her off him, but Krea's grip was even stronger than his own. He tried to push his weight up against her, and immediately regretted it.

"Ah, there," she crooned. "See? I knew you'd change your mind." Her head dipped and her lips touched his neck, one hand trailing from his shoulder to reach down between them.

Oh, dear Aveia. Or Valsana. Or whichever damned deity on Verragos is listening. I'm sorry for calling you all out as cowshit, but, if you're there, now would be a good time for a little divine intervention.

———— • ————

Gorven led the way through the city streets and side alleys, the whole time offering small-talk about landmarks they passed and waving perfunctory greetings to the few cityfolk on the otherwise empty streets. Their host, who claimed to be both 312 and 39 years old, depending on how you looked at it, deftly sidestepped Jalis's attempts to pry meaningful information from him, such as Dagra's alleged predicament.

171

If he hadn't taken the accursed jewel, there seemed only one answer. Oriken had been right. Jalis had to rebuke herself for allowing Demelza to run home. They should have kept her at camp until they set off at sun-up. But then, the girl would have had plenty chance to sneak away after Dagra took the last shift and Oriken went to sleep. The end result wouldn't have changed; they'd still be where they were now, and still without the jewel. Its whereabouts were now of considerably less concern than leaving this place alive.

She couldn't accept that Dagra was somehow moored to Lachyla for no good or obvious reason, but she also couldn't explain why he'd left camp and ended up in the Chiddari mansion. His pensive mood wasn't helping matters, either. If only he would share his thoughts with her like he'd always been able to do – trust and openness were driving factors within any good team in the Freeblades Guild – but Dagra wasn't talking, and any words directed at him just glanced off like water from oil. It was frustrating. And Jalis wasn't confident that this Sabrian, whoever he was, would manage to shake him from his malaise. She also hoped that the man wouldn't provide proof to reinforce Krea and Gorven's claim.

With Dagra at her side, she followed Gorven into an alleyway with tall buildings to either side. A strong breeze funnelled down the alley, causing Jalis to pull Oriken's padded leather jacket tighter about herself.

As she leaned into the wind, she realised that aside from the mildew between many of the flagstones, Lachyla was the cleanest city she had ever seen. There wasn't a stray piece of litter in sight, nor any festering piles of sked, bird droppings or rodent leavings. And there were no unwashed bodies lying beneath rags and raising palsied hands to beg for coppers. If not for the stale weight of the blighted dead pressing on her mind – not to mention the blighted living – Lachyla would be a welcomingly prepossessing place. But then, if the graveyard was replete of the walking dead, and the city was populated with typical citizens, it would be filled with a much more recognisable corruption.

They reached the end of the alleyway and the view broke out onto an open plaza. Dominating the centre of the plaza was an iron statue on a circular plinth. The figure was struck in a heroic pose – chest puffed, hands on hips, his crowned head tilted to gaze out over the rooftops. The heavy stormclouds behind the statue's profile lent an ominous aura to the moment. A burst of sunlight knifed through a gap in the clouds to wash over the towering figure, casting its strong features in a contrast of light and shadow.

"Yes," Gorven said as they passed the statue and headed for the entrance of a wide street, "how could our beloved liege, poised in all his splendour, possibly go unnoticed?"

Jalis wasn't sure if she'd detected a hint of sarcasm in his tone. "King Mallak," she said. "It seems he's a focal point of your city's legend."

Gorven glanced from her to Dagra. "I'd like to hear what the modern world is saying about our city," he prompted.

"You're in my mind, so why don't you pull the legend out of it and have a look for yourself?" Dagra turned his red-rimmed eyes to Gorven. "I can feel you in there, prodding away at the edges. Do you think I want to chat about your fucking king after you've dropped a proverbial rock on my head?"

"Ah. Of course. My apologies."

Jalis stepped close to Dagra and placed her arm around his shoulders, grateful when he didn't shrug her away.

"I don't much care for your apologies," Dagra said. "I want to keep my thoughts to myself." He reached to his shoulder and gave Jalis's hand an appreciative touch. "And I want to go home. Fuck your jewel, fuck your city and fuck your king."

An alarmed look crossed Gorven's face. "Please don't say that." As if searching for a reason to drop the conversation, he scanned the street ahead and pointed to a modest-sized house with an equally compact but decorative yard. "Here we are. And here comes Sabrian."

The door opened, and a man who appeared to be in his late twenties stepped out. He sported a neatly-trimmed goatee and moustache, with chestnut-coloured hair that hung in thick waves about his face.

Sabrian beamed them a wide grin and gestured cordially for them to approach. "Welcome!" he called. "I can't tell you what a pleasure it is to meet someone from my neck of the woods after so long!" He aimed his words at Dagra but also gave Jalis a warm smile. "Please, come in. You really must tell me how life beyond the Deadlands has changed since Lachyla became my home."

They gathered in Sabrian's small but homely living room, each settling into one of the four armchairs that formed a half-circle around a wooden table, its top fashioned from the trunk of an oak, with expertly-carved etchings of a young woman and a small boy beneath the varnish.

Jalis kept her eyes on Sabrian, who sat in the farthest chair from her, speaking in hushed tones with Gorven beside him. She was as unsure of what to make of him as she was of the whole macabre yet mystifying situation. Thoughts whirled through her mind as she tried to find sense in the events that had unfolded from yesterday until now. Gorven and Krea's claim about Dagra seemed fabricated, but to what purpose? She decided that patient observation was the answer, for now, and would allow Sabrian the chance to speak. Scrutinising the man, she supposed he was handsome; even those black-tainted slivers of flesh between eyes and lashes were not unattractive, and one could perhaps overlook the disconcertingly dark gums. Was the discolouring of raw flesh somehow a characteristic of their alleged long life, or of the blight they carried?

The risk of contagion was a growing concern, but, without knowing the source, there was little she could do except to keep direct contact to a minimum. But if the blight was in the air, there was a chance they were all already doomed.

No, she thought. *Gorven wouldn't be putting all the focus on Dagra if Oriken and I were also infected. Unless something more is going on here than they're letting on.*

Thinking of Oriken, she hoped he was okay back at the mansion, alone with Krea. The way the girl had knocked him to the ground was quite the surprise, but it had gained Krea no respect from Jalis. It might have been an amusing sight in any normal circumstance, which this was not.

Centuries of life have honed Krea's skills, she mused, *as perhaps they have for all who live here. If what they say is true, then age has transcended meaning in this place, just as death has transcended meaning for the corpses in the graveyard.*

She suppressed a shudder as Sabrian finished speaking with Gorven and turned his attention to Dagra.

"I understand you're having some difficulty in adjusting."

Dagra shifted his weight in the armchair and regarded Sabrian with narrowed eyes. "I don't see what there is to adjust to," he said acidly, nudging a thumb at Gorven in the armchair beside him. "I've already told *him* all there is to say."

"Then, if I may," Sabrian said, "let *me* tell *you* a little about myself." He arched his brows, an empathic expression on his face.

Dagra waved a hand dismissively. "If it makes you feel better. But don't take all day about it, because we'll be leaving this accursed city soon."

Sabrian nodded and leaned forward. "Just as you came in search of Lachyla, so I also came in search of the fabled city, one hundred and twenty years ago."

Jalis pressed her lips together. She felt a tightness in her core as she guessed where this was going.

"I was not alone," Sabrian said. "My three companions and I crossed Death's Head Land—"

"You mean the Deadlands?" Jalis asked.

Sabrian's brow furrowed and he looked at Dagra, then nodded. "The Deadlands. Indeed. After many weeks, we finally glimpsed the great battlements of Lachyla in the distance. Well, I'm sure I don't need to tell you what that was like."

"Hmph," Dagra said.

"We never made it to the wall," Sabrian said sombrely. "But, before I continue, I'll let Gorven tell you about a certain place not far from here."

Gorven crossed one leg over the other, resting his elbows on the chair's arms as he steepled his fingers. "During the Days of Kings, there were a number of mines in the south of Scapa Fell, all belonging to the kingdom of

Lachyla. Prior to the Uprising, many of the mines became depleted and the kingdom had no more use for them, nor for the settlements beyond the city walls. With the land barely arable and not producing anything of much worth, the villages were abandoned, one by one. The reach of Lachyla retreated until most of Scapa Fell was discarded as worthless except for a couple of strongholds which were the homes of governing lords.

Only the manor near the southernmost mine, which still ran plentiful, remained occupied. Lord Albarandes governed the place and lived there with his family, while the miners lived in a scattering of surrounding shacks. Before the blight took hold, it was to Albarandes Manor that many of the escaping Lachylans converged. A village grew around the manor – a village that would come to be known as Minnow's Beck."

Dagra grunted.

Demelza's village, Jalis thought.

"With that in mind," Sabrian said, "I'll tell you how it is that Lachyla became my home. It was turning dusk when my companions and I saw the distant wall, so we set camp for the night. Perhaps we had been lucky, encountering nothing of much danger during the whole journey. Stupidly, we set no guard. We were attacked while we slept. As captives, we were led to a village; I didn't know its name then, but I do now. At midnight, as Haleth shone full overhead, the leaders and Warders of Minnow's Beck lined us up beneath an oak tree, our hands tied behind our backs. They meant to execute us."

"For what?" Jalis asked.

Sabrian cast her a grave look. "For intruding upon their peaceful existence."

She shook her head. "Ignorant of their own irony."

"Such attitudes are the epitome of irony," Sabrian said. "We offered them no harm, and yet they saw what they wanted to see, what their strange ways had them believe us to be: intruders."

"A society's true nature is let loose when an unknown element is introduced," Gorven said.

Sabrian shared an agreeing glance with him. "In this case, the unknown element was four outlanders. One of my companions pleaded for his life, babbling in desperation. Another wept quietly. The third stared out into the heath and whispered for his mother, but of course she never came. Me, I was too terrified for words or tears. The order was called for the first of us to step forward and drop to his knees. I watched him comply. He was commanded to lower his head upon a wooden block." Sabrian let out a low, long sigh. "He did so, with nothing but a quiet sob. When the axe fell, I ran. I didn't care where to, I just barged through the hunters and ran into the night, my arms trussed behind me. They gave chase.

"I got an arrow in the shoulder, but I kept going till I was running blind, not just from the dark night, but from fear and delirium. I stumbled often, but never fell; if I had, I would not be here to tell you. I was losing blood. By then, I was nothing more than an animal controlled by mindless terror, fleeing from an inevitable death. A second arrow punched into my side; rather than drop me, it filled me with new panic. And then I saw the wall."

"The graveyard?" Jalis asked.

Sabrian gave a brief nod. "The eastern wall, looming against the night sky. That's when I fell, down and over into the gods knew where. I landed hard on one of the jutting arrows, driving the head deeper into my flesh as the shaft snapped, and I lost consciousness. I awoke to silence and blackness, and agony. I crawled, and kept on crawling. I don't know how I managed to do so. Finally, I reached a dead end, a wall of smooth, flat stone. Somewhere in the distance I heard the faintest of noises. I thought it was the villagers, that they'd found me.

"Time stretched on. In the blackness, I crawled into the corner of the wall. The muted commotion above never drew closer. I was going to die, not by their hands, but from my wounds bleeding out. I knew my fate, so I slept, sure I would not awake again. But then I roused to the sound of stone grinding upon stone. The wall shifted beneath my shoulder and I pitched sideways, dimly aware that a voice was telling me I would survive. I was lifted by strong arms, and for the second time I lost consciousness."

Sabrian settled back in his chair. "And that's how I came to Lachyla. Not sauntering into the graveyard as I hoped, but in a nightmare of mortal fear, blind panic, pain and finally solitude, resigned to a death in an unknown cave at the far end of nowhere. But I didn't die. As an unrelated aside, my rescue wasn't the end of my torment. But you don't need to know the rest. Suffice to say, it was not Gorven who took me from the cave. Anyway, this all happened *many* years ago, yet I sit before you now as a man in his twenty-seventh year. Somewhat remarkable, don't you think?"

Jalis puffed her cheeks. Despite Sabrian's light-hearted end to his otherwise sombre tale, she detected something more in his tone, something unresolved, perhaps. "I've been a freeblade for over a dozen years, since I was a fresh-faced girl of nineteen. I've had a few terrifying ordeals in that time, both before and since my friends joined the guild." She glanced at Dagra. "Not the least of which was having to escape from that graveyard. So, to a degree, I can empathise."

"Aye," Dagra said. "As can I. But I don't see what relevance it has to me."

"The relevance," Sabrian said with a tight smile, "is that I, an outsider, was given another chance. One might argue that I was born again. Either way, I accepted my lot and it took some of the locals quite a while to accept me in return – not all are as amenable as good Gorven here – but I managed to find my place in Lachyla. And so can you, Dagra. I know that all your instincts are shouting for you to fight it, but you must accept the certitude of your fate."

Dagra shook his head. His face was set in stubborn resolve. "You're all claiming I have this blight, but how can you know that? Your mouths, your eyes... Do mine look like that?" He turned to Jalis and she shook her head. "See?" he said, rising from his chair. "Your story is sad and terrible, but I'm not blight-ridden like the two of you." He glowered at both Sabrian and Gorven. "I'm *not*."

Gorven sighed and pushed himself from his seat. "Not yet, you're not. Or, I should say, you're not showing the later-stage physical symptoms. But I don't doubt you're showing the early ones. Would you open your shirt?"

"*What?*"

"Humour me, if you will. One more minute of your time, then you can do whatever you please."

Dagra shrugged. He pulled the toggle on the drawstring of his shirt, then loosened the criss-crossed cord, half-revealing the poultice that Jalis had applied to the deepest of his gouges. "Counting the seconds here," he told Gorven.

Without warning, Gorven stepped in close and ripped the poultice away.

"Gah!" Dagra reeled back, his legs bumping into the armchair. "What do you think you're doing?"

"Take a look in the mirror," Sabrian said, gesturing to a dress mirror on the wall behind Jalis.

Dagra approached it. Standing before the mirror, he eased his shirt open and looked at his reflection. "Oh, my gods." He turned to face Jalis.

She stared mutely at his chest. The deep scratch was now nothing more than a faint red line. Most of the scab had already fallen off.

"It's healed," Dagra said, then crumpled to the floor.

177

CHAPTER TWENTY ONE
BEFORE THE STORM

Adri stood within the front entrance of Albarandes Manor. She looked out over her sister's shoulder across their garden to the village green and the small assemblage that were gathered there.

"It's a fine group you're taking with you," she said. As she rested a hand upon Eriqwyn's shoulder, she felt the tautness in her sister's muscles. "But what on the goddess's green heath made you include Shade, of all people? What did she say to you?"

"The woman practically begged to be included," Eriqwyn said sullenly, then shrugged. "So be it. The one idiot can keep the other company."

"Oh, Eri," Adri chided. "You won't hear me defend Shade, but you must show Demelza a little leniency. Old Ina did what she could for the girl, goddess rest her sweet soul."

Eriqwyn grunted softly.

"Demelza may be lacking in certain aptitudes," Adri continued, "but she does possess strengths. She's fended for herself while living alone in Ina's shack for almost six years. It can't have been easy."

Eriqwyn turned to face her. "She's not the only one who had a tough time growing up."

"Our father was still alive when we were her age. And Mother—"

Eriqwyn scoffed. "Mother? She's scarcely more than a ghost these days."

"Even so, we've always had each other," Adri said softly. "But let's not digress. All I ask is for you to know that Demelza would benefit more from your guidance than your contempt."

Eriqwyn sighed. "I will try, *after* we return. There is no place for softness where we are heading, nor with what we must accomplish."

Adri let the matter drop. "Tell me about Shade."

"She claims to be privy to more knowledge concerning Lachyla than anyone else in the village. She further claims that such knowledge would aid us in our search for the outlanders."

"What could she know that the rest of us don't?"

"Apparently, the whereabouts of another entrance to the graveyard."

Adri frowned. "The gate is the only way in."

"According to Shade, there's an underground system that would cut our travel time exponentially. She says it leads beneath the central section of the eastern wall."

Adri opened her mouth to speak.

"I know," Eriqwyn said. "I'm as suspicious as you, sister." She cast her gaze to the ornate sundial in the centre of the garden, its shadow pointing almost to the eleventh hour. "If true, I could be there shortly after noon. The alternative would get us to the same point more than two hours later. I've wasted far too much time already in discussing the matter with the council, and I'm achieving nothing by standing here with you."

Eriqwyn's tone was not disrespectful, and Adri understood her eagerness to be gone. "If it turns out that Shade is lying—"

"It would be beyond foolish," Eriqwyn said. "And with no obvious benefit. If she's misleading us in an attempt to delay or obstruct the mission, then she will be visited with some dire judgement in accordance with the laws."

Adri nodded. "Well then, I won't hinder you any longer. Speed of the goddess to you." She gently squeezed her sister's shoulder, wanting to embrace her but knowing it would not be prudent to show softness in front of the group and the few onlookers who, despite the approaching storm, had ventured from their homes to watch them leave.

For a moment, Eriqwyn's eyes softened as she smiled, then she gathered her pack and bow from beside the door and set off to join the others.

As Adri watched her walk away, their mother's muffled, emotionless call came from within the house. "What's the commotion out there?"

"Nothing, Mother," she sighed. "Nothing at all. Go back to sleep." With a last look at her sister, she added under her breath, "Be careful, Eri. I need you. We all need you."

Wayland rested against the manor's garden wall, his fingertip idly tracing the inscriptions in the iron of the wood-axe at his belt. He cast a cool gaze across Eriqwyn's group, trusting that he gave the appearance of casual confidence despite his reservations, not only about the mission, but also about the group itself. There was no denying that most of the chosen could look after themselves, but how they would operate as a unit raised a few concerns in his mind.

Demelza stood silently beside him, fidgeting with the satchel at her shoulder. A sheaf of arrows hung at her hip, and she clutched her bow tightly. Wayland understood Adri's insistence that the girl accompany them. Like Adri, he knew that Demelza was not as useless as Eriqwyn and others presumed her to be; a little under-nourished perhaps, and still a touch childlike although practically a young woman, but there was more to her than most were aware of. Admittedly she had her troubles, but Demelza was a good person, and that counted for a lot. He did not want her tainted with murder. Theirs was a necessary task, but not one that should fall onto the shoulders of one so young and innocent.

Living in Minnow's Beck was hard enough on the girl, and in the last year Wayland had learned of a couple of the village men taking advantage of Demelza's situation. At first, in her naivety, she had allowed it to happen. That changed after Wayland became involved. There was nothing in the Founding Laws that permitted him to punish the men, but still he had taken each into a quiet corner and persuaded them to stay well away from her. But Demelza was not his greatest concern today. Not by far.

Onwin stood, serious-faced, on the short grass of the village green. His lips flapped as he looked from Lingrey to Tan, drawing half-hearted nods from his captive audience. His bow dangled from his fingers. A sheaf of arrows were slung over his shoulder and on top of his cloak.

Always likes to be different, that one, Wayland thought. *Even if it means being impractical.*

He and Onwin were the same age. The hunter could have been promoted to Warder if he hadn't spent his life holding delusions above his station. Onwin considered himself the equal of Wayland, while showing Eriqwyn and Linisa a grudging respect tinged with mild disregard. Despite his lofty attitude, he was one of the village's most capable hunters, but the wrong rash decision could spell trouble for the entire group.

Lingrey, the hardest-working and most weather-beaten farmhand in the village, leaned like a crooked post beside the seasoned hunter, a pitchfork held easy in his hand, its curved tines beside his grey hair. Wayland knew something of the farmhand's past, and agreed with Blachord's recommendation for him to join the group. He also agreed with Fahrein's suggestion of Tan, although, as he observed the blacksmith now, something about the young man bothered him.

Tan wore a decorative gladius he had forged himself a couple of years back. It was a fine piece to look at, but swords were of little use in their isolated existence and the gladius was more of a bragging right for the young blacksmith. Wayland hoped Tan would find the nerve to use the weapon against the outlanders if it fell upon him to do so.

Although seeming to be listening to Onwin's continued monologue, the blacksmith was stealing glances towards the pale-skinned, raven-haired Shade. Wayland sighed inwardly as he empathised with how distracting the sultry seamstress could be, especially now. She was dressed in attire that was borderline scandalous for village-wear, even in this warm season, and utterly unsuitable for their mission. For a seamstress – and the village's finest, at that – Shade didn't waste much material on herself. As she stood alone and gazed pensively towards the wooded hills beyond the village, she seemed unaware of

Tan's glances. Wayland would bet a day's catch of food that she knew the blacksmith's eyes were on her, and that she secretly revelled in it.

Every member of the group needed to remain focused, and, in that regard, the seamstress could be a problem. *Not only for Tan, but possibly also for Eriqwyn*, he thought, knowing the First Warder as well as he did.

Shade was one to be kept at arm's length or risk being burned – or consumed – by her fire. There was no doubt that the woman was a feast for more than merely the eyes. Today she wore her typical gossamer finery – a silken ankle-length skirt that clung to every tender curve, and a silken sash draped over one shoulder and wrapped around the middle of her torso, leaving her abdomen and one breast almost entirely exposed. Despite the late morning heat, thunderheads were rolling in from the ocean and would be overhead before long; while the rest of the group wore hooded cloaks in preparation for the storm, Shade would be drenched to the bone. Whatever role she played here, the lack of a weapon showed that she had no intention of being involved in combat, which was all well and good but might cause her to be a liability. Wayland hoped that once her role was done – leading them to a supposedly secret passage into the graveyard – the seamstress would head back to the village alone.

I'd swap all of them for Linisa, he thought. Sensing Demelza looking up at him, he glanced at her wide-eyed expression and gave her a conciliatory wink. She seemed to relax a little. *Failure will mean consequences that affect the whole village, but success will mean consequences for each man or woman's conscience. I'll take that burden, but I mustn't falter by trying to ensure Demelza does not share it.*

Several villagers were gathered at the far end of the green along with a number of the hunters, all looking over at Albarandes Manor and the small group that waited before it. Linisa and her twin sister Laulani's buttercup-coloured hair caught the sun as they emerged from the crowd to cross towards the manor. When they reached him, Wayland greeted them with a feigned smile.

"The hunters are not happy at being excluded," Laulani told him.

He stifled a sigh of exasperation. "The choices were not based on who can hunt animals for meat and skin and bones, but on usefulness and having the mettle to brave the Forbidden Place and catch a group of outlanders."

"Not catch," Linisa said. "Kill."

Wayland inclined his head in acquiescence. "This isn't about mindless animals, it's about fellow humans, regardless of them being outlanders. The decision is not ours, but Adri's and Eriqwyn's. Our leader and First Warder have spoken. Whether we like it or not, the safety of our home *is* paramount."

Reluctantly, Linisa nodded. "Eri requested some torches." She passed him a thick oilskin filled with enough torches for each member of the group. Accepting it, he slung the bundle over his shoulder.

"Linisa is prepared to join you, should Eri change her mind," Laulani said. Her long hair was tied back with a leather thong, unlike her usual loose, flowing style. "As am I, even though I'm not a hunter."

"Eriqwyn? Change her mind?" Wayland barked a soft laugh and glanced from Laulani to Linisa. "You may yet be needed, but I hope it doesn't come to that. For now, just as we can't afford to lose hunters, the village also can't be left without a Warder." He shrugged. "Besides, I doubt you'll be missing much, Lini. I'd let you take my place, but you know I'm a sucker for the shit jobs."

The twins' expressions showed that they appreciated his attempt at levity, but Linisa was clearly ill at ease at not being included. But it was a necessary and sensible decision, and she knew it.

Linisa glanced into the manor's garden. "Here she comes."

Eriqwyn was striding down the path towards them, a hunting knife and a sheaf of arrows at her hips, and her bow in hand. Wayland opened the gate for her to pass through, catching her eye as he did so.

To Linisa, Eriqwyn said, "Minnow's Beck is in your hands. Perhaps, when this is over, the two of you can have your planned day at the beach, but not today."

Linisa shrugged. "The storm would have ruined it anyway. Be careful, Eri." Her eyes flicked to Wayland. "Both of you."

"It's just three fortune-seeking outlanders," Eriqwyn said.

"It isn't the outlanders we're worried about," Linisa said.

"It's the Forbidden Place," Laulani finished.

Eriqwyn nodded. "That's why I'm taking the others." She looked at Linisa and lowered her voice so that Wayland could barely hear her. "As callous as it may sound, Lini, they're all disposable. Warders are not. You know I'd have you at my side otherwise."

Wayland inclined his head to Laulani. "We appreciate *your* offer of support too, Lani."

"We understand," the twins said in unison.

"Then time is of the essence." Eriqwyn's eyes softened a touch as Linisa caught her gaze. Turning to the remaining members of her group, she called out, "You all know why you're here. I will brief you on the finer points as we go. We are heading directly towards the southern reaches of the eastern wall"—she turned a brief but hard glance on the seamstress—"where Shade has informed me is a passage into the graveyard, which will save us the much-needed time wasted on village politics. We have three objectives, to be accomplished in this order: dispatch the outlander threat, return the deadstone to its crypt, and lower the portcullis before leaving the graveyard. None of us want to go in there – it is the Forbidden Place for a reason, after all – but your bravery will be recognised and remembered. Our success is imperative. I'll be setting a brisk pace, and I expect all of you to keep it. Now, let's move!"

182

"Ayup!" Lingrey croaked, quite unnecessarily.

Wayland gathered up his bow and glanced at Demelza. Her chest was rising and falling as her breath came in short gasps. "Don't fret, lass," he said. "You remember what we discussed?"

She nodded.

The portentous, creeping shadow of the black eastern sky rolled towards them, and the knot in Wayland's heart tightened as he set off to catch up to the First Warder.

Chapter Twenty Two
Strumpets And Sovereigns

"Dagra! Hey!" Jalis slapped her unconscious friend across the cheek. After a moment, his eyes fluttered open to unfocused slits. "Ah, finally," she breathed, then clicked her fingers before his face. "Come on, Dag, get it together. Look sharp."

He groaned and lifted his head. "Huh?"

Taking his arm, she hauled him to a sitting position. "You had me worried," she told him, casting a relieved look to Gorven and Sabrian.

Sabrian smiled. "We told you he'd be fine. It's not easy to be anything other than that in Lachyla."

"Uh," Dagra proclaimed. "What happened?"

"You passed out is what happened."

"I did what?"

"After you saw your chest."

He grunted and scratched his beard. "It's usually the ladies who swoon when I open my shirt."

Gorven took Dagra's other arm and helped Jalis bring him to his feet. "Best you sit down a while."

Dagra nodded and sank into the nearest chair.

Sabrian passed him a glass of water and cleared his throat. "Ah, I hope this doesn't sound selfish of me, but would I be right in gleaning that your other friend, Oriken, has some tobah?"

Dagra frowned. "Did you pick that out of my mind? I wish you wouldn't do that."

Sabrian looked humbled. "My apologies."

"He's trying to give it up," Jalis said. "Done quite well, actually. But, yes, he's got some."

"Ah, then I shall have to ask him later if he would allow me to indulge for the first time in twelve decades."

"Starting that again would not do you any favours," Gorven advised. "Your physiology is not what it was."

"True." Sabrian nodded. "But one roll wouldn't kill me."

Gorven turned to Jalis. "What say we leave Dagra in Sabrian's fine hands and return to Oriken and Krea? Let Dagra recover his strength while they finish their discussion. Shall we?"

Jalis looked at him. They'd left Oriken behind because Krea claimed she had something vital to show him. Jalis didn't like it, but, despite Krea's evident physical aptitude, Oriken was a big boy and could hold his own. Besides, though she didn't fully trust these people, Jalis's instincts told her that if they wanted her and her friends dead, it would have happened already.

Reluctantly, she turned to Dagra. "Will you be okay?"

"Aye," Dagra rumbled. "If Sabrian's got more to say, he can say it."

Jalis gave his shoulder a gentle squeeze. "We'll figure this out. We have to."

Gorven led her to the front door and opened it to a storm-darkened street. A fine rain and a warm breeze filled the air, but the whorling mass of black clouds was quickly drifting towards the city. Jalis slung her arms into Oriken's coat. The cuffs reached to her fingertips as she fastened the clasps at the front.

"Dagra doesn't seem so ill now," she said as she followed Gorven onto the street.

"It's the change," Gorven explained. "We were all like that to begin with." He wiped a hand across his rain-misted face. "I have to say though, he's coping with it quite well."

Jalis grunted. "I understand what you're saying, but you have to realise that we can't just leave him here. There must be something that can be done."

"That's your wishful thinking talking, Jalis. And I think you know it. Dagra is doing exceptionally well, considering, but don't let his apparent health fool you. You saw his healed chest." He paused, then said, "When it first hit the rest of us, back in the beginning, the city became chaos. Some thought it a blessing, at first. But imagine the elderly, the children... the babes. Those poor things. There is ugliness to this strange existence, without doubt."

She mulled over his words with growing horror, whispering, "Oh, my," as they entered the plaza. *What a cruel fate.* A mist of rain shimmered through the open area, with the towering shape of King Mallak in his dramatic pose ruling over the emptiness. The darkened statue gazed into the muddy sky like a fabled stormcaller of old. "What happened to them?" she asked.

Again, Gorven paused, considering his reply. "For many, their tales were tragic. Although the oldest regained the health of their younger days, they were still physically old and wrinkled. Some had been blind or nearly blind. Their sight returned. It was a miracle, or seemed like one at the time. There were joyous moments, but for some it didn't last. The torment of having the vitality of youth returned, but being trapped in an aged body compared to the luckier of us, it was too much for them. Some committed suicide."

"You said that wasn't possible."

"I said nothing of the sort, young lady. What I said is that it is difficult to die here. Not impossible. It wasn't just the elderly that wanted none of this limbo existence; there were others, of good age when the change occurred. Whole families, even, in some cases. Some helped each other to die, decapitating their loved ones. When that didn't work, they set the pieces on the pyre, which, up until then, had only been used for burning the horses and livestock.

"They listened to their children and parents, husbands and wives, scream in the flames and burn till they were charred husks. Only then did we feel their departure. Others wandered into the ocean, never to re-emerge. Still more decided to walk out onto the heath to whatever fate or destiny awaited them. With each who left, we who remained in Lachyla felt their consciousness fade away, with not one exception. Some believe they died a true death, others suggest the distance freed them, breaking the bonds which kept them in limbo, allowing them to return to mortality, as it were." Gorven scoffed. "More wishful thinking, considering the proof to the contrary."

They reached the alleyway they'd walked through on the way to Sabrian's. The narrow space had darkened since earlier, and wind gusted ahead of them into the high-walled channel.

"I don't understand," Jalis said, speaking loudly into the wind. She was horrified and perplexed at Gorven's story. Each of his comments begged for further clarification.

"They didn't understand, either," Gorven said. "Some *knew* they would survive when they left the city. Others *knew* they were leaving to die. Ultimately, it doesn't matter what we believe, does it? There is only one truth out there, and only one truth in here. The former is death, the latter is not."

A knot tightened in Jalis's chest. The temptation was still strong for the three of them to just leave, but it was Dagra's choice, not hers, and she had to let him reach it himself.

"Life in Lachyla is not as bad as it may seem to someone from outside," Gorven said as he caught her bleak expression. "There are adjustments to be made, it's true, but those of us who accepted those adjustments have done our best to give meaning to our lives. Most of us, at any rate. We've had centuries to master the skills still required for maintaining a city: metalwork, mining, tailoring, building and repairs. And, with the abundance of time we were granted, we've explored spiritual pursuits; well, I should say those of us who still put stock in such things, of which I am not one. The truth of existence is a hot topic around these parts. Quite the trend, actually. The days I have spent ruminating over self-awareness and our purpose upon Verragos..." As they exited the alleyway, Gorven raised a hand to point into the whorling skies. "Indeed, some of us believe we've solved the mystery of the great Void, the stars, the moons, warts and all. Life, for those who choose to call it that, does not have to be boring here. It doesn't have to be quite the bleak fate Dagra thinks it is."

Jalis had journeyed throughout the three lands of the Vorinsian Arkh. She'd glimpsed the awe-inspiring mountains of the Ÿttrian Wedge and the city of

Midhallow nestled between them, its towering Needle a thin line bisecting the sky. She'd sailed the Sea of Furies and travelled much of Himaera, including the Isle of Carrados where the monks brewed their wines deep within the Maze. By comparison, spending the rest of her natural days in one small area would feel like imprisonment, and extending those days to eternity would be nothing short of torture; not the worst of fates, admittedly, but the limitations would drive her to insanity.

She and Gorven turned a corner and the Chiddari Mansion loomed into view at the end of the street, its windows shuttered, its domed and angled roofs dark against the rainclouds. No sooner had Jalis glimpsed the antiquated structure, than the clouds decided to empty their load. She drew the collar of Oriken's coat tight around her neck as the fat raindrops quickly drenched her hair, leggings and shoes. Gorven seemed to relish in the downpour, keeping at a steady stride as Jalis burst into a run for the mansion. Soon, she was through the iron gates and sprinting along the path towards the shelter of the entrance's portico.

Oriken was sitting in the shadows of the eaves, a dispirited look on his face as he blew out a steady billow of tobah smoke. Jalis bounded up the steps and slowed to stand before him. As she regarded him, she drew her hair over her shoulder and squeezed it, letting the rain run from it in a rivulet.

Oriken nudged a finger against the brim of his hat. "I was trying to kick the habit," he said despondently, "but now seemed a good time for reconsidering the notion."

His cheek was swollen from Krea's punch, and the skin around the side of his eye had turned purple. Jalis stepped forward and gently touched his cheek, causing him to wince.

"Are you alright?" she asked.

"Sure." He cast a moody glance to the steps as Gorven reached them. "Although, I may have to rethink one or two fundamental principles."

"What do you mean?" Jalis frowned, then sighed. "Oh, Orik, you didn't."

"I really don't want to talk about it."

Gorven chuckled as he joined them. Oriken glared at him and took another pull of tobah.

"The smart bee," Jalis said sternly, "does not sip from the fallen flower. No offence, Gorven."

"None taken. I think you'd fit in quite well here, Jalis."

She scoffed. "Dream on. Not this girl."

Oriken flicked the stub of tobah into the rain and rose from the bench.

"So," Jalis said. "What else have you learned from the duplicitous madam? Anything actually useful?"

"That's a matter of perspective." He pushed the mansion's door open and stepped into the foyer.

Jalis followed him in. "Where's Krea?"

"Upstairs sleeping, I guess." Oriken shrugged "For all I know she could be preparing the sacrificial altar."

"Ah." There was a note of concern in Gorven's voice, and a distant look on his face. "I was worried this might happen."

"Hey." Oriken stabbed a finger towards Gorven. "I didn't start anything Your beloved little—"

"You misunderstand," Gorven told him. "I've just received word that King Mallak has requested your presence."

Jalis's jaw dropped. "Wait, what? Mallak's alive?" She sighed. "Of course he is. What's he want to see *us* about? Don't say the jewel."

"Not you, Jalis. Only Oriken." Gorven fixed Oriken with a grim look. "And I wouldn't delay, were I you. Years may pass without anyone even sensing the king – he's a private person, you understand – but our liege has, shall we say, an erratic disposition. I suggest we ambulate with all due haste."

"Great." Oriken folded his arms and scowled from beneath his hat. "Crypts and corpses, strumpets and sovereigns. I can't wait for the encore."

Chapter Twenty Three
Den Of Dire Secrets

A fire roared in the hearth while candles lit the corners of Sabrian's living room. Beyond the windows the street was dark and melancholy as the wind whipped rain against the panes. Immersed in the cushions of the armchair, it was an effort for Dagra to move even slightly.

Feel like I'm melting into this thing, he thought, rallying against the myriad of voices that whispered in his mind as if from across a great divide, willing him to relinquish his grasp on wakefulness, on life.

"We're done here," he said. The words were slurred, but the sound of his voice helped to ease the incessant internal babble. "I want to get back to my friends."

Relaxing in his own seat, Sabrian regarded him from across the table. "You will see them shortly."

"Oriken—"

"He speaks with the king, while Jalis awaits with Gorven. Their business will be concluded soon."

"What business?"

"That, I fear, I do not know."

"I need to get out of here," Dagra said miserably. "I want to go home." He lifted his head from the cushion and blinked, trying to push the drowsiness away. "Did you not want to leave, to go back to your village, your family?"

Sabrian nodded. "I did, at first. How I wish I could see my wife and son again, but, alas, it will be many years now since they took the swan's path. I rallied against staying here, just like you, but my entry into Lachyla was not quite as... *comfortable* as yours." He barked a mirthless laugh. "I was, shall we say, in the wrong hands to begin with. But I was already close to death. And then it happened. However misguided my saviours, they did still rescue me when they could have left me on the other side of that door to rot, or worse. In comparison, you have had a warm welcome into the city and, unlike me, you were not suffering mortal wounds when you arrived. You were quite healthy."

"I *am* healthy," Dagra corrected.

Sabrian's nod was acquiescent, but it was clear to Dagra that the man didn't agree with him.

"The corpses," Dagra said. "That's what did it to me, isn't it? Those damned creatures."

"Perhaps we're all damned creatures," Sabrian mused, "whether cursed by a goddess or cursed by mortality. But, no, the denizens of the Gardens are not responsible, not in your case."

Dagra loosed a rattling sigh and rested his head back against the cushion. "What, then?"

"Do you recall the tomb you were in? The one belonging to Gorven and Krea's family?"

"Of course I bloody well remember it. Horrible place."

"That's where you were taken by the blight."

"*What?* How?"

"The broken vault."

"The burial hole?" Dagra frowned in confusion. "The one full of cobwebs?"

"Curiosity, my friend," Sabrian said softly, "can be quite the killer. Not every small thing is as innocuous as it may seem."

"I don't follow."

"In the graveyard and the city, you will have noticed a fungus that grows upon the tree-bark, between the flagstones and the cracks in the soil. That fungus is potent, but more so in its natural habitat beneath the ground, especially in, well, let's not beat around the bush, in places where corpses can be found."

"I remember it. Black stuff with pale sacs and red veins. Ugly."

"Do you recall what you did?"

He did recall. All too clearly. It had been a trifling moment, buried in the midst of his fear and forgotten through the terror that followed. *The blisters. Those swollen, white cysts. I poked one, and it burst. Burst into my face. Oh, you damned fool.* He held his hands over his eyes. "Surrounded by the desiccated dead, and I'm taken out by a piece of fungus."

Sabrian nodded. "Spores. Simple, yet deadly."

"Well, I won't give up so easily. You say I can't leave, and you expect me to just take your word on that. If you wanted to see your family so badly, didn't you ever try to get out? Not even once?"

Sabrian tapped a finger against the side of his head. "In here was, and is, the knowledge of all those who chose to leave Lachyla. None survived. I could not have reached my home so far away. But, I do leave the city on occasion; many do, but infrequently and never in large numbers, and always under the cover of darkness to avoid unwanted attention. It would be impossible to maintain a society without wood and other supplies. And then there are the times we feel nostalgic for the taste of meat, fish or vegetables."

"What do you mean?"

"We don't need to eat. Fresh water provides enough nutrients. Well..." He shrugged. "But everyone has the occasional urge to indulge. A juicy side of roasted deer, a boiled egg, a dish of scallops. Unfortunately, that which keeps death at the door also binds us to its proximity. Where there's a boon, there is often also a bane. We can leave, but we cannot remain away for long. It is... what it is..."

Sabrian's voice was small as it merged with the sibilant whispers. His eyes were growing larger, and the walls and furniture of the room were all wrong – bulged, pinched, or stretched.

"I'm so tired," Dagra said.

"I know. Close your eyes. The time will pass faster until you see your friends again. Rest. You need it."

"Aye. I do..."

"Then sleep. Now."

And Dagra slept.

———·•·———

Shade glided gracefully along beside Eriqwyn, her hips swaying, her skirt swishing like fronds of fern in the gentle breeze. Her bare breast, coated in a sheen from the fine rain, scarcely moved.

Damn her, Eriqwyn thought, casting the seamstress a cold glance. "I'll be blunt, Shade. I don't like you. I have never liked you. And you have put yourself in a no-win situation. If this tunnel of yours does indeed exist, you will be recognised as helping us today, but there will be questions. On the other hand, if it doesn't exist—"

"You always claim to despise me," Shade said, her eyes mocking, her fingertips lightly touching her breast. "But the only person you're fooling is yourself. It's a pity, because I *do* like you. I admire a woman who possesses"— her gaze drifted momentarily down Eriqwyn's cloaked body—"such confidence and strength of character."

Infuriating woman, Eriqwyn thought. *The insolence!*

"My information *is* correct, Eri. When that proves to be true, you can... reward me, later."

Eriqwyn glowered. *How dare she call me Eri? As if we were ever friends!* She gave a sniff of disdain and opened her stride to catch up to Wayland, who was taking the lead a short distance ahead. As she strode away from Shade, she could sense the wanton woman smiling at her. *Goddess forfend*, she thought. *Demelza is easier to cope with than that lustful witch.* Reaching Wayland, she sighed as she fell into pace with him.

Long moments passed as the two walked swiftly without comment, the swell of the ocean a constant, subdued roar.

"You shouldn't let her get under your skin," Wayland said quietly.

She nodded. "Now more than ever. In truth, I don't know how she manages to vex me so."

"Aye, well, let it be a problem for another day. You have other concerns. So do I. What do you need of me?"

She moved closer to his side and kept her voice low. "Shade is less than a weak link in our chain – she's an open lock waiting for a chance to slip free. As for Lingrey, bless his soul, he's a fine man."

"That he is."

"When it comes to hard work, he's second to none."

"That's a given."

"I only hope he can hold up against an opponent if he has to fight to the death. None of us go to this task with cheer, and the fulfilment of it will undoubtedly fall on you and I, but—"

"Lingrey once killed a man," Wayland said, his voice barely above a whisper.

Eriqwyn glanced at him. "This is news to me."

"Well, it was long ago. Reckon he must have been in his late twenties at the time. I was a lad, in my eighth year, out in the fields spying on Jessa's mam, goddess rest her soul. Spotted her getting flirty with one of the young men, having a bit of a tumble in the hay, as it were. The feller, he started getting rough, pushing her around. When he slapped her, she screamed at him. Well, around the corner of the hedgerow comes Lingrey, pitchfork in hand – could've been the same as he's carrying now, truth be told. He watches the feller take a swipe at Jessa's mam. Down she goes, and Lingrey shouts. The feller swings round."

"And Lingrey killed him?"

"Let me tell it, woman," Wayland said in mock irritation. "The feller says to Lingrey it's none of his business. Calls him a retard, says he'll be getting some of the same as Jessa's mam. Well, Lingrey looks at him and says he shouldn't oughta be hittin' on a woman, so he shouldn't. Mayhap he oughta leave 'er be. Feller steps over to Jessa's mam and hoofs her right in the middle, asks Lingrey how he liked that. Then he does it again."

Eriqwyn bristled. "Bastard got what was coming to him."

"Aye, that's the truth."

Wayland flicked a glance over his shoulder, as did Eriqwyn, but the old farmhand was striding along at the rear beside Onwin, his pale eyes gazing about his surroundings. Tan had ventured closer to Shade, while Demelza walked several paces to their side.

"So," Wayland continued, "Lingrey stomps over to the feller, swings his fork across, whacks him right on the 'ead. Down he goes on his back, all a-daze, and Lingrey stands over him and says he shouldn't oughta have done that. Them's the last words the feller hears. Lingrey raises his fork and brings it

192

down, tines-first, and the feller gets the middle two spikes right through his eyes an' starts twitching, you know like they do when they don't know they're dead yet. And then he's still."

"Sweet Valsana," Eriqwyn breathed. "I would never have guessed."

"Aye." There was a distant tone in Wayland's voice. "When he pulled the fork out, the eyeballs stayed stuck on the tines, like skewered beans. I never lost that image."

"Neither will I, now."

Wayland mumbled an apology.

"I never heard a whisper of this," she said. "How did they keep it hushed up?"

Wayland glanced at her. "Because it never happened, that's how. Man deserved it. Lingrey didn't deserve to face the laws for that."

"He certainly dodged a stern reprimand, possibly even death, but for once I'm glad to hear of it."

"Jessa's mam, she were lucky to have had Jessa nine months later, despite who the girl's father was – a man whose name didn't matter then and don't matter now. Lingrey got rid of the body. Jessa's mam swore she'd never say a word to a soul. As for me, I hid there till they went away. Neither of them saw me. Lingrey never knew I was there, and I never told a soul till now."

Eriqwyn knew there was no need for him to mention trust; he had hers implicitly, not that the farmhand could be tried now for a murder that took place four decades earlier. "Well then," she said. "That's three strong enough links with you, me, and Lingrey; two that will hopefully stay back and not interfere; Tan, who needs to keep his mind on the mission; and Onwin."

Wayland laughed softly. "I've got no tales about Onwin that you don't already know, and we share the same opinion of the man. In his mind he's probably out hunting animals, which, callous as it may sound, is probably for the best. We'll see how he fares."

Eriqwyn sniffed. "Lingrey would make a finer hunter than that one, but it's a good thing that he never did. Maybe we could count on him to keep half a mind on Onwin."

Wayland smiled. "Aye, Queenie, maybe so. Some might say that half a mind is all Lingrey's got, but I wouldn't recommend them to voice it to his face."

From some a dozen paces behind came a faint, "Ayup."

Eriqwyn glanced back at the farmhand, whose long-handled fork rested easy over his shoulder. "Ayup, indeed," she said quietly.

Within minutes the rain gained in intensity, reducing visibility, with the occasional errant gust preceding the full storm, pulling it further inland. The group closed to a tighter formation, Shade taking point, with Eriqwyn and Wayland directly behind her. All hoods were drawn and cloaks clasped at the chest, and those with bows held them beneath protective garments.

Shade's hair was plastered to her shoulders and back, the fine material of her dress and sash clinging even tighter to her body. The only part of her that stayed dry were her feet, covered by soft, calf-length boots. She almost seemed to enjoy the deluge whipping at her exposed skin. Glancing back, she said, "Not far now. Half-way between those hillocks."

Eriqwyn's eyes followed Shade's pointing finger to a pass between two rises that ruffled the land in a sweeping quarter-circle, five minutes distant. In the shadowed dip between the hillocks, the eastern wall of the graveyard was just visible against the sheet of rain. Although she had passed close to the wall a thousand times and more, the sight of it now gave her a deeper feeling of dread, knowing she would all too soon be on its other side. When she glanced at Wayland, he pulled his hood aside to meet her gaze and gave her a wink that told her he had her back.

Behind Eriqwyn, Lingrey cleared his throat. "I'm mighty glad you opted to bring the stone back to its rightful place," he called against the growing wind.

Beneath her cloak, the pack containing the deadstone pressed into her back. She'd felt mildly sick during the whole journey, having to keep it in such close and constant proximity.

"The tragedy of the boy and his parents," she said, pausing as thunder rumbled over the ocean, "must never be given the chance to repeat itself."

"Ayup," Lingrey said. "Happen I'm not meaning that, though. I'm meaning what daft notions the folk had afterwards. Keeping a-hold o' that foul hunk o' stone. Should'a oughta taken it right back."

"What do you mean?" Wayland asked.

"What's that, feller? Ah, me pa told me. He were a young man when it transpired." Lingrey leaned over Eriqwyn's shoulder. "No offence to yer, but it were the Lord Albarandes what delayed the stone's return. Ayup, your 'cestors kept the accursed thing a while, 'cause someone had the notion that the problem were that the bairn was already dead. See? So they reckoned maybe if the stone were around someone what was alive, it might cure 'em. Har!" The old farmhand retreated from being immediately behind Eriqwyn before he hawked and spat a wad of phlegm into the rain.

"I heard there'd been a delay in returning the deadstone," Eriqwyn said. "But what of it?"

"Well, it were daft, weren't it?" Lingrey barked a laugh. "Anyways, I forget his name, but it were your pa's pa who was the lord; he were still alive when I were a bairn. Only, his lady, the wastin' disease were takin' her. Cut story short, same shit came as afore, beggin' the young misses' pardons for me manners, an' all."

Eriqwyn glanced back. "Are you saying there was a second incident after the boy?" Returning her eyes to the front, they glanced over Shade's glistening skin and rain-soaked skirt that managed to highlight the subtle sway of her hips.

"That's right," Lingrey said. "The lord thought that to keep the stone by his lady's side would stop the wastin'. It did, for a while, so me pa said, but only a while. Then she died. Then she woke up."

"Blood of the old gods," Onwin said from beside the farmhand. "Shameful business. Bloody shameful. He should'a known better than that, bein' the lord."

My great-grandparents, Eriqwyn mused. "The Beck is turning out to be a den of dire secrets," she muttered.

"Mm-hm," Wayland sounded in assent.

"The stone, you see," the farmhand continued, "it weren't strong enough to stop her from dyin', but it were strong enough to bring her back as soon as her heart stopped beatin'. Trouble was, she weren't some poor, mindless critter like the bairn. She still had her ken about her – well, some of it. Didn't last, though. Weeks wore on an' she started utterin' a whole heap o' crazy talk. And festerin'. Stinkin' the place down."

"Foul work," Onwin said. "No business messing with the goddess's plans."

Lingrey leaned in to Eriqwyn. "It were only then when they opted to take the rock back to where it belonged. The lady died then. A blessin' she were put from her misery afore she turned vicious like the bairn. Can't have the likes o' them risin' up again, so good for you is what I say. Ayup."

CHAPTER TWENTY FOUR
AMMENFAR

Oriken sweated beneath his fleece-lined jacket. His sodden trousers chafed against his thighs. The rain drummed upon his hat's wide brim. He was in no mood for politeness, and certainly in no mood to be subservient to anyone, least of all a king.

This whole fiasco has gone to cowshit, he thought. *And now I'm soaked to the skin on the summons of some turgid cock of a king. The nerve of it!*

With the deluge blanketing the city in a darkened shroud, there wasn't a single positive thing he could see at that moment. "Shouldn't have camped last night," he mumbled into the wind and rain. "Should've kept on walking." A gust of wind lashed into his face, and he pulled the hat tighter onto his head.

Gorven was setting a quick pace for the castle. Occasionally Oriken would glance to the side to see a lone figure, or two or three, stood behind panes of glass or open shutters in the shade of their houses, looking out at the so-called 'outlanders' as he and Jalis passed swiftly by with Gorven Althalus. Silent, staring, blighted figures, every last one of them. All the while, the hulk of Lachyla Castle loomed on its low hill at the rear of the storm-darkened cityscape, its domes and towers and spires melting into the louring squall.

Thank the stars we done away with the rest of those things long ago. Who wants an unsightly horror like that as a neighbour? I'd say curse this whole city if someone hadn't beaten me to it. His earlier suggestion of looting the place seemed now a naive and wholly unsavoury notion.

To Gorven's other side, Jalis's shorter legs were working double-time to keep up. She held tight to the hood of her cloak as the wind whipped it around, exposing her drenched leggings to more punishment from the storm. "What is this all about?" she asked, spitting the rain from her lips. "What does Mallak want with Oriken? And why only him? Are we heading willingly towards trouble?"

"Whatever the reason," Oriken shouted across to her, "he'd better have a solution that'll help Dagra." To Gorven, he said, "I don't care for being called on the whim of this Mallak fellow. He may be king here, but he's no king of mine. Himaera got rid of his sort with the Uprising, and it's doing fine without them."

Gorven's hair was plastered to his scalp like a skullcap, but he seemed almost to be enjoying the downpour. "Not that I've experienced a post-Uprising Himaera," he said, "but I don't entirely disagree with you. As to why you've been summoned, though, I'm afraid I cannot say."

"Cannot?" Oriken asked. "Or will not?"

"Cannot. King Mallak shares his thoughts only when he chooses, just as I have closed my mind while we speak now."

"It doesn't surprise me," Oriken said. "He doesn't exactly win votes as the most benevolent leader. Paranoid and isolationist, history says. Shut the gates to keep the influence of the other kingdoms away from his own."

"You have to understand that Mallak wasn't a bad king," Gorven said. "Mostly, anyway. Show me a king who isn't' a tyrant, and I'll show you a man who isn't a king. Ostensibly, it's true that the gates of Lachyla were closed due to the king's paranoia, but the reality is that the portcullis was lowered – and remained so – to keep the growing blight contained within."

"He imprisoned his own people?" Jalis asked.

Gorven's expression was tight as he answered. "The blight was new to us. We didn't understand it, and it frightened us all, including the king. What started as a slow outbreak of symptoms grew into a city-wide epidemic. Some of the visiting merchants and ambassadors from the northern kingdoms witnessed the earlier stages and quickly left, no doubt spreading word of the contagion. Even while still in Lachyla, they had begun referring to it as the Blighted City. It was a rumour which we didn't encourage, but, behind closed doors, many of us believed it to be the curse of Valsana. It was months before the king finally called for the gates to be closed – not just the heath-side gate, but also the ocean-side gate." Lightning streaked behind the castle, silhouetting the colossus and striking down behind it into the ocean beyond. "So," he continued, "yes, at that time we were prisoners in our own city, but we would have been so whether the gates were closed or not, for our fates were already sealed."

"I take it the dead hadn't started kicking out the slabs of their tombs at that point?" Jalis said.

A strong gust whipped into Gorven's face, slashing rain into his eyes; he blinked it away, then nodded. "For the most part, that's true. The first to turn were the newly, as-yet unburied dead." A haunted look clouded his black-lined eyes, there and gone in a moment. "By that time, those who hadn't escaped the city endured a waking nightmare. Our loved ones died but did not *truly* die, for the curse, or the blight was not as strong then as it is now. Accidents happened, suicides and murders were attempted, many unsuccessfully, as I told you." He nodded to Jalis. "We had little choice but to accept our undeath – or unlife – somewhere between the two, for what could conceivably stretch into eternity."

197

Jalis scoffed. "I can scarcely conceive of what eternity truthfully means, let alone living for as long as you have. What purpose could there be to enduring an unending existence in a confined space? It would drive me crazy. And yet there's little choice but to accept what I've seen. The restless dead, Sabrian's story, you taking a bolt in the chest from Oriken..."

Oriken cleared his throat. "Yeah. Sorry about that, I guess."

Gorven shook his head. "Ignorance, as they say, is bliss. We Lachylans found it more difficult than you can know to accept what the future held for us. That's why we want to help Dagra as much as we can. Is life without purpose a life at all? The flowers and grasses are alive, yet we would not say they have discovered a reason for living; they merely exist. We can only leave these walls for hours at a time, or, for the strongest of us, days at the most. We spend our time ruminating over the mores and morals of society; our fears; our philosophies, and how they might be forced to change between the perceptions of mortality and immortality; the ultimate futility of mysticism and deific worship, by ones such as us, to ones such as Morta'Valsana, Banael, Haleth and all the other gods. Many of us here have concluded that our dear curse-casting goddess belongs only with the Taleweavers, their myths and legends to be spun for historical interest and entertainment, that Valsana and her cohorts should be cast into the realm of fantasy along with the likes of dragons and orcs and jotunn."

"But jotunn do exist," Jalis said. "We have a friend who's a halfblood."

Gorven raised his eyebrows, then blinked as rain flurried into his face. "Is that so? Hm. That will prove an interesting topic for future discussions. Still, the point remains."

"I have to admit," Jalis said, "that in a world where corpses can rise from their graves, and humans are somehow transformed into undying beings, I'm beginning to wonder what else might be out there on Verragos."

"Make no bones about it, dear girl, there is nothing magic about the restless dead; the mindless occupants of the graveyard are a sad by-product of Lachyla, much closer than we in the city to the true death they once enjoyed. Nor is there anything mystic about people who have seemingly transcended mortality."

Feeling the need to add something to the frankly tedious discussion, Oriken said, "Oh? How so?"

"The truth, I fear, is something quite mundane, and yet, perhaps, also much more chilling. But we are almost there. I must open my mind to his liege and announce our presence."

Great, Oriken thought. *May as well have kept my bloody mouth shut.*

As he frowned up at the sprawling behemoth of Lachyla Castle that now dominated the view, the image of a hangman's noose flashed into his mind, followed by a chopping block. The thought occurred to him then, that there was a good chance he was being led by the shepherd to the slaughterhouse.

They turned onto a wide walkway that cut straight through the centre of the hill. The flagstones shimmered with carved, rain-filled whorls. At the end of the walkway was a set of steps, beyond which Oriken could see the upper halves of two armoured guards standing rigid in their glistening armour before the castle's entrance. Stone arcades enclosed the way to the steps – two walls of arches housing statues that brooded within their niches, gazing impassively across at each other.

A real show of splendour, he thought with a sneer. *Looks like half a job to me.*

The aged timber of the entranceway was studded with large, black nails, with an intricate, wrought iron crest adorning the centre of each door. The guardsmen completed the ego of the place: clean-shaven, wearing polished greaves and ringmail, with half-cloaks clasped to their shoulders by silver buckles. The guard on the right wore a braided burgundy cord from armpit to shoulder, which Oriken supposed marked him as the superior. As he drew closer, the guards lowered their pikes to bar the way.

More show. And I'd wager it's put on just for us. Does the king get an abundance of visitors these days? I think not.

Oriken came to a stop before the doors. "Right," he announced. "Your king – that's the fellow who lives here, unless we're at the wrong house – he's expecting us, so you can drop the act." As an afterthought, he added, "Because I'm not impressed."

Both guards completely ignored him.

Gorven nodded to the one with the fancy rope. "Greetings, Ellidar, old friend. It has been too long."

"Indeed, it has," Ellidar replied impassively. "His Majesty is expecting you—"

Oriken thrust his hands in the air. "Aissia's tits! Didn't I just say that? What am I, invisible?"

Jalis leaned behind Gorven and shook her head. "Leave it alone," she whispered.

"Please follow me," Ellidar said to Gorven. Fixing his pike into a bracket beside the double doors, he walked across to a smaller door set into an adjacent wall, pushed it open and stepped through.

The second guard tilted his pike back to a vertical position, but remained at attention. Oriken leaned towards him. "You should get yourself a little niche," he advised, poking a thumb over his shoulder at the statues beyond the steps. "You'd fit right in with that lot. Ow!" He scowled at Jalis and rubbed his arm where she'd pinched it.

She cast him a flat look, then followed Gorven into the castle.

"I'm just saying it like it is," Oriken called after her. He shrugged at the guard. "Women, huh?" The guard didn't even blink. *Not getting a rise out of this one.*

Oriken stepped through the side door and peered ahead. The one Gorven had called Ellidar who had set a deliberate, stiff-backed pace along the corridor. "All right," Oriken said. "I get it. You haven't had a chance to do this in, what, two centuries? Three? You're clearly getting a buzz of nostalgia, so go ahead, have at it."

Jalis spun on him. "Oriken, you fucking dolt. You're not making things any better, you know?"

He snorted. "Could they get much worse?"

The corridor walls were festooned with drapes, curtains and tasselled ropes. He glared at each from beneath his hat as he passed them by, until Ellidar paused to open a side door and led them into the main entrance hall. A bronze candelabra dangled from the high ceiling with a hundred or more candles, all unlit. Weapons, shields and a plethora of decorations adorned the walls, set above low pedestals, upon which helms nested like metallic eggs. A faded canvas hung over a wide arch at the rear of the hall, depicting what Oriken supposed was a map of the Lachylan Kingdom.

The place was filled with callbacks to the Days of Kings. For each sign of grandeur, there was another sign of disuse with a hint of neglect. Still, he had to admit that Lachyla Castle was considerably less ugly within as without.

Beneath the arch, ornately-carved doors barred the way. A red carpet stretched from them all the way back to a second set, which he guessed was the main entrance they hadn't been invited through.

Several full suits of armour were positioned within corners. It took Oriken a second glance to realise that the two beside the ornate doors contained guardsmen, each standing perfectly still and clasping a longsword in leather, silver-backed gauntlets.

Ellidar nodded to the guards. In unison, they pulled the doors open and Ellidar took a step over the threshold. "Your Highness," he called, his voice echoing within. "I bring you Oriken of Eyndal."

"Alder's Folly, actually," Oriken muttered.

"Send him in!"

That's my cue. "Right. Listen up." He strode past Ellidar into the room. "Yes, we took your jewel. No, we don't know where it is. Something's wrong with our friend, and you— Oh."

"Oh, indeed." A large bronze throne, embellished with gems of all colours, dominated the far centre of the room. Set into its high back, the metal shaped as if holding it like a claw, was a deadstone. The hard-faced man who had spoken was slouched upon the throne. He flicked his hand in a bored gesture.

The doors clicked shut behind Oriken. He spun about to see Ellidar positioned before them, leaving Jalis on the other side with Gorven and the two guards.

Oriken half-turned and eyed the throne and its occupant sidelong. He'd never seen a king before, other than on sketches, murals and portraits, because

200

they were all dead, like this one should be. Mallak oozed regality and decadence in equal measure, for as much as his wide-shouldered posture, strong nose and penetrating, brown-eyed gaze spoke of strength and sureness of character, his gilded crimson shirt, waxed leather leggings and fur-topped boots hinted at an era lost in time. A black swordbelt was strapped to his hips, edged with maroon embroidery and sporting an ornate silver buckle. The handle of the attached gladius was nestled between man and throne. The lack of a crown on the king's head was more than reconciled by the gladius's golden, gem-studded scabbard, its mirror-finish glinting with the light from the myriad torches upon the walls.

Dagra would love that sword, Oriken thought, transferring his gaze to the deadstone above Mallak's head. The king rose, blocking his view of the jewel, and stepped from the dais. Oriken waited with jaw clenched as Mallak made his way along the red carpet.

"I know what you're thinking," the king said. "You're thinking that everything about this place"—he swept a grand gesture around the throne room—"is little more than a shambolic pretence of might and splendour." His eyes hardened as he came to a stop before Oriken. "Including me."

He pursed his lips, then shrugged. "You got me there." *No point in denying it.*

Mallak nodded. "As I thought. And, if you're wondering, I didn't read your mind; you are, after all, not one of us. But I *can* read your face, and your contempt for this"—he cocked his head—"this *lifestyle* is written all over it."

Oriken crossed his arms. "Can you blame me? We do quite well without the despots that once plagued our land. Sure, there are bandits, and other problems, but we freeblades do a fine enough job of keeping things in order. The ways of kings are a thing of the past. You"—he stabbed a finger at the king—"are a relic, an arachnorism."

The king stifled a laugh. "An anachronism."

"Hey, however you like to say it is fine with me."

Mallak cast his eyes about the throne room, at the walls bedecked with weapons, burning torches, shields emblazoned with coats of arms, fading drapes of regal colours, and the tables and niches that were stacked with pierced breastplates, broken swords and helms, and the skulls of men and monsters.

"Would it surprise you if I said I understood your sentiment?" the king said with a sidelong glance at Oriken. "Well, I do. If you had spoken to me so a mere hundred years ago, I might have had Ellidar remove your head, strip it to the bone and place it on one of the shelves. Most likely I would have done the deed myself. But today... Let us just say that you catch me in a somewhat different mood. To that end, let's dispense with the insults and the façade which a king must otherwise wear. I called you here for two reasons, and you have my gratitude for responding."

201

"It didn't seem like I had much choice."

"No. And perhaps you didn't. So, then, will we talk? Not as equals, of course, but as one man to another?"

"I'm listening."

"Good. In that case, there is something I would very much like to show you."

The king smiled, and Oriken didn't like it. Not one bit.

CHAPTER TWENTY FIVE
ONE BIG MOTHER

King Mallak led Oriken down a gradually descending, winding corridor, the gentle *chink-chink* of Ellidar's ringmail drifting to them as he marched ahead. Flags, plaques and portraits decorated the walls, as well as a variety of masks and shields, with flaming torches in gilded sconces lighting the way.

"A man's life is his crime," Mallak said conversationally as they walked. "It is also his judgement, and his penance. This is true for none more so than a king. I made my mistakes and I paid dearly for them. This bubble of existence called Lachyla is set apart from the rest of Verragos, and yet remains eternally outside of the Spirit Realm." He turned a hard eye on Oriken. "This is a ledge of the Pit itself, risen to the surface of the world; a purgatorial polyp that even the birds and the worms shy away from. The dark centuries of suffering have brought me to one nugget of wisdom: that I have served my penance in full, for there is no man left within this shell. A king? Perhaps. But a man? No."

"If you're sick of life, why not just wander into the ocean? Gorven says—"

"Gorven Althalus speaks the truth. And yet... Tell me, would you take the coward's way out?"

Oriken shrugged. "I don't know what it's like to wish for death, to prefer the prospect of that over life. But, hey, I'm not in your shoes."

Up ahead, Ellidar grunted softly. Mallak quirked an eyebrow at the guard's back then flicked a glance at Oriken. "Ellidar knows. All my knights know. The people of the city, those who remain, have come to terms with the changes, even improved their lives because of them, and many have made peace with their pasts, presents, and futures. But here in the castle, what does a knight have left to occupy his time?"

Oriken shrugged. "Weekly tourneys of lob-the-lumber? Horse-grooming contests?"

"You are being facetious, I know, but what horses? They were all put to the pyre within the first year of the gates being closed. Driven mad, you see. Couldn't take the babble of noise from the minds of... us humans. I had no choice but to order the creatures destroyed."

"There are next to no horses left in Himaera," Oriken remarked. That he was indulging in a conversation with an undead sovereign of a bygone time felt utterly surreal, but he allowed it to go along in the hope that it was leading to information concerning Dagra.

"What happened to them?" Mallak asked.

"Word is that after the Uprising they were mostly all sold to the Arkh." He shrugged. "Don't ask me why, I ain't got a clue. Best we got now is mules, for the most part. You've heard the expression 'a one-horse town'?"

The king shook his head.

"Well, we're less privileged in the Folly, and mules ain't so good for riding. I reckon they'd be useless for your knights."

As the corridor arced around, Ellidar came to a stop before a plain bronze wall.

"Huh? A dead end?"

"No," Mallak said. "Now we go deeper."

"Deeper? We must already be fifty feet below."

"Indeed we are."

At a nod from Mallak, the guard drew aside a drape and took hold of a lever secreted behind it. As he pushed it upwards, the fake wall slid to the side and disappeared into a niche to reveal a wooden platform with an iron wheel and a mechanism of cogs. A series of pulley wires ran down beyond the structure, indicating to Oriken that it was used for transportation up and down the chute. Ellidar took a torch from the wall and stepped onto the platform.

The ghost of a smile played on Mallak's face. "I did mention that this is a ledge of the Pit, did I not? Ah..." He tugged a flag from the wall and passed it to Oriken. "A precaution. To put over your face. The risk is somewhat higher down below. We don't want you catching anything, do we?"

"Such as?"

Mallak shrugged as he stepped onto the platform. "The blight, perhaps?"

Oriken folded the flag in half, secured it over his nose and mouth, and tied it behind his neck. "If I catch that shit," he said from behind the makeshift mask, "I'll kill you."

"A fair warning, and duly noted."

With the scarf secured and tucked into his shirt, he joined them on the platform. Ellidar handed him the torch and, for the first time, made eye contact with him; it was a brief but hard look which Oriken took to be a warning, though of what, he had no idea. The guard grasped the wheel and began to turn it with ease. The contraption juddered slightly, then began a smooth descent. After a while, Oriken glanced up into the shadows of the chute to see the faint glow of the corridor some twenty feet above; he watched as it dimmed and shrank from view. Soon the rough-hewn ceiling of a wide tunnel rose up beside them, and the contraption came to a stop. Ellidar took the torch from Oriken and unclipped the platform's side. As he stepped out, the light fell upon a set of iron tracks upon which sat a mine cart.

"Are you taking me digging for rocks?" Oriken asked with a feigned grin. "If so, I should warn you – I don't know one end of a pickaxe from the other."

Mallak cast him a sidelong glance. "Yes, you do. But worry not, our destination is not much farther."

They followed Ellidar to the cart. Once all were inside, the guard took the rear lever in one hand and pumped it down and back up, repeating the process. The cart rattled along the tracks, slowly gaining speed.

"I've been thinking," Oriken said as the tunnel walls cascaded by. "If all life in Lachyla got blighted, then where did all the creatures and insects go? You've told me about the horses, but I've seen no bugs, no flies or spiders – thank the stars for *that*. And the trees are nothing but standing fossils."

"Aren't we all?" Mallak mused. "Most of the animals vacated the place early, no doubt sensing the change in the balance of nature. All the small things know, you see?" The king cast Oriken a pointed look. "Only the curious creature of man lacks the sense to avoid Lachyla."

"Now hold on a minute—"

"That was no low jab, dear outlander, merely an observation. The animals give the city and the graveyard a wide berth. Even the grasses shy from the walls as if sensing the difference within. The fish, too, out below the cliffs, do not venture into the shallows. Humans, on the other hand, have lost these primal senses, if indeed they ever possessed them at all. As for the trees within the walls, they were rejected as vessels. They cannot ambulate as we, you see? That, coupled with their lack of flesh and blood, makes them redundant as anything but fungal hosts – something at which they excel. Do not venture too close to the trees, for they possess a fruit which all year round is ripe for the picking; or, rather, for the popping. Many of my subjects were turned in such a fashion. The pustules are *quite* pernicious."

Oriken gave him a flat look. "I hope you don't talk to your dinner guests that way."

The king chuckled. "Dinner? I've scarcely eaten more than the rare morsel for over two hundred and seventy years! Ah, there's that confused look again. All will become clearer in just a moment." The cart slowed to a crawl as they approached a curve in the tunnel, from around which spilled a wan, spectral glow. "We are here."

"Where?" As the cart made the curve and jarred to a halt, Oriken stared dumbfounded at the monstrosity that dominated the huge cavern before him.

"Welcome," Mallak said, "to the Mother."

Oriken reached for his sabre.

"Stay your hand, outlander," Mallak said quietly as he stepped out of the cart. "Even if you went at her like a berserker with that sliver of steel, all you would accomplish is to antagonise her. You do not want that."

Reluctantly, he released his grip on the sword. "*Her?* How in the black fuck is that thing a *her*? It's a..." He stared at the entity that filled the far reaches of the cavern. "What *is* it?"

"The Mother is nature's highest pinnacle, the result of untold aeons of trial and change, culminating in a lifeform that is quite on top of the food chain; an ancient, impervious hybrid of animal, plant and mineral. Her roots stretch deep beneath the ocean. Her shell, tougher than anything on Verragos, encases her heart. And her pods"—Mallak gestured to the cavern's ceiling—"bears the sweetest and the most bitter of fruits."

As the faint echo of the king's words faded, Oriken became aware of an almost inaudible *thrum-thrum, thrum-thrum* that could only be emanating from the creature before him. He lifted his gaze from its thick body to the cavern's lofty reaches, where rainbow motes blinked like a thousand watching eyes. Myriad vines hung from a network of inky-black cylinders; at the end of each, a pale, cocoon-like oval emitted an effulgent glow, putting him in mind, not of the skins of fruits, but of the egg sacs of some enormous spider. Suppressing a shudder of revulsion, he turned his eyes away.

Mallak strolled into the cavern and squatted to his haunches, picking up an object that fit into his fist. He gestured for Oriken to approach and held it out for him to see.

Stepping out of the minecart, Oriken walked slowly towards the king, his muscles tensing as he drew closer to the hulking entity. Looking down at Mallak's open palm, he bit back a terse laugh. "A deadstone." It was smaller than the Chiddari stone and the one set into Mallak's throne, but the likeness was unmistakeable. "Sure. Why not? You were mining jewels, and you unearthed a monster."

"I don't believe you understand," Mallak said. "These are the fruits of the Mother. When they are ripe, they fall, and we gather them. Here is the safest place to keep them now." He rose and handed the stone to Ellidar, who carried it towards the cavern's far corner; there, a large mound glittered in the shadows like a dragon's hoard.

"Khariali's teats," he whispered beneath the scarf. *A pile of countless jewels. Except they're not just jewels, are they?* But if their client wanted to *believe* they were...

Any might pass for the Chiddari stone, even without the silver banding, so getting his hands on just one would land them the five hundred silver dari that waited for them back in the tavern's safe-room.

With a sigh, Mallak said, "I expect it would have been prudent of me to order the burial jewels to be collected and brought to this cavern. But, even now, that would still likely incite an uproar among the citizens. Our transcendence notwithstanding, traditions must still be respected."

"By Maros's warty arse, traditions!" Oriken shook his head at the king. "You spent your whole reign defending your city and its people from outside threats—"

"And still we were conquered." Mallak nodded, an expression of sadness and supreme weariness clouding his features. "Not from outside, but from within, at the very heart of the kingdom."

As Ellidar returned, the three stood in silence, Mallak casting a long look at the cavern's colossal inhabitant. Glancing at the stalwart guard, Oriken wondered what thoughts were running through the unreadable man's brain. As for Oriken's own thoughts – other than the distant hope of getting his hands on just one deadstone – he knew exactly how he felt about the otherworldly entity that was single-handedly responsible for turning an entire city into condemned, limbo creatures. For a decade he had wandered Himaera, first with Dagra and later as a freeblade, oblivious that something so bizarre could exist. Clearly there was no killing the creature – it had been here for a long time, and was here to stay. But if word got out that a trove of jewels was secreted deep beneath Lachyla, the death's-head-on-palm symbol would be completely ignored. People would swarm to the Blighted City in the hope of finding a fortune to save them from a life of hard and ungratifying labour. Not that there was anything wrong with treasure-seeking, but he didn't want it to be a free-for-all. If the Chiddari jewel alone was worth half a thousand silvers, then three sackfuls of the stones would bring…

Forget it, he admonished himself. *Some things go beyond wealth, right into the realm of Leave It The Fuck Alone.* He cleared his throat. "So, er, you call this thing your mother, right? I can't say I'm seeing a huge family resemblance."

Mallak's gaze lingered on the creature before he turned to face Oriken. "More correctly, she is *the* Mother. My own mother's body lies quite at peace within her tomb beneath the castle courtyard, mercifully untouched."

"Huh." *Like I could care less about your rotting mother.* "So, this is the piece of shit that's done to Dagra what it did to you and all your people. What about me and Jalis? Are we infected, too? Will we all have to stay in this—"

"Calm yourself, outlander. You and the lady Falconet are not infected. But the longer you stay, the greater the chance you will be." The king drew a breath. "Please understand, there is no malevolence here. Only natural instinct."

"So you say." He nodded towards the behemoth. "Is it aware? Of me, I mean."

"She is as aware as any lifeform that dwells in the shadows of Verragos, though her perception is unfathomable, even to us. You might say she is a queen."

"Like a bee?"

"A closer approximation would be a forest's heart tree, or another theory put forward by a few of my citizens is that she is akin to the never-seen catalyst of a fairy ring." Seeing the confusion in Oriken's eyes, he added, "Mushrooms."

"Yes, I know what a fairy ring is!" Oriken shook his head. "But do *you* know how crazy that sounds?"

The king eyed him shrewdly. "You are a man who believes what he sees. That much I know from Dagra's mind and from reading your character. The truth is here, right before you."

Oriken barked a laugh. "Oh, I do believe it. It's just absurd. The queen of the mushrooms. I guess that would make you all her fairies."

"Your fatuousness is duly noted, but the dynamic between the Mother and ourselves is considerably more complex than mushrooms and fairies. She dominates Lachyla." Mallak gestured towards the hill of deadstones. "Those are her fruits, or, more accurately, her clones. Trees, as I mentioned, are her hosts. And we humans are her vessels."

"Vessels," Oriken echoed. "So, the moral of the story is don't let a weird fungus grow in your mines. Why didn't you just kill her – *it* – when you had the chance? You could have avoided so much tragedy."

"Not so. For all her strength, she is only an extension of something much more primal. Out across the ocean, in the heart of a colossal mountain far beneath the waves, is the First Mother – the true progenitor of her species."

"This is too much." Oriken twisted his hat, then secured the scarf tighter beneath his shirt. "Why the necessity to reanimate corpses? And why turn the living into... whatever you are?"

"As I mentioned, it is about the blood and the meat." Mallak's tone was matter-of-fact. "*She* is flesh. She is plant. She is stone. She is formed of the living and of the dead. From the First Mother to the Mother, to the newest of her clones and vessels, we are all a part of the greatest and most dominant organism on and under Verragos."

"You're all part of a rotting nightmare, if you ask me."

"Don't misunderstand me. I'm not advocating any of this. My stance on the whole sordid situation is not too dissimilar to your own. I find it quite deplorable, in fact." Mallak nodded to the hulking creature before them. "And the Mother senses it. There is nothing she can do, of course. Well, there is much she *can* do, but it goes beyond her nature to shrug off a compatible vessel. More's the pity."

"Why did you bring me here?"

"Because I want you to understand."

"Nothing you've shown me is of any use to Dagra."

"No, I'm afraid it isn't."

"Well, I reckon I've seen and heard all I need, enough to know I should leave this cavern right now. How's that for understanding?"

Mallak cast him a flat look, and nodded wearily. "It is the minimum I expected. But, in time, I know you will look back on this moment with a more... enlightened perspective. Well then, let us return to the throne room." The king barked a mirthless chuckle, then added, "Before the Mother takes a liking to you."

———— • ————

Shade opened her pace as they neared the pass between the two hills, cutting around the side of a knotted bogberry thicket. A peal of thunder clapped as they cut into the grassy pass, and a sheet of lightning lit the sky. Shade jogged ahead to the edge of a cluster of bushes at the base of the hillock, then turned to face the group.

"We're here," she said.

Eriqwyn stopped as she reached the woman and peered around her. "What am I supposed to be looking at?"

Poking a thumb over her shoulder, Shade said, "Round the side of that bush at the base of the hill you'll find the entrance to an old nargut's den." She flashed the group a smile.

Onwin strode past her to approach the prickly shrub. "Let me take a look."

"Don't fall in," Shade advised, a mocking tone in her voice.

"Don't mind me, missy." The hunter crouched to sweep the sodden grass from beneath the bush. "I've a way with the old nargut."

"None down there. Hasn't been for a long, long time."

"How do you know that?" Eriqwyn asked.

Shade's eyes trailed down Eriqwyn's body as she drifted closer. "I know because I've been going into that hole"—her mocking gaze lifted to meet Eriqwyn's scowl—"for a *long* time."

Eriqwyn clenched her teeth. The innuendo was not lost on her.

"How long?" Wayland asked.

The seamstress kept her eyes on Eriqwyn as she answered. "Oh, twenty years? I was... quite young."

I'll bet you were, you bedevilled creature, Eriqwyn thought as she edged past her to Onwin.

The rain tamped down onto the hunter's cloak as he clutched hold of the grass at one side of the concealed entrance, eased the foliage aside with his hunting knife, and leaned in. A long moment later, a muffled grunt issued from the hole and he emerged. "Can't see any nargut spoor. A few rodent leavings, but it looks like the feller who dug this den is long gone."

Wayland glanced at Eriqwyn, and she gave him a brief nod. He passed her his bow and the wrapped skin of torches, kicked the grass aside and lowered himself in.

Eriqwyn waited in the rain for her group to descend into the hole. Once Lingrey had eased himself in, she handed him the torches, quivers and weapons, his cumbersome pitchfork going in last. As she prepared to enter, a muffled cry issued from the tunnel.

"What's going on?" Eriqwyn hissed.

"Sorry there, young'un," she heard Lingrey say, then his voice rang clearer as he called back to her, "My fault! Stuck me fork in the lad's rump."

Muttering a curse, she lowered herself into the nargut's den, her boots slipping but finding purchase in the damp dirt. As she crawled into the blackness, the muted rumble of the storm faded behind her. Up ahead, she heard Lingrey climbing to his feet as he reached the others in the first hub of the den. The strike of flint on firesteel resounded through the cramped space, and within moments an orange glow banished the deeper darkness as the first of the torches was fired up.

She struggled along the nargut-sized burrow until she emerged into the hub, where the stooped forms of her group were cast into striking silhouettes by the torchlight. She climbed to her feet and looked around. This was where the creature would have stored its kills, but no remains were in evidence now. Stooping beneath the low ceiling, she accepted her bow and arrows from Tan, and a torch from Wayland.

"How much further?" Tan asked of Shade, his eyes betraying him as they glanced from her face to her muddied, rain-wet body.

The seamstress's features teased into a smile. "Oh, not far now, darling. But we have the tightest gap to enter yet."

The blacksmith stifled a cough and looked around the group, eager to shift the attention away from himself.

"Lead on," Eriqwyn told Shade.

They continued into the den, keeping the torches low to avoid dousing them on the low ceiling. After a minute, Shade's voice rang clear within the enclosed space. "The way opens up a little further ahead."

Before long, the wider tunnel began to descend and the damp soil gave way to packed clay. After a minute of heading deeper underground, the way levelled off and the group emerged into a much larger area.

"Har!" Lingrey exclaimed, standing upright and stretched his back. "Damn, but that weren't good fer me old bones. Aye-yup! Ah, that's better."

"Sh," Wayland hissed at him. "Not so loud."

"Sorry, feller."

Eriqwyn held her torch high, and the flames illuminated a bumpy, domed roof that flickered with sharp shadows cast by small stalactites. She cast her gaze about the cavern, noting the myriad stalagmites that dotted the floor.

"Watch your footing here," Shade said. "Or you'll risk impaling yourselves."

Let the woman have her moment, Eriqwyn thought, signalling to Shade to choose a route between the spiky columns.

"Burrowing through into this cave, the old girl who lived here struck gold," Onwin remarked.

Shade gave a low chuckle as she stepped easily between the obstacles. "Luckier for me than for the nargut."

"Why so?" the hunter asked.

She shrugged. "If it wasn't for that creature choosing to build its den where it did, I might not be here at all."

"What do you mean by that?" Tan asked, but the woman merely glanced over her shoulder with a sly smile. After a moment, she said, "Incidentally, Onwin – if you're interested, over there is what's left of her." She pointed into the corner of the cavern to a shallow pool where the partially-submerged remains of a large, adult nargut lay, its skull resting over the edge. A droplet fell from above into the pool, setting the water rippling with the glow of torchlight.

Onwin grunted. "She crawled as far into her home as she could to die."

"It were like that long before I ever came in here. Hasn't moved a muscle in all these years." As Shade angled past the last of the stony mounds, she added, "Which is less than can be said for others around here."

Eriqwyn wasn't far behind her, and within moments had stepped out of the obstacles onto flat stone when a shout filled the cavern, followed by a crash and a clatter. She spun about to see Lingrey on hands and knees, his torch fizzing out in a puddle.

"Ayy! Darned went and slipped on something." With a grimace, he held his hand out for her to see the bloody gash across the palm. "Smarts," he announced. "But I'll live." Reclaiming his fork from the ground, he grabbed hold of the broken stalagmite beside him and climbed to his feet, pausing to peer down at the crushed body of a rat, a mess of innards spilled from its rear end. "Well, what do you know? Damned critter tripped me up. Sorry, feller."

Eriqwyn sighed. Behind her, Shade laughed softly. "I did warn you to take care."

"Lingrey," Eriqwyn said, "I need you at your best. I chose you from three hundred villagers for good reason. Show me that I was right to do so." Her glare shifted from the farmhand to the others who were still negotiating the stalagmites. "That goes for all of you. Now let's move this cursed mission onwards. Shade."

"Ready and waiting, dear." Shade stood with her back against the cavern's far wall, her hands resting atop her thighs. Beside her, a narrow fissure ran from floor to ceiling.

Eriqwyn eyed the gap. *That's the way forward?*

The seamstress gave a single nod. "It doesn't last for long." Glancing at the group, she said, "Some of you may want to rearrange your clothing and

211

belongings before trying to squeeze through. It does get a little tighter for a moment a ways inside." She turned to the fissure and began edging her way through.

Eriqwyn lay her torch on the stone and removed her cloak. As Lingrey reached the end of the obstacles, she passed it to him without a word, then shrugged out of her backpack and unbuckled her belt with the arrows and hunting knife attached. "Wayland—"

"Aye, I'll come last after passing the gear through," he said, one step behind Demelza as they traversed the spiky ground.

Taking up her torch, she held it before her through the crack and edged herself in. The sides of the fissure scratched at her tunic as she inched along. The gap gradually narrowed, causing her to wince as the rock pushed and scraped against her breasts.

From the darkness ahead came Shade's voice. "Pass it to me," she said, looming into the torchlight and reaching for its source. Her hand clasped around the stave and Eriqwyn released it. Edging back out of the fissure, the seamstress stood in the open space with the flickering light spilling over her dirt-smeared chest.

Eriqwyn pulled her eyes from the salacious woman, but felt Shade's on her as she continued to struggle through the gap. Reluctantly grasping Shade's proffered hand, she squeezed through the last of the fissure into a rough-hewn tunnel, clearly dug by human tools.

One by one, the others emerged, and the equipment was passed through until only Tan and Wayland were left.

The blacksmith shuffled through the crevice with confidence until he reached the narrowest section. Try as he might, he couldn't squeeze his muscular frame through. "It's no use," he gasped. "I'm stuck."

Eriqwyn gritted her teeth. "Goddess above. Wayland, can you pull him back out?"

"You may have better luck crawling on your belly in the dirt," Shade called to Tan. "It's wider down there, but not by much."

Once Wayland had helped him out, Tan got down and dragged himself along the ground by his elbows with no room over his head to spare, grunting and cursing the whole way. Lingrey reached a long arm into the gap and heaved the blacksmith through the final stretch. Clambering to his feet, Tan glanced to Eriqwyn with a silent apology.

Despite her growing anxiety, she gave him a curt nod and began to reattach her equipment while waiting for Wayland, her gaze roving over each of her group as she did so. Tensions were beginning to mount. It was not going quite as well as she had hoped, and they were not even inside the graveyard yet.

"We're almost directly beneath the perimeter wall," Shade said, as if reading Eriqwyn's mind. "Not far now."

"You told us that before," Onwin snapped.

"And I told you true. Don't put the delays on *my* shoulders, hunter."

Onwin growled under his breath, but said no more.

Truth is, Eriqwyn thought grudgingly, *aside from Wayland, she's been the best asset so far. Nor can I fault Demelza; the girl hasn't uttered a single word.* Taking a clean cloth, she gave her bow a quick wipe down, followed by Wayland's. When he emerged from the fissure, they shared a brief look as she passed him his weapons.

"What lies ahead?" he asked of Shade.

"Very soon, the surface. And the storm. And death." With a shrug, Shade turned on her heel, and Eriqwyn's thunderous glare bore into her back as the seamstress melted into the shadows.

I'm trying to keep everyone at their best, not put the fear of the goddess into them. "Onwards," Eriqwyn growled. She marched after the irascible woman, and the rest of the group fell in behind her.

They walked in silence, and she could feel the emotions of each of them, along with her own, the sensation permeating the musty air. Within minutes they reached the end of the tunnel, marked not by hewn rock and crossbeams but by a smooth slab of granite, a bronze lever jutting from a pillar beside it.

"We are entering through one of the crypts?" Eriqwyn asked.

"Yes," Shade said, reaching for the lever.

At Eriqwyn's side, Wayland said, "I don't suppose it's the one we need?"

Shade gave a melodious laugh as she pulled the handle. "That would be far too easy, don't you think?" The oblong stone pivoted at its centre, and she stepped through.

"Which of the families does it belong to then?" Eriqwyn narrowed her eyes at the woman. "I'm beginning to suspect that you didn't just stumble upon this den."

"How astute of you, dear." A smile worked its way from Shade's lips to her brown eyes as they reflected the flickering flames. She spread her arms as if welcoming them to the darkened hallway, and said, "These are the tombs of House Galialos."

"Never heard of 'em," Onwin rumbled, with a similar mutter of assent passing from the other members of the group.

"I have," Eriqwyn said, fixing Shade with a level look. "From the archives. They were not among the families that escaped the city."

"Oh, but they were. They fled through the very tunnel you now stand in, built during Mallak's father's reign, years before the curse. The man was even more of a tyrant than his son, by all accounts. But, you know"—she placed her hand on her hip and cocked her head—"not every member of the upper class enjoys flaunting their privileges."

Eriqwyn balked. "*You?* Descended from nobility?"

The seamstress gave a sweet, sickly smile and fluttered her eyelashes. "Not *descended* from nobility, Eri. I *am* nobility. Just like you. We are, as it happens, equals."

CHAPTER TWENTY SIX
A SHADOW THAT BEARS HIS FORM

Ellidar held the curtain open for the king, letting it fall after Mallak stepped through. With a frown of irritation, Oriken pushed the velvet drape aside and followed them into the throne room.

"Unless I'm mistaken, you said there were two reasons I was summoned here. The first was to show me the true ruler of this kingdom – that abomination down below – so what's the second?"

"Ah, yes." The king sighed. "I did say that, didn't I?"

"Well?"

A tight smile creased Mallak's features. To Ellidar, he said, "You may leave us now."

Ellidar regarded the king, his face set. As the knight turned to leave, the king stopped him by clasping a hand to his pauldroned shoulder. Mallak stepped around to face Ellidar, and grasped the knights arms in a grip that spoke not of a liege and his protector but of friends, albeit ones who masked their emotions for the sake of duty and propriety. Ellidar held the king's gaze, and Mallak gave the briefest of nods. Oriken sensed that an understanding of sorts had passed between the two, but of what, he could not say. Nor could he say why his heart was beginning to race, but something more than the oddity that pervaded the place was prickling his freeblade senses.

The king released the guard, and Ellidar strode across the throne room to the double doors. As he opened one and stepped through, Oriken caught a brief glimpse of Jalis sat with Gorven, and then the door clicked shut.

Mallak paced across to the far wall of the grand chamber. Pulling the cork of a crystal decanter, he brought it to his lips and took a deep drink. "Ah," he sighed, turning to Oriken and holding the decanter in offering. "Wine?"

"Thanks, but the stuff tastes like piss to me."

The king chuckled. "Of course. I can't say I've had that particular privilege, but each to their own."

Oriken's irritation was mounting. "Look, my friend is in some sort of predicament thanks to that monster under your castle, and, frankly, I'm having a hard time believing that he can't just walk out of here. If you don't have any pearls of wisdom to offer in that regard, then our business here is concluded. So why did you really summon me?"

The king set the decanter down, reached to his waist and unsheathed the jewelled gladius. "To kill you," he said.

And there it is. "Why am I not surprised?"

The king stepped around the chamber in a circular route towards Oriken, the sword hanging casually at his side. "Your friend seems to consider you a fine swordsman. Is his assessment accurate?"

Oriken shrugged. "I'm all right. What about you? The stories say you're not so bad with the blade yourself. I've heard Taleweavers talk of how you bested three princes years before you came to the throne. You even cut down your own champion in a fair duel, to prove your might, I suppose. Waste of a good man, if you ask me, but there you go." Mimicking the king, he added, "Are the assessments of the Taleweavers accurate?"

Mallak sneered and brandished the gladius, its blade gleaming amber in the torchlight. "Why don't you draw your sabre and find out?"

Oriken pressed his lips together. *Just another lunatic. No different from a thug or a bandit. Really? No different? This one's had three centuries to hone his skills, and if he's anything like Gorven with that bolt in his chest...* He whipped his sabre from its sheath. "You want it?" he asked the king. "Then come and get it."

Mallak circled closer, holding his sword in an easy pose, his footing light and precise. His black-lined eyes held Oriken's as they stepped around each other, each sizing their opponent.

"Why send your lap-dog away?" Oriken taunted, hoping to jibe the king to anger. "Didn't want him to see me whip my sword across your arse? Is that it?"

Mallak grinned. "You read me too well, outlander. Now, will you stand and bleat all day or are you going to attack?"

Oriken edged closer, as did Mallak, circling one another like a slow-moving whirlpool. Both stretched their blades forward, touching steel upon steel, and a quiet chime echoed through the throne room. Mallak sprang into action, his sword slashing and swiping and stabbing, his muscular frame lending weight to the attacks. It was all Oriken could do to keep the deadly gladius at bay. Sensing that he was being pushed closer to the wall, he skirted around the king and back into open space. Mallak launched a backhand slash aimed straight for his heart. As Oriken swerved back, the gladius's tip sliced cleanly through the leather of his jacket. Backing away, he drew deep breaths and eyed the king, the confident posture, the grace of his movement. With grim determination, he brought his sabre to bear as the undead sovereign of Lachyla charged in.

---·•·---

The clash of steel rang behind the entrance hall's doors. Jalis turned an alarmed look on Gorven sat beside her and sprang to her feet, Dusklight and Silverspire instantly in her hands.

"What's going on?" she demanded.

Gorven rose. "I have no idea." He turned to the three guards standing before the double doors. "Ellidar?"

The guard in the centre said nothing, merely stood with his hands clasped before him, the knuckles white.

Jalis paced towards him, and the guards on either side raised their swords. "Open these doors," she told Ellidar. His eyes turned to her, but he said nothing. "Open them!"

"What is this?" Gorven asked as he approached Jalis.

As Ellidar's hard gaze turned to him, Jalis reversed her blades in her palms and grabbed Gorven's coat, driving him backwards and slamming him into the wall. Keeping her eyes on the guards, she whisked Silverspire up and touched its slender point beneath Gorven's chin. "I know it won't kill you," she spat, "but I'm sure if I slide this blade into your brain it will indeed fucking *rankle*! Your king is killing Oriken in there. Tell them to let me in!" Her glare flicked from Gorven to the guards. "Or was this a trap to separate my friends and I? Is Dagra already dead? Do the four of you intend to dispatch *me* together?"

Gorven took her wrist in a gentle grip. "Jalis, I swear I do not know what transpires within the throne room. You must believe me."

"I must do nothing of the sort. We've been following your lead since we entered your cellar, and it stops here." Releasing him, she stepped backwards onto the red carpet and pointed Dusklight at Ellidar. "I'll give you a final chance. Let me through. Or is your king too afraid to face more than one mortal at a time?"

A shadow passed over Ellidar's unyielding expression as he folded his muscular arms over his muscular chest. "None may enter." His liquidy voice cracked, betraying an inner emotion.

Jalis sized him up, along with the two sentries. All armed. Two with longswords, the last unarmed but looking as hard as a smith's anvil, and with any number of weapons within easy reach. Against mortal men it would be a tough battle with no sure outcome, but against immortals, she stood no chance. She flicked a glance to Gorven. "Are you with me, or against me?"

Gorven sighed. "I can be neither. Please, do not be impetuous." He stepped past her to approach Ellidar and looked him square in the eyes. "We haven't communicated much, by mind nor mouth, for quite some years, as is the passage of time in this place. But we are still friends of sorts, yes?"

The guard commander grunted. "We are."

"Then tell me, as a friend, and as a member of one prominent family to another, what game is our good liege playing here?"

217

Ellidar's jaw clenched, and for a moment he looked past Gorven's shoulder and his black-lined eyes moistened as he fought whatever emotions were inside him. When he looked back to Gorven, the knight's expression was once again set.

"Oh, no," Gorven whispered. "No…"

"What?" Jalis said. "*What?*"

Neither man responded. By the door, the two sentries remained impassive.

"Right." Jalis drew a breath and readied her daggers. "So be it. Today is a good day to die."

"Not for you, lady," Ellidar said. "Not for you."

———— • ————

Mallak paused his attack and backed away slowly, a sneer upon his face. "Your little woman grows anxious."

Shaking out the tightness in his tiring shoulder, Oriken frowned at the king. "Huh?"

"Did you not hear the commotion beneath the clash of our blades? When fighting, you should extend your senses – focus on the fight, but be aware of everything in the sphere around you." Mallak sighed. "I was referring to your outlander woman in the hall beyond, not the harlot you left at the mansion."

"You don't know what you're talking about."

The king laughed. "Oh, I know. I touched her mind when the two of you were alone, so softly that she could not sense it. I witnessed every… sordid… detail."

"You witnessed nothing."

"As you say."

Mallak readied his stance, and Oriken did likewise. Deftly, slowly, they stepped around one another.

"Why are you doing this?" Oriken asked.

The king barked a terse laugh. "I'll tell you why. These black centuries have left me as little more than an empty husk, a blighted ghost inhabiting this flesh and this castle. I am bored, outlander, and you are sport. Now, raise your weapon before I gut you like a pig."

"I'll show you guts."

"Promises, promises."

Mallak swarmed in, his gladius a whir of motion. The chime of steel filled the air as Oriken fought for all his worth, barely deflecting the flurry of blows that rained upon him, forced back across the floor by the king's sheer ferocity. With a snarl, Mallak changed to a frenzied beat attack, aiming each thunderous blow at Oriken's sabre.

In the briefest of pauses, Oriken saw an opening. With a flick of his wrist, he circled the sabre beneath the gladius and swept the king's sword aside, following up with a backslash that tore across Mallak's chest.

The king merely grinned and lashed a fist into Oriken's jaw, sending him careening away. Planting his feet firm, Oriken groaned as pain swelled across his face and the stars in his vision faded. Casting Mallak a black glare, he wiped a sleeve across his bloody lips. No sooner had he done so than the king came at him again.

On they fought. Mallak angled him further and further back into the centre of the chamber. Oriken's boot-heel snagged on a ruck in the carpet and he toppled. Holding his sabre out wide, he tucked his knees to his chest as his back touched the carpet, and he rolled with the fall. His feet arcing over his shoulders and touching ground, he sprang into a stance and danced away as Mallak's blade hummed through the air where he had stood.

"For crying out sodding loud," Oriken breathed.

The king smiled and flicked a glance to the frayed edge of the red carpet. "My apologies for the untidiness of the place," he said in mock civility. "It really will not do. I shall have to have the servants slain for such ineptitude. Oh, wait! They're already dead!" The smile widened to a grin as Mallak held his arms out in a theatrical shrug.

"Side-splitting," Oriken muttered. Lunging forward, he thrust the sabre between Mallak's ribs and drove it deep.

The king grunted and cast Oriken a baleful glare. With a snarl, he hammered the pommel of the gladius onto the sabre with enough force to snap the blade and wrench the handle from Oriken's grasp. Weaponless, Oriken backed away. With deepening dread, he watched Mallak clasp the broken sabre and draw it from his torso. Tossing the bloodied blade to the red carpet, the king's expression turned from hate to admiration.

Oriken looked around in desperation for a weapon, but he couldn't be further away from those that adorned the walls of the voluminous chamber. If he turned to sprint to the wall behind him, Mallak would tear his back open, but to reach those on the opposite wall he would have to get past the king. That left the hunting knife. A pitiful weapon against the heavy gladius.

I'm fucked, he thought. Casting a grim look at Mallak, he unclasped his jacket to reach the knife.

Mallak grinned. "You can leave that toothpick where it is, outlander; I may as well be fighting an unarmed man, and that would be against the rules. Here." Mallak tossed the royal gladius across the space between them.

Oriken snatched it from the air and frowned incredulously at the gleaming blade, then at the king. "Why?" he demanded.

"No sport," Mallak replied as he turned his back and strolled with confidence across the throne room.

I drove my blade into him, and the man barely reacted. Oriken shook his head as fatigue began to creep in.

"That was your chance to run me through," Mallak called over his shoulder. "Again. But you're a man of honour. I respect that." Reaching the wall, he plucked a considerably less-ornate gladius from its bracket and tested its weight. Nodding in satisfaction, he strolled back to Oriken and, without any further preamble, he resumed the fight.

Stars a-fucking-bove! Oriken thought. Unaccustomed to wielding a gladius, he fought to manage the weightier weapon. Sparks flew as the short, wide blades danced and clashed. Sweat ran beneath his hat into his eyes, down his face. Fatigue was creeping in, and his shoulder ached from the constant clashing of blades, but the king seemed not to be tiring at all. *How in the fiery Pit am I supposed to defeat this creature?*

---·•·---

With Eriqwyn at Shade's heels, the inscrutable seamstress led the way up the Galialos vault's stairwell. The four men and Demelza trudged mutely behind, each no doubt contemplating the task that awaited them. She could sense their trepidation, their fear, and she understood it; never had her nerves been tested so since becoming a Warder. Over the years, she had often paused at the bars of the portcullis during her patrols, and through them glimpsed movement in the shadows or heard a distant crooning that was nothing like any creature of the heath, and it had never failed to leave her skin prickling with gooseflesh. But the ghouls within the Forbidden Place were an obstacle, not an objective.

Her scrutiny of the outlanders on Graegaredh Knot had allowed her to commit their appearances to memory; that, and Demelza supplying her – albeit under duress – with their names, had allowed her to build a profile for each of them and share the descriptions with her group. The hunt was not for a nameless, faceless enemy, and that gave her an advantage. She was prepared, and the graveyard was almost upon her.

"You have my appreciation for showing us this route," she said to Shade. "But you must know that the council are likely to call for the cave to be sealed."

"That would be unfortunate," Shade replied, her voice drowned by the staccato echo of rainfall that drifted from the vault's entrance.

"Moreover," Eriqwyn said, "we will have no choice but to hold a hearing to determine the punishment for entering the Forbidden Place without permission – not once, but repeatedly. I imagine it won't be treated lightly."

"I fully expect so."

Eriqwyn cast the seamstress's rear a wilting scowl. *You're being remarkably calm for a woman in such a tenuous position.* She pushed the thought from her mind as they turned onto the last flight of steps and a grey curtain of rain loomed into view, leaking wan daylight onto the stairwell's landing. She doused her torch and placed it within a shallow niche by the wall, then selected an arrow from her sheaf. As she waited for the others to join them, she gazed out at the bleak vista of the graveyard.

She had been twelve years old the first time she glimpsed the inside of the Forbidden Place. She'd stared between the portcullis bars with nervous fright, fascination and the thrill of naive youth. She'd knelt and reached through to touch the mist that licked at the cracked earth, and listened to the muted sounds that ignited her direst imagination. Now, she was inside that place, and the first wisps of fog curled upon the rain-pelted mud, the downpour filled the air, and the rumble of thunder rode the black clouds that darkened the day. As a Warder, it was weather she was accustomed to; with the wind and rain masking sight, sound and smell, it could give her a tactical edge against the outlanders.

"Thank you, Shade." Eriqwyn turned to the seamstress as the last of the group reached the landing. "You have aided our mission greatly by leading us here, but your presence is no longer required. You may return to Minnow's Beck and report to the Lady of the Manor." Now that Eriqwyn knew of Shade's noble lineage, she could see it behind the woman's smile – it was one of patience, the sort that Adri showed to the common folk when they approached her with their trifling problems.

Stroking a finger slowly down her chest, Shade said, "Oh, I think rather that I might stay a while."

Eriqwyn cast her a level look. "I have no time for this. Do as you will, and face the consequences later, but do not hinder us. If you compromise our—"

"Yes, I know," Shade sighed. "You'll shout at me and wave your finger in my face. Spare me the misdirected anger, Eri, *and* the spurious gratitude. It is not me you should be worried about." With her torch still ablaze, she headed for the stairwell.

"Where are you going?" Wayland asked as she angled past him.

"To pay my respects to my relatives." Shade's gaze fell across the whole group. "Watch yourselves in this so-called Forbidden Place. There are things here that are more dangerous than a trio of outlanders."

"We know that," Onwin said.

"No, hunter. In this, you know nothing." Ignoring his dour expression, Shade crossed to the top of the steps where Demelza stood nervously clutching her bow. Placing a hand upon the girl's shoulder, she said, "Don't be afraid, little one. You will do what you know you must when the time comes. As will we all." And with that, the seamstress headed back down into the depths of her family vault.

She is of no concern, Eriqwyn told herself. "Wayland, you will take Tan and Demelza and scout the far side of the graveyard for the outlanders. Circle

221

around to the Chiddari vault and wait at its entrance. I will meet you there. You remember its location from the archives map?"

Wayland nodded. "Aye."

"Onwin and Lingrey, you are with me. If anyone sees the outlanders, try to dispatch them from a distance. If they see you, we have lost the element of surprise, in which case you should alert the rest of us by any means necessary. But, as Shade rightfully reminded us, do not forget what else lurks within these walls. Any questions?"

"What if..." Demelza began.

Eriqwyn looked past the rest of the group to the girl. "Yes? Speak up."

"What if one of us gets lost?"

"We cannot waste time or attention in retrieving any who stray," Eriqwyn said firmly.

Wayland gave Demelza's shoulder a gentle touch. "Stay by me, lass. But not *too* close."

Eriqwyn turned her attention to the whole group. "If all else fails – goddess forbid – and if you can retreat to the cave or the northern portcullis, then do so. Otherwise we strive to achieve our objectives. Valsana be with you all."

Five solemn faces regarded her, and when she caught Wayland's eyes her strength bolstered. This time, his subtle wink was aimed not at her, but at the girl by his side. And then he was striding past her, stepping out into the storm with Demelza and the blacksmith in tow. Eriqwyn watched the three cloaked figures angle around a bronze statue that lay half-submerged, its face pressed into the dirt. *Like ancestor, like descendant*, she thought, detachedly, as the three cloaked figures moved away.

She glanced up at Lingrey as he appeared at her side. "Ayup," he said, smacking his lips as he gazed out across the rows of headstones. "Just another field, is all. Just another field."

———— • ————

"What troubles you, outlander? Not so brash now, hmm?" Raising an eyebrow, Mallak lunged for Oriken's chest.

Oriken swept his blade across and the swords clashed, deflecting the thrust, but not enough. The edge of the king's gladius sliced through his jacket and bit into his shoulder. Gritting his teeth against the pain, he flashed his sword across to meet Mallak's next attack, but the king's blade dipped and he over-swung, leaving his side exposed. A blur of motion was the only warning as Mallak's fist hammered into his face.

He was down, cheek mashed against the hard stone, his vision awash with a rainbow of colours. Willing his body to move, he slapped a hand around the floor in search of the jewelled gladius. *Twice in one rotting day*, he thought.

222

Only, this time, it wasn't Krea he faced. *I'm a dead man. Get up, damn it!* He eased himself to his hands and knees, every moment expecting Mallak's sword to plunge into his back, but the blow never came. Slowly, the throne room swam into focus and he looked across to see Mallak grinning from ear to ear, all white teeth and black gums. The king's shirt was stained from the wound in his side, and the chamber floor was pockmarked with dark droplets, but the wound itself seemed no longer to be bleeding. Between Oriken and the king lay the jewelled gladius.

He glanced back up and frowned at the king's expression. Was that a shadow of pain that flitted across Mallak's face, the briefest wince that the ruler of Lachyla had let slip? *So, you do feel something, after all.* The thought gave him hope.

"Perhaps if you kept your mind on the moment rather than elsewhere," Mallak suggested, stepping to the fallen gladius. "Because it seems to me that your friend's assessment of your swordsmanship is sorely lacking." Nudging a toe against the sword, he slid it across to Oriken.

The haft slid into his open hand. He upturned the tip onto the stone and leaned upon the pommel, using it to climb to his feet. His face throbbed – both from the punch and from striking the stone floor – and the inside of his sleeve was slick with blood. He clutched the gladius and held his other arm to his side, and regarded Mallak with a baleful glare.

"That was honour repaid," the king said. "In a duel, it is the height of bad manners to attack an unarmed opponent, just as it is the height of impropriety to *not* attack an armed opponent." He lifted his sword in a mock salute.

Fuck your honour. Oriken lunged and swiped his sword in a backhand that bit deep into Mallak's raised forearm. "No more games," he growled, whipping the blade away.

"Only the endgame," Mallak said, his voice thick with a liquid crackle, the casual amusement slipping from his face. He swapped the sword to his off hand and held his injured arm to his chest, soaking his shirt in even more blood.

Oriken flicked a half-hearted jab at Mallak which the king swatted aside. Oriken's optimism surged as he circled his blade back around in a savage reverse slash. Mallak's parry came too slow, and Oriken's sword tore across the king's abdomen.

With a deft back-step, he grinned in satisfaction as Mallak clutched the wound, his slick, blackened entrails spilling about his fingers. "I got you, you bastard. I got you good."

The king's mask of pretentiousness dropped altogether. "You did say you would show me some guts," he spat. "Come on then, don't stop now! Be a good sport!" He lunged, but his movement was sluggish and Oriken easily side-stepped the thrust.

Ignoring the pain that pulsed down his arm, Oriken raised his sword in a double-grip, reversed the blade and plunged it into the soft flesh between Mallak's chest and shoulder. The king's arm dropped to his side, but the sword remained in his grasp.

With a shake of his head, Oriken stepped back from the grievously injured king. "Give up, damn you."

"Don't you dare spare me any quarter!" Mallak snarled. "I hold a weapon yet. Have at me!" He ran at Oriken, his blade flapping up in a feeble attempt at attack.

Oriken swiped his sword into Mallak, then a second time, and a third. "Curse you!" he yelled into the king's face. Mallak's black gaze shone with defiance as he locked eyes with Oriken, but still he refused to fall, refused to let go of his weapon. Oriken tore into him, swiping the royal gladius across the king's torso, slicing his face over and over, until finally he reversed the blade in a sweeping overhead arc and hammered it down. The wide tip smashed through the king's collar-bone and plunged deep into his chest. With a gurgling sigh, Mallak's hand fell from his stomach and his innards spilled to his feet. He crumpled and sank to his knees amid the pool of his bowels, staring towards his throne as he teetered, a bloody, broken mess. His sword slipped from his grasp and clattered to the stone.

With the last of his strength, Oriken pulled the gladius from Mallak's body and sank to a knee before him, leaning upon the royal sword, its tip pressed against the blood-soaked stone.

Mallak's breath came ragged, and blood, darker than wine, frothed at his lacerated lips. "There's no need... to show deference now, Oriken of Eyndal."

"It's Alder's—"

"Folly. I know." Mallak's eyes closed and he fell backwards, his head landing with a soft thud upon the red carpet.

"You were toying with me."

A gurgling cough issued from the mess that was Mallak's face. "Perhaps. Just... a little."

"Why?"

"I could have taken my own life... a thousand times and more... but that is not the way of kings, it is the way... of cowards." This time when he coughed, blood spumed from his mouth and he fell silent but for the crackly, liquidy, burbling of his breath. He lifted a hand and motioned for Oriken to draw nearer. Oriken lay the gladius down and shuffled closer. Mallak's hand shot down and gripped his wrist, his grip strong for a man who should be utterly dead. Oriken made to pull away, but there was no attack left in the king. Mallak's mouth opened. A bubble popped at his lips as he tried to form a word.

"What, damn you?" Oriken lifted his arm and grabbed the king's wrist, trying to pry him off. "Still have something to say? Why won't you just let go?" With the last word, he wrenched himself free of Mallak's grip, and the king's arm fell to splash into the mess at his side.

Mallak's gaze locked with Oriken's. There was no malice in his eyes now, he was back to the man with whom Oriken had earlier conversed. "Thank you," the last king of Lachyla whispered, and his eyes closed.

CHAPTER TWENTY SEVEN
UNHOLY COMPULSION

Swathes of rain whipped Eriqwyn's cloak about her as she trudged through the mud. A tumbleweed, bouncing along between the tombstones, snagged on a tilted cross before tearing free and flying past Lingrey. Struggling against the wind and loping between graves with pitchfork in hand, the angular farm labourer could have passed for a Servant of the Slain, sifting a battleground for the fallen dead.

As she turned from the portentous image, Eriqwyn peered into the storm towards Onwin. The hunter tramped along a narrow pathway that ran parallel with the perimeter wall, an arrow nocked to his bow. She stumbled as her foot caught in the mud and was almost blown to her knee by the fierce wind. Steadying herself, she pulled her boot free from the mud and frowned down at the hollow it had created, the sides lumpy and risen, recognising with disgust the sunken shapes of a torso and pelvis.

"Merciful goddess," she whispered.

She called out for Lingrey and Onwin to wait, but her voice barely carried in the ever-changing gusts of wind. The farmhand paused, glanced back and raised his hand in acknowledgement, but, heedless of her call, Onwin continued on. Eriqwyn stepped over the corpse and picked up her pace. She opened her mouth to call to the hunter a second time when he turned and waved for her attention. Onwin pointed ahead, but whatever he wanted her to see was blocked from view by a vault entrance. She lifted her gaze above the structure and saw the hazy shape of a large, domed roof a hundred feet beyond the vault. Tucked into the corner of the graveyard, with the stark, grey perimeter walls rising above it, she envisaged the manor's archive map of the graveyard and recalled the crude circles that dominated each of the four corners. When she had been a Warder-in-training, the First Warder had instructed her about the ghouls within the Forbidden Place and given her a basic description of its layout; she remembered now that each of those circles represented a chapel. It was possible that the outlanders sought sanctuary from the weather beneath one of the domes.

Perhaps, she mused, *but it is equally likely that they wait the storm out in one of the many vaults. I cannot second-guess myself. And what of the ghouls? I have seen hide nor hair of them so far, yet I know they are here.*

She signalled for the hunter to wait, but he was already slipping from view behind the vault. "Onwin!" she hissed, not daring to shout too loudly in case the outlanders were in hearing distance. "Damned fool!"

A muffled shout rose over the wind from beyond the vault entrance. Sharing a glance with Lingrey, Eriqwyn broke into a run for the far side of the obstruction. She paused at the edge of the vault and peered around it. Onwin backed into view, then promptly slipped and plummeted into the mud.

In the corner of her eye she saw Lingrey point his pitchfork at the fallen hunter and shout something unintelligible. With her arrow taut in her bowstring, Eriqwyn stepped out from the cover of the vault.

"Blessed Valsana," she whispered. The scene before her was from every villager's worst nightmare. "On your feet!" she called to Onwin, loosing the arrow into the horde of ghouls that swarmed towards him. Turning on her heel, she broke into a stumbling run between the gravestones for the southern dividing wall. Through the sheet of rain her keen eyes sought and found the crooked line that ran from the wall's base to its battlements. "Steps!" she called out. "To the ramparts!"

Whipping another arrow from her sheaf, she looked back at Lingrey to see him striding and slipping, thrusting the haft of his pitchfork into the mud as he went. She flicked a glance over her other shoulder and immediately wished she hadn't; the ghouls were closing in, scores of the creatures streaming through the chapel's high pillars from the shadowed interior, heading straight for her.

Heart and mind racing, she fixed her gaze on the narrow steps ahead, swallowing a scream as the rain and wind pushed her back, seemingly in alliance with the monstrous swarm. Her Warder training wavered as unwelcome thoughts spilled into her mind. *They see me. They smell me. They want me. Goddess, give me strength.*

And then she was at the wall, floundering up the rain-slick steps, clenching her bow and arrow in a fist and slapping her other hand upon the stones for purchase. As she scrambled onto the battlements, she spun and crouched, her eyes darting over the nightmarish scene. From her vantage point she could see far and wide to each of the perimeter walls. The grave-studded vista was filling with ghouls, spreading out not only from the closest chapel but also from the one beyond the Litchway at the far end of the dividing wall. Pockets of movement in the extreme distance told her that more of the creatures were pouring in from the northern reaches. Beneath the storm-black sky, the long, shadowed rectangle of the graveyard was a quagmire peppered with tombs and trees and vaults and ghouls; beyond the walls, nothing but a haze of rain. It was a diorama of death, disconnected from the outside world.

227

Beneath her, Lingrey loped through the mud a stone's throw away from the steps. A single ghoul ambled into view beside the wall and paused. It lifted its countenance to Eriqwyn as if sniffing the air, then, with a rasping moan, it turned on Lingrey. Eriqwyn loosed her arrow. The projectile punched into the ghoul's head and it pitched sideways into the mud. The farmhand ran past the fallen ghoul and slid to a halt against the wall. He glanced up at her, his expression haggard, then took to the steps. Behind him, the ghouls rose back into sight and lurched forward, snatching at his heels, pulling Lingrey's mud-caked boots over the slick stone and bringing him crashing face-first to the steps. The ghoul fell onto him and sank its teeth into his rear. Lingrey cried out and kicked frantically, and the creature released its grip. As it slid to the ground, its talons raked down the back of the farmhand's legs, dragging him to the base of the steps. He flipped over onto his back and swatted the fork at the creature's face, then slammed his boot-heel hard under its chin, sending it careening away. He scrambled to his feet, but more of the ghouls were upon him.

"Lingrey!" Eriqwyn shouted. She reached for an arrow, but stayed her hand as she realised with sickening horror that too many of the monstrosities had closed around him, and wasting arrows on creatures that didn't feel them was an exercise in futility.

Lingrey held his ground, spinning his weapon all around, swatting their reaching hands and holding them at bay. The pitchfork was a blur of motion as the curved tines slashed furrows from the ghouls' ravaged flesh, but still they pushed forward as the throng grew.

One ghoul made its way onto the steps. As it neared her, she whipped out her hunting blade and swiped it into the creature's face, sending it careening into the horde. She watched hopelessly as a taller ghoul lumbered between Lingrey's swipes and grabbed him by the shoulders. Its lipless maw lunged for his face, and the rotten teeth sank into his cheek, pulling a chunk away. Lingrey thrust the ghoul back into the crowd and plunged the pitchfork into its chest.

"Ayyy-yup!" he screamed, and swung the stuck creature in an arc, the momentum lifting it from its feet. "Har!" With a flick of his wrists, the ghoul went sprawling from the tines into the mass of its brethren. "You shouldn't oughta have done that!" he shouted at the fallen creature as he ran at it and rammed the fork's spikes into its gore-filled sockets. As he whipped the weapon free, the horde closed in behind him and a score of hands clutched at his cloak and arms, wrenching the pitchfork from his grasp. They tore at his neck and face, and dragged him to his knees.

"Ayyyy…" A tumult of moans drowned the old farmhand's last utterance to the world as the ghouls swarmed over him.

"I'm so sorry," Eriqwyn whispered.

"*Warder!*"

Her gaze darted over the graveyard for the source of the faint call. A flash of movement on the eastern wall caught her eye. Peering through the rain, she saw a figure waving to her from between the parapets. *It can only be Onwin,* she thought. Two stretches of walkway separated the hunter from her, and a partially-collapsed tower rose behind the chapel's dome in the corner between east and south walls. It would be perilous, but the hunter might be able to join her if he could climb between the rubble. But she had to reach Wayland. All others were expendable.

"Onwin!" she called. "To me!"

The ghouls had taken to the steps. The nearest had almost reached the walkway. Delivering a swift kick into its face, she broke into a run for the central Litchtower.

A gust of wind whipped through the battlements and sent her sprawling to the wet stones, but she picked herself up and soon the drum tower came into view. Beneath it, flurries of ground-fog buffeted across the crumbled Litchway. She scanned ahead into the shaded interior of the Litchtower. Her eyes fell upon the winch mechanism nestled against the forward wall, and the seeds of a plan began to form in her mind.

She reached the tower's side arch and passed beneath it, not slowing until she exited the other side. Fifty feet along the walkway the graveyard's rear watchtower stretched higher than all the others, its width reaching out beyond the battlements. An iron door was set into the watchtower's circular side. Coming to a halt halfway between the two towers, she leaned through the walkway's risen sides and steadied herself between two merlons out for a view of the graveyard. Ghouls peppered the immediate area, ambling within the rising fog. Though the greater gathering of the creatures amassed closer to the western chapel, they were heading slowly but inexorably her way. She scanned the ground for Wayland and his team, her heart thumping as she looked from ghoul to headstone, from tree to vault entrance with no sign of them. *I need Wayland,* she thought, staunching her rising panic. As her gaze passed over a vault entrance almost directly ahead of her, a figure stepped into view with its cloak whipping behind it and its axe raised.

Thank the Goddess, she thought as Wayland lunged forward to smash his axe through a nearby ghoul's face. Calling out his name, she waved her bow high. "Up here!"

He cleaved into a second ghoul, splitting the head in two before glancing up to her. After a pause, he raised his wood-axe and bow in acknowledgement. As two figures stepped out from behind the vault, a warning cry spilled from Eriqwyn's lips before she recognised Tan and Demelza. Gathering his team to him, Wayland ran closer along a side path adjacent to the Litchway.

"Get to higher ground!" Eriqwyn pointed her bow towards the watchtower. "Can you get inside?"

Wayland glanced across, then shook his head. "No entrance!" His voice barely cut through the wind. He pointed to a section of wall hidden beyond the tower, and Eriqwyn caught the last of his words. "...steps further along!"

"Get to them! I'll attract the ghouls' attention. Reach the battlements and find a way into the city. I suspect the outlanders are in there, and they are still our priority."

As Warder and blacksmith set off between the gravestones with Demelza in tow, Eriqwyn could only hope he had properly heard her. As the men paused to dispatch a pair of ghouls that staggered into their path, Eriqwyn nocked an arrow. Selecting a ghoul that faced the trio with its back to her, she gauged the wind, took aim, and released. The arrow tore through the air, pulled by the gusting wind, but found its target, plunging into the creature's shoulder. It turned, seeking the source of the attack.

She waved her arm and shouted at the top of her lungs, "To me, you cursed dog! Get over here!"

The ghoul lifted its visage to the battlements and staggered towards her. As it passed another of its brethren, the second turned to follow.

"That's it!" Eriqwyn yelled. "Come and see what I've got for you!"

More of the nearby ghouls paused in their meanderings and turned to face her as she continued to shout down to them, and one by one they waded through the fog to gather beneath her section of the wall. A glance to the east told her that the creatures that had swarmed from the first chapel were making for the Litchway in droves.

With a last glance at Wayland's team as they weaved through the creatures for the steps, Eriqwyn eased herself out of the embrasure and back onto the walkway. She would have to trust in him to reach the safety of higher ground. Running back into the Litchtower, she cast a grim glare at the line of ghouls that headed along the battlements, then stepped to the tower's forward wall to glance through a murder hole at the Litchway below.

Yes, she thought, seeing the creatures gathering before the gate. *That's it. Come to me.* Moving to the winch, she slid a finger over the chains; they were rusty, but slightly slick with grease. Frowning in puzzlement but shrugging at her good fortune, she placed her bow on the floor and grabbed the winch handle. At first it refused to budge, but she planted her feet and heaved upwards and, with a grinding of metal on stone as the chains shifted, the handle began to turn. Slowly, the chains passed through their apertures in the floor to either side of the mechanism and inched their way upwards to coil around the barrel.

The outlanders have entered the city, she told herself. *Given the potential for looting, that is their most likely target. They must have avoided the ghouls by staying on the Litchway and heading straight for the battlements.* Thinking of Lingrey, she hissed a curse. *As I too should have done.*

Intent on turning the winch, she almost didn't register the rasping moan as a ghoul shuffled into the tower's small room, its outstretched hands reaching for her. She released the handle, whipped her dagger out and plunged it through the ghoul's palm. As the broken nails of its other hand scratched at her head, she dug her fingers into its scrawny neck and shoved backwards, slamming it into the side of the arch. She glared into its dead eyes as it snarled and snapped, then with a cry of defiance she squeezed its neck and wrenched the creature and herself through the arched doorway. For a sickening moment she imagined them turning, her blade through its withered hand, their faces inches apart as they pirouetted across the walkway like some macabre dancing couple. With bile rising in her throat, she tore the dagger free and ducked beneath the ghoul's reach to step behind it. She wrapped her arms around it, pinning the ghoul's arms to its sides, and heaved it into an embrasure. She slammed its face to the stone and grabbed a fistful of its ragged clothing, then pushed it through the gap and watched as it plummeted into the teeming mass beneath.

Readying herself for the next of the ghouls that filed towards her, a sudden shout drifted over the wind from somewhere behind them. Several paused and turned, giving Eriqwyn the opening to peer along the ramparts, but beyond the ragged, rotten procession she could see nothing.

"Onwin," she called. "Is that you?"

"Aye, Warder!"

The nearest ghoul was almost upon her. Grabbing it by the shoulders, she rammed a knee into its groin; decayed bones crunched from the impact, but the creature's ghastly visage showed no reaction. She stepped back, planted the flat of her boot onto its chest and kicked it to sprawl at the feet of its fellows.

Swallowing the acrid taste that rose in her throat, she shouted across to Onwin. "Draw their attention! I'm raising the gate to lure them into the city. It's our only chance."

Onwin's response was drowned beneath a fierce gust and an overhead crash of thunder that shook the stones beneath Eriqwyn's feet. The ghouls paused, mouths agape as they lifted their faces to the sky. Eriqwyn ran into the Litchtower and resumed her turning of the winch. The hunter's shouts slowed the ghouls and kept her from being their singular intent, but still a number of them continued for the archway. Switching glances constantly between the advancing ghouls and the mechanism, she watched as inch by slow inch the chains turned until several rows were coiled around the barrel.

Seeing the first ghoul step under the arch, she ran forwards with a snarl and thrust it backwards to slam into three more of the creatures, sending them all slipping to the stones.

"Cursed abominations!" she hissed. Returning to the winch, she turned the handle with as much speed as she could muster. Onwin's shouts were not drawing all of the creatures to him, and the few beyond the arch were already back on their feet.

Surely that must be enough. "Onwin!" she called. "It's done! Take to the roofs!" As the ghouls staggered into the Litchtower, she gave the winch one final turn, snatched up her bow and ran for the opposite arch, passing several gaps in the rear ramparts before skidding to a halt and hauling herself up into an embrasure.

Her jaw dropped as she glanced out into the rain-filled distance as, for the first time, her eyes fell upon the city of her ancestors. Its network of buildings and streets, alleyways and plazas blanketed the expanse within the metropolis's high walls, the castle's towers stabbing into the storm-black sky at the rear of it all, the fortress itself sprawling atop its hill like in the vellum sketches of her family's archives. Sheets of lightning coursed over Lachyla amid a rumble of thunder, and for several seconds the cityscape flashed starkly between dark and light. For all the horror the Gardens of the Dead instilled in her, the sight of the true Forbidden Place almost brought her to her knees. As she stared at the scene, she understood what immeasurable wealth and grandeur, elegance and luxury Valsana's curse had stripped away.

And yet somehow those elements still remain, her Warder senses told her. *And not merely as vestiges.* Something about the place was very wrong, more so than the horrible truths of deadstones and the deceased; everyone in the village had always known it, though only ever spoke of it in hushed and secret whispers.

Ghouls stumbled onto the walkway from the Litchtower, their yellowed orbs and empty sockets fixed on her. Steadying herself between the merlons, she eyed the gap between herself and the sloping roof of the nearest building – at least six feet across and as many down. Clenching tightly to the grip of her bow, she thought, *I can do this.* As the ghouls' decayed hands reached for her, she leaped from the battlements.

Time slowed, a second becoming an eternity as she coursed across and down the divide, her cloak billowing over her head as she was buffeted by the strong winds. In that moment, she envisaged herself plummeting to the flagstones, to the ghouls that spilled through the raised Litchgate and streamed into the city.

Goddess, what have I done?

She hurtled towards the sloping roof-side and slammed into it, the breath punched from her lungs. Her fingertips curled over the lip of the rooftop above, and with a snarl of exertion she dragged herself up and over onto the flat stone. Gulping air as her breath returned, she crawled across the roof and leaned back against its domed centre.

The deadstone in her pack pressed into her spine, and, with what was almost becoming a mantra, she answered her own question. *The course is set. I will see it through. I am the First Warder, and the safety of the village is paramount. I have done what is right.*

CHAPTER TWENTY EIGHT
FACING THE RAVEN

In Krea's dream she swam naked and free above the ocean bed, drifting idly through swaying fronds as schools of fish darted away from her. Diving and rolling, she sank to her back and lay motionless upon the sandy floor, basking in the languid life of the shallows as a group of tiny sunfish flitted down to nibble harmlessly at her skin.

In the waking world she ventured often into the shallows, but the fish always kept their distance, and the plants beyond Lachyla's cliffs were not tall and vibrant but pale and lifeless, just like her. And so she dreamed of things as they would never be, things that could not happen even if she really was just a girl and not a three hundred year old woman trapped in an undead girl's body.

A shadow fell over her, scattering the radiant sunfish. She gazed up into the waters at a nebulous shape with spumes as of ink flowing from its mass. But as it drew closer she saw it was no squid or octopus but a man, and the ink was blood. Lots of blood. His face loomed closer to hers, and although she could not recognise his features, shredded as they were and obscured by the crimson cloud, she knew, with certainty, who he was.

"Highness!" Krea's eyelids fluttered open to the darkness of her bedchamber as the lingering dream-image transferred to a signal within the hive-mind. She threw the bedsheets aside and jumped from the four-poster, ran across to the window and threw the curtains open. As the grey light of day spilled into the room, King Mallak's scream coasted the undercurrent of the city's linked consciousness. It was an offering from sovereign to subjects, the pain of his passing as a final farewell. One by one, the cityfolk stirred as they felt their liege's life ebb from his body. Krea had never been close to the king, but she knew the few who had, and, through them, she shared the sorrow as their liege turned to face the swan's path.

She unlatched the windows and pulled them inward, gripped onto the sill and leaned out into the rain and wind to look towards the distant castle. As she did so, she called upon her training of three centuries, focusing, pushing the emotions of the king and the citizens to the corners of her mind. Because something was amiss. Something other than the king's impending departure.

She could feel it swirling at the periphery of the hive-mind as a similar sense to that which led her and Gorven to Dagra as he slept out on the heath. But this was different somehow. Casting her gaze across the rooftops to the city's main thoroughfare, her high vantage-point afforded her a view of the Litchtower – just a pinprick at this distance, but as her eyes fell upon it she sensed more than saw the focus of her concern. It was a frenzy of wrath awakened, the greatest failure of the blight, the deepest shame of the conjoined mind as of a child discarded into a cellar. And the child was loose, and looking for its Mother.

"Oh, no," she whispered.

Closing the windows, Krea whisked her negligee off and hurried into more congruous apparel, all the while glancing to the wall and the slender, crossed swords that hung there.

---------- • ----------

The knight commander opened the throne room doors. "You may enter now," he said in a strangled voice.

Jalis barged through the doors, coming to an abrupt halt at the sight of Oriken alive and kneeling beside an eviscerated, blood-soaked body. *Is that the king?* "By the gods," she whispered. The words echoed faintly through the chamber.

"Not even close." Oriken cast a tired, sidelong glance.

Ellidar strode along the red carpet and Jalis followed, prepared for the knight to show the first hint of attacking Oriken, but instead he lowered to a knee beside Mallak. "My liege," he said, taking the king's tattered hand into his own.

Jalis crouched beside Oriken and wrapped an arm around him to help him to his feet. He winced, and she gently touched his cheek to turn his face to hers. One of his eyes was all but swollen shut within a circle of livid purple that merged with the darkening bruise Krea had given him. "Orik," she whispered, tilting her head to the side. "I thought you… They wouldn't let me…" A tear fell from the edge of her eye.

Oriken held onto her. "I know."

She looked down at the king. His features were all but stripped away by a score of deep cuts. Only the eyes were intact; as she looked at the speckled green irises, he blinked and met her scrutiny.

He's still alive. The realisation sickened her, the pain he must be in, and then she recalled Gorven's stories about how their loved ones had committed suicide. *Of course he's alive. Lachylans die hard, remember? He's only lost half the blood from his body and is wearing his guts around his ankles.* Holding tight onto Oriken, she aimed a question at both him and the king. "What did you do?"

234

Oriken shook his head and flapped a hand weakly at Mallak. "He gave me no choice."

"It is true. His Highness has imparted as much to me." Ellidar turned a stony look upon Oriken. "He says I should not blame you."

"Then don't," Jalis said forcefully. "And be glad that Oriken bested him, because if this had gone differently you would already be lying next to your king in a similar fashion."

"Please, Jalis." Gorven came to stand at her side. "It is over. The time for threats is passed. Sire, why do this? He is just an outsider. You could have commanded any one of us to a duel."

"He desires oblivion," Ellidar said. "He would not leave any of his subjects with the knowledge that they had ended his life."

"But his life is not ended!" Gorven exclaimed. "Your Highness, you know from experience what must be done to achieve that."

Mallak's torn lips fluttered, and a gurgling sigh escaped them.

"He would speak to you," Ellidar told Oriken. "Listen and show your gratitude."

His voice no more than a raspy whisper, Mallak said, "The royal sword... It is yours. You have... earned it."

Oriken looked mutely at the blood-streaked gladius at his feet.

"His Highness affords you the highest honour and privilege," the knight said. "Gratitude, outlander. Now."

With a sigh, Oriken stepped out of Jalis's hold and looked from Ellidar to Gorven to the king. "Damn right I earned it," he said with a nod. Casting a gaze across the throne room, he wandered across to retrieve his fallen hat, regarding the battered old thing with a wry chuckle as he returned to hunker down beside Mallak. "As far as items go, this one means the most to me. I've held onto it for more than a decade, and I reckon it's time to let it go." He placed the hat upon Mallak's chest, then rose to his feet. "It's yours. You earned it." The king's eye fixed on him, blinked, and Mallak gave a gurgling grunt of acceptance. It was done.

Blood burbled at Mallak's lips, and Ellidar placed a hand upon the king's shoulder. "He is too weak for more words, but he conveys his gratitude strongly." He unbuckled the jewelled scabbard from Mallak's waist and took up the royal gladius. Accepting Gorven's proffered kerchief, he wiped the sword and scabbard clean before sliding the blade reverently into its sheath. Rising, he looked into Oriken's eyes for a long moment before holding the gladius out for him to accept, which Oriken did without a word.

"Your Highness." Gorven's voice was pained. "Please, do not ask this of us."

"It is my charge," Ellidar said. "And I accept it as my final duty to my liege."

Jalis frowned. "Final duty?"

"His pain has been long suffering," Gorven explained. "He seeks peace. There is a sense of communal preservation that has nurtured and strengthened our society. When one of us chooses to leave this life – which, these days, is rare – they take the matter into their own hands, either by entering the ocean or the heath, or by climbing into the forge. The king would never choose these ways. You, Oriken, have bested him in combat, but, this time, the final blow must be dealt with fire. There is no other—" Gorven's expression turned aghast. "Oh, no."

"What now?" Jalis asked, unable to mask the irritation in her voice.

Ellidar looked up sharply and rose from the king's side. "Go," he told Gorven. "Prepare the citizens. I will join you presently."

"Open the outer door!" Gorven shouted to the guards stationed between the throne room and the entrance hall. Glancing to the king, he inclined his head in deference. "Farewell, my liege," he said, and then fled from the throne room, shouting commands to the guards and the cityfolk who amassed beyond the castle's entrance.

"What's going on?" Jalis demanded as Ellidar strode across the chamber.

Taking a lit torch from its sconce, he ripped a velvet curtain from the wall and paced back towards the king. "The denizens," he said. "They have infiltrated Lachyla. All of them. You should go now."

Casting the knight a grim look, Jalis took Oriken by the arm. "We have to get to Dagra."

"What impeccable timing," he sighed, clipping the royal sword to his belt.

Together, they ran from the castle.

———— • ————

A crack of thunder pealed across the sky, thrumming through the roof as Eriqwyn crept across it. She reached the edge, and lightning forked to strike down into the city's eastern reaches. The wind suddenly abated, its roar fading beneath the rasping ululations of the ghouls as they flowed between the buildings below. As the rain thinned to a drizzle, she scanned the rooftops for signs of Wayland. Several rows along, she glimpsed a crouching, cloaked figure as it skulked between the elevations of a row of buildings. A second, smaller figure followed it, and then a third, moving less nimble than the others. Her keen eyes caught the shape of Tan's self-made sword, affirming that her friend and fellow Warder had made it to safety from the horde of ghouls. But it was far from over. Wayland and his team were unreachable with the narrow streets separating each row of the city's outermost buildings.

Hundreds of ghouls ambled along the main boulevard across the roof to Eriqwyn's left, filing between the thin alleyways between the buildings, and still more crowded beyond the Litchgate. Dread washed over her, and she closed her eyes. It was not supposed to happen this way. In raising the portcullis, she had hoped only for a distraction to pull the ghouls' focus away from her and her group, but instead, despite their spreading into the city like some hideous, unfurling flower, it seemed that they were not content with merely entering the place. She had lost their attention, but she was fast running out of rooftops to cross and soon would have no choice but to relinquish their safety and vantage points; the choice was either stay up here and wait in the hope of spotting the outlanders, or take to the streets, among the ghouls. Finding the outlanders in the metropolis of Lachyla would be like seeking a needle in a hay pile.

It would be much easier with the streets empty, she thought. *If I hadn't raised the gate… But who's to say that the ones I seek are here at all? What if they're still in the graveyard?*

Biting back a curse, she jumped across the narrow gap to the next roof. Creeping along beside the low parapets on the far side away from the main street, she peered down into a fenced-off courtyard. Ghouls filed along the back street beyond and out of the cramped alleyways to either side, but considerably fewer than those that teemed down the main thoroughfare. None of them looked her way. Taking to the streets and avoiding the creatures was her only option. Slinging her bow over her arm, she swept her cloak aside and climbed over the parapets. Sending a silent prayer to any god that wished to listen, she dug her fingers into the crannies between the stones and began to scale down to the courtyard below.

———— • ————

"In here," Wayland said, running across the roof to a mould-riddled shack that nestled in its corner.

"Why we goin' in there?" Demelza asked.

"There are no hatches on the roof and no ladders leading to the ground." The pathways below were almost devoid of the undead creatures, and he knew what Eriqwyn would be doing. "No one builds a roof-shack without access to it, which means the way into the building has to be inside here." Putting a shoulder to the warped door, he nudged it inwards. A wet, musty smell wafted from the shadowed interior, and among the rotten crates he spotted the iron rungs of a ladder leading down through a gap in the stones.

"Why we need to go down?"

Ah, lass, he thought as he crossed to the ladder. *Enough with the questions.*

"Because we do," Tan said.

"I know, but…"

Demelza's voice trailed off as Wayland descended into the blackness. The bulky, rectangular shapes of stacked crates filled the floor; beyond them, grey daylight peeked through gaps between shutters along the walls. As his eyes adjusted to the scant light, he meandered between the crates to the warehouse's door. He waited for Demelza and the blacksmith to join him, thankful for the reprieve from the ghouls and the fading storm. His clothing was soaked, as were the arrows in the quiver at his waist, and in the pause he suppressed a shiver as his wet skin pricked with goosebumps. Scraping the mud from his boots onto the corner of a crate, he eyed Tan as he approached with Demelza at his side. "The stakes are much higher now," he told them. "I'm sorry that you had to be a part of this. But it is what it is. In here we are safe, but the outlanders are out there somewhere and the mission must continue. You have both held up amazingly so far, and for that alone you deserve a commendation." Tan held grimly onto his sword and gave a curt nod, while Demelza's expression was altogether miserable as she gripped her bow. "We will avoid the creatures wherever possible, while making our way through the city in search of the outlanders. Be on alert for any movement, for any one of the bodies out there may not be a ghoul. Are you prepared?"

"Aye," Tan said.

Demelza's lips pressed into a line, looking as if she might cry, but still she nodded and Wayland's heart warmed at her bravery.

He grabbed the door handle and eased the door open a crack, eyeing the interlacing pathways beyond. Aside from two or three ghouls that wandered along unhurriedly, the coast was clear. Picking a route, he pulled the door open fully. "Stay close," he said over his shoulder, and ran from the building.

———— • • ————

Dagra slept, and yet was aware that he did so. His consciousness hung suspended, a mote trapped in the cage of his skull. Within his darkened mind-prison, the grey edges of the dream circled the periphery of his vision like fleeting, unformed spectres that swam and danced and soared away; their meaningless whispers ensconced a distant but unending scream, symbolised as flames licking into the morass of his thoughts.

I'm trapped! Trapped inside myself!

His rising distress swatted at the fires, brushed at the confines of his bone cell only to find it not hard but yielding. I have to get out! He was rising, pushing through, and suddenly he was out and floating inside Sabrian's living room, but only for a moment – up he went through the ceiling into the room above, and passed through the roof into bright light that faded to a rain-shimmered, pastel-painted Lachyla, and exhilaration coursed through him.

I'm free! he thought. But there were none to applaud his efforts, for the ghosts of the cityfolk focused their attention elsewhere.

"Welcome to your new life, my friend."

238

Dagra whirled around, but saw no one. It was Sabrian's voice, but Dagra knew that Sabrian was still sitting in his armchair. He had communicated merely with a thought. Though disembodied, Dagra felt himself smiling. He looked out across the city and began to drift above the rooftops, untouched by rain, wind or any other physical senses.

"Dagra, come back," Sabrian sent. A note of anxiousness was in his voice. "You do not want to—"

"But I do," Dagra replied. "It's beautiful."

"Not now! Can't you hear them?"

As he soared over the streets and buildings, he became aware of a discordant note among the whispers, a guttural moaning he recognised all too well. And, still beneath it all, that single cry of agony. The dead, he thought. *I can hear the graveyard from here.*

"No," Sabrian sent. "The denizens, yes, but not the graveyard. They have entered the city. You must return to the house."

"Nothing can harm me here," Dagra replied, shutting Sabrian out and gliding towards the centre of the city He caught glimpses of figures below, some walking, some lurching between the dwellings and along the walkways. Forms made not of flesh and bone but of shadow and fog. Denizens of the graveyard and the people of Lachyla.

But there are no true humans in this place, he thought. *Not even me any more. Only Oriken and Jalis...* As he remembered his friends, without warning he veered and soared in another direction, the mansions and monuments a blur as he sped between them until he reached a pair of running figures, and slowed to hover above them. As indistinct as all others, their wispy greyness trailed behind them as they ran, but Dagra knew these were his friends. They entered the plaza of King Mallak's statue, and he realised they were on their way to him.

I have to get back to my body. As soon as the thought formed, he slammed back into the prison of his skull. With a gasp, he cracked his weary eyes open.

Sabrian pounced from his seat and bolted from the living room. Disoriented, Dagra groaned and held a hand to his forehead. He heard Sabrian swing the front door open and shout something into the street, but Dagra's thoughts were still a whir. *Did that really happen? Or was it just a dream?* Footsteps tamped along the garden path, and he struggled to his feet, gripping the chair's arm as dizziness took him.

"Quickly, the pair of you, get in!" Sabrian's call echoed down the hallway, followed by a rustle of activity as the door closed and a deadbolt was slid into place.

A drenched Jalis stepped into the room, shrugging off her cloak. She paused as their eyes met, then crossed quickly to stand before him. "Are you okay?"

He nodded. The nausea was passing. "I'm fine." To avoid meeting Jalis's gaze, Dagra took her cloak and crossed to a coat-stand in the corner of the room. As he draped the garment on a peg, from the corner of his eye he caught Oriken entering the room. Oriken's arm was pressed stiffly to his side, one eye was purple and half-closed, and blood was splattered all over his clothes. "By the gods, man," Dagra said. "What happened to you? And where's your hat? You look like you've been dragged through the Pit face-first."

Oriken winced. "That's a fair approximation. Look, Dag, the shit's about to hit the sidewalk and we have to be ready to get out of here."

The undead, Dagra thought. "I saw you both." He looked from Oriken to Jalis. "I saw you running. And the corpses. At least I think I did…"

"First things first." Jalis took hold of Oriken's jacket and eased it over his shoulders. "Let me see that wound. Sabrian"—she turned to their host as he stepped into the room—"do you have needle and thread?"

Sabrian nodded and turned on his heel.

Jalis helped Oriken out of his shirt. Dagra frowned at the slash across his friend's shoulder. His eyes fell to the jewelled gladius at Oriken's hip, and suddenly he understood. The screams. The king. There was a dull sense of knowledge that Mallak had passed – or was passing – and that something had occurred between Oriken and the king. "What did you do? By Cherak's stones, Oriken, *what have you done?*"

"Later," Jalis said. "There are bigger problems right now."

Dagra frowned. "Aye, lass. I know. It's our fault, and it's only right that we help."

Sabrian returned and handed Jalis a needle and a length of thread. "The blame sits on a multitude of shoulders," he said. "You are not the only ones at fault in this. It is not your fight."

"We fought through that horde once before," Dagra said. "Just the three of us. We can lend our blades this time, too."

Oriken quirked an eyebrow. "I'm not exactly in the best shape at the moment, and neither are you."

"There are hundreds, if not thousands, of the graveyard's denizens swarming into the city as we speak," Sabrian said. "Practically the whole cursed lot of them."

"Except for the legless one we saw on our way back in."

"Really, Orik?" Jalis sighed as she stitched his wound.

"Please," Sabrian said, "wait in my home and let the Lachylans deal with the denizens; they are… better equipped than any of you. No offence, of course. Dagra is in transition and still weak. Oriken is wounded. And Jalis…" He shrugged. "It is senseless for you to risk your lives."

"Actually," Dagra said, "I'm feeling stronger by the minute. If we hadn't come here at all, this would not be happening. Oriken can stay here. Jalis, you too. But I will fight."

"Are you sure, Dag? After last time—"

"I recall it all too well," he said. "But it changes nothing." He patted the shabby old gladius at his hip. "Are we tail-tuckers or are we freeblades?"

Sabrian smiled. "Well said."

Jalis sighed. "It does seem there are some folk who might benefit from our assistance."

Oriken's hand moved to the pommel of the sword at his side. He shook his head, but said, "Fine. My sword arm's uninjured, so count me in. A team's a team."

Dagra eyed the jewelled scabbard and marvelled at its silver and gold craftsmanship, at how the metals gleamed between the specks of dried blood, at the assortment of gems embedded into the sheath and haft and crossguard. A clearer picture of what had transpired filtered into his mind. He glanced at Sabrian before regarding Oriken with a soft grunt.

"Yeah." Oriken said. "So *that* happened."

Dagra nodded. "What's done is done. I take it you've learned how to use that thing?"

"I had a rather pointed lesson."

"Good. Then we've got an unwritten contract to fulfil." To Sabrian, he said, "Coming?"

"Wouldn't miss it for the world."

Jalis finished sewing Oriken's wound closed, then tied a knot in the thread. He pulled his shirt and jacket back on and they followed Sabrian from the room.

At the front door, Dagra looked out through the fine drizzle at the dozen or so corpses along the length of the street.

"Having a change of heart?" Oriken asked.

Dagra drew his sword and stepped into the rain. "This city's not falling to those creatures," he said, touching the pendant of Avato at his neck. "Not while there's breath in my body."

————— • —————

Eriqwyn crouched behind the low wall, waiting for a chance to move. Her eyes darted over the ghouls as they filed down the street, ensuring that none turned her way. As several of the creatures wandered past her hiding place, she noted that the horde seemed to be heading in a general direction towards the south of the city. Risking a glance over the wall to the street behind, she saw that the nearest of the approaching ghouls was far enough away.

Without a pause she vaulted the wall and sprinted away, dipping into a side path. Her steps brisk and silent, she nocked an arrow to her bow as she neared the end of the pathway. Pressing her back against the wall, she inched along to peer out onto a large courtyard, and stared agape at the chaos before

241

her. Ghouls were everywhere, but they were not the only creatures in the area; dotted amongst them, Eriqwyn spotted not one but several figures which clearly were not ghouls but humans. Each wielded a weapon, each fought separate from the others, battling through the horde with fierce skill. Her mind raced through the possibilities. These were not members of her group. Even at a distance she recognised none as folk from her village.

More outlanders? she wondered.

Most wielded wide-bladed swords, the likes of which hung as decorations on the walls within Albarandes Manor, reminders of a violent, bygone age. But the garments they wore…

Like the depictions in the archives of life before the blight.

Their blades danced and gleamed under shafts of storm-pierced sunlight. Ghouls lurched around them, seemingly incapable of deciding who to target. Eriqwyn watched as one of the fighters fell beneath a swell of the creatures. But rather than linger upon their prey, they quickly moved on and the man pushed himself to his knees, dark blood spurting from his lacerated throat. The blood slowed and the fighter rose to his feet, wiped a hand across his neck and ran to rejoin the battle.

That wound severed his jugular, Eriqwyn thought. *He should be dying. The blood should not have coagulated so quickly.* "It cannot be," she whispered.

Intent on the fighter, Eriqwyn's attention had wavered from the rest of her surroundings. She glanced the other way in time to see a group of ghouls crossing the courtyard not far from her. One turned its twisted features in her direction and she raised her bow to take aim. A young girl darted into view wielding a pair of thin, straight-bladed swords. She was dressed in a tight black tunic and black leggings, her raven hair clasped into a loose tuft at the crown of her head. Without pause she ran straight for the ghouls and tore into them as if they were nothing but training dummies.

By the goddess. The girl is a whirlwind. Eriqwyn lowered her bow and eased off the string. Within the space of a minute the group of ghouls were writhing on the floor, their legs either hamstringed or completely severed below the knee. The tips of the girl's blades lowered to her ankles and she turned to Eriqwyn, locking the Warder with a piercing blue gaze. The moment stretched. As if reaching a decision, the girl raced off into the city.

"Who *are* these people?" Eriqwyn muttered to herself. *They cannot be here. Generation after generation living within the city for three centuries? We would have known.* But the walls of Lachyla were high and thick, enough so to conceal and mute any activity within, certainly with the vast graveyard before it. It was possible, but why remain inside all this time? Somehow, bizarrely, it was easier to understand the presence of the ghouls; reports of such sightings had trickled through the village since its founding, since those who fled the city had first flocked around Albarandes Manor and began to build. Even in recent decades, despite the Gardens being the Forbidden Place, the occasional curious villager had reported ghastly sights and sounds beyond the gates of the mist-filled graveyard at night. They had become a part of folklore as much as the goddess Valsana herself.

Pushing the disbelief away, Eriqwyn plotted a course between the ghouls to the south side of the courtyard. Returning her arrow to the quiver, she drew her hunting blade and made a dash for it, weaving around the clusters of creatures and ignoring the few humans that fought them, and soon she was out of the courtyard and entering a pathway that snaked between the gardens of manor houses. Slowing to a brisk pace, she passed between the low walls and skeletal remains of ancient trees. Glancing over her shoulder, she saw that two of the creatures were entering the pathway behind her. Breaking into a jog, she returned her attention to the front and screamed as she ploughed face-first into a ghoul that had appeared out of nowhere. Falling over the creature, she rolled from its grasp and staggered to her feet.

My knife! She had dropped it in the struggle, and the weapon now lay beneath the ghoul, which was clambering to its hand and knees, ooze drooling from its mouth to the flagstones. It began to rise, hunched over like an elder crippled with the rheumatism. Eriqwyn kicked hard into its face. The head snapped backwards and the creature flopped over onto its side. She snatched up her blade and ran, turning through an open iron gate and slamming it shut behind her, driving the latch into place.

The enclosed patio was empty, the large house ahead dark and hushed against the backdrop of distant fighting. She took a shuddering breath, then crossed the paved area and dropped to squat with her back against a stone well. In the temporary safety, the horror of it all washed over her, catching up with the instinct for survival. Her head swam and bile rose in her throat. Swallowing it down, she ran a hand over her forehead. She thought of her sister, and sent her a silent apology.

This is beyond my training as a Warder. Far beyond. How did it come to this?

Cursing herself, she climbed to her feet and continued through the garden and out onto an empty boulevard. Off to her right, a distant procession of ghouls filed down a main street, and she turned to look in the direction they headed, a grim chill coursing through her as she beheld the castle of Lachyla.

If that is their destination, then it is mine also. Perhaps I will find the outlanders there. She pressed her lips together and broke into a jog. Along the street, an armoured fighter clattered into view and spotted her, but, like the girl in black, he ignored her and ran off towards the procession of ghouls. *They don't see me as a threat, she thought. Or, rather, they ignore me because they have a larger and more immediate concern with the creatures.* Who these people truly were was a problem she would have to face, but, like them, her core mission remained in place.

The deadstone nestled against her back beneath the cloak seemed almost meaningless compared to the legion of undead that coursed through Lachyla. Terror, Eriqwyn now knew, was something she had never fully experienced, not like this. And, for the first time in a long time, surrounded by monstrosities and strangers, her group lost and possibly overwhelmed, she felt truly alone.

———— . ————

As Jalis slammed her heel down onto a corpse's spine, Dagra stepped in and hacked his gladius into its neck. The pair shared a grim nod and waited for Oriken and Sabrian to dispatch the last of the stragglers within the king's plaza.

"How's the shoulder holding up?" Dagra asked.

Oriken forced a grin as he wiped a sleeve over the sweat and drizzle that coated his forehead. "The exercise is just what it needs. Where to next, Sabrian?"

"The larger mass of the denizens are headed down the main boulevard. The castle doors are closed. The knights and a group of cityfolk wait to hold them off at the steps, but the numbers need to be thinned from the flanks."

"Then that's where we're headed," Dagra said.

"No. We will not put Jalis and Oriken at the heart of the battle. That would be suicide. Dagra, I admire your courage, but there are many more denizens elsewhere other than the main bulk."

"I'll second that," Oriken said. "I don't fancy being pulled apart by an undead legion. Not today."

Dagra blanched. "Then lead the way," he told Sabrian.

As Sabrian turned to move, a tremor shook the ground, hard enough for Dagra and Oriken to lose their balance. As Dagra went to one knee, he looked up at Sabrian. "What on Verragos?"

"I'm not sure," Sabrian said as the tremor subsided. "But I think it might be—"

"Teuveyr!" Dagra yelled, staring up beyond Sabrian and the statue of King Mallak behind him, to the sun-dappled clouds of the abating storm. "The Arbiter!" he cried, pointing at the light and dark shape into which the stormclouds and sunlight had coalesced.

"Oh, my," Sabrian exclaimed.

"You see his sword-axe?" Dagra said to his companions. "All shadow-etched and gleaming, like it's written?" He turned to Oriken. "You see that?"

"Yeah, Dag, I see it." Oriken grimaced as he climbed to his feet, just as a second tremor vibrated through the flagstones.

"The Battle God!" Dagra cried. "All this carnage. It's awoken him!"

Oriken slid his sword into its sheath. "I don't give a rat's hindquarters about the pretty shapes in the sky, nor so much about what's causing the ground to tremble. You wanted to do this, so let's do it. Or has the sight of the Battle God put you permanently on your knees?"

Dagra's jaw dropped open as he glared at his friend, then he snapped it shut. "Damn you, no it hasn't."

"Then get your soft arse up off the floor." Oriken grabbed a fistful of Dagra's shirt and hauled him up. To Sabrian, he said, "Ignore Dagra's imagination. Let's go."

Sabrian nodded. Glancing at the statue, his eyes widened and he backed away.

"Oh, come on," Oriken exclaimed. "Not you, too." Behind him, Dagra issued a curse and then backed into view alongside Sabrian. "Oh, for the love of— Jalis, can you slap a little sense into this pair?"

"Get over here, Orik," Jalis said.

The tone of her voice gave him pause and he looked over his shoulder. A ball of light the size of a man's head was drifting down towards the crown of the statue. "I don't like the look of that," he muttered, turning on his heel and running to join his friends who already were putting distance between them and the statue. "Hey!" he called. "Wait for—" A deafening crash filled the air, sending Oriken sprawling to the ground in mid-run. The sky flashed behind him and he scrambled to his feet, half-running, half-staggering to where his friends crouched, shielding their eyes from the brightness. No sooner had it begun though, than it was over, and when he reached the three he turned to stare at what remained of Mallak's statue – its upper half aglow like a blade in a forge, the head melting onto the shoulders.

"I told you!" Dagra blurted. "I said it was Teuveyr."

The colossal apparition was still in the sky, the Arbiter's glistening weapon etched with shifting thunderheads. The flagstones beneath Oriken's feet vibrated with a steady *thrum-thrum*. Giving Sabrian a sharp look, he said, "Is that what I think it is?"

Sabrian nodded. "Someone is displeased, but it is not Teuveyr."

"Who, then?" Jalis, asked. As she stepped in closer to Sabrian, he regarded her with a steely look.

"It is the Mother."

———— ·•· ————

Eriqwyn slashed her knife across a ghoul's face and slammed her boot into its knee. As it toppled, she drove her heel down onto its jaw, then swiftly retreated to scan the area and assess the situation. In the middle distance, the wide street was lined with battle as humans fought the procession of the undead. And how they fought! Even the elderly among them fought with a tenacity and skill equal to – no, surpassing – that of Lingrey. They fought well, but for every human there was a score and more of the undead. The outlanders were not among their numbers. Nor had she seen any sign of Wayland, and feared for his safety. Splitting the group into two had made sense from a hunter's perspective, but she now doubted its validity. Hunting deer was a far cry from fighting a legion of ghouls.

Holding her balance as the shaking ground increased in intensity, she wheeled about at a noise behind her. From around the side of the nearby building a figure staggered into view. As she raised her bow, Eriqwyn recognised the scant attire that clung to the woman's body, and stayed her hand. Shade took a faltering step forward, then stumbled against the wall and slid down it to a sitting position, resting her left arm in her lap. As Eriqwyn crossed to her, Shade looked up.

"One of them got me." Shade's voice was weak as she held her arm out for Eriqwyn to see the four deep welts that ran down her inner forearm onto her wrist. A rain-mingled scarlet droplet fell from her fingertip.

"You have lost much of your lifeblood," Eriqwyn observed.

Shade nodded. "I know."

"The bleeding needs to be staunched." Eriqwyn knelt to cut a strip from Shade's dress, but the woman shook her head.

"It's too late," she said. "Just... Hold me, Eri." She reached out to her. "I know you hate me now, but you didn't always. Please."

Eriqwyn stared at her for a long moment, then sighed. She glanced around to ensure no ghouls were heading their way, then sheathed her hunting knife and took Shade in her arms.

"Thank you," Shade whispered, her warm breath upon Eriqwyn's neck. "I'm sorry, Eri."

"Sorry? Sorry for what?" Eriqwyn tensed, understanding too late. Searing pain stabbed into her back and coursed through her chest as she sagged within Shade's strong embrace. *Dead*, she thought as her vision darkened. *Killed by a wanton whore...*

"It will only hurt for a moment," Shade whispered sibilantly. "You won't be alone any more. You can let go now, Eri. Let go..."

The hypnotic thrum of the earth faded from her senses, and Eriqwyn slipped into death.

———— • ————

After all he'd been through in the last 24 hours, Dagra realised he had become numb to the horror and madness. Gone was the terror that consumed him as he fought his way out of the graveyard, replaced with a grim determination. Dispatching the undead was almost cathartic, and he was starting to see it as an act of kindness.

Stepping behind a reaching corpse, he ran his sword through its torso then moved aside. "You should have done this ages ago," he told Sabrian.

With a nod of agreement, Sabrian hacked the creature's head off and watched it bounce and roll into the gutter. "By the time I arrived here, the routine was long since set. The problem is that these are the ancestors – and in some cases the immediate families – of the people who live here."

Dagra chewed on that thought, turning away as Sabrian spilled the next corpse's innards to the flagstones. A brittle near-skeletal figure stood in the centre of the street, swaying gently much like the first corpse Dagra had laid eyes on in the graveyard. He regarded the creature, wondering how he might feel if it were his own mother, twenty five years dead now, or his Grandpa Gafrid or Grandma Ilhdra, both still alive, or so he hoped; he hadn't visited them in three years, and suddenly he felt profoundly sorry for that. The skeletal creature half-turned, its blind face seeming to sense his proximity.

"Mindless, tortured souls," he muttered, walking around the corpse and thrusting his gladius through its neck. The head flopped forwards, hanging to its chest by a sliver of leathery skin, then the corpse pitched over. The tips of its finger-bones scratched at the stones, its wasted form too ravaged to return to its feet.

"Mindless, yes," Sabrian said. "But proportionate to how long they were dead before the blight took them."

Dagra wheeled on Sabrian. "Why?" he demanded.

"Why what, friend?"

"Why does the blight cure wounds, like with Gorven, you, *me*, but it leaves these creatures in a permanent state of decay?"

Sabrian chuckled mirthlessly. "Some say the gods work in mysterious ways. Or merely the goddess. Or, more accurately in this case, the Mother." Turning to Jalis and Oriken, who had finished dispatching a cluster of corpses, Sabrian gestured for them to move on. Setting a fast pace into the nearby alleyway, he added, "The truth of it is simply that the power which holds sway over the city – aye, and the graveyard – maintains each of its vessels in the form in which it first entered them, at least in most cases. For me, I was close to death. For the majority of Lachylans, they were very much alive. As for the bodies buried in the graveyard…"

Dagra understood, but shook his head. "It isn't right."

"The world we live in doesn't care," Jalis commented from behind. "Nature knows nothing about right or wrong."

"This isn't nature," Dagra argued.

"Actually," Jalis said, "I'm beginning to think it is. Out of control, perhaps, but nature nonetheless."

"From what Mallak said," Oriken added, "and from what I saw with my own eyes beneath the castle, I have to agree with you."

"Piss on your nature," Dagra muttered beneath the noise of the dead as they passed by the far end of the alleyway. "A turd by any other name is still a turd."

"The front of the monastery is just around the corner," Sabrian announced. "The denizens are passing directly by its garden, which is enclosed by iron railings. Once we get in there—"

Dagra stopped as one of the passing corpses paused and turned their way. Its mouth opened and it staggered into the alleyway. Several of its brethren instinctively followed, and suddenly a crush of the creatures was pouring into the confined space.

"Retreat!" Sabrian shouted. "There are too many!" He raced back the way they had come, but more corpses were filing in from ahead.

Hot on Sabrian's heels, Oriken swung about. "We're trapped!"

"They've broken through a section of the railings." Sabrian pointed to an iron ladder fixed to the wall. "Quickly! Take to the roof!"

Dagra sheathed his sword and ran behind the others for the ladder. *Surrounded,* he thought, a surge of the terror returning as he swung this way and that, his eyes on the corpses that filled both ends of the alleyway. Oriken was on the ladder, with Sabrian grasping the ladder, ready to follow.

"Damned shoulder," Oriken growled.

"Faster!" Jalis called up to him. She pushed Dagra towards the ladder. "Go!" she ordered.

There was no time to argue. He snatched at the rungs and hauled himself onto the first rung, then the second... The metal beneath his palms shook as the quaking ground intensified. He glanced down to see Jalis reaching for the ladder. The nearest of the corpses was fast approaching.

"Move it, you bastards!" Dagra called up to the others as Jalis took to the ladder. The creatures were upon her. She kicked at their grasping hands and hauled herself up.

Beyond Sabrian, Oriken reached the top of the wall and rolled out of view onto the flat roof. Dagra glanced down to see Jalis gripping the rungs tightly, one leg dangling in the grasp of the creatures. Their claws were on the hem of her cloak, dragging her down. As he watched, her hand slipped from the ladder.

"Jalis!" he cried.

She unclasped her cloak and let it fall onto the corpses' heads. She wrenched her foot free and scrambled out of reach of the reaching hands.

"Thank the gods," Dagra breathed.

He scurried up the remainder of the ladder. The metal pulsed with the Mother's ire and rattled as the undead clutched the bottom rungs. The roof was almost within his reach when the ladder shifted and pitched, its lower supports ripped from the wall. He clung on and stared helplessly at the upper joists as they slid from the crumbling stonework. The ladder dropped. Its feet thumped down onto the alley floor.

Sabrian reached over the lip of the roof and grasped Dagra's hand firmly, then hauled him up and over the edge. Down below, Jalis frantically climbed the teetering ladder. Dagra stretched to grab hold of the uppermost rung, but it tipped backwards out of his reach. His breath caught as the ladder swung out with Jalis gripping onto it.

"No!" Oriken yelled. "Jalis!"

Her back slammed into the far wall. Her foot slid between the rungs and one hand was jarred from its grip. She hung there, dazed and tangled, the ladder jittering as the creatures tugged at it.

Oriken thumbed a bolt into the crossbow. He fixed the string and fired into the mob, then hastily fumbled a second bolt into the chamber.

"Conserve your ammunition," Sabrian warned. "It won't help."

"Fuck off!" Oriken shrugged Sabrian's hand from his arm and fired into the corpses.

"She's moving!" Dagra cried. "Come on, lass!"

Jalis had both hands back on the ladder. She pulled her leg free and swung around to the outer side and began to climb.

"That's it!" Dagra called as a third bolt twanged past him and disappeared into the throng.

The ladder was too far below the opposite roof, but to Jalis's right was a set of closed shutters. Dagra shouted to tell her. She gave him a quick glance, then reached for a narrow lip that ran the length of the wall and passed beneath the shutters.

It's closed from the inside, Dagra thought. *She'll never get it open.* With growing desperation, he watched as she eased her way along the wall, clinging on only by her fingertips, her feet dangling above the mass of reaching bodies.

"Stop!" Sabrian hefted his gladius and stood at the edge of the roof. He brought the sword over his head and launched it at the shutters. His aim was true – the sword's tip struck slightly off centre and the left shutter flew inwards. The gladius dangled for a moment then dropped into the swarm of corpses. Jalis resumed her course, inching along the lip, her knuckles white with the effort. The creatures below her stretched their taloned hands as if ready to catch her should she fall.

"Go on!" Oriken called.

Finally she was beneath the shutters. Flinging a hand up, she grabbed hold of the sill. The toes of her shoes scrabbled for purchase against the wall as she heaved herself up and flung an arm into the gap. Swinging her leg up, she snagged her foot onto the narrow lip and hauled herself through the shutters. As she disappeared into the shadowed interior, Dagra loosed a sigh of relief.

"Thank the gods. She made it. You made it, lass!"

Jalis's face appeared and she looked up at them. "Go!" she called, catching her breath. "I'll be okay!"

With no way to reach her, Dagra nodded, and she dipped from sight.

"Suffering fucking stars," Oriken growled, helping Dagra to his feet. "If she'd fallen... I would have jumped right down there. I would."

"I don't doubt it," Dagra said as they followed Sabrian across the roof. "That's the sort of friend you are." *Yes*, he thought, a knot tightening in his throat, *but could I say the same for myself?*

———— • ————

Jalis sat beneath the shutters, groaning as she rubbed at the back of her head where it had struck the wall. She regarded the dusty storeroom before her, pushing away the lingering image of her terrifying ordeal. Dozens of nightmare countenances swam across the stacked wooden chests and floorboards like a ghastly tableau.

She reached to her throbbing ankle and touched the livid welts caused by the grasping talons.

That was a close call, she thought. *Possibly my closest yet.*

Releasing a shuddering breath, she checked her weapons. Her throwing daggers were all present, and Silverspire and Dusklight were still in their sheaths, thank the stars.

I need a weapon more suited to the task. Something with more immediate damage. Rising and crossing to the nearest of the chests, she lifted its lid. *Parchments*, she thought wryly. *Not a great deal of good against corpses unless they were willing to hang around while I paper-cut them to a second death.*

She opened a second chest, and her breath caught. The coffer was filled with ancient silver dari, with more than a peppering of gold pieces thrown in for good measure. In all of her years in Himaera, she'd seen only one golden dari piece. The dust of centuries permeated the room, and she knew these coins had been forgotten and were worthless to the folk here. Snatching up several gold pieces, she realised her hypocrisy as she stuffed them into a pocket of her leggings.

The next chest contained figurines. She took out an exquisitely-shaped brass depiction of a naked woman and hefted the ornament, testing its weight. It was solid, and the base was heavy. It would do as a cudgel.

The storeroom's door clicked and she sprang into a stance, waiting as the door swung slowly inwards... but there was no corpse on the other side, just a boy of four or five years dressed in a brown robe and holding a hooked stick.

"So!" he exclaimed in a high-pitched voice as he hung the stick on the door handle. "You're a worshipper of Aissia?" He nodded to indicate the figurine in

Jalis's hand. "Well, you can take her. It's for a good cause, after all. Sabrian sent to me that you'd dropped in. Not that I needed to be told, mind you; there was enough racket with that ladder clattering around. Ah, don't worry." The boy waved his hand indifferently as Jalis stared. "I am Brother Lewin, custodian of this house of the gods. I'm afraid I can't leave the monastery to assist in the cleansing of those poor souls – too small, you see – but I will show you to the door." He turned to leave. "Come, follow me."

Jalis opened her mouth to reply, but the words died in her throat as a vigorous tremor shook the building.

CHAPTER TWENTY NINE
BETWEEN TWO ETERNITIES

Ellidar strode from the castle entrance as it closed behind him, and approached the top of the steps to gaze out across the city. Before him, his knights waited in an arrowhead formation upon the marble stairs. Only two knights remained behind in the castle, along with a contingent of cityfolk. Deeper inside the fortress the king's body sat upon the throne, a roaring pyre at Mallak's feet as he burned to char. His liege had passed to the true death, but Ellidar had no time to mourn.

"They're almost upon us!" one of the knights called.

As if I can't see that. Ellidar shielded the thought, his eyes intent on the mass of denizens that filled the wide street. Three hundred strong, they stumbled over each other as they drew ever closer to the Mother, their moans an almost rapturous cacophony.

A vicious tremor pulsed through the foundations of the castle. Ellidar's knights held their balance, while a number of the denizens toppled, their fellows trampling over them but scarcely slowing the relentless approach.

An idea came to him, and he sheathed his longsword. "Stand ready!" To his second, he said, "Their mass is unstoppable by us alone. They will reach the doors like a slow battering ram. We must disrupt their advance, but to do so from a frontal defence is not enough."

"Your orders, sir?"

The horde reached the steps, and the knights at the base met them, their maces swinging into rotting faces.

"The command is yours, Heilin."

"Sir?"

"Change nothing. Hold the steps at all costs. I will break them from within." Steeling himself, Ellidar charged down the stairs and ploughed into the horde.

Dagra floundered upon the rooftop as the building shook. From his vantage point he could see the undead on the streets below stumble and pause. One woman, caught off-balance, teetered backwards into a group of the creatures, and Dagra watched as their talons and teeth tore into her.

"Gods above and below!" he cried.

A violent tremor shook the building anew and he fell to one knee, planting his hands on the shaking timber of the roof. As sunlight burst through the clouds and washed over him, he glanced into the sky. A tall column of dissipating cloud sloped upward from a darker mass, a thick crescent of sun shining through its apex.

"The Arbiter casts his judgement," he muttered.

"Hold on!" Sabrian called as the planks began to shift.

Oriken was on his hands and knees. "Shit! We're gonna—"

The timbers collapsed, and Dagra's heart lurched into his throat as he plummeted through the roof and crashed into the room below. Stunned, he rolled onto his back amid the fallen planks, and groaned. As the tremor subsided, he stared up through the broken roof to see Sabrian peering down.

"Are you both alright?" he called.

Somewhere behind Dagra, Oriken loosed a stream of obscenities.

"Yes," Dagra called as the tremor began to subside. With a wince, he pulled a large splinter from his palm. "I think so."

"Gah, that smarts," Oriken said. "Damned shoulder!"

Sabrian lowered himself to a supporting beam and dropped into the room, then stumbled across the debris to help Oriken to his feet. "I am needed elsewhere," he said. "The advance on the castle is being broken as we speak, but there are still many denizens to be neutralised. The best assistance the two of you can give now is to help cut down the stragglers between here and the Litchgate."

Dagra shook his head. "Jalis—"

"I have observed that your friend is more than capable of fending for herself, and she is currently in the good hands of Lewin. The bulk of the denizens are under control, though barely." He ushered them across the fallen planks to a set of stairs leading down. "There are few Lachylans assigned to the main boulevard. Please lend your blades there. Your help is important."

"You've got it as long as my shoulder holds up," Oriken said. "I think the fall pulled the stitches."

"You freeblades are as tough as old leather," Sabrian remarked as he eased the door open to peer through the gap. "Right, I'm off to collect my sword then join Gorven. I'll see you again when this is finally over." Swinging the door inward, he raced out of the building and disappeared around the side.

The wide street was littered with body parts and peppered with pockets of corpses, perhaps a hundred or more, but Dagra could see only a handful of

Lachylans battling their blight-ridden forebears. The few cityfolk between here and the Litchgate looked worse for wear, but were still in the fight.

Oriken gestured for Dagra to lead the way. "After you."

"Jalis better be safe," Dagra growled. Drawing his sword, he stepped out onto the street.

"The Arbiter is gone." Oriken flicked a glance into the sky. "That's got to be a good sign, right?"

"You're a mocking bastard, Oriken, but, you're right."

"In that case"—Oriken unsheathed the royal gladius—"I'd say we've got a street to sweep."

———— · ————

"Go with the gods," Brother Lewin squeaked beneath the hum of battle as Jalis opened the monastery door. "Not literally, of course. That would not be good."

Jalis nodded her gratitude and set off down the path, her eyes on the rear of the large column of undead further down the street.

"Oh!" Lewin called.

Jalis glanced back at the little monk.

"One thing my brothers and I strive for in our cenobitic monasticism is discretion over ruthlessness." He gave her a sly wink. "Purchase not impetuously, Jalis, but rather spend sensefully."

"I… How…" Despite the immediate horror beyond the monastery's fence, Jalis felt her face heat up.

Lewin's lilting chuckle took the edge off her guilt at pocketing the gold pieces. "One boon of the goddess's blessing is excellent hearing." Shrugging, he added, "True, another is being stuck in a four year old's body forever, but swords and horses, eh?" He stepped back inside the building and pushed the heavy door closed, leaving Jalis shaking her head in bemusement.

With the Aissia figurine in her hand, she assessed the corpses that dotted the street. The ones here were mostly of two sorts – heavily decomposed, and looking to have been in the grave only a matter of weeks or months. Sabrian's earlier comment came back to her as she stared at the fresher of the corpses: "*For the majority of Lachylans, they were very much alive. As for the bodies buried in the graveyard…*"

"Oh, stars," she whispered. "Can some of these creatures still think? Or feel?"

In that moment, her heart went out to them. All these years… The one she was staring at turned and caught her gaze. A woman. Fleshy. Swollen. The yellowed eyes looked almost kind as the cadaver shuffled towards her, closing the gap between them. Kind… and then not. Bursting forward, Jalis hammered the figurine into the dead woman's face. The heavy base cracked the

254

cheekbone and she launched a second blow, smashing the jaw to the side and causing the woman to stumble. Rushing around her, she aimed the makeshift weapon at a kneecap. The leg bent backwards at the joint and Jalis cracked the brass weapon down onto the back of the woman's head. The woman pitched to the floor and Jalis made quick work of bashing her brains in. Stepping back, she leaned against the fence and realised with disgust that she'd been thinking of the creature as a woman, not as a dead thing. But what if they do think? 'Cleansing', Lewin had called it, and perhaps it was the most apt word.

A battle cry resounded from close by. Jalis glanced to the main mass of corpses in time to see one of the knights burst through with a triumphant shout, smashing two of the creatures together in his gauntleted hands and casting them aside. He staggered forwards and paused for a deep breath before striding along the street towards Jalis.

"Ellidar?" Although sheened in sweat and grime, she recognised the knight from earlier in the castle.

"My lady." Ellidar stopped before her and gave a brief bow. "Care to join me?"

Loosing a terse laugh, Jalis shook her head, shrugged, then smiled. "I'd be honoured to, knight sios."

Returning the smile with a thin one of his own, Ellidar said, "Actually it's knight-paladin." Jalis quirked an eyebrow as the knight strode past her, beckoning her to join him. "Your friends are heading for the Litchgate. The last of the denizens are still trickling through. It's a clean-up operation now." He snatched his longsword from its sheath and drove it into a corpse's mouth before kicking the creature away.

A one-armed corpse came stumbling towards them. Jalis raised the figure, but Ellidar caught her wrist. It was only then that she noticed the creature was carrying its arm in the other hand, and as she stared in sickening dismay she realised it was not a corpse, but a Lachylan.

"For the gods' sake, Emil!" Ellidar snatched the arm from the man's grasp and shoved the bloody bone-end into the ravaged shoulder muscles, loosing a cry of agony from Emil. "Hold it firm and get it stapled back on. You do want to keep it, don't you?"

Emil nodded, clearly in shock despite the Lachylans' healing abilities.

"You did well," Ellidar told him, ushering him across the street as a door opened and an elderly man stepped out to assist.

Ellidar turned to Jalis, swatting a head off a corpse as he did so. He motioned for them to continue.

"I nearly brained that man," Jalis muttered.

"I was only a second ahead of you," Ellidar admitted. "Which is lucky for Emil – it takes much longer for the motor functions to reaffirm themselves after a decapitation – but not so lucky for many of my fellows, I fear. The casualties are extreme, but, gods willing, there will be no more true deaths this day. I left my knights defending the attack from the front," Ellidar said. "Ten men in total, plus my second. I know that the castle doors have held, gods be thanked, but I fear that half of those men, along with too many other folk of this city, are in as bad a condition as Emil." He sighed. "Or worse."

Conversation ceased as they continued up the boulevard, together dispatching each corpse along the way. The sounds of fighting behind them grew quieter by the minute, and Jalis knew that the battle was over and had turned into a rout.

Except the enemy was no enemy, she thought. *Just a mass of unthinking creatures following their instincts.*

As they drew ever closer to the Litchgate, Jalis peered ahead past a handful of Lachylans and the few corpses that still stood upon the street that was littered with their brethren. "There they are!" she cried, spotting the unmistakable forms of Oriken and Dagra in the distance, their backs to her.

Ellidar peered ahead and gave her a respectful nod. "Go to them."

———— • ————

Treading lightly along the mansion's side pathway, Wayland edged around the dead trees beside the corner of the house and froze as he stared into the empty sockets of an emaciated ghoul. The creature hissed at him through its rictus grin, and he smashed his axe into the top of its skull, cleaving it in two. Kicking the ghoul to the ground, he took a calming breath and gestured behind him for his group to follow. He heard Demelza's soft footfalls as she hurried up to him. Frowning, he glanced back and beyond Demelza to the far corner of the mansion.

"Where's Tan?" Wayland whispered.

Demelza glanced around. "Dunno."

"He was right behind you!"

"Aye, he was." She shrugged. "And then he wasn't."

"Damn it. Wait here." Running back the way they had come, he glanced around the rear of the mansion, but the blacksmith was nowhere in sight. He sighed. *And then there were two.* Casting the despondent thought aside, he hurried back to Demelza. "Nothing to be done for it," he told her. "Stay close. *Very* close. You hear?"

She clung tightly to her satchel and bow, and gave an abrupt nod.

Together, they crossed the mansion's garden, through a side gate and into the next garden, staying out of sight of the nearby street. The tremors now were nothing more than subtle vibrations beneath his feet – a small mercy for which he sent a silent thank-you to Valsana or whichever of the elder gods were listening.

256

A lone ghoul stood beside a cluster of skeletal saplings. Shuffling into the open, it took several steps towards Wayland and Demelza, then paused, swayed on the spot for a long moment as if in indecision, and loped away. *Again*, Wayland thought as he watched it wander towards the garden's corner. The longer he'd been in the city, the more the creatures had exhibited such behaviour, as if something of more interest had won their attention. Or something was repelling them. Glancing at Demelza, he rested a hand on her shoulder, drawing her wide-eyed gaze away from the retreating ghoul.

His plan was to avoid unnecessary contact, not only with the ghouls but also the enigmatic residents of the city, by keeping to enclosed areas but holding the tactical position of observing without being seen. He'd conserved his remaining arrows, using his now gore-encrusted axe to dispatch any ghouls that attacked them. If the true targets showed up, then ranged weaponry would be a distinct advantage against the three outlanders.

The open expanse was devoid of greenery save for the carcasses of standing trees, but otherwise well-kept. Waist-high stone pillars topped with bronze balls marked each corner of the garden. As he reached the sundial in the centre, the mansion's front door creaked open and Wayland froze, readying his axe. A shadowed figure stood within the doorway, its features gaunt and wrinkled; not a ghoul, but an elderly woman. Bizarrely, he felt like a child caught stealing apples, though there were none to steal, and the city was swarming with the undead. "I mean you no harm," he called out, wary of his voice travelling to the street.

"Good that you don't," the old woman croaked. "You tried anything clever with that axe of yours, I'd be putting you over my knee, young man."

Spotting the next adjoining gate, Wayland sidled across to it, casually saying to the woman, "I'm looking for someone specific. I don't suppose—"

"Ha! Aren't we all?" she crooned, then gave a lascivious cackle.

"Yes, er, we're also trying to find our companions. Have you—"

"I'm afraid I can't help you there either, lovely." The crone smacked her lips.

I'll get nothing from this old biddy, he thought. "We'll be on our way." He forced a tight smile as he took Demelza's arm and quickened his pace for the gate.

"Such politeness." The woman turned her beady eyes to Demelza. "And what a *charming* girl. Do come back any time!"

"Yes, of course." Wayland glanced into the next garden. "It was, er, lovely to meet you."

"You mind yourselves out there, young man and little missy."

He ushered Demelza to hurry through the gate, leaving the old woman watching them from her porch. In the next garden, he sighed despondently and dropped all pretence of stealth.

257

What is the point in creeping around? If I could just find Eri and the others, go home, forget that any of this ever started... We long knew of the ghouls within the graveyard. But the city... The curse of the goddess runs rife here. And yet it teems with people living in dwellings as grand – or grander – than Albarandes Manor. If I had to guess, I'd say it's been this way since the blight. Lachyla was never fully deserted. These are our cousins.

"The dynamics of the mission have changed considerably," he muttered, then sighed. "But orders are orders."

"Huh?" Demelza looked quizzically at him.

"Nothing, girl." He patted her shoulder. "It's nothing."

Spotting a gated arch that led out onto the main street, he headed towards it. A ghoul ambled into view beyond the iron bars and turned to regard him. He waited, and the creature continued on. Reaching the gate, he glanced through. The street was sprinkled with twitching bits of ghoul, and few still stood among the mess. Several of the city's inhabitants meandered between the fallen ghouls; beyond them, in the far distance, he caught sight of two men headed in his direction. A third figure – a woman, if his eyes didn't deceive him at this distance – was running up behind them. Something about the three gave him pause, something that spoke to his Warder senses that they didn't quite fit in with the inhabitants of the city. The men working in unison – one taller, the other short of stature – and the woman of slight build but graceful confidence. *Is it them?*

Stepping back from the arch, he pulled Demelza before him. "Look down the street," he told her. "Far down. And tell me if those are the ones we seek."

The girl stuck her head out. After a moment, she turned to him. "Aye. That's them."

Ah, goddess. Wayland's heart suddenly felt like lead. *This is it.* "The moment is here, Demelza." He slung the axe into his belt. "It's time for you to go, like we discussed."

Her brow furrowed, her eyes misting over.

"Run for the graveyard. And don't stop. You hear?"

"Aye." Demelza's voice cracked. Her eyes were downcast, her fear held just beneath the surface. "I hear."

"You're the bravest lass I know, little Dee," he said softly. "Now, run."

When she didn't respond, he turned her roughly about. Her shoulders hunched and she loosed a small sob.

Ah, girl, I'm so sorry. "Go!" he hissed, and nudged her forward. She stumbled, then broke into a run, padding across the garden. Wayland watched her go, then turned to the archway. Notching an arrow, he steadied his nerves and waited for the outlanders to draw nearer.

———— • ————

Blackness. She floated in a painless place; not her body, only her mind. Pain held no dominion in this space so far from the stars. The emptiness loomed in from all sides, ensnaring her in its web of nothingness. The Void. The thought came without attached emotion. This must be the waiting room between Verragos and the Spirit Realm. But where is the goddess? She will come for me soon, take me beneath her wings.

A grey cloud materialised before her, and a soft sensation intruded upon her contemplations with a thrum-thrum, thrum-thrum *like a colossal, invisible beating heart. The Void whorled and opened like a flower's petals unfurling, and a flicker of doubt grew into a torrent of fear as the cloud bloomed into a yawning vortex. Unable to control it, she began to turn; the motion quickly grew into a dizzying spin and she plummeted towards the widening maw. The gyre brightened. She hurtled through, and burst out into blinding light...*

Pain coursed through Eriqwyn's body and she cried out, snapping her eyes open. Dazed and disoriented, she stared up into blinding daylight. With a gasp, she arched her back, feeling her shoulders press into hard ground that buzzed with a rhythm like a heartbeat. As her eyes became accustomed to the sunlight, a hazy figure hovered into her view.

"...fine now," the silhouette said. "Rest easy."

She took a gulp of air. "It hurts."

"It will fade." The figure laid a hand upon Eriqwyn's shoulder, holding her to the ground. "Give it time, Eri."

I know that voice. And the memory flooded back as the face swam into focus. "You! You killed me." She grabbed Shade by the shoulders and pulled her to the ground, rolling on top of her. The woman struggled, but Eriqwyn snatched at her wrists and held her in place. Pain still seared through her, but was quelled by her rage. "You fucking whore," she spat. "What have you done?"

"I freed you, Eri. I made things right."

"You tore me from the afterlife!" She let go of Shade's wrist and slammed a fist into her face, rocking her head to the side. Shade gasped, then grinned and pulled Eriqwyn down, rolling over onto her and straddling her waist.

"So feisty," she purred. The woman's strength was unnerving. "That's another trait I admire in you."

"No ghoul attacked you, did it?" Eriqwyn spat as she struggled within Shade's grasp. "You did those wounds to yourself. You'd already bled out before coming to find me. It was all an act. They're all like you, aren't they? All those people in the city. All ghouls! And now you've made me the same."

"You'll thank me for it one day. Perhaps not *this* day, but eventually. You can live out your dreams here, your fantasies. You can do all the things you ever wanted to do but were held back by your... inhibitions."

259

Eriqwyn fought to free herself from Shade's hold. "You took that choice away from me. I would never have chosen this. Never!"

Shade nodded. "You were too afraid of yourself. Which is why I did it *for* you, Eri. Don't you see?"

"Minnow's Beck needs me," Eriqwyn argued. "It needs a First Warder. *Adri* needs me. You will not keep me here!"

"There were First Warders before you. There'll be others after you, too, for those who choose to remain in the village. Not all will want to remain after this. They will flock, when they learn the truth." Her eyes glistened as she smiled. "I waited my whole life for this."

"You are mad," Eriqwyn hissed. "I will kill you."

Shade laughed. "Ah, Eri," she said with a lustful grin. "That which is once dead, dies not twice so readily." Leaning her weight down, she pressed her lips to Eriqwyn's. With their lips still touching, she whispered, "You won't hate me forever. You may even come to love me."

Eriqwyn screamed into the woman's face. A surge of strength welled in her and she forced Shade away, throwing her to the ground. Eriqwyn climbed to her feet. Standing over Shade, she drew her knife.

Shade leaned back on her elbows and locked her dark eyes onto Eriqwyn's. With a soft laugh, she said, "What is more important, Eri? Me, or your mission?" Before Eriqwyn could reply, the woman sprang to her feet and ran.

With a snarl and a curse, Eriqwyn snatched her bow from the stones and took pursuit.

———— • ————

With Oriken at his side, Dagra stepped between the downed corpses, lopping heads from necks with a detachment that he knew would soon be replaced with facing his own predicament. *It should have been easy*, he thought, crushing a reaching bony hand beneath his heel. *It almost was. We had the jewel. We were out on the heath. And then...* He looked up from his grisly work to see a corpse stood in the street. Its partially crushed head hung askance, the jaw dislodged. Blade-slashes covered its half-eaten features, and its yellowed eyes stared at Dagra with a quiet madness beneath which he sensed a taint of misplaced kinship.

"You." Dagra pointed his sword at the corpse. "I know you."

"Want me to get this one?" Oriken asked.

"No." To the corpse, Dagra said, "I gave you a beating once. You're back for more? Fine. I'm not afraid of you. Not this time." He readied his gladius. "Have at it, then."

Rather than advance, the corpse raised a mangled hand to its chest. The broken jaw shifted and crunched. "*Lie*," it rasped.

Dagra nodded. "Yes, I know. You told me that before."

"Shitting stars!" Oriken said. "Did that thing just *speak*?"

"Uhuh. Believe me, now?"

"Damn, that's wrong on so many levels."

"*Lie*," the corpse repeated. "*Liar...*" The gnarled hand tapped at its chest over its dead heart, then it stretched its hand towards Dagra as if trying to point a twisted finger at him. It repeated the gesture at Oriken. "*Ree*," it said. "*Liar!*" The eyes narrowed and it took a step towards Dagra.

"That's enough of *that!*" Oriken pounced. The royal gladius descended and hammered into the corpse's head.

"Dagra! Oriken!"

Dagra whirled around to see Jalis jogging towards them, a grin of relief upon her face which he couldn't help but return. "Ah, lass!" he called, to the sounds of Oriken finishing off the corpse behind him. "There you are." But Jalis's smile slipped and she slowed to a halt. "What?" He turned, and found himself staring down the pointy end of an arrow aimed right at him.

As the rangy one rose from finishing his business with the decapitated ghoul, Wayland shifted his aim from the bearded man. "You," he said.

"Whoa there, friend." The tall man raised his hand. "We're on your side."

"Deceivers as well as outlanders." Wayland snorted. "I know your names." He glanced to the short, bearded one. "Dagger." Then behind to the woman. "Chalice!" he called, then turned back to the lofty one. "And you are the Orc King. Don't look much like an orc to me. Nor a king. But what do I know? Your greatest folly was in venturing to this place."

"Hey," the Orc King said with a shrug. "You know the old saying. When from the Folly—"

"Not now, Oriken," Chalice hissed.

"Hm. Oriken, is it? Fair enough. Can't blame Demelza. She's not so good with names. Now, I'm afraid you have to die."

"You won't pull off more than one shot before the rest of us rip you to shreds," Dagger said. "You must know that."

Wayland nodded. "And yet I have no choice."

Oriken leaned forward. "There are always choices."

"Why?" Dagger lowered his sword. "What have we ever done to you?"

Wayland's heart was thudding in his chest. He'd hurt his fair share of men in the past. It was a part of village life. But he'd never killed a man, and the bearded fellow that stood before him now, asking his question in earnest, was no mindless creature, not even a gobshite in need of a painful lesson. These three were not animals to be slain for meat and skin and bones. But if he were to let them go...

"You should never have ventured into the Fell," he told Dagger, training the arrow across to him. "Outsiders are not welcome here."

261

"You're not wrong, on both counts," Dagger said.

"Your knowledge of us threatens our existence." Wayland flicked a glance across the three of them. "You have to die."

A wry smile creased Dagger's scraggly beard. "Now *there's* a point I've been reckoning with lately. So, are you going to do it?"

A man of solid muscle stepped up alongside Chalice, dressed in the armour of the bygone days. He planted the tip of his longsword between his metal-clad boots and fixed his eyes on Wayland.

No matter, Wayland thought. *I'm already a dead man.* "It's nothing personal," he said. His hands were trembling for the first time in decades. "I can't allow—"

"If you're here to kill us," Dagger snapped, "then get the fuck on with it. But don't insult us by trying to excuse the fact."

A figure ran into Wayland's sight. Nearly naked from the waist up, there was no mistaking Shade as she darted across the street behind the two men.

Dagger lunged forward. Before Wayland could react, the bearded man doubled over, his sword clanging to the stones, and pitched to the ground, an arrow jutting from his upper back.

"No!" Oriken dropped to his knees beside his companion.

Taking a step back, Wayland glanced across to see Eriqwyn at the street's edge, notching an arrow to her bow as she brought it to bear on Chalice.

"My first shot was meant for another," Eriqwyn said. "But that one can wait. The safety of the village is paramount."

She pulled back on the bowstring. As the armoured knight stepped before Chalice to shield her, a flash of movement behind Eriqwyn caught Wayland's eye. The arrow flew, and the bow dropped from Eriqwyn's grasp. The projectile clattered against the knight's ringmail. A stupefied expression creased Eriqwyn's face, and her gaze dropped. A slim shaft of steel protruded from her breast.

Oh, goddess, Wayland thought. *Please, no.* Helplessly, he watched as the steel slid from the First Warder and she dropped to her knees. Behind her stood a young girl dressed in black, a slender blade in each hand, her eyes as midday blue as she coolly regarded him.

The whole tableau was thrust into brightness as sunlight streamed down. Down the sights of his arrow, Wayland cast a baleful glare upon the raven-haired girl as she squinted against the sun. He loosed his arrow. A blur of motion and a clang of metal, and it ricocheted away from her. He snatched at his sheaf, fixing a second arrow to his bow even as a slash of pain flared in his neck and a wetness trickled beneath his collar. He fired, and this time the arrow thumped into the girl's chest. She flinched, then flashed him an entirely mirthless grin.

He clasped a hand to his neck, his fingers brushing against something small and hard that slipped from his flesh and fell to the ground. Blood pumped between his fingers. His senses swam.

"You," he spat at Eriqwyn's attacker. "You are not our cousins!"

The raven-haired girl sneered. "No, boy, we are your elders, and you are interfering children who are long overdue a punishment." She nudged a toe against Eriqwyn's shoulder, and the First Warder toppled sideways.

"Eriqwyn!" he cried, his voice a hoarse croak.

He watched Chalice run to her fallen friend. His head reeled as he watched her crouch before the bearded man. Wayland blinked, then glanced at the ground at his feet, at a tiny knife that lay within a spray of slick crimson. *My blood,* he thought. *Huh.*

"Hey, shitface." Oriken sprang to his feet, dodged around his friends and hammered a fist into Wayland's face.

The world turned in spiralling flashes, then all was still. Wayland opened his eyes. Eriqwyn was inches away, the side of her head resting on the flagstones, her expression calm.

"Queenie," he whispered.

A small gasp escaped her lips, then her face blurred and the daylight dimmed to black. The street was soft beneath Wayland's cheek. Soft and warm...

This can't be happening, Oriken thought as he stared helplessly at Dagra, at the spread of blood that darkened his shirt around the shaft embedded in his back. Despite all they'd been through, the moment felt surreal.

Dagra shifted his face to the side, and blinked.

"He's alive!" Oriken squatted beside him, looking desperately to the Lachylan onlookers as more of the cityfolk came to stand beside Krea and Ellidar. "Help us!" he pleaded of the knight, then looked beseechingly to Jalis beside him. She shook her head. *It's a killing blow,* her expression said, *and you know it.*

Dagra loosed a shallow groan. "Oriken..."

"I'm here. Lay still."

Ellidar dropped to a knee at Dagra's other side. "Are you ready?" he asked. Dagra nodded weakly.

As the knight reached for the arrow, Oriken grabbed his arm. "What are you doing? You pull that thing out and you'll kill him!"

Ellidar held his gaze calmly. "I think you know I won't."

The knight's meaning was not lost on him. He looked bleakly to Dagra, whose eyes flicked to meet his gaze.

"Do it," Dagra whispered.

"No," Oriken protested, but his resistance slipped as Jalis pulled him away.

"It has to happen," she told him.

263

"Hold him down for me," Ellidar commanded her. She knelt and placed her hands firmly on Dagra's shoulders as the knight tore a strip from Dagra's shirt, wadded the material into a ball and shoved it into Dagra's mouth. He grasped the wooden shaft and wrenched upward. Dagra's muffled scream lasted only an instant as the arrow slid free, then he went limp.

"He sleeps," Krea said, stepping to Ellidar's side. "That is all."

Ellidar nodded as he rose. "He will live." With a nod to the two fallen assailants, he added, "As will they."

"Is that what you call it?" Oriken squared on the knight. "*Life*? What the fuck good is *that* to Dagra?" He gestured down the street to the subdued remnants of fighting, and out to encompass the whole of Lachyla. "This isn't his home. These aren't his friends." He barked a terse laugh. "Your king called this city a ledge of the Pit itself. He wasn't wrong."

Krea stepped between them and looked sternly up into Oriken's eyes. "Shouting at the world right now won't get anyone anywhere. Take your friend to my mansion. Remain there with him if you must, or return and help us put this mess in order. It makes little difference to me; the situation is controlled and the Mother is calmed. Go." She slipped a key from her leggings and handed it to him.

"Oriken." Jalis took hold of Dagra's arm, who even now was already stirring. "Help me get him to his feet."

Oriken glowered at Krea. "You could try showing a little compassion," he told her, moving to Dagra's side. "It wouldn't change anything, but it wouldn't hurt."

"That's a lesson you can teach me later," she countered with a tight smile.

Oriken and Jalis lifted Dagra to his feet, and he spat out the wad of material. As Oriken bent at the knee to wrap an arm around his friend's waist, he caught Ellidar's eye as the knight moved off. "Thank you," he said, though gratitude was not at all among his current emotions.

By all rights, he ought to be dead, Oriken thought to himself, casting a sidelong glance at Dagra's haggard features. And yet, despite his protestations, he realised that he *was* thankful – thankful that his old friend was still with them, in whatever horrific form of life – or non-life – he had slipped into.

CHAPTER THIRTY
ROTTEN LUCK

Demelza ran down the long alleyway alongside the towering western wall of the city, briefly quickening her pace as she passed each connecting pathway between the buildings to her right. It was quiet here with the commotion of activity muted and far behind her – quiet enough that the sound of something sliding and scraping across the rubble brought her skidding to a halt.

From around the corner of the next adjoining pathway, a ghoul crawled into view through the dirt, scratching at the ground to drag itself onwards, its backbone trailing behind it like the tail of a snake. Demelza let out a small scream and clasped her hand to her mouth. Stumbling back, she tripped over debris and landed hard on her rear. With fumbling fingers, she pulled an arrow from her sheaf as the ghoul's milky eyes locked onto her. It snarled, and its fingers dug with sudden urgency in a bid to reach her.

Her scalp tingled with terror as the creature closed the distance. With shaking hands she fitted the arrow to her bow, drew back on the string and let loose. The ghoul showed no reaction as the arrowhead sank into its shoulder. It snatched for her foot and she pulled it away, scrambling backwards and climbing swiftly to her feet.

As she stared at the bloated features, the air around the ghoul shimmered, becoming denser. She pressed her back to the wall, keeping her focus on the rotten thing as its eyes melted, glowing dimly from within. The flesh over its ribs began to bubble and smoke. With a gurgling moan, it dropped its face to the ground. The stench of roasting meat assailed her and she swallowed the rising bile. The ghoul ceased its movements, all but one hand clutching lethargically at the cracked paving.

Quelling a whimper, Demelza darted past the ghoul and onwards, all the way to the perimeter corner. Gravel scraped beneath her shoes as she slid into the wall and used her momentum to sprint on, not stopping until the wide main street came into view, the dividing gate's towers high above. Pausing at the building's edge, she peered around the corner and down the long street. A few of the strange people crossed back and forth in the distance, stooping to grab fallen ghouls and drag them away. Taking a deep breath, she dived for the portcullis and scrambled beneath the spikes, crawled across the mud to the inside wall and stared out at the expanse of graves. It was only then that she allowed herself to cry, but quietly and just for a moment.

The immense vista was empty, just as it had been when she first entered the place. Sunlight streamed across the rain-wet pathway and the muddy puddles, making it all sparkle. Taking breaths to calm herself, she brought to mind the faces of the group that she hadn't felt a part of – the First Warder, Waynan, the round-bellied hunter, the blacksmith, the old farmer man, and Shade. Lost in her thoughts, she glanced to the side and gave a start at the sight of a tall, hunched figure standing beside the wall with its back to her. She rose slowly, wiping her muddied hands on her leggings and frowning at the figure's dirt-caked cloak and cowl.

Ain't one o' them dead'uns, she thought. Then she saw the four curved spikes beyond the figure's hood. "It's the farmer," she whispered to herself. "Hey!"

He half-turned, paused, then completed the movement.

Demelza recoiled from the sight. It *was* the old farmer, but half of his face was torn away, his clothes and cloak a bloody mess, and what was left of his insides trailed down his trousers like a string of sausages. His grey eyes looked at her.

She took a step backwards. "I... I'm leavin' now," she stammered. "You, er..."

His teeth gnashed in mimicry of how he used to smack his lips, and he shuffled forwards a step, using his pitchfork as a crutch. "Dead," he said, raising a hand to touch the side of his head. "Can... feel it."

Demelza did cry then. Not a stifled sob, and not for her, but for the farmer man. His pale eyes looked sad and in pain. She made to move towards him, but he raised his hand.

"No," he drawled, then pointed his fork northwards across the graveyard. "You go. I... Ayyy..."

With a wail, Demelza threw her bow to the ground and ran, ran onto the broken pathway and kept running, not looking back, not even once.

———— • ————

The sound of a door slamming shut and a click as of tumblers turning roused Tan from his slumber. He didn't remember falling asleep. Didn't remember anything. Groggily, he rolled onto his side and pushed himself to his hands and knees, gazing around at the shadowed room. A sliver of sunlight knifed down across the carpeted floor of an ornate but small chamber with closed doors on two sides and an open door to his right.

He touched his fingers gently to the back of his aching head and felt a lump below the crown. He remembered bringing up the rear behind Demelza while Wayland scouted ahead. The next thing he knew, he was waking up here.

"Tan..."

The sibilant voice came from beyond the open door. He pushed himself to one knee and peered through, his brow furrowing in confusion at the sight of the bottom steps of an elaborate staircase.

Am I back in the village, he wondered. *Have I been taken into Albarandes Manor?* "Who's there?" he called.

A figure stepped into the doorway.

"Shade?"

She trailed a hand up the door frame and leaned upon it.

"What's going on?"

"You were hurt. I dragged you in here to safety."

He climbed to his feet. "But the—"

"Shh." She smiled. "Everything is fine. It is over."

"But..." He trailed off as his eyes took Shade in. Her hair clung wetly to her face, encircling her beauty. Her wet garments revealed her near-nakedness with almost as much detail as if she wore nothing.

She turned her back to him. His gaze drifted down the dark strands of hair that trailed her back, still further to the curves of her waist, the diaphanous material clinging to her buttocks and falling in neat folds down her thighs. She paced slowly away from him, and he watched, the madness of the city outside all but forgotten.

With liquid grace she turned back to face him, her hips swaying. "Come," she said, curling a finger to beckon him through.

Something felt wrong, but he couldn't place it. Warily he followed her, his eyes flicking to right and left to see the darkened interior of an entrance hall, much like what he had glimpsed several times beyond the double doors of Adri and Eriqwyn's house.

"What's going on, Shade?"

"What is going on?" She smiled sweetly. "The mission is over. The outlanders are dead and Eri has returned home. There is no rush. We are not in danger here. Let us take advantage of the moment." Her hand was atop her thigh, and she traced it up over her side to squeeze her breast. "You like what you see, don't you?" It was an observation, he knew, not a question.

He lifted his eyes to hers. For some reason his heart was thumping wildly. He nodded.

"You would like more of what you see, yes?" Shade drifted close to him, her fingertips light on his shoulder, her back arched, her chest rising and falling as she pressed her hips against his.

"But we have to—"

She touched her finger to his lips. "Shh."

267

"But—"

"Do you want me, Tan?" Her lips brushed against his cheek. The warmth of her breath upon his skin made his heart thud louder.

"Yes," he said, wincing at the squeak as his voice cracked.

"Then you should take me," she whispered. "But first, there is someone I would like you to meet."

"Who?"

Shade stepped away and turned her gaze up the grand staircase, an open smile blossoming upon her face. "Hello, Aunt Elimae," she called.

An elderly but attractive lady stood at the top of the stairs, a hand upon the polished banister, her other hand toying with a circle of starstone in a fine pendant at her neck. She smiled down at Shade, then turned to regard Tan. "Hello, young man. Welcome to House Galialos."

"Gali—" He frowned in puzzlement. "I don't…"

"You don't need to," Shade purred. "Don't be rude, Tan. Say hello."

"Er… Hello?"

Aunt Elimae laughed sweetly as she descended the stairs. "Oh, but you've put him ill at ease, the poor thing. He's confused. Likely concussed from the blow to the head. Shade, dear, you should explain that you call me Aunt only as a term of affection."

"Yes, of course." Shade turned her dark brown eyes on Tan. "Aunt Elimae is over three hundred and fifty years old," she said casually. "Which couldn't really make her my aunt, now could it?"

Tan took a step towards the double doors. "What's this about? What kind of game are you playing with me?"

There was a rustle of movement further down the entrance hall. From the shadows came a third woman, almost the double of Shade. With the same graceful motions, she swayed along the hall and paused beside the foot of the stairs to rest her hand upon the varnished post.

"Mama." Shade stepped across to the woman and kissed her upon the lips. With a smile, she glanced to Tan and said, "Look what I've brought us."

Tan blanched as he recognised the woman. "You're dead! *Fifteen years* dead! Your grave—"

"Is clearly empty," the woman said with a laugh. "Oh my, but it is nice to be recognised after all this time. And how are you, Tanriel Ebran? You have grown into quite a man."

"This isn't happening," he muttered as more women drifted in from the shadows on both floors. Turning to the double doors, he wrenched at the knobs, but the doors were stuck tight. Wheeling around, he backed against the wood and grasped for his sword, but the scabbard was empty. "Who *are* you women?" he demanded, turning on Shade. "You knocked me unconscious, didn't you?"

She sighed. "You had to make it difficult, didn't you?" Slowly, she stepped towards him, the other women at her heels. "We are the family Galialos. And this is your new home."

"We do hope you enjoy it here," Elimae called from the stairs, then her smile disappeared as the women closed in on him. "You *will* enjoy your stay, won't you, dear?"

———— • • ————

With his friends' help, Dagra lowered himself to the sofa in a downstairs room of the Chiddari mansion. "Thanks, lass," he rasped as Jalis pulled his boots off. "You should go. You're needed out there."

"We're staying with you," Oriken insisted.

Jalis reached to a set of shelves beside the sofa and took out a blanket. "I'll stay," she said, flicking the blanket open and draping it over Dagra's legs. "Oriken can go help Krea and the others. Besides, I need to clean and stitch your wound – something that is becoming a trend of late."

Dagra barked a laugh, then grimaced. "I have a feeling I'll not need stitches." To Oriken, he said, "Watch yourself out there."

"They don't need me. Everything's under control. But, hey, if you want rid of me..." He held Dagra's gaze for a long moment, then nodded and turned to leave.

Jalis followed him into the hallway. "Oriken, wait..."

As her words trailed away, the quietness gave strength to the babble of disconnected whispers within Dagra's head. He tried to push them away, and they diminished but did not silence.

I don't want this, he thought sullenly. *I don't want to die, but I can't live this way. Except I'm not alive. I'm dead. Dead and back again. I just didn't notice it happening. I was dead before the arrow took me. Sabrian's armchair, that's where it happened, but my fate was sealed the moment I inhaled that accursed fungus.*

His mind took him back to the crypt, once again reliving the moment when he crouched before the web-filled burial hole, spotted the strange, dark-as-char growth with its pale, crimson-veined cysts, and curiosity killed him.

Damned rotten luck, he thought, releasing a deep sigh.

Jalis re-entered the room and perched upon the sofa beside him. "How are you feeling?"

Dagra grasped the Avato emblem on its cord around his neck and managed a smile. "Strong as an ox, lass, as Maros would say."

"You're a terrible liar," she chided. "You always touch your pendant when you lie."

"Aye, I do. You know me well. But sometimes a lie is better than voicing the truth."

———·———

Oriken closed the mansion doors and crossed the porch. Pausing at the steps, he cast a dispirited gaze across the garden and the city beyond. "How did it come to this?" he mumbled to himself. Lachyla was filled with treasures beyond belief, but he was sure that so was Brancosi Bay if you searched hard enough in its secret corners. The problem wasn't the undead – not the rotten variety, anyhows – it was the *people* who dwelled there, the *people* who called the Blighted City their home.

You can't just go stealing shit from a place that's inhabited, even if the inhabitants are blight-ridden to the last. If Lachyla had been empty, and if we'd been prepared... Yeah, and it's a world full of ifs, ain't it?

With a shake of his head, he reached to pinch the brim of his hat, only for his fingers to close on empty space. Images of King Mallak Ammenfar surfaced then: Mallak showing Oriken the monstrous jewel-mushroom-tree-fish-whatever creature that dwelled in the depths; Mallak luring him into a fight; Mallak sinking to his knees, shredded by countless cuts and stabs from his own royal blade; Mallak's twitching body as he sat upon the throne, placed there by the loyal knight, painted from crown to boots in the darkest red of his own blood while flames consumed the last of his life – not that Oriken had seen that final image, and he was glad he'd missed it.

Then came memories of Dagra: Dagra's growing consternation over the foolhardiness of their contract as they drew deeper into Scapa Fell; Dagra's fears – along with Oriken's own – being tested as they ventured into the Chiddari crypt; their narrow escape from the fog-filled graveyard and the monstrosities that lurked there; Dagra's conversation with Oriken before he offered to take over the guard shift, and his subsequent disappearance. Oriken's throat tightened with regret as he remembered the venomous words he'd spewed about his friend while he and Jalis searched for Dagra.

I was so angry. I blamed him for taking the jewel, as if that fucking stone ever mattered. A few hundred paltry silvers, enough to keep us right for a long while, but what good will that do Dagra now?

Briefly he wondered at whatever had happened to that beautiful yet disgusting bauble. Even if the girl, Demelza, had taken it, Dagra was always going to have upped and left camp whether the jewel remained or not. Oriken wanted to hate the girl for playing a part in the ensuing nightmare, but found that he couldn't; she was just a simple peasant lass – tricky, no doubt, but he'd sensed no malice in her. If their two attackers were from Demelza's village, then their actions were not necessarily hers to answer for. Those two got what was coming to them, but what did the girl deserve?

Shrugging, he jogged down the steps and made his way across the garden to the street. Far to the south, a cart angled into view onto the wide boulevard, pulled not by horses but by people. A second cart followed behind. *Litchwagons*, he guessed, casting his eyes distastefully along the lines of corpse bits that had been dragged to the gutters. Turning his back to the wagons, he strode in the direction of the graveyard, casting a hard look at each of the cityfolk he passed. The minutes flew unnoticed beneath his melancholy contemplations, and soon he reached the spot where it had all come to a head.

And there's *the head it all came to,* he thought, stepping to the street's edge and looking down at a half-chewed, severed head that sombrely returned his gaze.

Despite the legion of corpses he'd battled yesterday and today, he easily recognised the less than handsome fellow that had stopped him and Dagra in their tracks, catching them off guard and unprepared for the bowman.

"Hello, chum," Oriken said. "Not so talkative now, hey?"

The yellow eyes regarded him pensively. The mouth opened, then closed.

Oriken lowered to his haunches before it. "What's that, sunshine? Liar, is it?"

Perhaps it was his imagination, but the head almost seemed to want to nod in agreement as its dead eyes turned from pensive to pleading. Oriken rose quickly. "No way. Stop messing with me. You hear?"

The head said nothing, though for some reason Oriken was sure it wanted to say not *Liar*, but *Please*.

"Ah, fuck off!" His frustration boiled over and he kicked the head and watched it soar down the street towards the approaching wagons. It struck the ground, then rolled and bounced until it came to rest a short distance ahead of the lead litchwagon. The men pulling the wagon stopped and one gave Oriken a thumbs-up while the other retrieved the head and tossed it into the cart.

"Oriken!"

He whirled around to see Krea beckoning him to her from further up the street, her blades sheathed upon her back. As he crossed the distance, he eyed the men and women that dotted the street. Some walked beside the line of piled corpses, thrusting blades into their heads to put the death-ravaged creatures further into lethargy. Other Lachylans were emerging from side alleys, dragging corpses and dropping them onto the pile. A small boy in monk's robes wandered along the corpse-filled gutter, waving a hand over each writhing body.

As Oriken reached Krea, he nodded to indicate the child. "What's up with that?"

Krea pressed her lips together. "Lewin is blessing them. It gives some of the people comfort. Tonight the streets and the graveyard will be emptied of all carnage, and the final vestiges of consciousness will be taken from the bodies by fire. Even now, a pyre is being constructed beyond the western walls out by the cliff-tops, where Lewin and his monastery bunch will perform last rites."

"Huh. That's gonna be one huge bonfire."

"Hmph."

"You don't approve?"

"I don't much care either way, as long as life returns to how it was before *you* showed up."

"You really mean that?"

"Truthfully? No, I suppose not. A girl can get a little crypt-crazy after three centuries within these walls, despite the occasional brief jaunt into the heathland."

"I thought you couldn't leave?"

"More than a few days beyond the walls and we'd lack the strength to return. Believe me, it has happened, not just the suicidal, but also the overly adventurous. Come." She turned on her heel. "Somebody is waking."

"Hey."

She wheeled back around. "What?"

"You know you have an arrow stuck in your chest, right?"

Krea sighed. "Thank you." She grasped the shaft, wrenched it out and threw it over her shoulder. "See? Three hundred years. I've become too accustomed to pain."

With a shake of her head, she snatched Oriken's hand and pulled him along the street towards what he'd presumed to be two corpses propped against a wall, but as they neared he realised it was the bowman and bowwoman from earlier, their bodies dragged into a clear space away from the others.

The bitch who shot Dagra, he thought, bristling at the sight of her. *And the fucker who stood us off in the first place.*

As they reached them, Krea released his hand and jabbed her toe into the woman's ankle. "Wake up, sleepyhead."

Oriken glanced at Krea in confusion. And then he understood. "Huh. When dead in Lachyla…"

The woman stirred. Her eyes flickered open, and for a moment she lay dazed until she spotted Krea standing over her. Reaching to her side, she bit a curse upon discovering her bow and arrows were not there.

"Looking for these?" Krea stepped nimbly to the weapons that had been piled close by. Selecting a bow and sliding an arrow from one of the sheaves, she cast them onto the woman's lap, who promptly notched the arrow and trained it on Krea. Pursing her lips, Krea cocked her head. "I've had not one but two rude awakenings today," she said, her tone matter-of-fact, "and, as you know, a lady can get snappy without her beautysleep. The second of those occasions was when the king died, at precisely the same time as *somebody* set the denizens loose into the city. *And* I've been shot once already, ruining my tunic which I'll have to darn. If you want to make a second hole, I welcome you to go ahead, but I should warn you that it will result in you burning to your second death on top of a thousand rotten corpses."

Slowly, the hate and misery clear on her face, the woman lowered the bow, her eyes narrowing as she held Krea's gaze.

"Your thoughts are mine now," Krea said. "Lachyla is the one place on Verragos where a person can truly be held accountable for thought crimes. While that's sinking in, I'll invite you to consider me a girl one more time – just once, and I swear I'll have a flaming torch in my hand quicker than you could get to your feet."

Flicking a glance at Oriken, the woman sneered and looked back to Krea. "You are in union with the outlanders."

Krea's smile was wicked as she glanced up at Oriken.

Beside the woman, her companion opened his eyes and groaned. "Wayland," she said, placing a hand upon his chest.

"Ah, good," Krea said to the man. "Welcome to your second and possibly short life." Her scowl encompassed the pair of them. "Let me tell you something. You people entered what you think of as the Forbidden Place, when you should have left well alone. You came, you meddled, and you paid the price. Just as Oriken's friend has paid a similar price. There is no moral high ground in Lachyla. Or, rather, if there is, then *you* do not own it. This is our city, and it was your forebears who chose to leave. Tell me, if you can, why did your ancestors not continue north further into Scapa Fell, or leave it altogether? Why remain but mere miles away from the place they fled? I'll tell you why. It's because they could not fully ignore the calling of home."

Neither of the captives spoke.

"That's right," Krea purred. "Dwell on that and be on your best behaviour, with your mouths – and minds – clear of malice. Your fate is still undecided, but you might yet see the end of this day."

Stepping away from the pair, Krea headed for the group of nearby Lachylans, and Oriken followed.

"Ah, Oriken." Gorven angled his way through from the back of the group. "Allow me to extend our thanks – not only for your support, but also for forcing our hand to do that which we should have done centuries ago. I trust Dagra is on the mend?"

Oriken grunted. "Such as it is."

Gorven glanced to the gladius on Oriken's hip and raised his eyebrows. "It may not mean much right now, but I would guess that sword could be one of the greatest single treasures in the whole of Himaera."

"You're right. Mallak lured me to the castle under false pretences, forced me into a fight, toyed with me the whole time, and refused to submit till he couldn't hold a weapon. How much do I care about any honour involved?"

Oriken shrugged. "You can gauge that from me giving him my hat. This sword is no recompense for losing a friend."

Gorven bowed his head. "If only you, Jalis and Dagra had knocked on our doors first—"

"If those doors were even open, maybe. But they weren't. To all intents, you gave the impression that Lachyla was a dead city – which, it turns out, is only half the truth."

"Hm. Perhaps that is something we should rectify in the future." Glancing to the Litchgate, he gave a start. "Ah! It looks like we have company." To the gathered Lachylans, he said, "One of you come with me," and promptly ran towards the half-raised portcullis.

Oriken peered past him to see a lean figure stood beyond the iron bars, a pitchfork in its hand. Gorven and one of the men reached the gate and dipped beneath it to stand with the figure. After a moment, they assisted it beneath the bars and guided it along the street. As they neared, Oriken pursed his lips at the sight of the tall stranger. The man would have been gaunt if his face were intact, but it was not. His neck was a grisly gorget of gouged flesh over a torn shirt. His middle was a sunken gap; what remained of the man's innards were now entrails that draped over his belt. What Oriken had at first taken to be cataracted eyes were a natural pale grey, and they were afraid, dumbfounded.

Poor bastard, he thought, suppressing a shudder as he realised that Jalis could have found such a fate if she'd fallen from the ladder.

Without any spoken words, one of the Lachylans brought a bandage from a nearby stash and held it poised to wrap around the man's middle, while a second Lachylan pushed the entrails back inside. The stranger just stood there while they worked, clutching his pitchfork with white-knuckled fingers – white because the skin was flayed away to reveal the spindly bones.

Another of the cityfolk stepped in to replace Gorven in holding onto the stranger's arm, and Gorven returned to Krea.

She cast him a flat look. "Any more surprises?"

"With luck, no." To Oriken, he said, "This one was killed earlier today. His name is Lingrey. He understands, but is in great shock, as anyone would be. He might heal completely, but then again…"

"Wait." Oriken held his hand up. "You mean he's not one of you, er, one of your…"

Gorven inclined his head towards the bowwoman and her companion. "He was with these two."

"I see." Oriken narrowed his eyes at the stooping man with the pitchfork. "So, you came to kill us?"

"Aye," Lingrey said. "Uh."

"How's that working out for you?"

The man's pale eyes lowered to the ground.

"What in the suffering Pit did we do to deserve your hate?"

274

Lingrey took in a shaky, phlegmy breath. "Egg cone."

Oriken shook his head and raised a questioning eyebrow at Krea.

"Deadstone," she said.

"Ah. It's all about the accursed jewel, is it?"

"Careful, Oriken." Krea smiled sweetly at him. "You and I may be... better acquainted now, but that's my family's burial stone you're talking about."

"Hey, if it wasn't for that stone, none of this would have happened. What's so important about it anyway? You've got—"

"Stop," Krea said flatly, flicking a glance at their captives. "The stone was quite happy in my ancestor's slab, and doing nobody any harm until you so-called freeblades showed up. Remember that."

He bristled, but couldn't disagree. "Well, if we're talking about blame, then I'd say our client, old Cela, was the catalyst for all this."

Krea nodded. "I've gathered as much from Dagra. We will talk later about your client."

"Uhuh." He glanced to Gorven. "So then, what can I do to help?"

"I'll tell you what you can do, my friend. You can return to our home and rest a while. You and your companions have done enough, and I mean that as a compliment." Gorven squinted his eyes against the sun and raised a hand to shield them. "The sooner we are finished, the better; it'll be evening in a few hours, and we all want to get out of this heat."

Oriken peered at him. "You okay? You're looking a little blistery there." He glanced to Krea. "You too."

"It's the sun," she said. "Water heals. Heat weakens. Same for anyone, I suppose, only more so for us."

"*Much* more so," Gorven said. "You know, some would say that the gods have a sick sense of humour."

Oriken scratched his stubble. "Why's that?"

"If we'd had weather like this the whole day, the denizens would've stayed in their shelters," Gorven said. "They only come out at night or when it's heavily overcast, especially when it rains. What Krea said about fire and water is also true, or *was* true, for the denizens, though the majority only operated on instinct, much like a turkey lifting its face to the rain. Except, of course, we blighted folk do not drown out of stupidity." Gorven flicked a hand dismissively. "But I ramble. Krea, you and your blades played a vicious and vital role today; why don't you escort our guest back to the mansion and get some rest? There will be plenty of work in the coming weeks, what with all the repairs the Mother's ire has made necessary."

The lead litchwagon rumbled slowly past. The two men pulling it trudged up the shallow incline like tireless mules. The second wagon rolled to a stop beside the group, and its pullers lowered the handles to rest. One of them walked to the rear of the cart. He reached in and snatched hold of a protesting, round-bellied and hard-faced man, dragged him from the cart and forced him to stand upright. The man's arms were tied behind his back. His captor gave him a rough prod to edge him forwards. The man's face was bruised, his nose swollen, his mouth caked with dried blood

The captive bowwoman sat forwards. "Onwin, where—"

A Lachylan man beside her nudged a boot into her shin. "Quiet, you!"

Gorven approached the newly-arrived prisoner and addressed the man holding him. "Amaran, you kept this one quiet. What have we here?"

Amaran tugged hard at Onwin's ropes. "My brother and I returned home after the fighting. Alamar heard a noise and went upstairs to investigate, thinking one of the denizens had entered the place in our absence. He didn't come back down. I followed him and found the loft hatch was open. I called for him but he didn't answer, so I climbed the ladder and promptly received an arrow to the gut." He gave another hard tug on the prisoner's bonds, and Onwin gave a snarl. "This craven was hiding in our loft. Got in through the roof shutters. Bastard shot Alamar right in the eye and sliced his throat wide open. Finished him off with a stab to the heart, or so he thought. Alamar will live, of course, but no thanks to this one's intent."

"I thought your brother was the Orc King!" Onwin protested.

Oriken growled under his breath. "Excuse me." He stepped around Gorven and snapped a thunderous punch into Onwin's jaw.

Onwin's head sank to his chest and he slumped within his captor's grasp. Amaran heaved him across to the other prisoners and cast him to the ground.

"That's right." Oriken raised his eyebrows and glanced around at the onlookers. "Did you see that? Out like a lamp." Flat expressions regarded him. "An oil lamp. No? Ah, forget it." He turned to Gorven and hitched a thumb at the captives. "What are you gonna do with them?"

"The one named Lingrey will stay with us," Gorven said, watching as the angular old man was escorted away from the group. "He knows it must be so, and we welcome him. After all, he did no harm to you and yours, nor to us, and his heart is good. As for those three, the consensus is verging on them being given two options: stay and adhere to our code of decency, or return to their home… and die."

Oriken puffed his cheeks. "It's your call, boss. Me, I'd be dragging their arses out of here, hobbling their ankles and leaving them to burn on the heath. Call me vindictive, but that's how I roll."

Gorven smiled wryly. "There is balance in all things."

With a bored sigh, Krea spun on her heel to walk away, then glanced back at Oriken. "Well? Are you coming, or will you just stand there like a spare part?"

"One moment." He walked over to the three villagers and squatted to his haunches before them. "Yeah, you," he said, ignoring the one he'd knocked unconscious and fixing the remaining two with a hard stare. "Do I have your attention? You came here to murder me and my friends, for your own misguided reasons. If you ask me, you deserve what became of you. And I'll say this: That which is dead, can indeed die again. I should know, I fought against the best of them. So believe me when I tell you that if you'd like to continue this fight, I'll be ready, waiting, and eager to tear you limb from rutting limb."

The woman blinked, her expression impassive. The man called Wayland pressed his lips together and gave a weak nod.

"That's all." Oriken slapped his hands onto his thighs and sprang to his feet, turning his back on the villagers and striding to catch up to Krea.

"I don't know about you," she said as he reached her, "but the first thing I intend to do is get out of these clothes and climb into a hot bath." She wrinkled her nose "I would suggest you join me."

Oriken burst into laughter, then quickly quelled it. "You sounded a lot like Jalis then."

"Please." Krea rolled her eyes.

"In truth, I'm hot, wet and stinking," he admitted. "Plus I'm aching all over and I could probably sleep for a week. Not to mention I'm also starving and parched. I might just take you up on the bath, but don't be surprised if I drink half the tub water and fall asleep in the other half."

Krea smiled. "You can bathe first and rest later, but between those there is a meal being organised for you and your friends. Some of us will join you."

"I appreciate that. But, for the love of any good that's left in this world, please – no jerky, and no damned bogberries."

———— • • ————

Oriken slumped back in the armchair, steepled his fingers and regarded Dagra. Their bearded friend hadn't yet moved from the sofa. Oriken had tried coaxing him to talk, but whatever Dagra was chewing on, he wasn't giving it up. Not yet, anyway.

"So," Oriken said. "Tomorrow, huh?"

Dagra peered at him, looking thoroughly miserable. "I don't know. And stop asking me." With a sigh, he added, "What would *you* do?"

I honestly have no clue, he thought. And then Gorven's comment about the villagers came back to him: *Go home, and die.* "Dag," Oriken said, "as far as prisons go, this one has to be the biggest and most open in the world. The alternative—"

"Just drop it. Please."

"Okay. Fine." He pushed himself to his feet. "You sure you won't go freshen up? I can take you to Jalis."

Dagra shook his head. "Soon. Gorven can run me a fresh tub before we head to this debacle of a meal. Let me snooze now for a while."

Dagra closed his eyes, and Oriken watched him for a full minute before slipping quietly from the room and into the entranceway.

He wandered to the back of the grand staircase and pushed a drape aside to reveal a secreted alcove. The shadowed corridor beyond stretched towards the outer edge of the building, then arced around to continue along a windowed wall. His muscles fatigued, he strolled the corridor's length, glancing only briefly through a window at the evening that descended over the mansion's lawn.

At the far end of the corridor a simple door stood ajar, a torch flickering behind it, casting an amber glow onto stone steps. He stepped through and pushed the door closed. The soft echo of rippling water drifted from the room below. His footfalls scuffed the worn stone as he descended to a heavy, velvet curtain. He eased it aside. The sweet scent of lavender filled his senses as he entered an expansive cellar.

Lit torches lined each wall, reminding him of Mallak's throne room; they illuminated a water-well in one corner and an iron cauldron in another, cradled above the ashes of a fire. A deep, circular bath was the only furnishing in the centre of the room, filled inches from the brim, a pile of folded towels upon the floor beside it.

Krea's head emerged from the water and she swept her hair back, the steam drifting around her.

"You're still bathing," Oriken said.

Torchlight caught her serene gaze, which he avoided as he unbuckled his swordbelt and quickly undressed. He climbed the steps beside the tub and stepped over into the hot water, then lowered himself to the submerged seat.

"Ah, that feels good." He dipped his head and stayed under, running his fingers through his hair. When he surfaced, Krea's eyes were on him, seeming to acknowledge that he'd positioned himself as far from her as the tub allowed.

"What are you thinking?" she asked.

He shrugged. "Nothing. Everything."

"I never dreamed I'd share my hot-tub with a world-class philosopher. It's almost enough to make a lady swoon."

"Huh?"

"Nothing, dear Oriken. My wit is too far beneath one of such esteemed free-thinking calibre."

"Free*blade* calibre," he corrected.

"Huh?"

He frowned, and Krea laughed. It was a good sound, with little mockery in it. In truth, the crackling, gurgling undertones in Krea's and everyone else's voices in the city no longer seemed so... wrong as they had at first. He was beginning to understand that the only thing these people had tried to do was to make the best of what cards they'd been dealt. He wondered if he'd have the fortitude to adapt as well as Krea had. He doubted it.

"What are you thinking now?"

"Just how I actually admire you," he admitted.

Her smile grew. "Ah, he admires me." She took a soap bar from the rim of the tub and stood, the water lapping at the tops of her thighs. An involuntary sound issued from Oriken's lips. He averted his eyes, pressing his back against the tub. Krea laughed lightly. "Admiration and restraint are such an attractive combination in a man."

"Really?"

"No, you dolt, not really. Life's too short for pretence."

"After you with the soap," he said, forcing his eyes to not slip from her face as she lathered the suds into her skin.

"You still see me as a girl, don't you?"

"How can I not?"

Krea sighed. "I'll forgive your ignorance, and your bull-headed disinclination to open your mind to reason. What you see before you is what your eyes tell you to be a 13 year old girl, yes?"

He shrugged, nodded.

"And what does your brain tell you?"

He barked a laugh. "My brain doesn't even know what it's telling itself, let alone what it's telling me."

"Hm. A self-explanatory statement if ever there was one. Well then, would it make your thought processes any easier if I reiterated that I'm approximately twelve times your age? What you consider to be an older woman would be someone twice your age, no?"

"I guess so."

"Which ought to make me more of a crone in your eyes than a naive child."

"Yeah…"

Krea sighed again. "Never mind. Here's the soap." She leaned forward and held the bar out for him to take. When his hand clasped around it, his eyes slipped to her chest. The puncture wound from the arrow was scabbed over, already peeling away to reveal pink skin beneath. *She's healing well*, he thought, his gaze straying from the scar. Sighing inwardly, he allowed himself to acknowledge that although Krea's was undoubtedly the figure of a girl – arguably a young woman – it was also more than that. Her muscles, though slight, were toned, and her face, though child-like, exuded an understanding of the world and of herself which no girl of her physical age could have amassed.

"That's better," she said, noticing his lingering gaze as she leaned back in the tub. "But let me tell you"—she flashed him a sweet smile—"next time you insinuate that I'm nothing more than a girl, I will show you how much of a boy *you* are. Understand?"

He nodded.

She sidled along the edge of the tub to scrutinise the wound on his shoulder. "You've torn some stitches."

"Doesn't matter. It'll hold. Stings like a bitch and the muscle's tight as fuck, but—"

"Are you aware that you have a penchant for cursing like a sailor? I thought you were trying to affect a penchant for decency?"

"Ah. Sorry."

"How did you get those red marks on your abdomen?"

"Hm?" He glanced down. "These? Some creature attacked me in my sleep, according to Dagra. Looks like they're starting to fade."

"You were lucky. The pygmy couldn't have been attached for long, otherwise it would have burrowed into your guts."

"The... *what?*"

"They're called blind pygmies. Curious little creatures. Innocuous-looking, but deadly if they catch you at slumber. Gorven has one in a cage. It's turned, of course, so can't die, but it's a poor vessel. Plus it's gone mad. He lets it feed on him occasionally to stop it from drying up."

"Close call. If Dag hadn't seen it, I would have missed all this fun."

Krea gave him a flat look and shifted away, but only slightly. "Well? Are you going to wash, or not?"

Oriken turned his back to her and stood, acutely aware of her scrutiny, and equally aware of his own body responding to it. He willed himself to think of the corpses being slung into a heap in preparation for the pyre. It helped, a little. Krea shifted further around the tub until she was side-on from him. He drew a breath and glanced at her. She said nothing, allowing him to wash himself in silence. When he was finished he placed the soap beside him and sank into the tub, splashing water over his head. Krea drifted across and rose before him, her legs sliding between his. She placed her hands on his shoulders, tracing one up behind his neck and the other down over his chest, inching herself closer.

"Gah," he muttered, flinching as her hand dipped lower.

"Mmm." There was no smile on her face now. "Such strength for a mere human."

"Krea—"

"Shush." She swung a leg over his, then the other. "No one will know.". Her blue irises sparkled with intent as she leaned in. Her wet lips brushed against the side of his mouth. "And I promise I'll be quiet..."

CHAPTER THIRTY ONE
LAST SUPPER

Trickles of subdued conversation ran the length of the narrow table. Almost forty were in attendance in what Gorven informed them had been a dining hall for the nobility, now rarely used. The tremors from the monstrosity beneath the castle had reached the building, and some quick repairs were in evidence. A couple of the windows were without glass, and one outer door sported a new upper hinge attached to a fresh square of stone in the adjoining wall.

Oriken fiddled with the puffy-sleeved shirt and plucked at the stretchy fabric of the black-cotton breeches Gorven had gifted him. To his left, Dagra was dressed in similar attire, but without Oriken's needlessly flamboyant collar and cuffs. To Oriken's right, Jalis wore a low-neck, white-cotton blouse with billowed arms that pinched above her elbows, covered by a coarse, embroidered thing that laced across her midriff and pushed her breasts up, which were half-covered by the soft undergarment. The numerous scratches criss-crossing her skin were the only signs of the harrowing events they'd endured; that, and the haunted look in her eyes.

"The fish is delicious," she remarked, slicing into the creamy-white meat on her plate, though to Oriken her tone sounded understandably less enthusiastic than her words. She glanced to Gorven opposite her. "What is it?"

"Kingfish," he replied, then forked a sliver of fish into his mouth. "Oh, my! I'd forgotten how good this tastes! It was Ellidar's choice, to which we all agreed. Mostly." A murmur of solemn approval cascaded along the narrow table, though some looked less than interested in the meals before them.

"How did you catch them?" Oriken asked. "I thought the animals gave this place a wide berth?"

Across from Oriken, Krea spooned some vegetables from a silver bowl and deposited them onto her plate. "Patience," she said. "Patience, a net, and the ability to breathe underwater. You should try it some time."

"Ah, I'll pass on that." He shifted his gaze to Sabrian, who sat between Krea and the toddler in the religious garb. Oriken shook his head at the sight of the child-monk in a highchair. Everything about the boy made him cringe, but,

281

despite that, he made a mental note to add the oddity to his growing list of prospective reassessments of the world.

"The Mother has never reacted so strongly," a woman along from Dagra was saying. "Such bloodshed. We must not allow the likes of it to occur again."

Sabrian nodded and looked pointedly to Dagra. "Even the Battle God showed up, drawn by the extent of the violence."

"Hmph," Oriken said, glancing sidelong to Dagra whose eyes were on his barely touched food.

The tiny monk leaned forward. "You disagree, friend?" he piped at Oriken.

"Damn right I do. That thing in the sky was just sunlight glancing through stormclouds. Why is every unusual sight always labelled as god-sent?"

The boy inclined his head in acknowledgement. "Perhaps it was merely sun and clouds – a warning formed by the goddess. As for the Mother, she *is* god-sent, and undeniable. After all, Valsana is the goddess of undeath as much as that of fertility, birth, life and death. We"—his eyes beamed, agleam with the fever of worship—"are her special chosen, granted the highest of her accolades."

"Right," Oriken said. "And by 'her', I'm guessing you mean both Valsana *and* the creature beneath the castle." He took some satisfaction in watching the boy quietly bristle.

Before the monk could reply, Jalis cleared her throat and said, "What of the sphere of light, Lewin – the one which melted the head of the king's statue and could have killed Oriken had he been much closer? Was that also god-sent? And, if so, by which god?"

"A good question," Lewin replied tightly. "This ball of white fire appeared as our liege was passing to Valsana. Although it struck his statue, it could instead have been aimed at your friend here"—he nodded to Oriken—"since it was he who brought our sovereign to his knees."

Oriken scoffed. "Revenge?"

Lewin shrugged. "Who are we to judge the actions of the gods?"

The woman beside Dagra leaned forward. "Maybe the light was a form of fae-fire."

"Or perhaps…"

Oriken glanced back along the table to the speaker, two seats beyond Gorven. The learned voice quietly commanded the attention of the dinner guests, and the academic but strong-looking man raised an eyebrow a fraction. "Rather than gods or fae, it *could* have been ball lightning."

Oriken smirked, then quickly hid it behind his fist and looking innocently at Jalis.

"I heard of a similar manifestation," Jalis said, "albeit on a considerably larger scale. It occurred in Midhallow. Allegedly, a large globe of light struck the tip of the Needle and travelled its length, but dissipated before reaching the citadel beneath."

Blank glances crossed the table among the guests.

"Forgive us, lady," Ellidar said. "Our knowledge of the free city is benighted at best."

"Let us change the subject," Gorven said, his tone polite as ever. "As you can see, the philosophies of Lachyla differ far and wide. Good Lewin is an acolyte of Valsana and the elder gods, extended in the monastery's beliefs to include the Mother. The fearless Ellidar is the city's singular guard commander and knight-paladin." He gestured to the woman beside Dagra. "Tamria is a mythologian and antiquarian, much like myself." Gorven inclined his head to the man two seats from him. "And our esteemed Cleve was a metallurgist before the blight, and quite the acclaimed academic. We're a mixed bunch, but the desire for wanton violence is thankfully all but extinguished; the events of the day are passed, along with any phenomena that occurred."

"I'm amazed at how you're all taking this so casual," Oriken said. "You've got a nearby village – populated with your descendants, by the way – that's probably got as many people living in it as the population of Lachyla. And they're pissed. You think they'll just take what happened today on the chin?" He looked across to Gorven. "What did you do with the prisoners, by the way?"

"The old fellow has agreed to stay, though not by force," Gorven said. "He is currently being cared for along with the worst casualties of the city, including many of Ellidar's valiant knights. The gentleman of rotund persuasion – the one found hiding in Amaran and Alamar's loft – was allowed to return home, and with him he took the other two."

Dagra shifted for the first time during the meal. "But won't leaving here mean that they'll... Ah, I mean wouldn't they..."

Gorven quirked an eyebrow. "Die? Yes, they most certainly will."

Dagra's expression was pensive. "So, they chose to go."

Gorven gave a slight shrug. "The woman insisted upon it. The man, well, to tell the truth I think he would have stayed, but his desire for life was less strong than his love for the woman, and so he returned with her."

"*Not* going to be an epic tale, that one," Krea muttered.

"How long will they have?" Dagra asked.

It was Sabrian who replied, eyeing Dagra levelly. "In the woman's case, she'll be lucky to last two days. Her wounds were grievous."

"Hmph." Krea tossed her head in indignation. "I only stabbed the wench once. I would have done it when I first saw her, if there weren't more pressing matters to attend."

"Someone beat you to it," Sabrian said with a sideways glance to his right, where an elegant elderly woman and an attractive younger woman returned his look with innocent expressions.

"It's true." Gorven leaned in to his daughter. "She was dead and risen before you reached her, Krea. None of us noticed with all else that was transpiring."

Dagra grunted. "So… you're saying that when she shot me…"

"Yes, my friend." Gorven gave a perfunctory nod. "She had turned before her arrow scratched your heart and completed your own turning, but her actions did not cause you to turn, just as Krea's actions did not cause Eriqwyn to turn."

A thought occurred to Oriken as he swallowed the last mouthful of his meal. "Wait a minute. If those two were dead – the woman and her man-friend – and since some of you cityfolk were with them before letting them leave, you could've pulled that trick you do with Dag; you know, had a look into their minds to see if they knew about the jewel." He glanced at Krea. "Ah, I mean, your family's burial stone."

Gorven gave a tight smile. "We did. But there was no need. The stone was in Eriqwyn's possession and she offered it freely. It is now safe in our home"—he glanced at Krea—"awaiting its return to Cunaxa's tomb."

Oriken nodded. The Chiddari jewel had slipped through their fingers after all. *No matter*, he thought, sharing a look with Dagra. The reward meant nothing now, and they had no choice but to renege on the contract – something every freeblade strived hard not to do. It was an unfortunate mark against the guild, but the only thing that mattered now was Dagra, whose sombre expression told Oriken much.

"They came to return the stone to its rightful place," Tamria muttered. "But at what a high cost."

Jalis pushed her fork around the remains of her meal. "That was only one of two reasons," she said. "The other was to kill three so-called outlanders, just like they did with Sabrian's friends before they even had a chance to enter the graveyard, let alone have a look around for treasures."

Gorven gave a closed-mouthed sigh. "It was an unfortunate by-product, born of generations of ingrained self-preservation and distrust of the unknown world beyond their home."

"No disrespect intended," Jalis said, "but that sounds not too dissimilar from a certain city I could mention."

"There is a marked difference," Krea said brusquely, not bothering to lift her gaze from her food to Jalis. "We have never sought to kill anyone, even for apparently justified reasons." And then she did look to Jalis, her expression serious. "Today I ran that woman through to save *you*, girl, because I know how much you mean to Oriken. Luck had it that Ellidar also had your preservation in mind."

Jalis blanched. "Er… thank you. I hadn't…"

"I know you hadn't."

"Krea speaks the truth," Ellidar said, placing his cutlery neatly upon his empty plate. "In terms of preservation, ours works both ways. If knowledge of our existence were to spread throughout Himaera, can you imagine the influx of pilgrimages to the city, by folk in search of the font of immortality?"

Gorven nodded. "As grandiose as it may sound, our secrecy exists to maintain the integrity of humanity, something which we ourselves have transcended."

"I don't know much about any of that," Oriken muttered.

"You don't know much of anything," a guest from further down the table said. "You outlanders brought this trouble upon us, strutting into the graveyard, casually taking that which does not belong to you, leaving the gate open – which we keep closed precisely to prevent anyone entering – and flaunting your prize to the locals. Without you luring them here, the Litchgate would never have been raised. And without your presence in our city, our beloved king would still be alive."

Oriken half-rose from his seat. "Now listen here—"

"Calm yourself, Josaius," Ellidar said. "Our liege is where he has wanted to be for a very long time. His torment is over."

As Oriken lowered himself to the seat, a young-looking man beside Lewin spoke. "It's true. These changes that were forced upon us can only benefit Lachyla. The denizens will be cleansed once and for all this night, and the city is no longer under the rule of a silent monarch."

"Be careful, Simri." Ellidar's tone was all warning. "I am still and ever King Mallak's bondsman, and will not hear his name slighted so publicly."

Simri nodded to the knight in acquiescence, then leaned in to the little monk beside him. "Too soon?"

Lewin nodded. "There is no grief greater than that for the dead heart. Your tact and timing are disgraceful, Simri, but Valsana still loves you, as does the Mother."

"Our liege was thankfully the only fatality today," Ellidar said slowly. "And, yes, he was the engineer of his own passing. There were, however, many injuries which, were we merely human, would instead have been deaths by the dozens. Five in particular – two citizens and three of my knights, including my second, Heilin – may yet decide after they're fully healed to relinquish their lives."

"Why?" Jalis asked.

"The onslaught of the denizens was brutal in its relentlessness," the knight said. "And those five men and women in particular suffered horrendous injuries. The details, I fear, are a touch too gruesome for the dinner table, but suffice it to say that our ability to heal, especially under such extreme circumstances, does not always yield perfect results."

Oriken ran a hand across his stubble, sighing inwardly as the conversation simmered down around him. Taking a sip of water from his cup, he flinched as a soft touch trailed up his shin and turned a hooded glance at Krea. Her full lips wore an almost imperceptible smile, her sky-blue eyes glinting with amusement as her foot crept around onto his calf muscle and she curled a toe into the crook of his knee.

"What of you, Dagra?" Gorven asked. "Have you made a decision?"

Dagra cast him a resigned look. "You ask me questions, when the answers could be easily plucked from my mind."

"We acquiesce to your wishes of privacy, my friend, as is the custom within Lachyla."

"You say that, but I can still feel you in here." He tapped a finger against the side of his head.

"Our presence, yes, but not our intrusion. You have not yet learned to partition yourself, and so your emotions are drifting through the city like wisps. It will come, with time."

"You won't be the only new arrival," Tamria said to Dagra. "There's the fellow named Lingrey…"

"And my dear niece has finally joined us. Isn't it delightful?" The elderly woman several seats along from Sabrian beamed a smile that encompassed everyone, then turned to the dark-haired woman beside her. "Aren't you happy, dear?"

"I am, Aunt Elimae," the woman replied, her tone languid and sensual.

"It is a pleasure to welcome the latest member of the Galialos family fully into the Mother's chosen few," Josaius said.

Sycophantic sod, Oriken thought. "No disrespect," he said to the table in general, "but the Mother doesn't seem to give a gutter rat's rectum who she turns into a vessel, least not these days. And what do you mean by 'fully'? From what I've been told, you're out until you're in, and then it's either death or Lachyla. Or did I miss something?"

"You missed nothing that wasn't imparted to you," Cleve's rich voice rumbled through the dining hall. "The Galialos ladies have ever been the eyes and ears of Minnow's Beck, since the turning and subsequent founding of the village."

"*What?*" Jalis's eyes were hard as she looked from Cleve to Gorven. "So you *knew* they were bringing the stone? You *knew* they were coming to kill us?"

Gorven shook his head. "It doesn't work like that. Shade, up until returning here today, was unturned and therefore incapable of sending her thoughts to us. She was, however, partially turned from frequent but short visits to her family."

Sabrian sucked air through his teeth, and Oriken caught his icy expression. The man was clearly ill at ease about something. Oriken glanced to the one called Shade. Her beguiling features were etched in wry amusement as she shared a look with her aunt. "Hold on a moment," he said, scratching at his stubble.

"Your rescue," Jalis said to Sabrian, her voice low enough to reach him but not to travel the length of the table. "You told us your torment didn't end there until Gorven intervened. This family..." Her eyes flicked to the two women at the far end of the table. Sabrian fixed her with a stern look and gave a slight shake of his head, as if telling her to leave it alone.

"One of the beautiful things about being turned," Shade said, smiling down the table at Jalis, "is the impeccable hearing."

"My family," her aunt said, a shadow crossing her face, "has been an invaluable asset to this city since time immemorial. Once in a while it is unavoidable for that help to be seen as something less." Her narrow-eyed glance to Sabrian lasted but a second. "You can please many, but you can't please everyone."

While Sabrian remained silent, Gorven cleared his throat. "You have indeed been an asset, Elimae, which is why the rest of us have turned a blind eye to your... indiscretions over the years, much as we left the denizens to roam the Gardens. But with the unfolding of today's events, it seems your family's duality in Lachyla and Minnow's Beck may no longer be required."

"No matter," Elimae said tightly. "My niece was unable to be with child, and so has left no legacy to continue our tradition. The secrecy of the two places has dissolved, and we believe the stability of the village is about to be tested."

"Others will come to Lachyla," Shade purred. "In time. And our family will yet find new members." Her brown eyes caught Oriken's scrutiny and her lips parted a fraction. She traced a fingertip over her breastbone, bringing his gaze down to see how visible everything was through the gauzy strips of material that served as her frock.

"Gah!" Oriken gasped as pain shot up his shin and turned a scowl on Krea, who raised an innocent eyebrow.

"Something troubling you, friend?" Gorven inquired.

"Just, ah, just my shoulder giving me gyp." He caught a glance from Jalis before she returned her attention to the glass of water in her hand.

Krea's foot rubbed gently against his tender shin, then she traced it up to the inside of his thigh. He turned a tight glance up and down the table in an attempt to feign casual interest in the dinner guests. Krea's toes trailed even further, and he puffed his cheeks, raising his eyebrows nonchalantly as he caught Sabrian looking his way.

"Ah, Oriken!" Sabrian called. "Would you mind ever so much if you and I had a... private chat, out on the courtyard?"

"Er, sure. Of course." Appreciating the tactful interruption, Oriken grabbed his cup and pushed his chair back. As he rose to his feet, he caught Krea's azure glare and turned away, striding past Jalis to the end of the table. Sabrian joined him, carrying a lit candle, and placed a companionable arm around

Oriken's shoulders to lead him from the hall. As they stepped out into the courtyard, Oriken breathed a sigh of relief.

"Thank you," he said in earnest. "It was getting a bit stifling in there."

Sabrian chuckled. "No problem. Anything to aid a fellow in distress. Besides, I was needing a breather myself."

"Yeah, what was all that about?"

Sabrian shrugged. "When I fled from the villagers who killed my friends, it was my luck to fall into a hole which led to a cave that just happened to join onto the Galialos family tombs. In short, I was held captive by Elimae and her women for three years. My introduction to dying and becoming alive again was a thousand days and nights of a nightmare paradise, where Elimae's harem sang their exquisite songs of pain and dark laments of desire."

"Wow."

"Indeed." A shadow crossed Sabrian's face, and he suppressed a shudder. "Now, on to more important matters, my friend," he said, holding up the candle.

With a nod, Oriken plunged a hand into his pocket and pulled out a thin brass case, popped the latch with a flick of his thumb and drew out a roll of tobah. "Jalis told me," he said, passing it to Sabrian who passed the cylinder beneath his nose and inhaled deeply.

"Ahh, now *there's* a scent I've missed."

Oriken tapped a roll out for himself. He held it between his lips as Sabrian lifted the candle for him to light it. He took a long pull, and blew the smoke out in a dissipating spume. Sabrian lit his own, then coughed and spluttered, taking a few short gasps to catch his breath. "Oh, my," he said, setting the candle down and taking a long drink from Oriken's cup. "And that's the part I didn't miss." He took another draw on the tobah, and this time managed it with scarcely a cough.

The two enjoyed the moment in silence, looking out across the serene courtyard. Oriken regarded the ugly statue of Valsana that decorated the centre of the open space, with its deep-set eyes, engorged breasts, and ridiculously oversized cleft below her belly. "Unsightly beast," he muttered, bringing the tobah to his lips.

Sabrian raised an eyebrow. "Hm? Oh, the statue? Yes, not entirely pleasing to the eye, is she? Mind you, some – like, perhaps, little Lewin in there – would say she's the definition of womanliness; fertility, at least."

"Well, she's not to my taste; not as a goddess and certainly not as a woman."

"Each to their own though, right?" Sabrian sucked smoke into his mouth and cast Oriken a shrewd glance.

"Yeah," Oriken replied carefully. "Each to his own."

288

"Tell me"—Sabrian leaned his elbows upon the short wall before them and looked out into the courtyard—"what do you really think of what's going on here in Lachyla? Not what happened today, I mean just generally."

Oriken adopted Sabrian's casual pose, and shrugged. "This morning I would have told you I find the whole situation deplorable, untrustworthy, violating, and bordering on evil incarnate. Now?" He sniffed. "I guess there's good and bad in everything."

"Evil *is* largely subjective," Sabrian mused. "What is evil to one is morally justified to another. But we're speaking in human terms. There is no thought behind the roots of what Lachyla has become."

"But you all share each other's thoughts. Because of that thing... that Mother down beneath the castle. Doesn't it all come from there? Or from the other one the king mentioned, out under the ocean? Mallak claimed that those creatures don't think, that they don't mean to do what they've done to you."

"The king was correct, in *that* if not in much else. Oh, there's impulse, but no forethought, no planning. The Mother doesn't twirl her moustache or wring her hands, cackling in glee over her sinister schemes. She merely *is*. The fish merely *are*; they swim around and eat and shit and fuck, but beyond that?" Sabrian shook his head.

"Still," Oriken said, "there's a part of me that's jealous of you being able to live forever. With the corpses gone, what you've got here isn't too bad, all things considered."

"Ah, but immortality comes at a hefty price. Would you rather remain in one place forever, or would you prefer the freedom of travelling the world, meeting new people, seeing fresh and wondrous sights, but knowing beyond doubt that you will one day die? Then again, can you imagine the experience of one who could combine immortality with freedom, to walk Verragos forever?" Sabrian sighed plaintively. "Me, I think I could enjoy that, but it is not the card I was dealt in life. I left a lot behind when I came here, but some of those who dwell in this city have pasts they cannot emotionally resolve, even after three centuries. The king, for instance."

"He wasn't a particularly jovial fellow, that's for sure."

"Nor would I be, in his situation. You know that he killed his champion? The act was warranted, from what I've learned. Mallak's wife gave birth mere months before the living of the city began to turn. When the boy was born, Mallak was convinced it was not of his blood. When he confronted his wife, after some... persuasion, I imagine, she confessed to a series of indiscretions with the king's own champion, no less. And so Mallak slew the man, but in a fair fight. After the turning, the baby was not half a year old – no physical state for any immortal to be locked in; poor Lewin suffers enough, but a baby?" Sabrian shook his head. "Before the first year was over, the queen took her dead lover's son in her arms and descended the trail to the beach. She walked into the water, and the king – along with all the cityfolk – felt her slow, fading passing along with the false but innocent heir as she waded deeper into the Echilan Ocean. So you see – for some like Mallak, three hundred years as a shackled ghost is not equal to even one year of living in freedom."

Oriken grunted. "It's a tragic story, but the world's full of them, and the rest of us have to live with ours. Define freedom, though. The freedom you talk of may be beyond your prison cell, but not beyond the whole dungeon. Perhaps it is not immortality, but mortality that comes at a price."

"That's a fair perspective for someone who hasn't spent the last century and more in the same city, staring out onto the same ocean and at the same stretch of heathland. Oriken, if I could trade my existence for yours, I might be sorely tempted to do so, despite the constant knowledge of unavoidable death. And, with my few remaining decades, I would head out into Verragos and fill my life with meaning. But"—again he sighed—"I am resigned to this life now. I might have traded places with you, were it possible, but I would not walk out into the heath in search of death."

"Who would?"

Sabrian turned to him, but said nothing. He looked down at the leafy cylinder in his hand. "Thank you for this, my friend. And for the talk. It was very nostalgic." He stubbed the embers against the wall. "I think I will keep a hold of this." He pocketed the half-finished roll of tobah. "See how many decades I can resist the urge to light it." Sabrian chuckled, and Oriken laughed with him.

CHAPTER THIRTY TWO
SUNSET TO SUNRISE

Dagra shifted upon the rectangular-cut boulder and looked out past the cliff's edge onto the grey ocean. No birds cried beneath the sigh of the tide or the crash of waves upon unseen rocks below, and none swooped before the orange orb of Banael as it melted into the frothing water. It was a beautiful sight, but barren of life.

This time yesterday I saw this place as the edge of the world, but what does a simple freeblade know? Maybe, somewhere far beyond the horizon, someone else is looking out onto the same churning expanse and thinking the same thought as I was.

Beside him, Gorven loosed a plaintive sigh. "I like to come here sometimes. Alone. To speculate."

Dagra huffed. "Is there anything left to wonder about after the years you've lived?"

"You might be surprised. Some questions, after all, are unanswerable; the more you consider them, the more they give rise to new, equally unanswerable questions."

"Such as?"

Gorven laughed softly. "Well, now…" As he pointed to the horizon far opposite from the sinking sun, Dagra followed his finger to a dim three-quarters sphere that hung low in the sky. "Do you see that?"

"Of course," Dagra said. "It's Haleth rising. The whole world knows that."

Gorven nodded. "Indeed it is. What more can you tell me about Haleth?"

"What is this? A history lesson?"

"History?" Gorven said with a grin. "Oh, but my dear Dagra, what makes you think my question has anything to do with history?"

Dagra shrugged. "Haleth is one of the old gods."

"True." Gorven leaned back and planted his hands on the stone behind him. "And this moon of Haleth, does she have a role in the stories of the old gods?"

Dagra sat up and frowned at the man. "Did you drag me out here so you could bore me into throwing myself off the cliff? Because, if so, it's working."

"Humour me. Please."

He let out an exasperated sigh. "Very well. Haleth is the Ethereal Goddess of the Air and the Void, cast there at the end of the Arkhaeon by the Arbiter for breathing life into the toys of the gods."

"And why did the Arbiter judge her so?"

"Because of the violence of the gods' creations. I guess she's supposed to not be able to come back to Verragos, condemned to forever watch the toys she helped create, but never again to interfere with the world."

"Hm." Gorven quirked an eyebrow. "But is any of this true?"

"Of course it is. I mean, look, there she is. What more proof do you need?"

"I see." Gorven lifted his gaze past Haleth, shielding his eyes from the rays of the dipping sun. "Ah, there." He pointed almost directly overhead at a small, indistinct smudge in the darkening sky. "Atros, the Grey Watcher. Emissary of the Dyad."

"Oh, you never gave me a chance," Dagra said drily.

Gorven smiled as he stared upwards at the smudge. "I don't seek to test your knowledge, my friend, but rather your understanding."

"What difference is there?"

"To some"—Gorven shrugged—"there is none. Now, tell me what you understand about that dirty little smear above us."

Dagra blanched. "You shouldn't talk like that. The Emissary watches us constantly."

"Ah." Gorven turned an amused eye on Dagra. "What will the Emissary do now, I wonder, that he has deigned not to do in all my years of blasphemous utterances? Shall we put it to the test?"

"No!" Dagra rose from the stone.

"Very well." Gorven waved a placating hand. "Please, sit. I'll behave, I promise."

Reluctantly, Dagra sat back down. "Why would you tempt the anger of the gods? You saw what happened earlier."

Gorven smiled ruefully, his gaze trailing across the watery expanse. "Truthfully? At first it was my own personal test, but I suppose it developed over the years into something of an indulgence, a game I've liked to play ever since the goddess died."

"Morta'Valsana? She didn't die. She deserted you."

"Perhaps that is true. But, after you have lived here as long as I have, a dead goddess or an otherwise absent goddess, it really makes no difference."

Dagra said nothing, and they lapsed into silence, each looking out at the tranquil ocean and the fading day. After some minutes, he felt Gorven studying him. "What is it?"

"I was just wondering what you were thinking."

He shrugged. "I was recalling something that happened a long time ago, back when me and Oriken were lads."

"I'd like to hear it."

292

Dagra barked a laugh. "I doubt it." He cast Gorven a sideways glance. "Fine, but I warned you." He drew a deep breath and released it slowly. "Me and Oriken, we were in our early teens. I'm a little older than he is, but I was as much a short-arse then as I am now, and Oriken was already turning into a beanpole, but there wasn't much strength to him. We'd been friends ten years or so, ever since he and his parents arrived in Eyndal. His pa, a good man named Kyne, was a mineworker. Both my parents were long dead. Oriken and I did menial jobs to help the miners – carrying supplies, relaying information, manning the doors.

"One day I entered the miners' rest area to see Oriken sizing up to one of the workers. The miner shoved him and he went down. I ran to help him up and the miner yelled at me to keep my friend from poking his nose where it didn't belong." Dagra looked at Gorven. "You know the sort."

Gorven nodded.

"Anyway, Oriken's shouting back at the man and telling me that the feller's got his pa's hat."

"Ah."

"Aye. Sure enough, I looked to the feller's head and there's the hat that Kyne supposedly lost some days earlier. So I voiced as much." Dagra shrugged. "You do, don't you, when it's your friend?"

Gorven brushed a thumb pensively over his chin. "Indeed you do."

"The mine worker shoved me away. I stumbled, but got a hold of him and we both went down. His hand clasped onto my throat, and he squeezed. He wanted to kill me. I could see it in his eyes. Somehow, I wrapped my hand around a rock. You don't stop to think when your life's in the balance. I smashed it into his head and he was out like a lamp. Oriken helped me up, and as he took his pa's hat I stared down at the miner. I wanted to pummel the rock into his face again and again, but I didn't. I let him live.

"Oriken returned the hat to his pa, and all was well with the world till the following week when Kyne died. Some accident down in the mines, it was said, but I called that out as cowshit. Couldn't prove it, but I knew it were the feller we'd altercated with, 'cause again the hat had gone missing." Dagra shook his head. "Damned business."

"There's a moral to the story," Gorven said.

"Aye, there's a bloody moral. That night I went to the feller's house and stuck the murdering bastard in the heart while he slept. Cowardly, maybe, but I didn't give a shit. Took the hat and gave it to Oriken. He's worn it ever since. Until today, that is. I reckon it's done him good to finally let it go. As for the moral, take your pick." Dagra shrugged. "For me, it's that cold-blooded murderous bastards may get what they want in the short-run, but in the long-run they damn well get what they deserve."

"And how do you feel about it now?"

Dagra pursed his lips and considered the question. "Maybe if I'd cowered, maybe if I'd just taken Oriken out of the mines instead of knocking the feller senseless, maybe Oriken's pa might still be alive. Maybe his ma, too. But probably not. Could be that someone else would've died instead, and that may have been Oriken. Would I change it if I could?" He shook his head. "I'm at peace with what I did. Just a bloody shame, is all. Still, maybe Kyne met his killer in the next life and befriended him. They say that the Underland makes the strangest bedfellows – mortal enemies on Verragos can be fast friends on Kambesh."

"Hm." Gorven looked thoughtful. "May I ask another question?"

Dagra gestured for him to do so.

"Do you worship the goddess Valsana?"

"I worship the Dyad," Dagra replied vehemently. "Svey'Drommelach and Aveia, and their prophets, Avato and Ederron."

"So, not Valsana, then. And is this"—Gorven indicated behind them at the towering battlements—"not what happens when a deity dies? Or if, as you say, she deserted us, then where now is she? Reduced to ruling over a single village innocuously named Minnow's Beck, when once she owned the whole of Himaera? Forgive me for saying so, but that doesn't sound like a goddess that can afford to pick and choose, especially these recent centuries with the Dyad invading her territory. Wouldn't you agree?"

"I don't know about any of that," Dagra said gruffly. "I only know I can't stay here."

"You cannot leave, Dagra." Gorven's tone was firm. "To leave is to truly die. When you walk away from the only place that can sustain you"—he held his hands palm-upwards—"then, like Valsana, you fade away."

Dagra said nothing. Gorven – and Sabrian – were newcomers to his life, and yet somewhere within him he knew them as intimately as he did Oriken, Jalis and Maros. To a lesser extent, the same was true with the entire population of Lachyla. He didn't know *what* he knew of them, only that the knowledge was either in his head somewhere or otherwise reachable. *Perhaps not knowledge*, he mused, *but more like an understanding.* "I refuse to stay in this blighted city," he said, "this limbo between life and rebirth where nobody's thoughts are fully their own."

"You will not endure beyond the reaches of Scapa Fell. That I promise you. You will never return to Alder's Folly, nor see your family in Eyndal again. The Mother's reach is only to Lachyla's perimeters. Beyond that, it is like being without food and water. Go for too long, or too distant, and you will not survive."

Dagra turned away from Gorven to the sun sinking into the rippling water. "Then I will die free," he said, rubbing a knuckle at the edge of his eye. "And in good company. With my friends."

The mansion doors clicked open and Oriken looked up from the unsheathed gladius in his lap, now polished to a gleaming shine. Gorven stepped through onto the porch and greeted them with a hospitable smile.

"Whenever the three of you are ready," he said, "I'll escort you to the guest quarters where you will each have a separate room with a comfortable bed. Krea has prepared fresh linen."

"We appreciate it," Jalis said. "Could we trouble you for a few blankets to take with us for the journey? We left our bedding at camp when we came to find Dagra."

"Of course. I'll leave some in the entranceway with your packs."

Jalis nodded her gratitude. "Thank you for retrieving them."

"Not at all. Ah, I also brought your light device from the tunnel. A lamp, do you call it? You see, I do pay attention. I had a little fiddle around with it. Quite practical, I must say. Cleve would be fascinated with it."

"I doubt we'll need that lamp again," Oriken said as he leaned back against the porch wall. "The guild has enough in stock. Keep it. Or give it to your friend."

"Truly? Well then." Gorven inclined his head. "My thanks. I'll leave you in peace. Come and find me when you're ready to retire for the night."

As Gorven withdrew back into the mansion's shadowed interior, Dagra reached for the jewelled sword in Oriken's lap. "Can I have a look at that?"

Oriken passed him the gladius. While Dagra scrutinised the weapon beneath the light of the torches attached to the wall, Oriken studied his face. It seemed to him that Dagra was only going through the motions, feigning an interest that, at any other time, would have been genuine. Faint shadows etched his eyes, the beginnings of what Oriken guessed would turn out like the thin black outlines on the eyes of every undead resident of Lachyla.

Undead. A tightness cramped his chest and he turned from Dagra to Jalis; she, too, had her eye on their friend, her expression solemn in the flickering shadows of the night.

"Fascinating," Dagra muttered, running a finger down the gutter at the centre of the blade. "This isn't iron, but it's not quite steel either."

"Steel wasn't made until after the Uprising," Jalis said.

"True," Oriken said. "Whatever it's made of, I can attest to it being stronger than my sabre."

"They must have created their own form of steel after the blight," Jalis suggested.

Dagra grunted. "Aye, so it would seem."

"What do the words say?" Jalis leaned closer. "I can't quite make them out in this light."

Oriken took the sword and rose to his feet. With the blade held close to one of the torches, he read the inscriptions out loud, struggling over the unfamiliar words.

Ammenfar Blaydos
Mallak Yldireth
Oerenos Lachyla Oanvaeld
Ay Ben Aevyknesa

"Whatever that means," Oriken concluded as he sat down and rested the weapon on his lap.

"*The blade of Ammenfar*," Jalis said as she stared across the dark garden. Her tone was almost bored, and Oriken knew that she, like himself, was playing at Dagra's act of interest. "Then it says *King Mallak*, I would presume. *Oanvaeld* might be *Kingdom*. The rest I don't know, but I would guess that *Ay Ben* could mean *I Am*."

"*Eternity*." Krea's voice drifted from within the entranceway, and a moment later she stepped out onto the porch. Rather than the black attire she'd worn while dealing with the corpses, she now wore sandals with laces wrapped around her lower legs, and a pleated dress, clasped at each shoulder with brooches of silver and garnet. "Very well done," she said, flicking a glance at Jalis. "You have a modest grasp of Old Himaeran."

"Language is one of my passions," Jalis replied tersely.

Krea crossed the porch to descend the steps.

"Going somewhere interesting?" Oriken called after her.

She scoffed and half-turned to look back at him. "Interesting? I'm going to play some games with an entirely deadlier weapon than the one between your thighs." She raised an eyebrow at the gladius on his lap, though her meaning was far from lost on him.

"Uh. Well. Have a good one, then." He raised a hand to tip his absent hat, muttered a curse, and ran his fingers through his hair.

Krea laughed heartily. "Oh," she purred, "I shall." Hurrying down the steps, she melted into the night.

Oriken caught Jalis's questioning look and pounced to his feet, slinging the sword into its sheath. "I don't know about you, but I think I'm ready for bed."

He awoke to his door clicking open. Instinctively he rolled from the bed to crouch behind the mattress, silently sliding Mallak's sword from its sheath and peering across the room. As his eyes adjusted to the darkness, he could just discern the edge of the door in the deep shadows. It swung slowly inwards, and a short figure materialised around its edge.

"Oriken?"

He released his breath and rose to his feet. "Gods, Dagra. You could have knocked."

"Jalis is across the hall. I didn't want to wake her." Dagra stepped into the room and held his hand out, wrapped around the neck of a bottle. "Gorven gave me this. I figured now's as good a time as any for a drink. Care to join me?"

"What is it?"

Dagra shrugged. "Damned if I know. Damned if I don't, for that matter." He pushed the door closed and perched upon the bed. "Smells as rank as an apothecary's concoction, and tastes like a liquid inferno. With a hint of bogberry."

"I'm surprised they brew anything at all down here."

"They don't. Or at least not much. Gorven says this bottle's 140 years old."

Oriken huffed. "Should be a good one then."

Weak amber light from beyond the window caught Dagra's haunting eyes. "Let's find out, my friend."

A tightness returned to Oriken's chest. *This is it. The moment I've spent the whole day dreading.* He glanced out the window. "What under the stars is that?" Out beyond the southern wall of the city, the flames of a large fire licked upwards into the night. "Oh, right, they're burning the corpses."

"Lewin is out there with the rest of his caste," Dagra said, "praying to the goddess to release the souls of the departed, and praying to the Mother to do the same. Half of the cityfolk are gathered above the cliffs to say a final farewell to their long-suffering relatives."

Oriken shivered despite the warmth of the room. "I don't suppose Gorven gave you any cups?"

Dagra pulled the cork, took a swig and passed the bottle. "Drink," he said. "You're going to need it as much as I am."

———— • ————

Adri paced anxiously beneath the Founding Oak. For hours she'd stayed at the edge of the village or within the guard station, looking out to the west and watching for her sister returning as the sun sank deeper into the horizon. Now night had fallen, the last purple tinges silhouetting the tree-studded mound of Dreaming Dragon Brae and the surrounding heathland. A thin mist had crept in from the nearby coast, tainting the darkness with a hazy sheen, and Adri knew that a similar mist would be forming in the Gardens of the Dead, bringing the ghouls out with it.

Stopping beneath the oak, she looked up its twisted trunk to the blackened skull that nestled out of reach in the lowest bough; its two ghastly companions were higher up, hidden behind the Founding Oak's leaves. *I wish they were all out of sight*, she thought. *I wish they had never been placed there at all.* The story of Daneira's dead boy flashed into her mind, the child feasting on its father as Daneira lay unaware beside them. A chill crawled over her skin and she hugged herself.

"Lady."

She turned to see Caneli approaching, a grim look on the physician's face, a satchel of medical supplies over her shoulder.

"They should have returned long ago," Adri said. "Something is wrong."

"There is much ground to cover in that accursed place," Caneli replied. "Not only above, but also below."

Adri sucked air through her teeth and shook her head. "Damn. I should have sent hunters before now. I will do so."

"We don't even know where Shade's entrance is located."

"Nevertheless—"

The physician grabbed Adri's shoulder and pointed into the heath. "There!"

Adri cast her eyes about the landscape until she saw the three figures heading slowly for the village. She squinted, but couldn't identify them at this distance.

Behind Adri, the guard station door opened and a hunter stepped out, fixing an arrow to his bow.

"Stop!" Adri ordered the man. To the figures she shouted, "Who is there?"

There was a pause, then a weak call drifted across the distance between them. "Adri?"

"Eri!" She breathed a sigh of relief at the sound of her sister's voice. She broke into a run to meet her, the physician at her side. As Adri neared the three figures, she could now recognise Wayland and the hunter, Onwin. She came to a stop before them and remembered decorum, once again resisting the instinct to embrace Eriqwyn. "It's a relief to see you," she said. "A great relief."

Eriqwyn said nothing.

"Where are the others?" Caneli asked. When no one replied, she grabbed Onwin by the shoulders. "*Where are they?*"

The hunter snatched himself away. "Get your hands off me, woman. I don't damned well know where they are."

"There's only us," Wayland said. "Lingrey was... He fought bravely, but succumbed to the ghouls."

Caneli gasped. "And the rest?"

Wayland shook his head. "Tan is lost. Shade..." He glanced to Eriqwyn, who gave a resigned nod. "She is also lost."

"What of Demelza?" Adri asked. "Eri, where is she?"

Again it was Wayland who answered. "Lady, she is dead. I witnessed it, but there was nothing I could do."

Adri's heart clenched and she closed her eyes. *Four lives lost.* "What of the deadstone?"

298

"And the outlanders," Caneli added.

As Eriqwyn drew a shuddering breath, footfalls sounded near the guard station. Adri glanced over her shoulder to see Linisa running towards them.

"The stone is returned to its rightful place," Eriqwyn said. "Two of the outlanders live. The third..."

"What is it, my sister?"

"The third is as dead as Wayland and I. We are... wounded."

Adri frowned, her gaze landing on the bandage that was wrapped around Wayland's neck. In the faint light of the rising moon, she could see the dark smear beneath his left ear. "I don't understand."

Linisa jogged to a halt beside them. "Eri," she breathed. "You had us all so worried."

Eriqwyn fixed her with a plaintive look and a sad smile. "Lini, Adri, Caneli, there is no partial victory here." She unbuttoned her tunic and drew it open to reveal bandages criss-crossed over her chest and middle, a bloody patch at their centre. She shared a brief glance with Wayland, then touched Adri's shoulder.

Adri placed her own hand over her sister's. "What are you telling me, Eri?" Seeing Eriqwyn's eyes glisten with moisture, Adri's also welled with tears.

"Wayland and I," Eriqwyn said, giving Adri's shoulder a gentle squeeze, "have come home to die."

And the tears fell.

"Nice hat!" Mallak flashed a black-gummed grin as he struck a pose in the middle of the throne room. He thrust his arm out dramatically, pinched the wide brim and twisted it to the side. "A fitting crown for the king of the freeblades, don't you think?"

Oriken frowned down at the spirited display from his seat upon the gem-studded throne. His fists gripped the onyx globes on the armrests and he leaned forward. "Hey," he said to the king, "shouldn't you be sat up here instead of me?"

Mallak laughed heartily. "No! That is your seat now! You earned it." He snatched the hat from his head and brandished it before him, taking a deep bow. "My liege."

The doors of the throne room swung inwards and Ellidar entered, his burly frame bulging through a jester's outfit. He danced along the crimson carpet, his muscles bunching and his bells jingling. Bouncing to a stop beside Mallak, he splayed his arms wide and cocked his head to the side. Gazing up at Oriken, he said, "Would you have this fool of a knight dance for you, my king? I serve only to amuse Your Highness. Does Ellidar the knight-jester amuse his liege?"

Oriken frowned. "Not really. I've seen better performances from gutter rats."

Ellidar's face turned aghast, the bells jingling around his head as he collapsed to his knees and thrust his arms in the air. "Oh! Woe! I have failed my liege. It is only fitting that I chop my own head off!"

"Don't be a fool," Oriken said.

"But that's exactly what I am!" A gladius appeared at Ellidar's waist and he pulled it from its scabbard, thrust his body to the floor in supplication, and whacked the blade down onto his neck. The head jingled along the red carpet and came to a stop at the foot of the throne's dais. Ellidar's mouth opened. "The lady Chiddari!" he announced in a loud voice, then gave Oriken a theatrical wink.

Into the throne room strutted Krea, full of confidence, wearing the sheerest pleated dress that revealed everything beneath. As she drew alongside Ellidar's prone, headless body, she came to a languid, sensual stop. Her hand rested upon her thigh and the other stroked her side, her thumb brushing the underside of her small breast. "My master summoned me?" she asked, her voice dripping with salacious intent.

"Uh, no?"

"Does this frock please my liege?"

"Well—"

"Or would you prefer me all in black?" The dress disappeared and she wore tight leggings with a tunic that clung to her delicate but toned figure, the neck so low it reached her navel.

"Er..."

Her sky-blue eyes glinted as she flashed him a suggestive grin. "I know how you want me." Her smooth skin wrinkled and sagged, and her raven hair lightened to grey, then white, flowing from her head like freshly-spun spider web. "Mmm," the crone warbled, grabbing a shrivelled breast in her bony hand. "My liege does likes them old, doesn't he?"

Oriken puffed his cheeks and exhaled slowly.

"Or, perhaps..." Krea's skin darkened, her lips curled into a sneer then were gone altogether, revealing blackened teeth hanging from shrivelled gums. The cobweb hair matted to her scalp, which split and peeled from her skull. "Does my liege find me sexy?" the Krea-Cunaxa corpse squawked. Then her lower jaw fell off and thumped upon the carpet.

Mallak the freeblade king side-stepped over the knight-jester's body and planted his hat upon Krea-Cunaxa's jawless skull. "Suits you, madam!" He beamed up at Oriken and winked. "Well! I believe my purpose here is done!" He strutted across the width of the throne room towards a bizarre metal contraption. "I really should climb into the death machine!"

Oriken wrinkled his nose in disgust. "You kept that one quiet."

"It's not easy being a king, you know?" Mallak said as he climbed into the contraption. "It isn't all merry maidens and archery tourneys! Sometimes a little torture is necessary!"

"That's not a torture device," Oriken pointed out. "It's a meat grinder."

"Indeed it is!"

The jawless Krea-Cunaxa staggered over and took hold of a winch handle. As she turned it, the freeblade king gave Oriken a theatrical wink, which he held as he was minced into a red pile that oozed from the base of the machine.

Ellidar's head tut-tutted at the macabre display. "Them undead girls," he said. "Can't live with 'em, can't die with 'em neither." His eyes rolled up to meet Oriken's stupefied gaze. "I believe my liege's taste in ladies is somewhat more exotic... and alive."

"Oriken!" Jalis strode into the room, utterly naked but for her dagger-belt around her hips, the prized Dusklight hanging from it, and Silverspire strapped to a lacy, white garter around her thigh. She kicked the jawbone and watched it tumble along the carpet to strike the back of Ellidar's severed head.

"Ouch!" the knight-jester exclaimed.

Jalis planted her hands on her hips and glowered up at Oriken. "What do you think you're doing?"

"What am I doing?" He cast his arm out to encompass the debacle. "What are you doing? What's everyone doing?"

Krea-Cunaxa hissed a throaty cackle. From within the death machine, Mallak gave a squelchy howl. At the foot of the dais, Ellidar squinted sidelong at the rotten jaw.

Jalis threw her arms up in exasperation. "Wake up, Oriken! For the love of the dead!"

"Huh?"

"I said get out of bed!"

He cracked his eyelids open and floundered within the bedsheets. A thousand hammers tapped at the inside of his skull. "Screaming stars," he croaked. "What in the—"

"Finally!" Jalis boomed into his ear. "Don't scare me like that!"

He pushed the sheets away, sat up, and swung his feet to the floor. *Suffering Pit*, he thought, gingerly touching his head. *What a concoction. And I'm still dressed.* Smacking his lips, he reached for a pitcher of water from the cabinet beside him and took several deep gulps. "Ugh. My mouth tastes like a burning sewer."

"From the smell of the room, I don't doubt it. Did you have fun last night?"

He shook his head, then groaned as the room spun. Pushing himself to his feet, he looked at Jalis, and a snippet of the previous evening came flooding back to him.

"I've made my decision," Dagra had told him as he took the bottle from Oriken. *"I know you think my beliefs are stupid, but they're my beliefs."* His

301

face had shown fear but determination, reluctance but resoluteness, and a preparation to face his fate. Oriken recalled what Dagra had said next, and he knew the words would be burned into his memory forever.

Jalis's expression softened and she stepped closer. "Not fun, then."

He took another mouthful of water and sat back down on the bed. "Me and Dag—"

"Dagra? You were drinking with Dagra?"

"Who else would it be?"

She gave a small sigh. "Never mind. I think I understand."

"Have you seen him?"

"He's downstairs, with Gorven." As she sat beside him, her thigh brushed against his. "What did he tell you last night?"

"Hasn't he talked to you?"

She shook her head. "He's not saying much of anything. Orik... we have to leave."

"I know." With a sigh, he placed an arm around her, and she rested her head in the crook of his shoulder. "I know."

CHAPTER THIRTY THREE
GIFT OF GOODBYE

Jalis waited by Oriken's door, leaning against the jamb. As he scraped and flossed his teeth with a soft branch of miremint, he glanced over to catch her staring at him, but her expression was distant. He knew how she felt. The two of them had to leave Lachyla. The place wasn't safe for a continued stay, and they had no reason to remain. But, for Dagra, the opposite was apparently now true. Oriken didn't believe it. Didn't *want* to believe it. Didn't *want* to test it out, for that matter, but there was nothing to be done.

With his gear repacked, he and Jalis made their way through the mansion to the east wing of the ground floor, where they found Gorven sat quietly in the room beside the entrance hall, his eyes on Dagra as their bearded friend stood facing out of the window. As they entered, Gorven looked over and shook his head.

"How are you feeling?" Oriken called to Dagra.

He snorted softly and turned to face them. "My head is fine. It's my heart that isn't."

"I thought your wound was healing?" Jalis said, crossing towards him.

"Oh, it is." He unfastened the top buttons of his shirt and pulled it open. Within the patchy hair nestled a line of pink, tender skin.

Jalis stopped in her tracks, her expression impassive as she regarded the healed wound.

Oriken shook his head ruefully. At this point, it came as no surprise for either Jalis or himself. "I suppose the Mother healed your hangover as well," he muttered.

"It's one of the boons of being blighted," Gorven said. "Swords and horses, and all that. Oh, I don't doubt the tonic you drank was as harmful to Dagra as it was to you. Gut-rot through and through, but under the circumstances..."

Jalis narrowed her eyes. "What do you mean, circumstances?"

Gorven glanced to Dagra and raised his eyebrows.

"I'm coming with you," Dagra told them. "You knew I would. Everybody knew. It is what it is, and I've made my decision."

Oriken shared a look with Jalis. "His mind's made up. You know as well as I do what that means. Since when could we ever talk him out of doing something?"

Dagra snorted. "You talked me *into* coming down here to chase dragons. No, don't look at me like that, I'm not blaming either of you. I got myself into this mess by putting my nose where it didn't belong."

Jalis closed her eyes, clenched her teeth, swallowed. Oriken watched her, and waited. When she looked again at Dagra, her eyes were misted over. "Fine," she said. "Then what are we standing around here waiting for?"

They walked through to the entranceway. Oriken's jacket and boots had been scrubbed by Krea, and the rip at the shoulder from Mallak's sword-thrust was expertly darned. He pulled his boots on and shrugged into his jacket, wincing at the tightness in his wound. As he stashed one of Gorven's blankets into his pack, he watched Dagra buckle his swordbelt around his hips and stare down at the old gladius, his hand on the pommel.

"Are you absolutely sure about this?" Gorven asked him.

"Yesterday you questioned me about where I stand with the gods," Dagra said. "If I remained here, that would be me turning my back on the Dyad. Aye, the Bound and the Unbound, too. I can't do that. I *won't* do it. I would just as soon—" He looked to Oriken, then to Jalis, and nodded. "Let's go."

Gorven gave a plaintive sigh. "I understand. And I respect your choice. But I had to ask one last time." He pulled the mansion doors wide open, and the light of morning flooded into the hall. "We're not keen on the sun," he told Dagra. "You'll find that, too, a little. I would suggest keeping your hood up in prolonged periods of direct sunlight."

"Thanks for the warning," Dagra said drily. "For what it's worth."

They filed out onto the porch to see Sabrian striding up the pathway. He held his hands out in greeting as they walked out to meet him, then reached inside his longcoat and withdrew a small book. "I heard you were all leaving," he said, passing it to Jalis.

She accepted the leather-bound tome, her brow furrowing at the words that were heat-stamped into its faded cover. "What is it?"

"Merely a token. A farewell gift, given your love of languages."

She opened the book and leafed through the pages. "Old Himaeran?"

"Precisely. It's not an original, but it's old, and was written by one of my friends here in the city. She was actually quite overjoyed when I asked if I could gift it to you."

"That's very thoughtful." A sad smile touched Jalis's lips. "Thank you. I shall treasure it."

Sabrian grinned and reached again into his longcoat, this time producing a small package which he passed to Oriken. "I hate to impose, but if you ever find yourself in the southern fringes of Grenmoor, between Grenmoor Forest and the River Huhe, there's a village called Harrowstone. You might have heard of it. I expect it could even be a town by now, after all these—"

"I'm sorry, Sabrian," Jalis interrupted. "The village of Harrowstone was razed by bandits from the forest eight years ago. It's gone." She caught Oriken's questioning look. "Maros and I were sent to assist in the aftermath," she explained.

Sabrian's shoulders slumped. "Well then," he sighed. "There's little sense in sentimentality so long after the fact, I suppose, but..." He gestured to the package. "It's just a memento. Of my previous life. A wooden toy." He chuckled in remembrance. "My son would never let me leave home without it. For good luck."

"Perhaps," Dagra said, his voice heavy, "its presence drove you on when you fled Minnow's Beck. Perhaps it brought you some luck after all."

"Yes, you may be right. Do what you will with it," he told Oriken. "I made my peace long ago. I'll at least be happy to know it is leaving the Deadlands."

Oriken nodded and stashed the package into his jacket. "I'll make sure it does," he promised.

"Ah, I almost forgot." Sabrian fished around in his trouser pocket and pulled out a tiny metal contraption with engravings and a hinge. "A joke, if you will," he said as Oriken took the proffered item. "It was made for me many years ago by another friend here in Lachyla." He chuckled. "Yes, I have a few. I'm sure Cleve made it to torment me, but he maintains he did so to remind me that the higher the mountain, the more satisfying it is when one manages to reach the summit."

"Cleve?" Oriken frowned. "He was at the meal, right? Where else have I heard the name? Wait, did he write a book?"

Gorven cleared his throat and glanced indifferently across the garden.

"Why, yes, he did," Sabrian said. "A tome on minerals, apparently. Not that I've read it. He misplaced it some centuries ago. I wasn't aware there was another copy. Have you read it?"

"Ah," Gorven interrupted. "I'm sure Cleve will have immense pleasure tinkering with his new light-source. No sense boring our friends here about some old book on the nature of minerals."

"That's it," Oriken said. "I saw it just before—"

"Well, we had best be off," Gorven said. "Don't you think? Sabrian, you mustn't keep our guests."

Sabrian shrugged, conceding the point. Pointing to the rectangle of metal in Oriken's hand, he said. "It's yours."

"Thanks. But, er, what is it?"

"Cleve calls it a heat lens. Flick the top open and you'll see a circle of glass. Don't ask me how it works, but if you hold the glass facing the sun it will glow hot within a minute or so."

"Ah, okay. And this is good for..."

"Why, for lighting your tobah, of course! But then, the idea, in Cleve's devious mind, is to keep hold of it to permanently remind you *not* to light one. The philosophically-minded of the city call it temptation therapy. I can't say that it worked for me, but my new temptation will be that half of a roll I saved. You might enjoy better luck." He shrugged, then smiled and glanced from Oriken to Jalis. "If you're ever in this neck of nowhere again, don't be strangers." To Dagra, he said, "May the gods go with you, friend." And with that, Sabrian turned on his heel, his longcoat swaying as he strode off down the path, and was gone.

They continued on their way, and when they reached the street, Gorven touched Oriken's arm for him to fall behind the others. He did so, and Gorven leaned in to quietly say, "I know Krea would have liked to say goodbye."

Oriken quirked an eyebrow. "Really? That's surprising after her comment last night, when she left the house."

"Ah. You should pay it no mind. That's just my daughter's way of... relieving her pent-up stress, you know?"

"Is that what you call it?"

"Oh, yes. In fact, I do it myself sometimes, but not so much these days. Krea though, she practices twice a week without fail."

"Practices?"

"Why, of course. Grandmaster swordswomen don't stay grandmasters if they don't train, do they?"

Oriken grunted. *Swordplay. So that's what it was.*

"Oriken, you didn't think she—"

"No. Don't be ridiculous." He drew a breath. "Listen, about Dagra…"

"There is no easy way to say it," Gorven said as they strolled a distance behind the others. "He will likely survive a night or two, perhaps even three, but it's unlikely. The two who returned to their village, they've been away from the city for, what, ten hours now? Being in reasonable proximity to Lachyla, Wayland may live a few days, since he died only from blood loss. Eriqwyn though, her wounds were altogether more grievous." He squinted at the low morning sun. "She may not see this hour tomorrow."

"I don't care a jot about those two," Oriken said. "Only Dagra."

Gorven stopped, and Oriken turned to face him. The man's expression was solemn. "You will lose him soon, Oriken, and forever. Are you and Jalis prepared to face that?"

Prepared? Of course I'm not prepared. How under the stars does anyone prepare to lose their closest and longest friend? "I understand his choice, but it's based on a skewed – and popular – perception of what's real. I wish I could convince him of that, but after all these years of knowing him, and especially after our talk last night, no words from me are going to change his mind. Short of locking him up somewhere in Lachyla, there's nothing that'll shake him from his conviction. And he would resent me forever for that."

Gorven gestured for them to resume their walk. "Conviction in the gods," he mused. "Well, three centuries of ruminating over the world's *ifs* and *maybes*, I still can't say with *absolute* conviction who is right and who is wrong, which gods exist and which do not, if any at all. Some would presume – mistakenly, I would say – that the Mother is a goddess, or that she is a personification of *the* goddess. But I don't think even the *First* Mother can claim that title. Are Dagra's gods of the Dyad waiting, ready to guide him into his next life?" Gorven shrugged. "I can't say. But he believes it, and has always believed it, and *that*, my friend, is what matters."

Oriken nodded. He stared ahead at Dagra's back as the bearded man walked beside Jalis. "I'll do what I must," he said, promising not just Gorven, but also himself. "Whatever he needs of me, I'll be there." His throat clenched, and he forced the rising emotions back down, down into the pits of himself; they would have their moment, but this was not it.

They opened their stride and caught up with Jalis and Dagra. When they reached the Litchgate, they stopped and Gorven turned to them. "There is one thing I must ask of you."

"Name it," Jalis said.

"We've spoken of what events could unfold if the truth of this place became widespread. It would be nothing short of chaos, for all of Himaera. Word eventually would reach the Vorinsian Arkh. In the worst case, war would break out between Himaera and the lands of the Arkh, perhaps even those beyond. Jalis, coming from Sardaya, you know this better than your friends do."

She nodded. "You have our word we will say nothing of you to anyone. The city was deserted, but for a few ancient, emaciated corpses, and fungus."

"Deadly fungus," Dagra muttered.

Gorven inclined his head in gratitude, then gestured to the sword at Oriken's hip. "Wear it well and with pride," he said, "but I would advise displaying it with a little more discretion."

"I'll wrap the scabbard and the grip in leather," Oriken said. "The pommel and crossguard might catch the eye, as certainly will the blade itself, but most folk who'll be seeing the sharp bit are unlikely to live to tell the tale."

Gorven gave him a rueful grin. "Very wise."

"And what of me?" Dagra asked. "What tale would you have us concoct for my friends and family? That Dagra died a meaningless death while out on a fool's errand in the arsehole of Himaera? Or, perhaps, Dagra died a hero's death for a noble and worthy cause?" He barked a dire laugh and held his hands palm-upward. "Where is the truth?"

Jalis touched his shoulder, and he gently but forcibly pushed her hand away. "You said it yourself yesterday," she told him. "Sometimes a lie is better than the truth. I know you agree that the reality of Lachyla must stay a secret, but where's the harm in compromise? We'll tell the truth, but only a fraction of it." She looked pointedly at Dagra, her eyes agleam with tears. "You fell ill in the

307

wilderness, and you died on the road. To the people who love you, Dag, it matters less how you died than how you lived." The last words caught in her throat, but she held his gaze.

He nodded, and took her hand in both of his. "Aye, lass. You have the right of it."

"In that case," Gorven said, spreading his arms, "it leaves me only to fare you well. And, as Sabrian said"—his gaze flicked momentarily between Jalis and Oriken—"our gates will always be open to you. Figuratively speaking, of course. The portcullis will be lowered after you are gone. Now that the denizens are gone, the consensus is that from now on we will post lookouts on the ramparts as a necessary means of protection." He gave Jalis a brief hug, then shook hands with Dagra, giving him a cordial slap on the shoulder and a nod of respect.

Taking the man's hand in a firm shake, Oriken said, "Give our farewells to the others, won't you?"

Gorven smiled, patted him on the arm, and walked away.

"Well," Dagra said as he watched Gorven stride down the sloping street. He turned a resigned look on Oriken. "I thought I might get a nice new gladius from this lifeless legend of a city. Just a good and sturdy blade with a secret story." His eyes flicked to the royal sword at Oriken's hip. "In a twist of irony, it was you who got it. You both got a trinket or two from this merry little jaunt. And what did I get?" He spun about and dipped beneath the Litchgate to stride off through the graveyard.

"Dag!" Jalis gave an exasperated sigh and rushed to follow him.

Oriken watched her go, then turned for a last look upon the sprawling cityscape. Far to the rear, the colossus that was Lachyla Castle looked less menacing than it had done two days earlier. One of its spires had toppled from the anger of the beast beneath, crushing a lower domed roof. The charred remains of the king were likely already interred, though the stench within the throne room would endure for weeks. Few Lachylans walked the now-clean boulevard, but it was not deserted. Without the disease that thrived here, the city could be a good place to live. Ships could sail along the coast to Brancosi Bay or across the channel to the Arkh. The Kingdom Road could be restored for folk to travel freely to and fro. And Scapa Fell would no longer be marked with the death's head symbol. It was a pleasing thought. Perhaps, one day, it might happen, but not in his lifetime, not while the secret of Lachyla remained kept.

He crouched beneath the iron spikes of the portcullis and looked ahead to Jalis as she walked briskly behind Dagra. *He wants a moment alone with her*, he thought, knowing with a sickening knot of certainty what he was to face out on the heathland. *I'll let them have their moment.*

Setting off at a stroll, he gazed around the deserted graveyard at the rows upon endless rows of weather-worn headstones, their bases all crusted in that foul, black rot, at one lonely statue after another, some with neither arms nor heads, and he wondered if that had been a portent of what ultimately befell the statues' long-undead likenesses at the hands of their equally undead descendants.

Or, he thought, *at the hands of Jalis, Dagra and me.*

The Chiddari crypt was a stone's throw from the Litchway. As he neared it, he muttered to himself, "I wonder whether old madam CC would appreciate a final farewell." He grunted. *Unlikely.* As his gaze lingered on the crypt, a diminutive figure stepped from the shadowed entrance into the daylight. *Krea.* He paused and waited as she crossed the distance to him. Her hair was tied up at the crown again, hanging like fronds and bobbing as she walked. A leather strap crossed her dress from shoulder to hip, and her face was set in a stern expression.

"Did you really intend to leave without saying goodbye?" she asked, coming to a stop before him and tilting her head to fix her scowling eyes onto his.

He drew a breath. "Krea..."

"I said I wanted to talk to you about your client. You never gave me the chance."

"I... I was..."

"With your friends. Yes, I know."

"And you—"

"Went to sword practice, you dolt. You could at least have woken me to say you were leaving so soon."

"I'm sorry. It was a rough night."

Krea nodded, her expression softening. "Yes, it was."

"And Dagra was adamant he wanted to leave."

She shrugged. "That's his choice. Personally, I would have liked him to stay. That way I might have been guaranteed the occasional... visit from you."

"Well—"

"Shush." She grabbed the strap at her torso and shifted it around, drawing a satchel from behind her. Lifting the flap, she dipped her hand inside and pulled out the Chiddari jewel, then held it out to him. "Take it."

"*What?*" He glanced to the distant figures of his friends far up the Litchway, then back to Krea. "Seriously? But what about Cunaxa? It belongs in her tomb, by rights."

"It belongs in the Chiddari *family*, that much is true. Which is what I wanted to speak to you about. Your client is a Chiddari. Cela..." She said it as if tasting the word, then smiled. "It's at least good to know that the line lives on."

"I guess so. But how?"

"To that, there is only one answer. Cela has to be descended from one of the Chiddaris who fled before the turning. Only two escaped. My mother and my brother. Gorven's wife and son. And now, none remain in Minnow's Beck – that we know thanks to the Galialos women."

Oriken frowned. "Why would your mother leave you?"

"She and my brother were among the last to leave. Gorven had been ill for several years. The wasting disease. He was house-ridden. He would have been dead within the next year or two. There was no way he could have left the city. Even walking to the garden gate was too much for him, back then. He forced them to leave without him."

"Okay. But that doesn't explain them leaving you behind. Or did you choose to stay, to care for your father?"

Krea gave a soft, shrill laugh. "No. I was the catalyst for them deciding to flee. I died, you see."

Oriken's mouth fell open.

"That's right. I'd been dead for a night and a day when they left. I never did get to say goodbye."

Great, he thought. *Now I really feel like the arsehole of the hour.* "You were dead."

"Quite so. And rigid with the stiffness of death." She fluttered her eyelids and flashed him a sweet smile. "You see these beguilingly blue eyes?"

He nodded. "How could anyone miss them?"

"They were brown before I died."

"Okay, that's—" He barked a laugh. "Actually, that's not weird at all. Listen, Krea, I... I guess I just didn't know what to say to you. I mean, well, after everything."

"Doesn't honesty taste better than excuses?" She pressed the jewel to his chest. "Are you going to make me hold onto this thing forever? For the love of goodness, take it already."

He closed his hands around the object that had given them so much trouble. His fingers brushed against Krea's as he took the jewel from her.

"You can fulfil your contract after all." She raised a finger. "But I'm only giving it to you because it's the Chiddari stone, and it's going to my"—she cocked her head—"great-great-and-so-on niece. Or something like that."

"Krea, I have no idea what she intends to do with it. I can't give you any guarantees it will remain in your family's lineage."

"Life, dear Oriken, comes with very few guarantees. What will be, will be."

"What about its power? I mean, we heard the story of the woman's dead boy in the village."

"Ah yes, Daneira."

"You know of her?"

"We had spies in the village, remember? Daneira was my last descendant. She fled Minnow's Beck eighty years ago, with child. That child must be Cela."

"Well, damn. You Chiddaris get around a bit, don'tcha?"

"Not nearly enough. As to your question, without a clone—"

"Wait, a what?"

310

"We call the jewels clones because they're the fruits of the Mother. Flora are her hosts, and creatures are her vessels. You were told all this by the king, and it was witnessed by Ellidar. Do keep up, Oriken. The Mother's reach alone holds no sway beyond the walls, but with the village's proximity to Lachyla, the presence of a clone – the one that Daneira's man took from the graveyard – made reanimation possible. If they'd procured it *before* the child died—"

"Hey." Oriken brightened as a thought came to him. "If Dag stays close to the jewel…"

Krea shook her head. "No. Its effect was only temporary in Minnow's Beck, and will be lost long before you leave Scapa Fell. Hold no illusion that it will be otherwise."

His shoulders slumped. "It was worth a try."

"Anything is," Krea agreed. "But for the choice your friend has made, there is no hope on Verragos of him surviving. You've already been told as much by Gorven, and by Sabrian."

"Yes," he sighed. "I know."

"So, then." She gazed up at him.

"Listen, Krea. I like you. I mean that. In other circumstances I think we could have been friends." He shrugged. "Who knows? Perhaps more."

"Hm." She planted a hand on her hip. "What are you telling me?"

"I've been giving the whole thing a lot of consideration since I arrived in Lachyla, and, admittedly, I'm not entirely surprised to hear myself say that I'd prefer living as you do to being dead. In that regard, me and Dag are on opposite ends of the rainbow. Something Sabrian said got me to thinking; I've spent nine years travelling Himaera, the last five as a freeblade, and the last three only in Caerheath till we came here. I've been wandering around with my eyes closed, and I think it's about time I opened them."

Krea remained silent, pondering him curiously.

"I'm saying that I love my freedom," he told her, "and what I've experienced here has taught me two things. One, that I need to stop being so presupposing about the world around me. And two, that if I ever get the cancer or some such, I may just decide to return."

"Is that what it would take for you to come back?"

He shrugged. "Right now, I don't know."

After a pause, Krea reached into the satchel and withdrew a piece of folded black cloth. "A little something I made for you," she said, holding it out for him to take. "Maybe you won't wear it, but once in a while it might remind you of me."

He accepted it from her. "What is it?"

"Unfold it and see."

Taking a corner of the thin but strong material, he shook it out and it spilled almost to the ground. Cream and tan and white threads were weaved into the edges in interlacing patterns, and at the top end the crossed blades of the

Freeblades Guild had been embroidered into the corner. "It's beautiful. Is it a scarf?"

"If you like. Or a sash. However you decide to use it."

Oriken drew a shuddering sigh, surprised at the wave of emotion that hit him. The thought that Krea had put into the gift... "I will wear it," he promised, "but not for the journey home. Thank you, Krea. I... I have nothing to give you."

She flashed a brief smile. "You have already given me more than you know."

He looked at her. "I do have something to give you." He unclasped the button of an inside breast pocket of his jacket, dug his fingers inside and took out a small pouch. After a moment of hesitation, he held it out for Krea to take. She loosened the drawstring and upturned it, dropping a delicate silver chain with tiny charms onto her palm.

"It's an anklet," he said. "It belonged to my ma. I'd like you to have it."

"I will treasure it," Krea said. "Well then, my outlander. If you ever decide to return, don't leave it too long. You wouldn't want to spend the rest of eternity all wrinkled and hairless, would you?" The black rims of her eyes glistened with moisture. "If you did, you might find me no longer interested." She curled her finger at him. "Come down here."

Oriken leaned down as Krea rose to her tiptoes. Her hands reached up to wrap behind his neck as his crossed behind her, and they embraced.

He crawled beneath the portcullis to find Dagra sat with his back to the outer wall, staring silently out into the heathland. Jalis stood a distance ahead, her petite frame seeming somehow smaller than usual. He recalled two evenings previous when she had stood in the same place, covered in gore and eagerly awaiting their emergence from the graveyard. Now, instead of the tattered chemise, her soft cotton garment billowed like clouds around her breasts and upper arms, her leggings a vibrant green. Red scratches laced her calves and ankles from her ordeal on the ladder, and she looked as unwilling to take another step into the heath as he did.

"Krea gave me something," he said.

Jalis looked at him flatly. "Mm-hm."

"Aren't you the lucky one," Dagra said as he climbed to his feet.

"It's not for me." Oriken deigned to mention the sash. "It's for all of us." He reached into his jacket and took out the jewel.

Jalis's eyebrow raised a fraction and she gave a brief nod.

Dagra barked a laugh and threw his hands in the air. "I was so wrong about that cursed chunk of crap. I actually thought it looked nice at first glance. Now I know it's the ugliest thing I've ever seen." He grabbed his pack and wandered past Jalis, muttering to himself.

312

Oriken understood their reactions. In both cases he felt the same. Jalis turned and he stashed the jewel into her backpack. Tying it tight, he set off on Dagra's trail, and Jalis walked at his side.

The ragged landscape of the wide valley stretched into the distant hills. Days of nothing lay ahead of them; nothing but walking, sleeping, eating whatever luck happened to bring their way, and waiting for the inevitable.

Jalis's eyes were fixed on their friend's back. Her thoughts were no doubt similar to Oriken's own – black thoughts that refused to leave, just as Dagra refused to stay.

Chapter Thirty Four
Footprints In The Sand

Maros swung along on his crutches behind the mill owner. His leg felt miraculously good today. *Must be all the exercise*, he thought, casting a glance to Henwyn who strolled a distance to his side.

"The burned building and the cravant corpse back-a-ways were definitely fresh," Maros said. "My gut says it was the work of our girl and the lads." With a grunt, he added, "Don't know why they'd burn a house down, though."

"It was a pretty big breadcrumb to leave us," Henwyn said. "Not that I'm complaining; their tracks are getting harder to spot since the downpour. Harder, but not impossible."

"You've the eyes of a hawk," Maros said. "Better'n these failing orbs o' mine. If premature old age don't take me first, I swear I'll end up as blind as a halfblood mole-bat."

"Ah, boss. Self-deprecation don't become you. I tell a lie; it does. But at least you're still the deadliest bastard with a greatsword in all of Scapa Fell."

Maros barked a laugh. "Hen, you do me a disservice."

"We should camp soon," Wymar said. "And by the way, just because I'm not mentioning it constantly, I am still hating every minute of being stuck out here with you freeblades. It's like being forced to endure a monotonous epic by a tireless, two-man theatre troupe."

Maros grunted. "If you can't beat 'em—"

"Which you can't," Henwyn added.

"Then you'd be best to… Oh, stars." Maros felt a sneeze brewing. "Ha… Haa… *Ha-akh!*"

"Aveia's teeth!" Wymar whirled on him and leaped backwards. "Would you do that in another direction? Or do I have a sign on my head asking to be covered in giant's phlegm?"

"Some folk pay good money for a philtre of halfblood humours," Maros said. "You could be onto a money-earner."

Henwyn chuckled. "No they don't, boss. Fairy tears, yes. But never Maros mucus."

"On with you," Maros told the mill owner. "That's it. Oh and you do complain every minute, but I think you're warming to us."

Wymar grumbled to himself as he trudged onwards.

"Don't hold his natural disposition against him," Henwyn said with a wink to Maros. "The two of you will be fast friends when we're back in the Folly."

Maros snorted. "I'd be as likely to marry a goat."

"Here, what's this?" Wymar paused to stoop over and reach into the low grass. Turning to Maros, he held up a leather strop.

"Well, I'll be buggered," Maros said. "Let me see that." He snatched the strop from Wymar and brought it to his eyes. "It's Jalis's."

"You sure, boss?"

"A strop is a strop, but the boys don't use 'em, and who else would be wandering this hinterland with a care to give their weapon a fine polish?"

Henwyn nodded. "We're on the right track, then."

Wymar hitched a thumb over his shoulder. "Not for long. We're almost out of road."

Maros squinted against the sun and peered ahead. The mill owner was right; fifty yards along the overgrown road, the aged flagstones disappeared beneath short thatches of reed that marked the edge of a swamp. "Rutting stars," he growled. "Hen, how far does that bog stretch?"

Henwyn scrutinised the landscape. After a moment, he said, "It's impassable, boss. We'll have to go around."

"Damn it!" Maros stamped his crutches into the grass. "In which direction?"

"We've got a few hours of daylight left," Henwyn said. "We may as well make camp here while I search around."

"I'll gather some firewood," Wymar said, wandering across to a nearby stand of trees.

Maros flashed a brief smile at the mill owner's back. Taking Henwyn's pack, he said, "That man is more amenable with each passing day. Not what I'd call convivial, but it's an improvement."

Henwyn bent to one knee to attach a string to his longbow. "I'll find their trail, and I'll grab us a meal while I'm at it," he said with confidence.

"I'm mighty glad I brought you along. Fancy a promotion?"

Henwyn rose with a grin. "You're funny, boss. The only promotion ahead of me is to become a quill-scratcher, and I ain't ready to fill your boots just yet."

"Quill— Bah, away with you!" He swung his crutch in a wide arc, and Henwyn easily danced out of its reach. With a sigh, Maros looked down at the leather strop in his hand. "We're coming for you, lass," he said as Henwyn moved off along the swamp's edge. "We're on our way."

Killed by a puffball. A sodding puffball. The thought churned within Dagra's head as they trekked across the lowlands. He'd accepted his fate, and yet a part of him still clung on to the dim hope that he might make it out of this bog-ridden backwater alive. He allowed himself a flight of fancy, imagining the three of them returning to the Folly and drinking a cup or five of Redanchor to celebrate achieving their objective.

Sod the cups, he thought. *Dust the tankards off. This is a celebration, not a damned wake.* He choked back a cry and rubbed a hand across his eyes.

"Dag?"

"I'm fine." He drew in a breath and stuffed his hands into his pockets. From the west, the sighs of the ocean drifted amid the warm breeze. "I want to walk along the coastline."

"Sure thing," Oriken said. "Whatever you want."

Dagra grunted. "You don't have to treat me like I'm—"

"Like you're what, Dag?" Oriken bit back. "Dying?"

"Come on, boys." Jalis stepped between them and wrapped her arms around their waists. "Let's go for a walk on the beach."

The sun was dipping closer to the ocean by the time they reached the coastline. This far from Lachyla, the air sang serenely with the cries of birds as they circled over the shallows. Jalis pulled her shoes off and ran onto the beach, curling her toes into the sand. Nearby, a crab scuttled into a rocky pool, and Dagra absorbed the scene with a mixture of sadness and gratitude. With their boots still on, he and Oriken stomped through the soft grains to join Jalis, and together they crossed to the tide and set a casual stroll along the wet sand.

"I've been thinking about the cave," Dagra said.

"Which cave?" Jalis asked. Her shoes dangled from her fingers, and her feet splashed along the water's edge to leave ephemeral prints that soon would be gone forever.

"I know which he means." Oriken shrugged his jacket off and draped it over his arm. "The one we found his sword in, seven years ago. Right, Dag?"

"We were seventeen," Dagra told Jalis. "Barely a year after leaving Eyndal."

"I didn't mean to start that rockfall," Oriken said.

Dagra shrugged. "At least between us we managed to get me out of there. I never blamed you for it; not really."

"I know. There were no ghosts in there. You realise that, don't you?"

"I know what I felt, and what I saw and heard. Look back there at Lachyla." He glanced over his shoulder at the shoreline far off to the south, where it climbed gradually from sea level to a steep promontory. They were a day and a half out of Lachyla and at this extreme distance the city was hidden from view, save for a spectral glimpse above the cliff's edge. But, for a moment, as Dagra regarded it, his bond with the dwellers in that place strengthened a touch.

He turned his attention back to Oriken. "Things exist in this world. Things that you've always doubted. They exist in the corners and between the cracks, in the darkness and the depths, and, sometimes, in the light. Remember that, Oriken. You'll *need* to remember. For me."

"You've been calling me Oriken a lot lately."

Dagra sighed. "Maybe because I'm not entirely myself any more. Maybe because I'm about to die, and the time for endearing appellations is over."

"Apple whats?"

"I'm a part of the blight," he explained. "Connected to the people, and to the Mother. I hate it. I didn't belong there, and it's fading, but it's still a part of me"—he tapped a finger to his temple—"in here."

"What do you need from us?" Jalis asked.

"I want you to burn me when... when it's over. I can feel the weakness already, I think. The voices are fading, and there's a shadow in my mind."

Oriken looked frustrated. "But, Dag—"

"When I feel that it's close, we'll head for the next copse of trees. If I can still go on, we'll continue to the next. That way, we won't be far from wood to build a pyre. Promise me you'll burn my body. Send me to the Underland properly, and with dignity."

"We promise," Jalis said.

Oriken blinked and turned his face away. "Yeah," he said, and Dagra heard his voice crack.

I know, my friend, he thought. *I don't want to lose you either. But I must.* "Give me some minutes, will you both?" he asked softly. "I just need a moment to... finish making peace with a few things."

Jalis nodded and dropped back beside Oriken, leaving Dagra to walk alone and use what little time remained him to make a deal with his gods.

"This is wrong," Oriken said.

"How long are you going to fight it?" Jalis asked. "There's nothing we can do. What will be, will be, and soon. I know it's hard—"

Oriken whirled on her. "What do you know?" She glared at him. "I'm sorry," he sighed. "That was uncalled for. Look, I've said I accept his choice. It doesn't mean I have to like it. It could easily have been any or all of us, Jalis. What would you do if it was you and not Dagra?"

"I've asked myself that question often over the last few days," she admitted. "I agree with you. His choice would not be mine. But at the same time I wouldn't want to live forever like Gorven and the others."

"What then?"

"I expect I would stay there. For a while, at least. Wait until I was sure what I wanted to do. But that's me. Dagra's decision seems impetuous to you and I, but it is his to make. And remember, his philosophies of the world are not ours."

317

"Bah! What Dagra has aren't philosophies."

"And yours are?"

He shrugged. "No, not really. I just know what I know. And I believe what I see. Where Dag's going – in his mind – is Kambesh. He's off to the Underland to be reborn as some… baby, I guess. Look, what happened back there, what we witnessed; at first it seemed unnatural, demonic, magical even. But at the heart of it, all the blight is is a parasite. Its only difference to a disease is that it doesn't kill people… unless they stray too far from its heart."

"A mutually beneficial symbiosis," Jalis mused.

Oriken shrugged. "Yeah, whatever that means."

"Except that this time it took an incompatible vessel."

Oriken bent to pick up a stone and skimmed it into the frothing water. "Incompatible by mind, yes. A shame it didn't sense that and ignore him from the offset."

"Just be strong, Orik." Jalis linked her arm in his. "For Dagra, as well as for yourself. And remember I'm here. I'm not going anywhere."

He gripped her hand. "I hope you never do."

Chapter Thirty Five
Interchange

Adri awoke with a start and sat upright in the chair. She cast a concerned glance to Eriqwyn who lay propped in her bed upon several pillows, a thick blanket draped over her legs. By the light of the room's few torches, her face was pale and drawn, and her eyes were closed. Wayland was slouched in an armchair at the far side of the bed, a frown creasing his brow even in sleep. Adri rose to her feet and hurried across to Caneli who occupied a stool at the near side of Eriqwyn's bed.

"How is she?" Adri asked, though she knew the answer.

The physician rose and motioned for her to follow to the door. Keeping her voice low, she said, "This is nothing that I've seen before, but I recognise the signs as sure as the last hours of the wasting disease. I'm sorry, Adri. She is on the way out, and Wayland fares little better." Pausing at the door, she passed a hand over her tired eyes and stepped out into the garden. "It's only a matter of time for them both, though I fear that Eri will not last the night."

Despair clenched at Adri's chest. "It is almost dawn."

"Aye." Caneli glanced to the purple hue that was rising over the eastern horizon. "It is."

Further along from Eriqwyn's room, the pantry door clicked open and the twins emerged, each carrying two steaming mugs. Laulani's golden hair was loose, spilling around her slumped shoulders, and the green blush around Linisa's eyes accentuated the shadows of worry and lack of sleep, even in the murky twilight.

"The village is in turmoil," Laulani said softly, passing a mug to Caneli. "Some are convinced that the outlanders never posed a threat to us. They are considering packing up and journeying north."

"I feared this would happen," Adri said, accepting a mug from Linisa.

"Others are saying that they can't stand to live here," Laulani continued, "knowing, as we now do, that we're not alone. They are considering heading to the city and requesting to settle there."

Adri closed her eyes in defeat. "Why would they do that?"

"They are in the minority," Laulani said, glancing to Caneli. "But some have sick children, or failing parents, or they themselves suffer from one ailment or another. It's the same fever that once gripped Minnow's Beck, only much worse." She paused to blow on her tea. "Eri and Wayland will be seen as martyrs, there is no avoiding that. Some of the villagers admire them for coming home to… to die…"

"While others question why they did not choose to remain," Linisa added, her expression turning hard. "And then there are those who are calling them ghouls. Ghouls!"

Adri gasped. "There is indeed a rift forming, and it was I who caused it. How can I heal it?"

"You did what you thought was best, Adri," Linisa said. "Now you must use the knowledge you have since gained, and once again do what you think to be right. There is not one easy answer, but whatever you choose, my sister and I are with you."

Laulani nodded in agreement.

"But can I stop those who want to head north from doing so? They could pose as great a danger to the village as any outlander who knew of this place. If they want to go, I can't force them to stay under penalty of the Founding Laws; there are no laws against leaving."

"And few ever have," Caneli said. "None in our lifetime." Drawing a deep breath, she added, "The fundaments of the Founding Laws are strict. Perhaps it is time to loosen them. You alone have that power."

"Hm." Adri looked long at the physician. "It is not something I could decide quickly, nor is there time to dwell upon it for too long." To Linisa, she said, "What of the families of the fallen?"

"Only Tan had any family. Lingrey lived alone in his cabin on Blachord's farm. Demelza, too, lived alone in old Ina's shack. And as for Shade…" She spat upon the grass. "I'd have that murderous whore's head alongside the others on the oak, if it were up to me."

In her heart, Adri agreed with the sentiment. Eriqwyn had told them how Shade had plunged a dagger into her back. Caneli had inspected the wound, as well as the second one mere inches from the first, and they were both fatal injuries. It was dark business, and Eriqwyn should by all rights be dead. Soon, she would be, but Adri refused to accept that Eriqwyn had already passed on once and was now nothing more than a ghoul. *Not Eri*, she thought. *Not my sister. She will die as the First Warder.* "Have you spoken to Tan's family?"

Linisa nodded. "His sister is worried sick with not knowing if he lives or is dead. Their father…"

"Yes?"

"He left their house several hours ago. According to his daughter, he brooded in silence the whole day, then after a visit from Onwin, he upped and left without saying a word."

320

Adri frowned. "Onwin? What is he up to? What else did Tan's sister say?"

Linisa shook her head. "That is all I know."

"Would you like me to speak with her?" Laulani offered.

"Yes, please do." Adri placed a hand on the taller twin's shoulder. "And hurry, Lani. I fear we are in the eye of the storm, and I would not put it past that hunter to be stirring up a hornet's nest of trouble."

Laulani passed her mug to her sister and hurried off across the manor's garden.

Watching her go, Adri said, "If some of the villagers are determined to relocate to Lachyla, then perhaps I should allow it. Our cousins, however distant and goddess-cursed, have dwelt within that place the whole time, secreted behind the battlements, while we ever presumed the city to be swarming with ghouls as much as the graveyard. And now those ghouls have allegedly all been disposed of." She shook her head. "How, after all of this, can I justifiably punish any who choose to enter?"

"We're entering an era of change," Caneli said, pausing to finish her tea. "I don't envy your position, but there are questions of morality at play here, and the villagers will need your guidance. Laws are necessary, but so is leniency. My advice, as a humble physician, is don't fight to keep them all; like any children, some will want to fly the nest, and that is not a right that we can earn – it is the right of freedom. Any who stay cannot consider themselves prisoners."

Adri smiled mirthlessly. "What have we come to, ladies? Is this what Minnow's Beck is supposed to be? Our ancestors left the city in the search for survival, but perhaps they got lost along the way." With a shaking breath, she turned on her heel to face the manor. "I must return to my sister."

As she entered Eriqwyn's sleeping quarters, Wayland stirred and looked across. The pain she saw in his eyes was a pain not of the body but of the soul. *You poor, brave man*, she thought. *I am sorry I sent you. I'm sorry I sent Eri. I'm sorry I sent Demelza…* The emotion rose and she clasped a hand to her mouth, her chest clenching with repressed sobs as her eyes welled with tears.

"Lady." Caneli's hand was on Adri's shoulder, and the physician reached to take her mug from her trembling hand.

Adri drew a deep breath to compose herself, then another. "I am fine. Please."

As Caneli withdrew to approach the bed, Eriqwyn's eyes fluttered open. Adri ran to her side and took her hand.

Eriqwyn gave her a weak smile. "I failed."

"No," Adri said, a tremor in her voice. "You did not fail. I think, perhaps, you succeeded."

"It was I who wanted to deal with the outlanders, Adri. In that, I failed. And it was my actions that led to the deaths of Lingrey, Tan, Demelza…"

"You can't blame yourself," Wayland said. "Nor Onwin, though it was he who disturbed the ghouls in the first place." He let out a rattling sigh. "The blame goes to all of us – we of Minnow's Beck, the outlanders, the cityfolk… even the goddess herself, I think."

Eriqwyn coughed. "Thank you, my friend."

Wayland's gaze lingered on her face, but he said no more.

"The village," Eriqwyn said to Adri.

"It will be fine," Adri lied. "You just rest."

"Sister, nothing will be fine any more. They will swarm from the north, and—"

"Then let them come. We will welcome them not with arrows and blades, but with lodgings, hot meals, and trade negotiations."

Linisa forced a smile as she looked down at Eriqwyn. "But any who *do* seek to hurt us will swiftly find my knife lodged in their innards."

"The Beck needs more Warders," Eriqwyn murmured, her voice becoming sluggish.

"It also needs a new *First* Warder," Adri said, the words feeling surreal as they left her mouth. "Linisa, you don't have to accept the role. I cannot force it upon you."

Linisa's eyes misted with tears. "It would be my honour, Lady."

"Congratulations," Eriqwyn said, and Linisa took her hand. "I stand… relieved."

Adri's mind was a torrent of emotions as her eyes fixed on Eriqwyn. She held her sister's gaze for a long moment, until Eriqwyn drew a rattling breath.

"Don't tell Mother," she said, her voice scarcely a whisper. "She couldn't take it. Let her stay in her dream-world. Perhaps she is happy there. Perhaps… it is a perfect place… where you and I are still little girls."

Adri nodded. She glanced through the window at the purple sky brightening to a dark red, and at that moment the tip of Banael winked into existence. She smiled. "Look, Eri, the sun is here. It is a new day." There was no answer. "Eri?" She turned to her sister, but although the first rays of sunlight shone in Eriqwyn's eyes, the life had left them.

Adri stared, unable to breathe, unable to speak, or feel. She watched as Linisa stooped to kiss Eriqwyn on the mouth. She watched, frozen, as Wayland gently touched Eriqwyn's cheek.

"Goodbye, Queenie," he whispered. "I must go soon, too."

And then it all rose up from the pit of her soul. She thrust herself at her sister's body, pressed her face onto Eriqwyn's chest and hugged her tighter than she'd ever hugged her before. Sobs wracked her frame but she clung on.

Don't leave me, Eri. I need you…

She was only distantly aware of footfalls running up the garden path and the door swinging open, someone entering and gasping for breath. Voices – first hushed, then raised.

"How many?"

"At least a dozen. Perhaps twice that number."

"To what end?"

"According to Onwin's father, to attain vengeance for what the outlanders have done to"—in the pause that followed, Adri realised that the speaker was Laulani—"to the brave souls who fought to protect Minnow's Beck, and who died trying."

"Damn!" Linisa hissed. "How long since they left?"

"Shortly after nightfall. Lini, they are half a day's march away now, and, knowing Onwin, he will be pushing them with intent."

Adri lifted her face from Eriqwyn's chest to see Caneli crouched beside her. "There is a choice to be made, Lady," the physician said softly.

She wiped a corner of the bedsheet across her face, composing herself as well as she could. "They will not be followed," she said. "Only Tan's father has the right of retribution, and even that is unproven. As to the rest, they knew the laws at the time of their leaving; the same laws will apply should they return. Let it be known that any others who decide to walk away, for whatever reason, may not readily be welcomed back." She pushed herself from her sister's body and fixed her eyes on Eriqwyn's serene, unchanging expression. After a moment, she turned to address Caneli and Linisa. "*We*, not I, will amend the laws. Linisa, choose a representative from the hunters to replace Onwin. He has forfeit his position. The council will meet tomorrow at noon. You have until then to decide."

"Understood."

A shout drifted in through the open door. Exchanging glances with the others, Adri stepped to the window and peered out across the long shadows of first light. At the far side of the village green, a number of individuals were stood outside of the guard station. The hunter on watch had his bow raised and pointed at someone out of sight beyond the sprawling Founding Oak. "What in the blessed heath is it now?" she hissed, wiping a sleeve across her eyes as she moved to the door.

"Be careful, Lady," Linisa said.

"I will be safe with you at my side." Adri strode through the door and onto the garden, Linisa and Caneli at her sides. Reaching the green, she fixed her eyes on the edge of the ancient tree until two figures came into view, and a moment later, two more. Pausing, she turned a worried look on Linisa. "The ones behind are knights."

"It would seem so."

She continued towards the guardhouse and came to a stop half a dozen paces from the front two strangers. Both men were unarmed. "I am Adriana, Lady of Albarandes Manor and Minnow's Beck. I presume, from your eyes, you are residents of the city."

323

"Indeed we are," the man on the right said. His voice was rich, his nose strong, the wavy hair and close-shorn beard as dark as the black traces around his eyes. "Although we are accompanied by knights, it is only as a precaution. On that, you have my – our – word. Your hunters can rest easy."

Adri motioned for the hunters to lower their weapons. They did so, albeit reluctantly.

The dark-haired man inclined his head. "Please allow us to extend our sympathies for your recent loss. It has been a… trying time."

Adri bristled, but calmed herself. "You arrive only minutes after my sister leaves this world, but I take it that is not the reason for your presence here today."

"It is not," the man on the left said. "Ah, but where are our manners?" He cast the fronts of his longcoat aside and hooked his thumbs behind his belt, casting a mildly amused glance at one hunter who had begun to reattach an arrow to his bow.

With a shake of his head, the man's gaze roved around the gathered individuals. "It's been quite a while since I stood here," he said, then approached the Founding Oak and stamped a foot on the ground beneath it. His features hardened as he added, "In this *exact* spot, as it happens." He turned to Adri. "You, Lady, won't recognise me. But were your great-grandfather still alive, he most certainly would." He pointed up to the boughs of the tree. "You see, the heads of my friends adorn your precious oak. I believe I may not have been mentioned in your great-grandfather's ledgers – something of an embarrassment, perhaps – but I am the fourth of the original outlanders from 120 years ago. My name is Sabrian, and I am the one that got away. I would say it's a pleasure to make your acquaintance, but, as you can imagine, relations between our peoples will take some working out. The gentleman over there is Cleve." He motioned to the dark-haired man, who bowed his head in greeting.

"We come as emissaries," Cleve said, "not as antagonists. Of that, I assure you. My friend here merely has some pent-up frustrations over his skull narrowly missing joining those of his slaughtered companions. You, Adriana Albarandes, recently made a similar decision. It was the wrong one. When your sister brought you the stone, you knew whose family it belonged to. You knew that the last member of that family fled your village eighty years ago. You could, therefore, have surmised that those who came to claim it might in fact have been her forebears, or someone working for them. If you had made that assumption, you would have been correct. Instead, you decided to eliminate what you perceived as a threat to your existence.

"Now, when I say this, I mean no disrespect because I do understand that a small settlement like yours needs tight preservation, but those outlanders were not in the least bit interested in your village. They had no intention of ever visiting it, nor attacking it, nor as much as mentioning it when they returned home." Cleve frowned and glanced to the manor house.

Adri followed his gaze to see Wayland walking unsteadily down the garden path as Laulani ran out to take his arm.

"It seems," Sabrian said as he straightened the lapels of his longcoat, "that there are those in your community who still insist on eliminating the new outlanders. I would advise against that." He looked across to the approaching pair. "Thank you for telling us, Wayland. We will rectify the issue."

"I've never seen you before," Wayland said, sounding as exhausted as he looked. "But somehow I'm not surprised at your words. You're talking about Onwin."

Sabrian nodded. "You are a good and honest man. Onwin is not." He glanced around at the gathering. "Many of you here are fair and true folk, and yet, when something foreign enters your small diorama of existence, you turn into rabid animals baying for blood, convinced that you are still doing the rational and decent thing. It is time to let that go."

Adri narrowed her eyes. "You haven't yet stated your business."

"Ah, no. Cleve, would you?"

Cleve stepped forwards. "In the name of peace, we offer a union, of sorts. Three centuries ago, our brothers and sisters, parents and children, fled from Lachyla, and many settled here. All who live in Minnow's Beck are their descendants – *our* descendants. We believe it is time, perhaps, to reunite old families now that the cat is out of the bag, as it were. As you can see, we are able to leave the city, and, yes, we have been doing so the whole time – at night, mostly, to avoid your prying eyes. But now..." He shrugged. "We would be happy to allow you to visit our city, for your folk to meet their predecessors, and we in turn would enjoy visiting your village for limited periods of time. If you agree, there will have to be precautions which must be strictly adhered to for those among you who do not wish to find themselves anchored to Lachyla – and to eternity – as we are."

Adri stared at him for a long moment. "Your generous offer will be passed to all who live here," she promised.

"That is good," Cleve said. "Ah, and speaking of family..." He took a step towards Adri and motioned to the companions at her side. "If I may?" She nodded, and he advanced slowly to stop before Caneli. "It is a pleasure to meet you, Caneli Hauverydh."

"I... I don't understand." The physician glanced to Adri.

Cleve's smile broke into a grin. "I am Cleve Hauverydh. Your uncle, of sorts." He thrust his hand out for her to take, and after a moment of hesitation, she did so. "It has been good to watch my family from afar," he said. "I was proud to learn that you followed in your mother's footsteps and became the village physician. The apple hasn't fallen from the tree at all, merely drifted somewhat sideways." He peered at Caneli's eyes and the black dye that ran from her dried tears. "You know, that would be quite a way for our women to blend in unnoticed outside of the city. Perhaps also some of the men."

Caneli stared at him, looked blankly at Adri, then stared at Cleve again.

He chuckled. "Don't mind me. It will take time. But time"—he glanced to Adri—"despite the current turmoil in your village, is something we have in abundance. Do not worry, Lady, nor any of you, about the coming changes; they will not be as tough as you fear, and you are already making steps in the right direction."

"I am glad to hear a vote of confidence, however small," Adri said. After a pause, she threw caution to the wind and added, "I would value your counsel in the coming days."

Cleve offered her his hand. When she took it, his grip was firm but gentle. His eyes fixed onto hers and he gave the briefest of nods – an understanding between equals. Silence gave way to distant mutters, and Adri knew that a small crowd of onlookers was forming around the edges of the green. Wayland coughed, and Adri turned to see him release Laulani and nod his appreciation to her before taking a tentative step forwards.

"Wayland?" Adri said.

He turned to face her. "I think you know, Lady."

She sighed inwardly, then nodded. "I do."

"If you would have me, I would continue my Warder duties, albeit part-time."

"Always," Adri said.

"Wayland," Linisa said, "what are you doing?"

"I have to leave, Lini. I returned only to be at Eri's side." He looked to Adri. "I loved her as my own sister... perhaps more, yet not in this world."

A lump caught in her throat as she watched the veteran Warder turn sideways and allow Sabrian to link his arm. One of the knights stepped forward for Wayland to grip his shoulder. Looking back, he said, "There are no more goodbyes today, ladies. I will see you soon." With a wink to Linisa, he let the men lead him away.

Cleve remained, watching as the others walked away. Once they were out of earshot, he turned to Adri. "A word to the wise, Lady Adriana. It would grieve my friend Sabrian if he were to see those foul objects in the boughs of your tree again. Might I request you remove them? I believe you might agree that they have outlasted their purpose."

Adri drew a long, shuddering breath. "I most certainly do."

As Cleve walked away, the Priestess Superior ran forwards from her chapel. "You cannot do this," she hissed.

"Oh, I can, Amiryn." Adri looked out at the gathering of villagers, their shadows stretched across the green. "I can, and I will."

CHAPTER THIRTY SIX
UNBOUND

At the far end of the white corridor, Ellidar gave the twisted metal of the fake wall a final heave and it shifted another inch, affording him enough space to poke a torch through and peer into the black chute. The wreckage of the transportation mechanism lay somewhere at the bottom, half-buried, he knew, beneath debris from the partially-collapsed shaft. When the major repairs to the castle and the rest of the city were completed, there would be more work ahead for himself and the knights to dig a path back to the Mother, but, for now, she was quiet and content to wait. A lesson had been learned by recent events – a lesson of peace over violence, reinforced by one whose nature included wrath as a reaction without thought, who took any compatible vessels and used them for its own survival. Ellidar sniffed in wry amusement, not altogether appreciating the irony.

As he strode back along the winding corridor, he picked up a faint sending and aimed his awareness out beyond the castle and beyond the city walls. A gust of urgency blew through his mind as he sensed Cleve Hauverydh calling to him, conveying to him an image of the outlander lady and her companions. He pushed his focus, and Cleve's warning became clear. Clenching a leather-gloved fist, he hesitated only briefly before bursting into a run along the shallow rise of the corridor, and projected his thoughts to Gorven Althalus. *"Did you sense the message?"*

A moment later, Gorven's reply reached him. *"I sensed Sabrian, but the meaning was muddy. Something about Dagra and the others? What did you get?"*

"Villagers. A sizeable group of them heading to intercept the wielder of the blade Ammenfar and the lady Jalis. She is a woman of valour and every bit the warrior, but there are too many."

"Our friends are a day and a half out of Lachyla already," Gorven sent. *"It is too far, and Dagra is weakened; he cannot sense anything more than the distant buzz of our collective mind. There is nothing we can do."*

"I am a knight. There is nothing I will back away from." Ellidar bounded for the hanging drape that led into the throne room. *"These villagers have caused enough harm already. I will not allow it."*

"But, Ellidar, you will die!"

He dipped beneath the drape, his eyes falling upon the dark stain on the floor and the scorched surface of the bronze seat. He ran across the throne room and burst through the far doors, snatching a longsword from the wall before crashing through the outer doors.

"There is no time for discussion," he sent to Gorven as he pelted down the marble steps. *"I go now. I go alone."*

———— • • ————

With each passing step, Dagra's breath was becoming more ragged as he trudged across the grassy heath, his arm around Oriken's middle, and Oriken's clutched around his. Half a mile ahead a thicket of conifers stretched across the rocky coastline, nestled beneath a steep crag. The swatch of green melted into the grey tide, the trees' spindly trunks swaying like flowers though there was no breeze to disturb them. The voices in his head were all but gone now, but in their stead came others – the voices of the gods.

"It's time," he said, his step faltering. "I'm ready."

Oriken gripped him tighter, and at his other side Jalis linked his arm. His senses reeled. He felt Oriken's shoulder against his cheek, Jalis's warm hand upon his. Somehow they were already nearing the edge of the thicket. His feet all but dragged along the ground; he moved only because his friends were there to help him onwards.

Stars and shadows swam in his vision though the day was bright, and the gods' voices sang in known and foreign tongues. The Dyad sang with their paragons and a choir of disciples. Khariali's lilting chimes blended with her sibling Cherak's baritone rumble, resonating along the golden rays of their son, Banael, to wash over Dagra's face. Pheranisa crooned a liquid lament, while Haleth's chords danced across her waters. Beneath an unfamiliar staccato of hooves, the Arbiter's judgement was a calmed roar. All the aspects and patrons added their voices to the sibilant dirge, and he even sensed the silent attendants at the edge of the deific choir, among them the Herald, the Grey Watcher, and that ancient Himaeran goddess, the blighter of Lachyla.

He also felt the presence of another – one he did not know, that seemed to link the rest together like threads in a fractured tapestry. This was the least of them, a worm, but somehow the most important, weaving the notes of the song in perfect harmony.

He was on his back, perched upon soft ground and staring up into the starred-and-shadowed dazzling sky. The faces of his friends, at first hazy, came into focus above him.

"Oriken. Jalis…"

"We're here," Jalis said, though he didn't see her lips move.

He felt a pressure upon his fingers and looked down to see Oriken's hand in his. Dagra lifted his eyes to his friend, and in Oriken's features he saw the boy and the man he had become, a solemn expression on his face, the corners of his mouth turned down within his stubbled cheeks.

"It's okay," he heard himself say. "They're all here, come to see me away."

"Of course they are," Oriken said. "They'd have to answer to me otherwise." Dagra thought he saw him smile.

He felt a smile of his own, though whether it reached his face he couldn't be sure. "I don't think… it's heresy to say… that not even Aveia holds a candle to you, my friend."

Oriken squeezed his hand, but said nothing.

"Tell my grandparents I love them."

Oriken nodded. "Of course," he said, his voice cracking.

"It's been… a life worth living. And no regrets." Dagra turned to Jalis. "It's beautiful, lass. As beautiful as you. You've been… one of the finest people in my life. Knowing you… has enriched me. Say goodbye to that big, wonderful giant for me, will you?"

Jalis reached towards him and touched her palm to his cheek, just as tears ran freely down her own. "I will," she said.

He glanced back to Oriken. "Orik, I can… hardly see you." His breaths came shallower by the moment.

"I'm still here." Oriken squeezed Dagra's hand tighter.

"I want you to have… my sword," Dagra told him. "Learn how to dual wield. I wish… I'd had time to spar with you… the way they used to."

Oriken's choking laugh reached Dagra's ears through the choral voices of the gods. "I'll wear it for the rest of my days, Dag."

"Jalis. Take my Avato emblem." He waved weakly towards the pendant around his neck. "You don't… have to wear it, just think of me sometimes."

Jalis sobbed quietly.

"Don't cry, lass. I'm just… a thread… in the unending tapestry."

One by one, the stars faded until all that remained was the black Void. The heavenly song grew, soaring through his mind as his body became lighter.

"Goodbye, my friends. I hope… I hope we…"

Svey'Drommelach's shadow enveloped him. The god gathered him beneath its wing, evaporating all that mattered. And he was free.

The world closed in around Oriken as he stared at Dagra's eyes, and the bearded little man stared sightlessly back at him. With a shuddering breath, he removed the ancient gladius from Dagra's belt. With a hand on Jalis's shoulder, he rose to his feet and unbuckled his swordbelt, slid the aged scabbard over the leather, and refastened the belt. The weight of the two swords, one on each hip, felt balanced. It felt right.

He looked down at Dagra. In death, his features were slack; not peaceful the way everyone glorified it, but empty.

"So long, Dag," he whispered, the words catching in his throat. "We found the adventures we were looking for, hey?"

It didn't feel real. It felt like a dream he must surely soon awaken from. But he wouldn't, and he knew it. Dagra was gone. Jalis got to her feet, the Avato pendant in her hand. She placed it to her lips, then slipped it into her pocket. Taking Oriken's arm, she leaned into him and silently wept. He clenched his teeth and swallowed the lump in his throat. With his hand over Jalis's, the gentle pressure of her body against his reminded him that he wasn't alone.

CHAPTER THIRTY SEVEN
FIRE AND TIDE

The sun melted over the hills as the morning stretched on and Jalis gathered wood for a makeshift pyre. She watched with concern as Oriken wandered listlessly through the trees, his face empty of emotion. Eventually a large pile of wood was stacked upon the grass beside the rocky shore, and she crossed to Oriken.

"That's enough," she said gently, taking his arm and removing the short branch he'd held for the last five minutes.

Without looking at her, he grunted and gave a brief nod.

"We need to carry him over."

He took a deep breath and released it slowly.

"Oriken."

"Yeah."

He walked over to the shallow rise where Dagra lay, and crouched to take him beneath the arms. With an inward sigh, Jalis joined him and they carried Dagra's body to the woodpile, lowering him onto the pyre. She positioned his arms neatly at his sides while Oriken retrieved the tinderbox from a backpack.

"Do you want me to do it?" she asked.

"I've got it." He knelt and began to strike the flint into the kindling at the base of the woodpile. Sparks flew, but the wood did not catch.

Perching herself on a mossy boulder, Jalis gazed out onto the ocean and back along the stretch of heath behind them. The languid hiss of the waves mixed with the sound of Oriken striking the flint. *Scratch, scratch, scratch...* A gull cried and took to flight from within the conifers, soaring along the rocky shore. The minutes stretched by, and she opened her senses to her surroundings. As the scratching stopped, she looked to Oriken to see him fishing a hand into his jacket and bringing out the small metal object Sabrian had given him. He flicked the lid open and held the circle of glass within towards the high sun, and waited. After a minute the heat lens began to glow and he touched it to the kindling. The wood crackled, but did not take.

"Bah! Fucking useless cunting thing." He flicked the lid closed and stuffed the device into his pocket.

Jalis rose and approached him, bent down and whispered in his ear, "We're being watched."

"Where?"

"Stay here. But be on your guard, just in case." She brushed past him and ambled inconspicuously along the edge of the thicket, heading to the far end where the trees met the craggy rise. Nonchalantly she stepped around the back of the trees to the scattering of boulders that lined the base of the crag. Approaching the largest of them, she peered behind it.

"Hello, Demelza," she said, frowning down at the crouching girl pressed tightly against the stone. "You're far from home."

Demelza's face turned white as she looked up at Jalis. "I weren't following you. Honest. You... you were following me."

Jalis's frown deepened into a scowl. "Shall we talk about honesty? You swore to the goddess that you wouldn't mention us to your people."

"Goddess never did nowt for me. Why should I do summat for her?"

"You also swore to *me* that you wouldn't tell. Do we have you to thank for those hunters finding us in the city?"

"I didn't know they'd want to kill yous. I swear. They forced me to tell. I was scared."

"Jalis!"

She turned to see Oriken heading towards her, Dagra's sword in his hand.

"It's all right," she told him. "You can put the sword away. We have an unexpected guest." To Demelza, she said, "You'd better come and join us."

Demelza clung to her satchel and climbed to her feet, and Jalis led her to Dagra's pyre.

"As you can see," Jalis said drily, "our number has shrunk by a third."

"I... I can help wi' that," Demelza said.

Oriken scoffed. "The wood's damp, girl. If I can't get it to catch, what gives you the sodding thought that you can do it?"

Something in Demelza's expression piqued Jalis's interest and she caught Oriken's gaze, giving him a look to ask for his patience. "Go on, Demelza," she said to the girl.

Demelza stared at the woodpile, a look of casual concentration on her face. The moment grew. Oriken sucked air through his teeth and opened his mouth, but Jalis touched his arm and shook her head. Demelza closed her eyes, and when Jalis looked to the branches she saw the air shimmer beneath them within the kindling. And, with a quiet hiss, it caught into flames.

Oriken tensed. "What did you just do?"

"She magicked fire from air," Jalis told him. "You can put that on the list of things you've seen with your own eyes."

He glared at her, then turned on Demelza. "How?"

The girl took a step away from him, but Jalis gently took her arm. As the flames grew around Dagra's body, Jalis said to Oriken, "You remember the girl a few years ago? The one who shrank an oak back into a sapling? She was a diachromancer."

Oriken barked a harsh laugh. "Do you think I'm—"

"Let me finish, Orik. The girl was a feyborn, and Demelza is a feyborn, too. More specifically, she's an elemancer."

Demelza turned a doe-eyed look on Jalis, and a tentative grin spread on her face. "A Melemancer!"

Jalis couldn't help but smile. "Yes," she said, patting the girl's arm. "A Melemancer."

The flames were licking higher and spreading around Dagra's body, and Jalis suddenly became aware of the smell that drifted from the pyre. She looked to Oriken, but he was glaring hard at the fire, his jaw clenched.

"Demelza," she said, "would you help us gather our things? We should continue on our way." She eyed the girl sidelong. "That is unless you're returning to your home?"

Demelza gave a vehement shake of her head. "Don't 'ave an 'ome no more. Ain't no one there likes the Melza. Not no more. Not now Waynan's gone."

Waynan, Jalis thought. Then, *Wayland. Yes, I see now.* "In that case, if you say we can trust you, and if you have no other destination in mind, you're welcome to travel with us."

"I do promise," Demelza said. "I meant it afore an' I mean it now. I ain't got no contrabibialities 'gainst yous." She cast a fearful glance at Oriken, who looked up from the flames and narrowed his eyes, first at the girl, then at Jalis before turning on his heel and stalking away to their belongings.

"He don't like me," Demelza said.

"He's just upset. You don't have anything to fear from him. And it looks like you don't need to help us with our gear, either; the Orc King's got it covered." Jalis gave the burning pyre a last look and sent Dagra a silent, final goodbye.

Several hours later, Oriken sat on the rocks and gazed down the winding coast to the distant stand of conifers, behind which Dagra's remains lay on a bed of warm ash. The numbness had faded, the anger was quelling and the true emotions were clamouring to reach the surface, but he pushed back against them for all he was worth.

Not yet, damn it! Not yet.

In his hand, Dagra's gladius was all that remained of his lifelong friend. He vowed there and then that he'd use the ancient, rune-etched short sword until his freeblading days were over and he hung it on the wall with the blade of Mallak Ammenfar in traditional freeblade style; the age-worn gladius would take pride of place, crossed atop its gleaming, regal counterpart. He slid the sword back into its scabbard and looked long at the horizon where coast met ocean, imagining a faint spume of smoke drifting out onto the glistening water.

He sat, lost in thought until the sun arced into its final quarter and Jalis's voice stirred him from his reverie. He glanced across to her. She was sat cross-legged upon a blanket, and, although engaged in conversation with the girl, she seemed small, lost, as if a part of her had gone with Dagra, which he knew it had, as had a large part of his own self. He rose and wandered across to join them, lowering himself to the blanket beside her.

She gave him a weak smile. "I was just talking to Demelza about her talent."

"Uhuh."

"She possesses one of the three accepted magic arts. I've seen elemancy a few times, but only once before with—" Her voice caught. "Only once with fire."

He nodded and glanced indifferently at the girl. "Interesting."

There was a long pause before Jalis said, "Demelza, did your mother have the same gift?"

"Dunno. She died afore I was born."

Jalis muttered under her breath, then said, "You know, there are places where girls like you can meet others with similar talents, and live alongside them. Places where your skills can be put to good use. Would you like to visit such a place?"

Demelza looked uncertain.

"There are temples within the Arkh," Jalis went on, and Oriken wondered how much of her chatter was to distract herself from facing her feelings. "When I was a girl in Sardaya, younger than you are now, I lived near such a temple. I used to go there and talk to the girls and the women." She smiled in remembrance, though it did nothing to diminish the grief in her eyes. "I admit I went there to see the Ashcloaks as well, the strapping temple guards. I was a little envious of the girls' skills, and of the beautiful temple they lived in."

"It sounds nice." Demelza untucked her legs from beneath her and stretched them out along the grass, leaning back on her hands. "What's the Arkh? And what's a Saddier?"

"Sar-*da*-ya," Jalis corrected, inflecting the correct syllable. "It's a land, like Himaera. But there's plenty of time to tell you all about these things on the road ahead. Demelza—"

"Waynan called me Dee," the girl blurted out. "It reminds me of deer. I like deer."

Jalis blinked. "Well, if that's what you like, then Dee it is."

"I think I'd like to see a temple, too."

"I'm sure I can arrange it…" Jalis's brow furrowed. "Perhaps I'll take you to Brancosi Bay; I could organise an escort to accompany you across to Vorinsia, where you would meet the Ashcloaks in the capital. I think our newest member, Leaf, would like the job of taking you. She's only a couple of years older than you. You'll like her."

A sudden rustling in the nearby underbrush caused Oriken to glance sharply and reach for the loaded crossbow, but Jalis was quicker. She snatched the weapon and eased the string into place, rising fluidly to a crouch and stepping lightly towards the thatch of shrubs. She squeezed the trigger, and an instant later the bushes shook and an animal screech issued forth. A young nargut crawled into the open, the crossbow bolt jutting from its lower back. Pulling Silverspire from its sheath at her hip, she dashed forward and quickly put an end to the creature's misery.

"Orik," she called. "I promised I'd catch you a nargut."

"As a pet, you said."

"Half a promise fulfilled is better than none at all. Would you rather a pet or a full belly right now?"

Oriken gave no reply, but climbed to his feet and trudged off to gather firewood while Jalis dragged the nargut across to prepare it for eating. When the fire was built, Oriken reached into his pocket for the heat lens but paused as he caught Demelza looking at him. With a shrug, he motioned for her to get on with it, then sat down to help Jalis cut the nargut flesh into shanks.

The roasted meat melted his hunger. With the meal finished, he scrubbed the skin and cut it into thick strips which he wrapped around the grip of the blade Ammenfar and its scabbard.

The sky to the east deepened to evening blue, while to the west the sun hunkered down upon the watery horizon. The camp was quiet, with Demelza sorting through her scant belongings in her satchel while Jalis occupied herself with studying the jewel. Oriken had replayed the entire events of the previous week over and over in his mind, from venturing into the Chiddari crypt to Dagra's final words. He recalled the first clues that something was amiss – the scuff marks in the dust that led only outwards from the crypt.

God's fearing fool you might have been, Dag, but sometimes you were right. I reckon it was more than just your imagination at play down in that crypt. I should've recognised the signs for myself, should've connected them to the legend; the legend that even you never paid enough mind to. Maybe if I'd been more attentive I might've prevented everything. He shook his head; thinking that way would do no good. *I never put much stock in any of your gods, Dag, but still, I hope I'm wrong and you were right. I hope we meet again, you stupid, stumpy little bearded bastard.*

He caught Jalis regarding him with a sideways glance. He half-turned so she wouldn't notice the dampness that threatened to spill from his eyes.

The sun winked out into the water. The shadows of evening deepened, and he considered Lachyla's story.

It scared me as a young boy, he thought. *And I scoffed at it as I became a man. But I'm not laughing now. I've seen the city uncloaked and unmasked, in all its horror and beauty. Taleweavers be damned, the truth of Lachyla goes far beyond its legend.*

"I'd like to sleep now," Demelza announced. With the grace of adolescence, she grabbed her satchel and sprang to her feet.

"Take a blanket." Jalis pointed to their pile of gear stacked at the base of a lone gawek tree a short distance away.

The girl gave a nod of gratitude and trotted over to scoop a blanket into her arms, then wandered over to the edge of the ridge overhanging the beach. She jumped over the edge and disappeared, landing silently upon the soft sand below.

"She's off into that little cave she scouted earlier," Jalis said quietly. "She's accustomed to living alone, and probably needs her space. Oriken?"

"I'm listening. I'm just not in a talkative mood right now."

"I understand."

He cleared his throat. "I picked up that bloodstone, you know?"

"Which bloodstone?"

"The one Dagra threw away when I was making a fuss about taking more gems." He pulled it from his pocket and showed her the smooth, dark green oval, rubbing a thumb across the red speckles. "I meant to hand it to him on our way home, as an apology, I guess."

Jalis frowned. "So why didn't you?"

"For some reason, a piddling little thing like that seemed to slip my mind." He drew a breath and looked out at the ocean.

After a minute, Jalis said, "I almost don't want to complete the contract. We've got the jewel, but it just seems... I don't know."

"We finish it," he said. "And we collect our earnings. Then we continue."

Jalis gave a serene nod. "Retrieve, return, report," she muttered, quoting the expression of the guild.

"And relax," he finished. That was the way of it. Get the job done, then forget about it. Move on. Leave your losses behind.

"Before we met you and Maros," he said, "me and Dag were out there on our own for a few years. You and I still have each other, Jalis. And we still have Maros, and Henwyn, Alari, and the others." He managed a tight smile. "The Mountain makes as good a tavernmaster as he ever made a freeblade."

"He is still a freeblade."

"As Official? He's an overseer, a peddler of sellswords with a set of rules."

"He nearly died last year from that wound to his leg."

"But he didn't die."

"What if..." Jalis shook her head and looked across the heath. "What if he had, though? And what if you or I—"

"It's not going to happen." Touching his fingertips to her chin, he gently turned her to look at him. "I promise."

She blinked and a tear ran down her cheek, but she held his gaze. Something new passed between them then, though whether for better or worse, Oriken couldn't tell.

They carried their belongings down a trail that led from the tip of a long strip of firs to a cove secreted beneath the ridge, a hundred yards from the cave where Demelza slept. The base of the jutting outcrop sheltered them from the wind that now swept across the heath, while the breeze coming in from the ocean was warm and gentle. The sky was peppered with swathes of stars, and high overhead Haleth shone full and bright, her reflection shimmering in the black waters.

The lapping of the tide blended with the undulating buzz of night insects as Jalis stripped from her clothes, padded across the beach and waded into the water until it lapped at her thighs. Oriken lay on a blanket and leaned on his elbow, watching her in the moonlight. She moved in deeper and dipped beneath the waves, while within the firs a nightjar chirred a lonely lament. Moments later, she re-emerged and, as she turned to face him, the light of the moon glistened over her wet skin. Even through the haze of his emotions, the sight of her managed to fire his blood.

We carry on, he thought. *For Dagra, and for us. I can get through this.* The tears came then, and a quiet sob gasped unchecked from his lips.

He sat up and pulled the shirt over his head, sighing as the tightness in his shoulder protested. When he looked again, Jalis was swimming further out, her head bobbing amongst the silver ripples. He removed his breeches and wandered across the sand, scarcely noticing the chill as he entered the water and waded out until it sloshed around his chest. A larger wave approached and washed over his head, giving the tears their chance to run unseen. Time crawled by as he stood gazing out across the rolling tide, his eyes on Jalis's head as she glided through the water. Finally she swam closer and circled behind him. When he turned, she was stood inches away, the listless waves lapping at the tops of her breasts.

"It will be okay, Orik," she said in scarcely more than a whisper, placing a hand upon his chest.

He nodded, and she drifted closer. She slipped her arms around his waist and pressed her body against his. He held her tightly, lowered his face to her wet hair, and sobbed.

After she returned to their bedding and belongings, he stayed in the water for long minutes and watched her within the shadows of the embankment, standing upon the sparse grass and towelling herself dry. As he stepped out of the water, she paused and watched him approach, a curious look on her face as if in serious contemplation. He reached her and stepped close, and she looked up at him.

"What are you thinking?" he asked.

Her eyes dipped from his and trailed down his body. The casual scrutiny stirred a reaction that he could not hide. Her lips parted, and he watched the steady rise and fall of her chest as she drew in a breath and released it.

337

"Jalis—"

She looked up to meet his gaze. Her eyes glinted with more than just the light of the moon and stars. Her fingers touched his chest, then her warm palm. "I can feel your heart beating," she whispered.

Her other hand touched his waist, slid down onto his thigh, then across. She took another small step closer until the tips of her breasts touched his skin. Between them, her hand closed around him, her fingers squeezing with growing need. The pounding of his heart seemed to thump throughout his whole body. He opened his mouth but could find no words.

Her eyes strayed down to watch as he swelled in her grasp, responding to her eager touch. "This is what you want," she said, her voice husky. "This is what you've always wanted."

"I… Yes," he faltered. "But—"

"Shush now." She released him and placed a finger to his lips.

Is this happening? Surely this isn't real…

She took him by the shoulders and pulled him down with her to the blankets. Again her hand reached for him, this time with more urgency, while her other dipped between her thighs and a short gasp escaped her.

"Jalis, I—"

"Don't you dare." Her voice was thick with animal need like he'd never heard before. "You do this," she said, "and you do it now." She pulled him close, guided him into her. He hesitated, and her eyes narrowed. "For the stars' sake, Oriken, fuck me!"

He blinked, nodded. She clasped her legs around him and pulled his hips onto hers, and, for a while, Oriken forgot everything else.

Afterwards he lay staring up into the midnight sky, Jalis's leg strewn across his middle with his hand rested upon her thigh. All the while, a quiet storm flooded his mind – the memory of their lovemaking juxtaposed with images of Dagra, and of dead things, and Krea, here in this moment between all they had endured and what was to come.

"You know," he said quietly, "for all the horrors in this world, for all the senseless losses and atrocities, the firmament above us is a painting of innocence. The stars and the moons – all those lights are untouchable, unknowable. Sometimes I imagine myself soaring like a dawnhawk through that celestial sphere. For every horror down here, be it corpse or cravant, monster or man, there's a twinkling beauty out of reach up there."

From the corner of his eye he saw her looking up into the sky. "Look there," she said, and he followed her finger to a thin silver line as it sliced its way slowly down and across the sky. "Some would say that's Dagra, on his journey to the Underland to be reborn."

"Yeah," he sighed. "Some would say that."

They lay in silence until Jalis said, "I can't do this again."

He turned to her, but she kept her eyes fixed on the stars. A sinking feeling washed over him, like a keepsake spilling from between his fingers to fall into deep waters, and all he could do was watch helplessly as it drifted from sight.

"I understand," he said.

"No, you don't." She placed her hand upon his. "I don't mean this. I mean I can't continue the freeblade lifestyle." Drawing a deep breath, she let it out slowly. "I've been in the guild for over twelve years, more than twice as long as you and... and Dagra. With Maros, the four of us were invincible, then we lost him last year when he hung his blades up. Now Dagra's gone, not crippled by a monster or defeated by a bunch of bandits, not even slain by a horde of undead, but fallen to a trifling thing that caught him in a moment, and none of us noticed."

He turned his face back to the night sky. Kheyron's Soul, the brightest star, seemed tonight to shine twice as bright as ever. He pressed his lips together and turned his attention to the constellation of the Galloping Lady, her reaching limbs eternally frozen in mid-movement.

"What comes next?" Jalis asked. "When might I lose you, too? Or will it be my turn next? I'm hanging my blades up when we return to the Folly. I just... I can't..."

He closed his eyes. "I understand," he repeated, and this time it meant so much more.

The next morning, he awoke to the sound of the tide as it swept across the sand. Jalis stirred beneath his arm, and he lifted his head to see Demelza wandering along the beach, the water cascading over her feet as it rushed across the sand and fell away.

Jalis rolled against him and smiled sleepily. "Good morning."

He returned the smile. "I hope so."

They ate a bland but filling breakfast of berries and leftover nargut meat before packing their gear and resuming the journey home, heading inland towards the marsh crossing.

CHAPTER THIRTY EIGHT
DEE AND THE ORC KING

The wetlands stretched endlessly to the east with only the occasional twisted gawek tree to break the flatness of the reed-studded vista. With Jalis at her side, Demelza ambled along the wide pass, squinting as the afternoon sun flashed from the handle of the sword at the Orc King's hip a short distance ahead. *O-ri-ken*, she corrected. A desire to pay closer attention to the names of people and things had been instilled in her by Jalis's patience and teaching. Jalis's name was easy now that she'd explained it to her. Some names *were* easy, like Adri's. A small pang of regret fluttered in her belly as she thought of the home she'd left behind.

*Except only Adri and Waynan – Way*land *– and a few others liked me in the village*, she thought miserably. *Some o' the men said they liked me, but that were only so they could come to Ma Ina's home and...* She shook her head and glanced at Jalis, then looked away with a smile. *She likes me.*

Since leaving the cove, Demelza had spotted Jalis looking at her several times but quickly turning away. *No*, she thought. *It's the other way round. It's her* catching *me* looking. With a sigh, she glanced at Jalis now, but her new friend's eyes were on the way ahead.

"There's something on your mind, Dee," Jalis said. "You can talk to me."

Demelza gasped. "I..." She lowered her gaze to the grass.

"Go on," Jalis prompted.

"I'm sorry," she blurted. "It were my fault. It were all my fault. If I hadn't told on yous—"

"You did what you thought you had to do, which, I expect, I might also have done were I in your shoes."

"You don't like my shoes?"

Jalis laughed. "Your shoes are wonderful, but we will get you a brand new pair when we reach our home. What I mean is, you lived in a secluded village far from the rest of the world, so how could you know that such a peaceful place would send hunters to kill us?"

"I should'a known, though," Demelza said miserably. "The skulls on the oak..."

Oriken whirled around. "What skulls?"

Demelza stopped. She grabbed Jalis's arm and pressed up against her. "The skulls," she muttered. "Of the three. On the Founding Oak."

Oriken frowned at her. "The three what?"

"The three what was caught. Back in me mam's mam's mam's mam's time. Me real mam, I mean, not Ina. They caught 'em and put their skulls on the tree. Um. Their heads, I mean."

"Sabrian's friends," Oriken said. "Poor bastards. That could've been us."

"No! Adri would never do such a thing. She... she sweared it."

"It doesn't matter now." Jalis motioned for Oriken to continue walking. "They didn't kill any of us. They wanted to. They tried. Tell me, Dee, why *did* you run away from your village? And why come to us rather than going your own way?"

The girl shrugged. "Not many liked me in the Beck. Most hated me. Eri most of all. Said I were a fool girl, good for nothin'. Lots said that, even afore Ma Ina died. It weren't home after that."

"And you thought that wherever we're headed might be a nicer place to live?"

Demelza shook her head, then frowned. "You was kinder to me than any 'cept Way... Wayland... when you oughtn't have been."

Jalis grinned and wiped a fingertip beneath the corner of her eye. Glancing at Oriken's back, she said, "Do you like Orik, too?"

"I dunno." Demelza shrugged as she watched the tall man stride onwards. "Maybe."

Jalis chuckled. Demelza frowned, and her new friend laughed harder. Demelza laughed too. It felt good.

"Crossing up ahead!" Oriken announced.

She peered past him at the strip of marshland that blocked the pass, stretching from the wetlands all the way to the ocean. A crude path of three lines of stripped trees angled across the obstacle, leading to dry land beyond. Off to the north-west, a range of steep hills tapered into the distance, obscuring the view to the coastline. Oriken reached the walkway of half-sunken trees first stepped onto it. Jalis ushered Demelza to go next. She waited for Oriken to reach the halfway point, then sprang onto the middle log and rose to her tiptoes. Taking small but quick steps, she crossed along the first tree, then the second, keeping the wobbling Oriken at the edge of her vision as she gained on him. He reached the end of the last log and strode onto dry ground, and a moment later Demelza hopped off behind him, pouncing to the side as he swung around to look at her. She clutched her satchel and scowled back at him, and he shook his head. Jalis jogged along the walkway and leaped nimbly to land between them.

"She needs to get used to me," Oriken snapped. "And quickly."

"She will. Give her time."

341

"Listen, I let you bring her along, and, frankly, I'm indifferent as to whether she's here or not. I've done nothing to make her uncomfortable. If anything, it's the other way around." He turned to Demelza. "I'm not an orc, damn it. Do you hear me? Sure, I ain't looking my best right now, but I'm no monster. Whatever reason you've got for not trusting me is in your head, and I don't plan on spending the rest of our journey catching you giving me the evil eye. From now on, you'll walk at my side, and we'll talk, until you stop thinking I'm a demon who's trying to fatten you up till you're plump enough to eat."

"Orik—"

"No. It's gonna happen. Me and Demelza – *Dee* – are going to bond, because I've had it up to here with wearing the mantle of the bad man."

Demelza took a step closer to Jalis. "Here, mister, I ain't bondin' wi' you. You said you wouldn't do that. You promised."

"What?" He sighed and shook his head. "I mean bonding as in getting to know each other. Verbally. With tongues— Ah, for the love of the rutting gods, you know what I mean."

She eyed him shrewdly. "Maybe."

"Right then."

Demelza turned to her friend for support, but Jalis only raised an eyebrow and shrugged.

"Come on." Oriken reached for her. She flinched as his hand curled around her shoulder, but his touch was gentle and she let it happen. "Let's you and I walk together."

He guided her down the dirt trail, and once they were walking side by side he removed his hand from her shoulder. Demelza glanced back at Jalis; she was following a dozen steps behind, but her attention was elsewhere.

"Right then," Oriken said as they strolled along. "First things first, little lady. You've probably got your reasons for being wary of me. I get that. And I've got my reasons for..." He puffed his cheeks and blew out. "Me and Jalis have just lost a friend. A close friend. A brother. But here's the thing: We're freeblades, and we have a code of conduct. Sure, we don't always achieve it, but it's there to separate the wheat from the chaff – to ensure that any who join the guild have at least a trace of decency in their bones. Do you follow?"

She frowned. "Dunno. I think so."

Oriken's fingers fluttered at his head, then he thrust his thumb behind his belt and muttered, "Damn it, I need a hat." He cleared his throat and cast her a sidelong glance. "Secondly and more importantly, I don't hate you for alerting your village to our presence. I tried to hold it against you, but I can't. How old are you? Fifteen? Sixteen? I was still living in my village when I was your age, not quite ready to hit the road with... with Dagra... and go discover what the world was like beyond the Kadelia Downs – that's the region where I grew up, a bit like Scapa Fell, only mountainous and more richly abundant, with lots of agriculture, fishing..." He stifled a sigh. "What I'm trying to say is, if our village leaders had tried to force something out of me that I knew about some random strangers I owed no allegiance to, I might have whistled on them just like you did. So let's move past that and concentrate on now. What do you say?"

"Uhuh." Demelza tucked her thumbs beneath her tunic and hitched them into the top of her leggings. "I reckon we can do that."

Oriken squinted ahead and flashed a lopsided smile. "The boat's left the harbour and we're tacking into the wind."

"Huh?"

Jalis's warm laugh drifted along the trail. In unison, Demelza and Oriken turned to look at her. "You know," Jalis said, "the two of you are not nearly as dissimilar as you might think."

"What's she sayin'?" Demelza asked.

Oriken shrugged. "Damned if I know."

As they turned to continue, a fat droplet of rain landed in Demelza's hair. She glanced up at bulging clouds that had drifted in from across the wetlands, and a second droplet splashed onto her forehead. A moment later, the clouds burst open. Jalis cast her pack to the ground and bent to unfasten it, while Demelza hastily rummaged into her satchel for her cloak.

As she withdrew the threadbare garment, Oriken eyed it and shook his head. "That'll do you no good," he said, spitting rain through the rivulets that ran over his lips. He slung his pack from his back and pulled out a sturdy cloak. "This ain't mine," he told her as he wrapped it around her shoulders. "Never needed one, not with my hat and jacket." He secured the clasp at her breast and pulled the leather hood onto her head. "Good. It fits you."

Demelza managed a smile of gratitude, and in that moment she saw a sadness in Oriken's eyes – even the eye that was swollen and bruised – and she knew he was a good man.

He looked at Jalis, then nodded towards the hills. "Caer Valekha's in that vale. What say we get some shelter till the rain passes?"

With her own cloak donned, Jalis nodded from within her hood.

"Everyone up for a run?" Oriken glanced at Demelza with a small smile.

"I can run," she said.

"Then let's do it."

She and Oriken set off together. Rain lashed into her eyes, but she kept his speed. Jalis quickly caught them up and matched pace at Demelza's side. They sprinted across the expanse, drawing ever nearer to the hills. The edge of a large stone construction came into view. Within moments, the whole hulking fortress gradually loomed before her. The square behemoth sprawled at the rear of a pass between two steep rises, its stones as ancient and pitted as the walls of the Forbidden Place. Demelza remembered the rotten ghouls inside that terrible city, and her scalp tingled as she imagined the large entranceway ahead to be hiding more dead things within its shadows.

343

Oriken and Jalis ran ahead as Demelza slowed to scan her surroundings. She noted with concern the expansive patch of grassless dirt before the fortress, and, as she drew nearer, her heart rose to her throat as she spotted a white bone nestled within rubble and weeds at the base of the imposing building.

Sunlight poked through the edge of the rainclouds and sent a short wedge of brightness into the entranceway, enough to reveal black arches deeper inside. Demelza paused at threshold, then, hesitantly, stepped into the fortress. For a moment the only sound was the rain drumming against the dirt outside, and its faint echo hissing within the large, empty room. "I don't like it here," she said.

Jalis pulled her hood down and shook the rain from her cloak. "It's not the most inviting of places, but we won't be here long."

"It don't feel right. Feels like death. Can't you tell?"

Jalis glanced at the scattered debris strewn about the floor. "It's just your imagination. I saw no footprints outside and I see none in here. There are no restless corpses in Caer Valekha. That ordeal is behind us now."

"It's true." Oriken cast his packs into the corner and ran his hands through his soaking wet hair. "Even I can see this place is deserted, and that's saying something."

Demelza wasn't convinced. "Maybe it is. Maybe not. What about the bone outside?"

He looked at her blankly. "I didn't see any bones."

Jalis laughed. "Dee, you might have a keener sense of your surroundings than our journeyman freeblade here."

"Bah." Oriken gave a casual swipe of his hand and strode to slouch against the wall. "Hey, Demelza. Jalis reckons you're a 'blade in the making. You like the sound of that?"

"No."

"Can't blame you there."

She cast a moody stare through a darkened archway along the wall from Oriken. As her eyes grew accustomed to the gloom, she realised she was looking at a cluster of grey shapes upon the floor, at the far side of the small room. Catching her breath, she turned to Jalis. "Something's in there. I ain't imaginin' it."

Oriken pushed himself from the wall and approached the arch. He dipped beneath it and entered the gloom. Jalis followed, and Demelza shuffled along close behind her.

"We should just go," she whispered. "Please. I don't—"

"Ah, there," Oriken said. "Yeah, *he's* going nowhere. Not a scrap of flesh left on him."

Demelza peeked from behind Jalis to see Oriken crouched under a second arch that led into a deeper darkness. At his feet were the objects she'd spotted – a scattering of spindly bones in the shape of a human hand. "I said death were here, didn't I?" she whispered, clutching Jalis's arm.

"Yes," Jalis said softly. "But this one's not only been dead for decades, it's stayed that way. Nothing but bones here, Dee. Bones and a few spider webs."

"Gah!" Oriken lurched upright and cracked his head on the underside of the archway. "Damn it!"

Jalis laughed. "You never learn." She nudged past him and leaned into the shadows. Demelza stayed behind, scowling at the rest of the skeleton. The jawbone lay separate from the upper portion of the skull, which sat upright as if it had tried to bite into the stone and lost its teeth in the process. The ribs were empty of all but a few straggly webs, and the base of the spine hung over the edge of a square hole in the floor.

"Looks to be a latrine chamber," Oriken said, rubbing the top of his head. "The poor fellow must have snuffed it while taking a shit."

Jalis suppressed a sigh. "Orik, really? You think he stepped waist-deep into a sked-hole and lay down to die? It's not a toilet, it's an oubliette. You can see where the trapdoor used to be. Well, I'll be damned."

"What?"

"When this stronghold was abandoned, they must have left the prisoners down there to rot."

Demelza gasped.

"Sorry. Bad choice of words. This is where the worst of criminals are cast. Other than being tossed scraps of food, they're left to fend for themselves. Conditions in such a place must be appalling."

"If it's for bandit scum, then they probably deserve it," Oriken said.

"Perhaps, but not all. There are always the wrongly convicted, and the ones used as scapegoats for the rich and powerful. But it seems the prisoners here didn't just curl up and die when everyone left, unless someone removed the hatch from *this* side. If not, reaching it from within would have taken—"

Demelza released her hold on Jalis and crossed her arms in annoyance.

"Ah." Jalis nodded. "You're right. Let's leave it as a mystery."

"Put it on the list," Oriken murmured as he strode through to the entrance room. "May as well use this as a food stop," he called over his shoulder.

As they followed him into the brighter room, Jalis said, "We have nothing to burn."

"Dee can do her fire trick."

Demelza shook her head. "No."

"Huh? Why not?"

"I can make a fire to roast a rabbit or boil a fish, but I ain't no witchy cook. You wanna try eatin' summat I heated from the inside, go ahead."

"Hmph." Oriken's eyes misted over and he turned away. "I'll find us some firewood," he said as he strode towards the rear arches. "Must be some old furniture around here someplace."

CHAPTER THIRTY NINE
ENCOUNTER AT CAER VALEKHA

"Looks like we're staying the night," Jalis said despondently. She stared out at the sheet of rain beyond the wide entranceway, where a hail of droplets drummed into a large puddle that had formed a short distance from the open doors. Despite the downpour, the air was muggy, and she pinched the thin material of her chemise to pull it from her sticky skin. "I had hoped to have cleared the marsh before nightfall, and be well on our way to leaving this desolate region forever."

Beside her, Demelza sat cross-legged with her back against the front of a solid stone bench that ran the length of the wall between two rear archways. "What's it like?" she asked. "Where you live, I mean."

"Alder's Folly?" Jalis snorted softly. "It's serviceable. Truth be told, I miss the city life a little, but I think you might not like that. You've been accustomed to a village with a population of, what, three hundred strong? The Folly is a small town, and I'd guess it covers more area than Minnow's Beck. There are maybe a thousand people between residents and visitors, but you won't even glimpse half of those on most days. I think you'll be fine there until we head to Brancosi Bay."

"Is that a city? Like the Keeler?"

Jalis smiled. "Yes, it's a city, but nothing like Lachyla. The streets are bustling with people, especially on market day. Many parts of Brancosi are never quiet, even throughout the night, but there are tranquil places to be found. I like the ambience of the harbour; it reminds me of, well, let's just say it takes me back to a time before I was a freeblade."

"How old are you?"

Jalis cast her a sidelong glance, then grinned as she caught the girl's innocent gaze. "I will be 34 in the first week of Genopreta. I was a harvest baby – a blessing in a year of plentiful crop."

"Where's your mam?"

"My parents live a long way from here," she sighed, "back in my homeland of Sardaya. My father and I didn't get along so well, but that's by the by. From my childhood home you can see the towering peaks of Syen's Forge – a dead volcano and one of the largest mountains in the whole of the Vorinsian Arkh. Across its foothills, Gaspreau Citadel sprawls like a thick belt of black stone. It is a sight to behold. There are many places of wonder across Sosarra."

"What's a Sara?"

"So-*sar*-ra. It's the name of the continent we live upon. A stretch of the Broken Sea known as the Burning Channel divides Himaera from the rest of Sosarra."

Demelza's mouth hung agape. "But... you can't break a sea. And water don't burn. I tried it. It just boils."

"Ah, Dee, there is so much to tell you about the world, but I think that is enough for now. One thing at a time."

Demelza nodded. "I'm tired. I think I'll sleep a while."

"Do you want to go into another room?"

"No. Can I stay here? Near you?"

Jalis reached out and stroked Demelza's hair. "Of course you can."

Demelza pulled a blanket over and curled up on top of it, and Jalis waited for the girl's breathing to slow into a steady rhythm of sleep. Rising quietly to her feet, she stepped through one of the rear arches and listened to the faint sounds of Oriken breaking apart something he'd found for firewood. She closed her eyes and drew in a deep breath.

A few more days and we're home. But what is home? What will I do now?

Leaning within the archway, she turned her head to gaze across the large room and out into the rain, seeing the long pass between the hills but recalling another place from long ago. The sounds of men and women busying themselves with rigging and cargo echoed from her memory, along with the face of a certain ship's captain.

Where are you now, Celique? With a shake of her head, she laughed quietly to herself. *The things we reflect upon in these rare moments. I haven't spared you a thought in years. You became another lost friend.* She smiled sadly as she looked out at the grey, wet landscape.

"What the..." Something far along the wide vale caught her eye. Quickly she tiptoed through the debris to stand beside the entrance and peer out. "There," she whispered to herself. Somebody was on the heath. *Three*, she counted. *One closer, two further behind. No. No... Stars above, is that... Maros!*

She cast a quick glance at Demelza, but the girl was still sleeping soundly. Without bothering to don her cloak, she stepped out into the downpour and angled around the large puddle, then broke into a run along the pass.

———— • ————

Maros stopped in his tracks. He peered ahead at the distant, blurry figure. "Damn my eyes," he growled. "Can't see through this rain. Tell me that's not a lyakyn."

"It's no lyakyn, boss." Henwyn grinned from beneath his hood. "It's Jalis."

"Praise the rutting gods!" Maros stabbed a crutch triumphantly into the mud. "You found 'em! You damn well found 'em, Hen."

"In all fairness, you can't miss the tracks around here, nor that hulking brute of stone up yonder."

"Does this mean we can turn back now?" Wymar blew the rain from his lips. "I swear I've never been so wet."

Henwyn barked a laugh. "That's a matter of opinion."

The mill owner's retort was lost in the rain and the squelching mud as Maros swung onwards, his boots slipping but the crutches finding purchase with each loping step. Pain pulsed along his bad leg, worsened by the humidity, but he pushed onwards as Jalis rapidly closed the distance between them.

"Well there's a sight for sore eyes!" he bellowed, quirking a brow at the drenched chemise that clung to her torso.

She slowed to a walk and glanced down at herself, then flashed him a smile. "Not as welcoming a sight as your handsome face." Stopping before him, she looked up to meet his gaze. "Come here, you big brute." Wrapping her arms as best she could around his voluminous torso, she pressed up against him.

"Ah, lass," he said. "It's good to see you, too."

She released him and looked up to meet his gaze, shaking her head in bewilderment. "What on Verragos are you *doing* here?"

"Came to find you."

She looked past him and grinned at Henwyn, who gave her a wink. Glancing at Wymar, her brow furrowed in confusion. "Is that... Is that the fellow who runs the mill?"

"How refreshing," Wymar drawled. "I'm as famous in the Deadlands as in Caerheath. Nice to see you too, miss."

"This has to be a dream. I'm really back in Caer Valekha and dozing next to Demelza."

Maros frowned. "Who?"

"We're definitely here," Henwyn said. "Let me prove it." With his bow and extra pack cradled in one arm, he flung his other arm around her in a tight embrace. "I'm glad we've found you safe and well, Jalis."

"You think maybe we could get out of this rain?" Maros said. "The gammy leg's giving me serious gyp right now."

Jalis led them down the pass. As they walked, she glanced up at Maros. "I still can't believe you're here. What's going on, old friend?"

"I'll tell you when I'm sat down." Wincing with each step, he peered into the stronghold, spotting a small figure curled in repose at the rear of the shaded room. "What do we have here? Is that Dagra? He looks different somehow. Has he shaved his beard?" The expression on Jalis's face gave him pause. "What is it, lass?"

She drew a shaky breath and looked away. "Like you said, let's get inside first. Orik's deeper inside gathering fuel for a fire. Maros, that's not Dagra you can see, it's a girl – well, a young woman, but... Demelza has never seen a halfblood before."

He growled under his breath. "If I get called a monster one more time, I swear—"

"She's been through a lot," Jalis said. "Especially recently. Please go easy on her."

"Aye, well, I've a way with the young'uns... when they behave. Ain't I, Hen?"

"That you do. Not so much when they're screaming at you, though."

Jalis stepped into the fortress. Maros dipped in behind her, thankful that the ceiling within was at least high enough for him to stand upright. His gaze fell on the bench of stone blocks by the sleeping girl, and he began to make his way across.

"Maros, wait."

Hearing Jalis's warning tone, he stopped, and she walked over to kneel before the girl. A full minute passed as she spoke to her in hushed tones, then she shuffled aside as the girl rose to a sitting position, and Maros locked eyes with the usual wide-eyed, horror-stricken stare he'd become accustomed to.

"Stay calm, Dee," Jalis said, wrapping an arm around the girl's shoulders. "No one here will hurt you. And please try to not hurt them either. Okay?"

The girl gave a small nod as she gazed mutely at Maros, and her expression began to soften.

Hurt us? Maros suppressed a sigh. *This little slip of a thing?* He released his crutch and raised a hand in greeting. "Hello."

"Oh, for a world-class nursemaid," Henwyn muttered.

"I heard that!" The girl's eyes grew wider, and he stifled a sigh. "Er, I'm Maros. I, ah... It's nice to meet you." *Can we stop rutting around and get me sat the fuck down?*

The girl glanced at Jalis, then opened her mouth. For a moment nothing came out, then she blurted, "I'm the Melz— Uh, I'm the... Dee." She grinned nervously. "I'm Dee."

He forced himself to return the grin. "Well then, it's a real pleasure to meet you, little Dee." He gestured to the two men. "These fellers are Henwyn and Wymar."

Henwyn raised a hand and flashed her a smile, while Wymar grunted and gave a brief nod.

"Ma... ros," Dee said. "Hennin—"

"Hen*wyn*," Henwyn corrected, hiding an amused smile behind his hand.

349

"Hen*wyn*," Dee said, then turned her attention to the mill owner. "Why, Ma?"

"That'll do," Wymar sighed.

Maros looked across to Dee. "You mind if I sit by you over there?" he asked. The girl gave an ambiguous nod. *Ah, sod it*, he thought. *A nod's as good as a shake to a half-blind halfblood.*

As he swung his way across the room, Dee shifted closer to Jalis and watched his every step. He reached the bench and lowered himself to the stone with a long sigh.

"I ain't as young as I once was," he muttered.

Dee cast him a sidelong glance. "How old are you?"

"Ha! I'm 42, lass."

"That ain't so old. Ma Ina were 80 when she passed."

Maros glanced at Jalis. "That so?"

"Yep." Demelza gave an abrupt nod.

A bounding of footfalls resounded from deeper within the fortress, drowned for a moment by what sounded like pieces of wood clattering to the floor and the ring of steel as a sword was unsheathed. Moments later, Oriken burst into the room brandishing Dagra's old gladius. "I heard voi— What in the— Henwyn? Maros? *Wymar?*"

"That'll be us, then," Henwyn said, easing himself from the wall and striding over to clap a hand to Oriken's shoulder.

"Gah. Mind the wound." Oriken sheathed his sword and gave Henwyn a brief embrace, then looked to Maros. "What in the tenth level of the Pit are you all doing here?"

"More to the point," Maros growled, "as pleased as I am to see you, lad, why are you carrying Dagra's blade?" Oriken and Jalis exchanged grim glances. Maros eyed them, his fist tightening around a crutch. "What's going on? Where's Dagra?" When neither of them spoke, he climbed to his feet. "*Where is he? Damn it, answer me!*"

"He's gone," Jalis said from her spot on the floor. She clutched the girl closer to her. "He's dead, Maros." A tear spilled from her cheek. "Now, sit down before I sit you down."

"Excuse me," Oriken said tightly. "I've got some chairs to smash into pieces." He strode through the archway, and Henwyn hurried through after him.

Maros lowered himself to the bench and stared across the room. When Wymar cleared his throat, he swung his head to glare at the mill owner. "Say one shitty thing – just one – and I'll come over there and tear you in two." Wymar returned the glare, then stormed off into the fortress. Maros lowered his head. "I knew it. I knew something was wrong. I couldn't reach you in time thanks to this *fucking* leg, and now one of my boys is dead."

"It was no one's fault," Jalis said. She sniffed, and rubbed her hand over her eyes. "It just happened. You can't be angry at yourself or at anyone else."

"What was it? A lyakyn? A cravant? We saw the one you killed back at the burned-down house."

Jalis shook her head. "It was no creature, and no man nor woman. What took him was as unavoidable as bloatworm."

"I shouldn't have sent you down there. If I'd known it'd happened before…"

"This'un's smart," the girl said, nodding at Maros. "I told yous no good would come of it. Nowt goes in, an' nowt comes out. Mostly. An' *we* was the mostly, 'cause yous *did* come out. Me, too."

"Shush, Dee," Jalis whispered.

Maros scowled at the pair of them. "What's she talking about?"

"Nothing," Jalis gripped the girl's arm and looked squarely at Maros. "She was wandering near the Blighted City when we found her. She doesn't know how she got into Scapa Fell, but she's been there a long time. Remember what I told you outside. Please don't press her."

"Fine," he snapped, then sighed. "I'm sorry, lass. You don't deserve my ire – not you, not even Wymar. All right, I'll calm down. So what killed the lad? How did he go?"

"Spores are what killed him. Just spores. And he went quietly, with dignity, as befitting a man of his…"

"Stature?" Oriken strolled through the arch and dropped an armful of rotten wood beside the wall.

Maros tried to smile, but it wouldn't come. "He was a short'un, wasn't he?"

"Yeah." Oriken's lip twitched. "He was. But his heart was as big as yours."

Maros ate in silence, as did everyone but Henwyn and Jalis who chatted quietly by the entrance. Demelza sat cross-legged on a blanket on the stone floor, flicking the occasional glance at one person or another and managing to look both bored and interested at the same time. Wymar sat a short distance from her, nibbling the last strips of flesh from a nargut bone. In the centre of the room, the embers of a fire filled the place with a wan glow and a haze of musty smoke, while beyond the open doors the rainclouds had cleared and the evening sun behind the fortress cast a long shadow down the pass. Stuffing the last chunk of meat into his mouth, Maros sucked the grease from his fingers and chewed slowly, an image of Dagra etched into the corner of his mind.

I was right, he thought. *They were in danger, but Dagra was dead no matter what, and Jalis and Oriken were on their way home with or without me. I made no difference.* He sniffed disdainfully. *Some leader I am.*

Beside him on the bench, Oriken had finished his scant meal and was sat with a stoic expression, his usual stubble grown to a short beard as if in memory of his lost friend. Gone was the carefree nonchalance, replaced with a

351

hard edge borne of a hard life-lesson, but Maros knew how these things panned out – the old cliché was tried and true that time closed most wounds, and that the typical Oriken would surface once more. As for Jalis, he'd been close to her for more than a decade and could tell when a deeper trouble was on her mind beyond what was known; now was one of those times. She and Oriken were holding something back. He's seen the glances between them, and at the girl Demelza.

So be it, he thought. *We all have our secrets.* Maros looked across to Oriken, at the two swords on his belt. "So," he said, trying to sound casual. "It's good to see he bequeathed you his blade."

"Hm? Oh. Yeah." Oriken glanced down at Dagra's gladius in its battered scabbard, ignoring the sword at his other hip, gleaming where it showed between the freshly-wrapped hide.

"Sturdy weapon, that," Maros said. "Not enough reach for my liking, but I reckon there's something to be said for how they used to make 'em. Sabres don't always cut it, do they?"

"No, I suppose they don't."

"What happened to yours, by the way?"

Oriken grunted. After a moment, he said, "Damned thing broke. Guess it wasn't tough enough."

Maros nodded slowly. "Must'a been cheap steel. Want to tell me about your second blade?"

Oriken stared into the fire's embers and shrugged. "Just a lucky find. Small bonus on top of fulfilling the contract."

"A lucky find indeed. Freshly wrapped bindings, a gleaming crossguard, and, if I'm not mistaken, a chunk of thunderglass in the pommel. Was it wielded by the stone golem you fought?"

"Huh?" Oriken turned to him sharply.

"I'm just sayin'. Quite the bruises you got on your face there. Can't imagine any creature of the heath putting those on you. Unless it was Jalis. Did you give her one too many lewd remarks, eh? Ah, never mind me. You don't wanna talk, that's fine."

Oriken blinked. "A lot has changed. Too much. And right now it don't look like we gained more than we lost. It feels like a lifelong story's reaching its end before the teller's left town."

"Ain't nothin' over till you say it is, lad."

"Yeah? But who decides what comes next? It's not like it's all up to me."

"Well then. Best you *make* it up to you. Best you *become* the teller, and weave the rest of the tale for yourself."

Maros watched as Wymar cast the cleaned bone into the fire, and Demelza frowned as it crackled within the ashes. The mill owner muttered to himself as he looked across at the entranceway, then, with a gasp, his eyes widened. "Arrows!" he yelled, then threw himself onto Demelza.

352

Agony flared up Maros's bad leg. He stared down to see a wooden shaft jutting from his shin. Fury welled inside him as the room burst into action – Oriken dashing from the bench to assist Jalis in heaving the doors closed; Henwyn staggering to the side with an arrow lodged through his forearm; Demelza, pale with shock as Wymar lay sprawled atop her – then the fury escaped and Maros launched to his feet with a roar that echoed through the fortress.

Snatching hold of a crutch and taking up his greatsword, he limped straight through the hot ashes to the entrance as Oriken slammed an iron bar over the doors' brackets.

"Let me pass!" Maros growled, but Jalis stood firmly before the doors as Oriken hurried away to assist Henwyn.

"There are three wounded," Jalis said, "an unknown number of attackers outside, and Demelza is under my protection. You think I'll let you run out to your death? For what?"

"Damn it, Jalis!" He stabbed his sword onto the floor, gritting his teeth as pain surged anew up his leg. "Who's out there? I thought this region was deserted."

"Not entirely. I'm stepping away from the doors now. Don't you dare open them, Maros. This isn't about you."

He glared at her, but nodded, and she ran across to where Demelza now stood shaking beside the prone Wymar. Another volley of arrows thudded into the doors as Maros glanced to Henwyn.

The veteran freeblade's features were drawn as he held his arm before him. "Bodkins," he gasped, nodding to the cylindrical, pointed arrowhead. "Just as fucking well." He looked Oriken in the eye. "Do it." Oriken gripped the shaft and slid it forwards out of Henwyn's arm. As the feathered flights passed through the exit wound, Henwyn released his breath and pressed his forearm to his belly. "Your turn, boss."

Maros scowled at his leg and leaned his sword against the door, his eye on Jalis as she crouched beside Wymar. The mill owner lay on his back, an arrow protruding from between his ribs.

That's a killing wound, Maros thought. He snatched at the shaft in his leg and ripped it out with a rising growl. "*I'm gonna destroy whoever's out there!*" he roared, turning and slamming his palms on the doors. "*I'm gonna tear your fucking heads off, one by one!*"

"That's unlikely," someone called from outside. "You're outnumbered! There are twenty six men out here, and only three of you!"

"And your giant," a second voice added. "Seen him through the doors. Couldn't miss a brute like that."

"There's nowhere to run, outlanders!" the first voice called. "We'll make sure you pay for what you did to ours!"

Maros glowered and glanced sharply back at Jalis.

"You're welcome to take us on," Jalis called from beside Wymar, "but you should know that we'll cut down at least half of you before we fall."

"Ha! I'd like to see you succeed where a chapel full of ghouls failed! Your heads will mark the Founding Oak alongside the others!"

"What in the blistering Pit is happening here?" Maros demanded.

"Onwin," Demelza said. "The fat hunter."

"*Him?*" Oriken spat. "These fuckers are beginning to get on my fruits. Hey, peasant! I knocked you senseless once already. I should've put an end to you there and then!" Grabbing the mini crossbow from atop their gear, he stepped up beside a murder hole a few yards along from the door and glanced through the narrow gap, flinching away as an arrow ricocheted from the stones outside. With a curse, he poked the crossbow through the gap and squeezed the trigger. The string twanged and a cry rang out. "You like that? There's plenty more where that one came from!" He looked to Jalis and shrugged as fists pounded upon the doors and a commotion rose among the attackers.

"They don't know about Henwyn and Wymar," Jalis said quietly, rising from Wymar's side. "Nor Dee. But they have the advantage of bows. We have one between us, and the crossbow is down to three bolts. Ranged combat is out of the question against so many opponents in close proximity. We need to remove their advantage." She glanced at each of the freeblades. "How?"

Oriken gestured to Demelza, but the girl shook her head.

"I can't," she said. "They're my people. They didn't all hate me. There might be some nice ones out there."

"My men have returned from checking the perimeter!" Onwin called. "There are no other doors, outlanders! You're trapped, like birds in a coop!"

"They'll kill us all," Oriken told Demelza. "In here, we're useless. Out there, time is on their side."

"Wait," Jalis said. "Birds. That's it. Dee, can you focus on the fletchings of their arrows? With their ranged attack taken away, we'd be a step towards levelling the field."

"Maybe." Demelza drew a breath. "Or I could try for the bowstrings."

"Even better," Jalis said. "It doesn't give us much, but it's better than nothing."

———— • ————

Ellidar stepped wearily from the walkway of sunken trees and bent to study the many tracks in the wet grass. This far from the Mother his senses were diminished, and the isolation from the collective consciousness felt at once both liberating and soul-destroying.

I'm close to mortal here, and thereby close to death, he thought with more than a touch of trepidation.

He scanned ahead to where the tracks veered to the west, and nodded grimly to himself; keeping his eyes on the black hills, he crept forwards until the crenellated edge of the fortress came into view, silhouetted against the deep evening sky.

Caer Valekha, he thought. His lips curled in a mirthless smile. *Once a mighty stronghold of the Lachylan Kingdom*, he thought, *now a forgotten shell. And perhaps deservingly so. How fitting that this is where it should end.*

A little further on and the front of the fortress was cast in a lambent light by the flames of a dozen torches, revealing twice as many figures standing before the doors. Hope surged within him that the lady Jalis and her companion Oriken had secured themselves inside.

A siege, then. So be it. Let the endgame commence.

Backing out of sight, he ran for the hill at the south side of the pass, keeping to the grasses and away from the slick mud to reduce the sound of his footfalls. Though his ringmail jingled softly, he was confident it could not be heard by the large group over the crackle of their torches and the babble of the night's hidden creatures. Within minutes the ground began to rise steeply, and he slowed to stride onto the hillside and meander through the trees and shrubs until he neared the crest of the hill.

Dropping to a crouch, he secured his longsword between arm and torso before wending his way around to the hill's north face. With the front of the stronghold stretching along his line of sight, he inched down through the shrubbery. Reaching level ground, he set himself behind a cluster of low bushes and peered through the gaps at the nearby mob of villagers. White-knuckled fists clutched bows, cudgels and long knives, and a murmur of voices drifted to his hiding place; with his centuries of observing others, he detected a plethora of emotions from the besiegers – among them hatred, exuberance, resolve, and fear-tinged bravado. He could use those against them, and perhaps turn a number of them away, but not the majority. Whatever the outcome, it was going to be bloody.

And that also means for me, he thought, acknowledging the irony that the attackers were not alone in their fear and resolve.

As he watched and listened, a commotion began among the group, and Ellidar stared in wonder as a flame wisped into life upon the string of the nearest man's bow. The flame licked its way higher, and the villager cast his bow to the ground. "Gods forfend!" he cried. "Me bow's on fire!"

"Witch magic!" another man shouted.

"Demons!" a third declared, and Ellidar frowned in familiarity at the speaker's paunched middle and flaccid, jowly features. "You don't scare us, outlanders!" he called through the doors. "Not you, not your giant, and not your witchery!"

Witch? Giant? What tricks does the lady Jalis have up her sleeve?

355

"You will not find victory here!" the man continued. "If you surrender now, I promise your deaths will be swift!"

"Not on my watch." Ellidar rose from the foliage, his sword at rest over his shoulder, and the gathering turned to face him in stunned silence. Several of the men raised their bows, only to cast them away as, one by one, the strings caught fire. As he strode towards them, a single arrow streamed through the group and grazed past his pauldron. "Stay your hands and live," he said, "or continue this foolishness and die."

"Oh, aye? What's this, then?"

He came to a stop at the edge of the group and cast a cool look upon the speaker. "Ah yes, now I know you, *Onwin* – the coward who trembled within a loft and put an arrow through a defenceless man's eye. A good shot, I'll give you that much. But how do you fare with a blade?" He raised his voice so the whole mob could hear, and, he hoped, Jalis and Oriken. "I have a message for you from an acquaintance of mine. His name is Sabrian. Your ancestors murdered his friends and placed their heads upon your oak. He will be greatly displeased if you kill the outlanders he has come to know as friends, and you should all know that I share his sentiment."

Onwin sneered. "Is that so? You have me at a disadvantage, stranger. I like to know the names of the outlanders I kill."

"You have never killed an outlander, *hunter*, and that will not change today. I am Ellidar, knight-paladin of Valsana, guardmaster of Castle Lachyla, sworn sword to King Mallak Ammenfar, and ally of the worthy. You and yours"—he slid the longsword from atop his shoulder—"are not among the worthy. Retreat now and return to your village."

"You would rob us of our vengeance, would you?" Onwin spat. "Even while a Servant of the Slain carries our First Warder away?"

"They killed our people!" one of the villagers exclaimed.

Ellidar shook his head. "They did not."

"They'll bring armies from the north!" another called from the rear.

"This is the brabbling of fools," Ellidar said tiredly. "Fools who do not want to listen. By my reckoning, fools who wish to die."

"We won't let them walk away from here," Onwin warned.

Ellidar chuckled. "Oh, come now, hunter. Drop the mask of bravery. The cowardice you displayed in the city suits you much better." He drew a breath and addressed the whole group. "You have been misinformed. Stop this and go back to your homes or follow this man and die."

A mixture of doubt and resoluteness passed among the faces of the villagers, but none spoke or moved except to clutch their weapons tighter.

"We have no choice," Onwin said.

"You *had* a choice." Ellidar gripped his longsword in both hands. "You just made it." He charged. The nearest man raised his club. Ellidar swiped the longsword and smashed the weapon from its wielder's grip. With a backslash, he tore the man's throat open. As he turned to the next man, he flicked a glance at Onwin and noted with disdain how the fat hunter backed away to the rear of the group.

The doors to the stronghold scraped inwards, causing all heads to turn as a man of considerable height and girth stepped over the threshold, the muscles of his arms like thick cords of steel as he brandished a wooden crutch in one hand and a greatsword in the other. The weapon dwarfed Ellidar's own by a full foot.

"Not too late to join the fray, am I?" the giant bellowed.

Oriken stepped into view beside him, the blade Ammenfar in one hand and a second gladius in the other. Then Jalis emerged with her daggers at the ready.

Ellidar grinned. "The more, the merrier!" he called, then loosed a battle-cry and tore into the mob.

Demelza stood behind Maros, clutching Henwyn's longbow with an arrow nocked to the string. The wounded bowman stayed to the rear of the room, attending the one who had taken an arrow to save Demelza's life. As her friends stepped into the battle, she raised the bow and pulled back on the string.

Shoot any who try to enter, Jalis had instructed, and although there were faces within the group who had never caused her harm or spoken to her with malice, she intended to do as Jalis said.

She watched the giant limp among the villagers, his huge sword slicing left and right, catching some of the men and spreading others away to be torn into by the one in the shiny clothes. Oriken's two swords were a whir as he hacked and stabbed, swiped and deflected the blows aimed at him. Jalis ran among the throng, seeming almost to dance as she glided up behind one hunter and drew her silver blade across his neck, then leaped away from a slashing dagger and ducked beneath a club to stab her black blade into another hunter's guts.

Clubs smashed into the shiny one, knives slashed across the giant, and the clash of metal rang out as Oriken swatted his wide swords against one long hunting knife after another. Demelza cried silently as the numbers of her fellow villagers dropped, and Jalis, Oriken, Maros and their new friend bore wound after wound.

She counted the remaining villagers. *Fifteen. Fourteen…* Maros stumbled and dropped to one knee with a roar that was cut short as a club smashed into his face. Releasing his weapon and crutch, he grabbed his attacker and half-rose, then sank back down to slam the man's spine over his knee. Demelza gasped as a distinct *snap* resounded through the clash of weapons and the groans of the dying. Maros rose once more, punching a villager who dared approach him and snatching up his huge sword. Jalis sprinted behind the giant and leaped towards the backs of two men fighting Oriken. As she landed, her daggers jabbed into their sides, and from out of nowhere Onwin stepped up behind her, his hunting blade flashing for her head.

"No!" Demelza screamed, but Oriken's sword was already smashing into the hunter's weapon to send it flying from his grasp. Onwin turned and ran, dodging around the shiny man as his sword plunged into another villager's middle.

Demelza's heart was pounding as she counted again. *Seven, six...*, Almost as one, the remaining hunters and other villagers cast their weapons to the ground and held their hands out for mercy. Demelza stepped out into the mud. Oriken glanced her way as she ran past him and sprinted for Onwin. Her shoes slid in the mud, but she gained ground with each step.

"Onwin!" she shouted. Dropping to a knee, she raised the bow.

He glanced back, then stopped and turned fully around as fury spread over his face. "You! I should have—"

"But you didn't," she said, and her arrow sank into his heart. Onwin stared dumbly from her to the arrow, then pitched to the mud. She rose, her whole body trembling as she walked back to her friends, stepping around the fallen men.

"You didn't use your magic," Jalis said.

"No." Her voice quivered. She glanced back at the lumpy shape with the arrow sticking from it as if pointing to the stars. "He's still dead though, ain't he?"

Oriken gritted his teeth against the pain of his fresh wounds. Staggering to the fortress wall, he leaned against it. "Well done, Dee," he gasped.

"Traitor," one of the downed men spat, casting Demelza a seething look.

"That's enough from you," Maros rumbled. Limping across, he plunged his greatsword deep into the man's torso and looked around at the remaining four survivors. "Anyone else have any prevailing quibbles they're just *dying* to get off their chests? No? I take it you all want to live, then?" He hobbled over to one man, who stared up at him defiantly. "Give me one good reason why I should grant you that wish?"

"Because they have lain down their arms." Ellidar's voice rang across the grim arena. "Show them mercy, good jotunn. There is more at stake here than mere slaughter." As the knight angled around the bodies, he closed his eyes and staggered but righted himself, pressing a hand to a bloody patch on his side between the silver rings of mail.

Maros issued a low growl. Narrowing his eyes at the middle-aged villager before him, he said, "What's your name, feller?"

"Dal Ebran."

"And why'd you come to kill us, Dal Ebran?"

"My son."

"Your son's one o' these, is he?" Maros gestured around the fallen men.

Dal shook his head. "He... Tan was volunteered for the mission to return the stone. He never came home."

Oriken shared a glance with Jalis, and together they crossed to the man. "I don't recognise the name," Oriken said. "And we sure as shit didn't kill your son. Didn't kill any of you, for that matter, until now. So what's your problem?"

Dal turned to Demelza. "I don't know why you're here, but you were with my boy in that place. Onwin said he was killed by the... by your companions. Please, if you know something of him—"

"I don't know nowt," she said. "I never not liked Tan. He weren't nasty to me. He were walkin' behind me, then, when I looked back, he were gone. If my friends say they never killed him, then they never killed him."

"I may know something of your son," Ellidar said, "and I may be able to reunite you with him. But you will have to do something for me in return."

"Anything."

"Go with me to the city."

Dal eyed him warily. "Is that all? And you say I will see Tan alive again?"

Ellidar inclined his head. "That is my hope. But I cannot say for certain. What I can say is this: Whether alive or... something other, I will ensure you speak with him again. And, Valsana be willing, he will return with you to your village."

"Why would you do this for me, after all this bloodshed?"

"Because I am a man of honour. And because... I will soon be dead. I need you to ensure I live again."

Dal blinked. "Have you turned my son into one of you?"

"I have done nothing to him. But another may have, which is why we must not tarry." Ellidar looked pointedly at him. "Dal Ebran, I will undoubtedly fall on the journey home, and for you to have any chance of seeing your son again, you must drag me the rest of the way. Do you agree to this?"

Dal gave an abrupt nod. "I do."

"And, if we extend mercy to your three acquaintances here, will you ensure that their hatred and fear does not subvert your promise?"

"You have my word in the name of the goddess, and in the name of my boy."

Ellidar nodded. "Take your men and wait by the wall. No harm will come to any of you." He looked to Maros. "Is this well, friend?"

Maros grunted. "It's anything *but* fucking well. Truth be told, I don't have much of a clue what any of you are talking about"—he glanced at Jalis—"and I reckon I ain't likely to find out, either, so have at it."

Ellidar gestured for the villagers to approach the fortress wall. As they did so, he looked to Jalis and his chiselled features cracked into a smile. "It is good to see you, lady. Very good indeed."

"You too. If not for you and Maros showing up, Oriken, Demelza and I would likely be three more bodies to join the skeleton within the fortress."

The knight's brow furrowed, then he shook his head. "No matter. You are safe, and all is well with the world."

"Not all," Wymar called weakly from within the fortress as he raised a hand for their attention. "Man dying in here, you sons of bitches."

"He saved me," Demelza said. "Don't let him die."

Oriken took a lit torch from the wall and made his way into the room, with Maros following behind.

Beside Wymar, Henwyn rose from a squat and shook his head. "I stopped his bleeding as best I could," he told them, gingerly touching the bloody bandage around his own forearm. "It's all we can do. The arrow's popped a lung." He glanced down at the ashen-faced mill owner. "I'm sorry, Wymar."

"Fuck yourself, freebl—" Wymar broke into a cough, and pink blood frothed at his lips.

"Perhaps there *is* a way." Jalis said from the entrance, turning a pointed look on Ellidar.

The knight regarded her for a long moment, then drew a breath and approached Wymar. "What skills can you offer a community?" he asked.

The mill owner glared at him. "Are you joking? I'm close to death here, and you—" Another bout of coughing wracked his frame. When he was finished, he glanced questioningly at Maros.

"Don't ask *me*," Maros said. "I'm just a barman and a quill-scratcher."

Jalis dropped to her haunches beside the dying man, her lips pursed in consideration. "Wymar, if there was a chance you could live, but there were severe restrictions, would you take it?"

"Damned right I would."

She nodded and looked up at Ellidar. "If it wasn't for this man, I'm guessing that Maros and Henwyn wouldn't have reached Caer Valekha when they did. If not for Wymar, it would be Demelza who lay there dying instead. And, not to undermine your own arrival – for which we're all very grateful – but, in a way, he also saved the lives of Oriken and I."

Ellidar smiled. "That is all I need to know." To the mill owner he said, "Will you join me?"

"Doesn't sound like I have much choice. Lead the way." He closed his eyes and drew several shallow breaths. "Tavernmaster?"

"Aye."

"You're not... a total arsehole, after all," Wymar rasped. "You can settle your debt... at a later date."

"That's mighty kind of you, friend."

"What about me?" Henwyn asked.

Wymar barked a weak laugh. "You? You're still a c—"

"Come now, miller," Henwyn chided. "There are ladies present. And do you really want to end on that note?"

"I suppose not." Wymar's eyes cracked open to regard Henwyn. "You're a gobshite, but I thank you for doing what you could. And you can take that... or leave it."

Henwyn nodded. "I'll take it."

"One more thing," Wymar said to Maros. "My son'll mind the mill, but you have my blessings to tell him... to get rid of that other gobshite, Renfrey. The man's a drunkard and an ingrate."

Maros grinned. "With pleasure."

Wymar closed his eyes again and, after a moment, Demelza knelt and tapped him on the shoulder. He cracked one eye open and gave her a weak nod.

"Thank you," she whispered.

"Any time, girl. Any..."

Oriken passed the torch to Henwyn and gently brought Dee to her feet. As the mill owner's last breath rattled from his body, she placed her head on Oriken's chest. Pausing only briefly, he put his arm around her shoulders and looked at Ellidar. "Well," he sighed, "we outlanders didn't win any popularity votes down here, did we?"

"On the contrary. You won the gratitude of many of the cityfolk, myself included." The knight raised an eyebrow at Jalis. "Both of you. *And* Dagra."

She smiled. "Thank you. We were thieves in your home and you showed us civility. Had we realised..." Her brow furrowed, and she said, "But how did you know they were heading to kill us?"

"The one with the axe and bow," Ellidar said. "Wayland chose to return, as Gorven predicted. He waited only for his friend to die. There is gallantry in that."

Demelza lifted her face from Oriken's chest. "Wayland?"

The knight inclined his head. "Yes, lady. He lives."

She rubbed her eye. "I'm glad. Will you see him?"

"I will."

"Tell him I'm safe. That's all he wanted."

The knight touched a fist to his chest. "On my honour."

Oriken cleared his throat. "Listen. I'm sorry about all I said back in the castle. Emotions were sort of high."

Ellidar inclined his head, then pointed to the sword on Oriken's hip. "You have accepted a charge as meaningful as my own. The blade Ammenfar contains the essence of Mallak, the last king of Lachyla."

Oriken blanched. "Really?"

The knight cast him a flat look. "Figuratively."

"Ah."

Turning to the open doors, Ellidar called for Dal Ebran. A moment later, the villager stepped to the entrance. "You may tell your companions to enter and carry this one outside," Ellidar said, gesturing to the dead miller. "He will accompany us."

Dal's face was stony, but he gestured for his companions, and together they carried Wymar's body from the fortress.

Oriken strode to the corner and snatched up his packs, wincing as he slung them over his shoulder. "You can forget it if you think I'm staying here tonight," he told no one in particular. Stepping outside, he caught a seething look from one of the villagers – a bearded fellow with blood covering half of his face, who looked him squarely in the eye.

"Do us all one favour," the man said. "Don't come back this way. Not ever."

"That's a promise I can't and won't make, but one thing I *will* say is that I'll never set foot in your village. I'd rather enter a city filled with the undead than a backwater hovel filled with misinformed, fear-mongering, murderous peasants."

The man glowered, but Dal Ebran placed a hand on his arm and said to Oriken, "You might have the right of it. Aye, you might."

One of the other villagers sighed disconsolately as he gazed at the ground. "Only came this way to head north," he muttered. "An' I weren't the only one."

"Then you joined the wrong fight," Oriken said. "Don't look to me for sympathy."

The man said nothing.

"Hm." Jalis eyed the villagers, then walked into their midst. "There is no place for any of you beyond Scapa Fell," she said, casting a pointed glance at each of them before gesturing to Maros. "The northlands are filled with these beasts – these behemoths of war – and I promise you, any man – or woman – who dares to venture beyond this fortress will be captured by the armies of the giants, and their suffering"—she spun to face the bearded villager—"will be legendary."

Her words were met with icy silence.

"Leave," Ellidar told them. "I will join you momentarily."

The four villagers hefted Wymar's body and, despite their burden, set off at a brisk pace down the pass, eager to leave – a sentiment with which Oriken could whole-heartedly agree.

"Well then, my friends." Ellidar rested his longsword over his shoulder. "Time to depart. I'm afraid I must shortly take a brief leave of absence from my otherwise unending watch, and I would like to be as close to the city as possible before that happens. Please try to stay clear of trouble. I have a second death to die, and a third life to begin with clearing a mineshaft, and frankly I'm not sure which I look forward to the least."

Oriken hooked a thumb behind his belt. "No offence to you," he said, "nor to... anyone else down there, but some things ought to *stay* buried."

The knight's nod was barely perceptible. He locked eyes with each of them in turn, leaving Jalis until last. "My lady."

Jalis approached and took him by the shoulders, rose to her tiptoes and gently kissed his cheek. She took a step backwards and affected a brief curtsy. "My knight-paladin."

With a sad smile, Ellidar's eyes lingered on her a moment. Then he turned and walked away, back to the Blighted City.

CHAPTER FORTY
ONE MAN'S FOLLY

Oriken looked long at the sign above the Lonely Peddler's saloon doors, basking in the familiarity of the safe haven he'd called home for the past few years. The pains from his various wounds had faded with each day they'd drawn closer to the Folly, but still he was weary beyond measure and he knew that much of it was not a fatigue of the body but of the soul – or whatever within him passed for one.

Tracing his eyes from the tavern's wooden sign to the brass plaque immediately below it, he regarded the crossed blades of the guild crest as it swung gently in the noon breeze, and a leaden feeling squeezed at his core. The skirmish with the villagers was nothing a seasoned freeblade wasn't accustomed to, but their opponents were usually a gang of morally degenerate bandits, not a gaggle of paranoid peasants. Never had he felt so despised by so many, and for no good reason. Still, what was done was done, and he'd soon be taking his turn at soaking his battle wounds in the tavern's hot tub.

He wandered to the fence, leaned against it and regarded his companions: Maros, hunched on his crutches with Jalis standing under his shadow as they talked; Demelza, staring across the way at the surrounding buildings in quiet wonder; and Henwyn, standing alone with his hand clasped over his wounded forearm, a distant and serious look on his face.

He's a good man, Oriken thought. *And a fine freeblade. I'm not the only one among us who lost a friend out there. I'm just the only one who's experienced it for the first time. I guess it happens to us all eventually, except for those who die early.*

Noticing Oriken looking his way, Henwyn wandered across to join him. "Boss says the bar's closed this evening. I'll be bringing the lads and lasses from the guildhouse to pay our respects to Dagra, and to get pissed in his name. No watered wine for me tonight." He paused to clear his throat. "I know you were closer to Dagra than the rest of us, and I know how hard it'll still be hitting you. I don't know all what went on down there—" He held his hand up as Oriken's expression changed. "No, and I don't need to know. I heard enough what was said at the fortress, and truth is I can't tell whether I missed out on the adventure of a lifetime or skirted the fringes of a nightmare."

"Perhaps a little of both," Oriken said.

Henwyn lowered his voice. "Jalis told me her decision to hang up her blades, so I reckon it must've been the straw to break the mule's back. Truth be told, I couldn't blame anyone for making that choice. As for me?" He shrugged. "I can't imagine another life, so I'd best be getting myself straight to the apothecary to have this wound looked at. But you, I'm guessing you're considering your own future right now; whatever you choose, you'll be one of us. Once a freeblade, always a freeblade."

Oriken considered the oft-spoken phrase. "I need to figure a few things out, but, whatever I do, these blades are staying right at my sides."

Henwyn nodded and clasped Oriken's arm. "Good man. See you tonight." Gathering his belongings, he glanced across to Maros and Jalis, touching his fist to his forehead in mock salute as he trudged wearily away.

The saloon doors creaked open and Luthan stepped through, whipped a towel before him and folded it into two. Several serving girls followed him out and filled their arms with the journey baggage. Watching them filter back into the common room, Luthan folded the towel once more and tucked it into his apron pocket. Turning his ice-blue eyes on the freeblades and Demelza, he regarded each of them, pausing on the girl only briefly before turning a composed look on Maros.

"I'm pleased to see the three of you return in one piece," he said, and Oriken noted the tactful acknowledgement of Dagra's absence; the news had clearly already spread.

"Luthan," Maros said, "if the guild handed out medals, I'd be pinning one to your hat right now. If it weren't for your suggestion, I'd not have found these two in time." He rested a hand over the chef's shoulder. "You should join us at Dagra's send-off this evening. He'd be glad to know you were there."

"Ah, boss…" A flicker of hesitation touched Luthan's features. "I wouldn't want to presume—"

"Nonsense. I'll hear no protestations out of you, man. You may not be a freeblade, but you're one of us nonetheless. Where it counts." He touched a fist to his chest. "Any problems while I was gone?"

Luthan shook his head. "Only Renfrey, once, but young Leaf turfed him out almost as spectacularly as you did."

Maros raised an eyebrow. "Is that so? Where's she now?"

"On her way to see you, I shouldn't doubt. She has news from headquarters."

"Do you know it?"

"Aye. But I'll let her be the one to relay it to you."

365

Maros grunted. "As it should be. You've done a fine job keeping the place in check in my stead. In the absence of a medal, I might have to promote you to bar supervisor."

The chef chuckled. "That wouldn't be a promotion. Separate a cook from his kitchen and you'll be witnessing an uprising within three meals."

"Hmph. This land don't need another o' those any time soon. Listen, there'll be no patrons tonight, and that means no evening meal. No breakfast neither, other than for the three of us"—he hitched a thumb at Jalis and Oriken—"plus the guests. How many do we have?"

"I'm sorry to say we've none right now, boss."

"Good! In that case, I'll settle for a simple bowl of slop in the morning."

"Careful, boss. There's no slop made here."

"There is when I'm making it. Take the rest of the day off, Luth. Full pay. You've earned it. Back to business as usual with lunch tomorrow. I've no doubt the kitchen's pristine, and the girls can keep the housekeeping ticking over."

Luthan inclined his head in gratitude. "I suppose there's no harm in neglecting a kitchen of its chef for *two* meals." With an amiable look that encompassed all of them, including Demelza, he added, "I'd be honoured to attend tonight." He stepped to the doors. "I'll see to a few things before I leave…"

"Luthan," Maros rumbled, and the chef paused. "What part of 'take the rest of the day off' did you not understand?"

With his back to them, Luthan quietly chuckled, then he turned and whipped the towel from his apron and shoved it into Maros's hand. "See you at the send-off, boss." With a nod to Jalis and Oriken, and a wink to Demelza, he strolled from the tavern grounds and onto the hard-packed dirt of the street.

Oriken watched him walk away, smiling to himself at the sight of the chef's apron and hat being the cleanest, whitest parts of the whole damned townscape.

"He'd have made a fine freeblade," Maros commented. "Glad he didn't go that way, though; the world could ruin a man like Luthan if it pushed him in the wrong direction."

"Maybe Dagra took the wrong path," Oriken said distantly. "He could've been a priest, wielding a book instead of a blade."

"He took the right path," Jalis said. "Come on, let's get inside." As Maros swung a door open for them, Jalis placed an arm around Oriken, the other around Demelza, and they stepped into the tavern.

Maros stood before the bar, planted the tip of his greatsword between his feet and rested his hands on the pommel. Lifting his eyes to the bastard sword nestled in its housings on the overhang above the service counter, he regarded the empty brackets to either side where, other than the occasional sharpen and polish, the greatsword had hung untouched for almost a year. The bastard sword looked lonely, brooding over its bigger brother's absence.

"Time to get you reunited, methinks," he muttered, hefting the greatsword and setting it in place. *Gods, I might one day be crossing my crutches up there as well. Hmm... That gives me an idea. But first things first.* He glanced to his ruined leg, now worsened by the hole from the peasant's arrow. "You've given me enough gyp for one lifetime," he told it. "Tomorrow you're coming off, and I'll sell the rutting bones; I hear there's a niche market for 'em in the Bay."

With a sigh, he glanced over to where Jalis sat with Oriken and the little one they'd picked up on their travels. *Curious lass. Turned up out of nowhere, did she? Wandering around in the Deadlands, no family, no home?* He shook his head and loosed a snort. It was an unlikely story, but not implausible. Still, if the girl had a secret, then that was that; who didn't, these days?

The saloon doors swished, and he turned to see Jerrick shuffling into the common room. One of the serving girls stepped out of the kitchen and glanced questioningly to Maros. He nodded. "Aye, Diela, you can serve this one. No others, though."

"Redanchor, Jerrick?" Diela called as the elderly fellow made his slow way to the bar.

"What's that you say?" Jerrick croaked.

"*Redanchor?*"

"Aye. Aye, that'll do."

"Sit yourself down. I'll bring it across."

He paused in mid-shuffle. "Why so? Someone upset you?"

Maros bit back a laugh. "You pour, lass. I'll see to it. Jerrick!" He gave the grizzled old man a cordial smile and motioned to a table along the side wall. Jerrick nodded and wandered over to take a seat, and Maros accepted the freshly-poured cup of ale from Diela. Limping across, he placed it on the table. "There you go, old timer."

"Thankin' ye." Jerrick smacked his lips. "Thankin' ye kindly."

Returning to the bar, Maros leaned over the counter and grabbed his high-stool, then hobbled across to join Jalis, Oriken and Demelza. As he eased himself onto the seat, Oriken looked up from his ale to meet his gaze.

"You doing all right, lad?"

"Yeah. Right enough."

Maros regarded him a moment longer, then turned to Jalis. "And you, lass? You sure you won't change your mind?"

She shook her head. "It's made, my friend. I've been at this game for long enough, and for one loss too many."

He could feel the girl Demelza staring at him. Casting her a sidelong glance in imitation of what he'd seen her do plenty of times over the last days, he completed the motion and turned to face her, his mouth widening to a grin. She recoiled, but only slightly, and gave him a nervous smile in return. "You're still not used to me, are you?" he said. "You know, halfbloods like me ain't so unheard of around these parts, they just ain't all quite so dashing as me."

Demelza frowned. "I don't follow."

"Reckon it must be a thing down there in the Caerheath sticks"—he eyed her levelly—"since we'll presume, for the record, that that's where you're from. Demelza of Dulèth. How's that sound to you?" He chuckled quietly at her confused expression. "You think I'm scary, you just wait till you're in the Arkh and you get your first glimpse of a *real* jotunn. Them boys are *this* much bigger'n me"—he stretched his arm to the ceiling, fingers pointing upwards— "and their arms are as thick as an ironwood trunk." He quirked an eyebrow. "The ladies, too."

Demelza blanched and looked worriedly at Jalis.

"Let her be, Maros," Jalis laughed. To Demelza she said, "He's only teasing. He can't help himself."

After a moment, Maros looked pointedly at Jalis and Oriken. With a sigh, he said, "You know, I'm finding it difficult to accept your disinclination to give me any solid details. Someone at Headquarters has dug through historical records about the guild and the Blighted City, and they're likely to look at my vague and frankly boring report and wonder what all the fuss is about. Now, call me a nosey bastard if you like, but I know there's a lot you're not telling me – things you don't want putting on the records, maybe – and as the Caerheath Guild Official it's my duty to keep the top dogs happy."

"They'll be happy with their cut of the reward," Oriken said.

Jalis took a sip of her drink and set the cup on the table. "What historical records?"

"We'll find out soon enough when Leaf arrives. I know you, Jalis, better than I know anyone. If you're sticking to the story that Dagra just fell ill after fiddling with some fungus, then so be it." He lowered his voice to say, "I heard plenty of things spoken by them villagers and the knight. Didn't sound like much to me at the time, but I spent the last days dwelling on it all. I get the secrecy over the details – believe me, I do – but what I don't get is just who you're covering it all up for. And don't say it was for that armoured fellow who don't seem to know what century it is. I picked up enough to fathom he obviously resides in the Blighted City, and whether with or without the peasants, he's not alone." Maros turned a shrewd look on Jalis. "It makes me wonder just *who* put the death's head on the map in the first place. But if what you've given me is what you're sticking to…"

Jalis placed her hand over his. "It is, old friend. And it has to be accepted as the whole story. Please, forget all you heard at Caer Valekha. Let the death's head stay on the map, and let no one else be tempted to set foot in Scapa Fell. There is nothing good to be found there, except perhaps by those seeking an end to this life."

368

"Fine, fine. My report will be straightforward, with no mention of knights, jewelled swords, some feller who's outlived his friends by generations while their heads are stuck in a tree – aye, I caught that bit, too – and, perhaps the most curious of all, the complete absence of Oriken's hat."

Oriken cast him a bemused look. "HQ don't know nothing about my hat."

"They don't know nothing about your arse-clingers, neither." Maros commented, flicking a glance at Oriken's legs. Nice trousers, by the way."

"They're breeches."

"Whatever you say. You got a pair in my size?"

As Oriken took a long pull of ale, the saloon doors swished open and Leaf stepped briskly inside. Spotting Maros, she hurried across and brandished a large, flat leather wallet at him.

"Papers, boss."

"Ah, well done, lass." He took the wallet and flicked a thumb over the parchments within. "Three sheets? Is that it?"

The girl nodded. "Job request, contract, and report. One for each."

He grunted. "Succinct. I'd expected more. No matter. Did you have any problems at the Bay?"

"Yeah..." Leaf said carefully, but her eyes shone with confidence. "Nothing I couldn't handle though."

"Good, good," Maros said distractedly as he riffled through the papers and brought one to his face. "That's what I like to hear. Hm. Writing's too faded. Can't read the damned thing. What's it say?"

Leaf took the parchment from him and read it out. "In the year six-four-one of the Fourth Age. Season of Reibhar. Seventh day of the second week of Silspri. Request made by one Cela Chiddari of Balen, age 20 years. Mission accepted by one Elijah of Alder's Folly, age 28 years. Officiated by—"

"Skip to the gubbins, lass."

She scanned the document. "Blah, blah... to retrieve one heirloom belonging by right to the family of the client... blah, blah... That's about it. The report's no better." Maros handed her the remaining two papers and she trailed a finger down the top sheet. "Mission failed... No return of one Elijah of Alder's Folly after six months following mission commencement. Reward returned to client minus ten percent, that being eight silver dari."

"Eight!" Maros shook his head. "This Elijah feller went down there for a paltry eighty silvers?"

"Aye," Jerrick drawled from his table along the wall. "That he did. Ain't nothin' paltry 'bout that, mind you; not now and certainly not then." The old man loosed a rattling sigh, culminating in a throaty cough. "Well then, you young'uns back there discover what happened to Lijah? Hm?"

Jalis's brow furrowed as she glanced at Oriken and whispered, "Sabrian was the only one. There was no mention of an Elijah."

Oriken looked long at her, and silence filled the common room but for Jerrick's phlegmy breathing. Maros studied Oriken's face, watching as his expression slowly changed, his mouth opening and his eyes growing wider. "Elijah," he said slowly, then glanced to Jerrick. "Lijah. Oh, gods."

Maros scowled. "You know something?"

Oriken looked stunned as he leaned back against the wall. "Oh, that's... And I...." Hissing a curse, he looked again to Jalis. "Lie," he said, his voice thick. "*Liar.*"

Jalis's hand flew to her mouth. "Oh, no."

"What's that you young'uns are muttering over there?" Jerrick called. "Did you find a trace of me old friend or not?"

"Yes." Jalis placed her hand over Oriken's. "We did."

"You'll have to speak up, girl. I can't hear you."

She rose and walked around to pull up a chair beside the old fellow. "Your friend Elijah fulfilled his mission," she said gently as his rheumy eyes watched her lips. "He found what he went for, but he fell on the way home." She brushed a tear away as it slipped down her cheek.

Jerrick nodded and patted her hand. "Thank ye." From his expression, he looked like he was about to say more, but instead his eyes grew distant and he frowned down at his cup.

"Lijah," Oriken muttered. "He recognised us as being like him. He only wanted to tell us his name, and I—"

"*Who?*" Maros's exasperation overflowed. "Are you saying you *met* this fellow? What, is he another who's been wandering around the heath for years? What in the tenth level of the Pit are you talking about? Who wanted to tell you what?"

"No one," Jalis said as she returned to her seat.

Maros grunted. "Why am I not rutting surprised?"

Behind them, Jerrick's chair scraped as he rose to his feet. "Reckon I'll be getting myself away," he mumbled. "Aye, reckon that's for the best." He lifted his cup. "To Lijah. May ye've found peace in Kambesh." Draining the last of his ale, he added, "I'll let your girlie know. Been visitin' her grave each year since she passed. Aye, mayhap the two o' you found each other on't other side."

Maros watched Jerrick shuffle away, and thought to himself, *Gods, the poor bastard. He ain't long for this world. May've been kinder to tell him nothing.* With a sigh, he added, *Then again, he'll likely have forgotten by the morning.* Drawing a breath, he turned to find Leaf waiting patiently at his side. "I got one more job for you, lass, if you'll accept it? Nothing that'll take up too much of your time."

She gave an abrupt nod.

"I need you to run over to Balen and bring back a feller named Randallen. I don't know which is his house, but ask around. There are only a dozen or so."

"Will do."

"Fast as you can, lass. And don't forget the send-off tonight." As the girl strode to the doors, Maros called after her, "Why'd they call you Leaf, anyway?"

She paused and glanced back with a smile.

"Is it the colour of your eyes? Your tunic?"

"Nope."

"What, then?"

"If I told you, boss, you'd be the only man alive who knew."

He nodded slowly, the warning not lost on him.

"I like her," Jalis said as Leaf rushed from the tavern.

"Me too," Demelza said.

"Who's this Rand-whatever you're sending the merchant for?" Oriken asked.

"The client of the whole sorry affair. Well, the beneficiary, at any rate."

Jalis frowned. "What do you mean, beneficiary?"

"Sorry." Maros shrugged. "I forgot to mention. Cela Chiddari died shortly after you left."

A shadow crossed Oriken's face. "Did she now? Reckon she could've done it a week earlier, then there might've been an extra person sitting here right now."

"Maybe so," Jalis said with a glance to Demelza. "And then again, maybe not."

The common room was devoid of patrons save for the first few freeblades to arrive for Dagra's send-off, sat with Oriken and engaged in quiet conversation. Sat upon his stool behind the bar, Maros paid them no mind as he stared across at the saloon doors and brooded – not for the loss of Dagra or how Jalis and Oriken had urged him to keep what he'd witnessed a secret, but over Jalis's imminent departure. The long years he'd been partnered with her had come crashing to a halt a year ago, but he and Jalis were still together even though he'd hung up his blades. Now she was doing the same, but, unlike him, she was leaving the guild completely.

Out with the old and in with the new, he mused, thinking of young Leaf. *The cycle of change is an unstoppable force, and there ain't no such thing as an immovable object in this guild; even the Mountain won't be sticking around forever.*

His ears pricked at the crunch of footfalls beyond the saloon doors. Peering across, he spotted a pair of lower legs striding towards the tavern, and a moment later Randallen Chiddari stepped into the common room, his plaid cap squashed upon his head like a flat mushroom.

"Tavernmaster—"

Maros raised a hand. "One moment." As he hobbled around to the front of the counter, he called for Oriken to join them. "The contract is fulfilled," he told Randallen. Nodding to Oriken, he said, "This is one of the three who retrieved your mother's heirloom."

Randallen looked Oriken up and down. "And the others? I should extend my appreciation to all," he said, his flat tone exuding no gratitude whatsoever, "and it would be easier to thank them all at once."

"One is upstairs," Maros said, "resting after her arduous journey."

"And the other?"

Oriken shot him a cool gaze. "Dead."

Randallen swallowed a cough.

"Ah, shall we take this into the office?" Maros suggested. "It is, after all, a sensitive matter." He led them behind the stairs at the end of the bar and along a short corridor into his private office. Oriken filed in last and closed the door.

Perching against the corner of his desk, Maros cleared his throat. "As I said, your mother's jewel has been retrieved."

"Mm." Randallen flicked a glance at Oriken, but kept from looking him in the eye. "It's... a relief to hear, I suppose."

"I'll bet it is," Oriken said.

Maros fished a keychain from his pocket and limped around the desk, unlocked the office safe and took out a package from within. He hobbled back to Randallen with it wrapped in his fist.

As Randallen reached for the package, Maros withdrew his hand. "Firstly," he said, grabbing a large quill from the desk, "I need your signature here"—he tapped the quill against one of several papers laid out on the desktop—"here"—he tapped a second sheet of paper—"and I'll need your statement of satisfaction and acceptance of completion, with a third signature"—he stabbed at the last parchment—"here."

Randallen drew an impatient breath, took the quill from Maros and dipped it in the inkwell. He leaned over the first piece of paper to scrutinise each word.

"I can assure you that these are the exact papers your mother agreed upon. You can see her signature already on the first two."

"Yes, yes." Randallen scrawled his name beneath his recently deceased mother's, then moved on to the second paper.

Oriken sighed. With a shake of his head, he paced across to the corner of the office and stood with his arms folded, his hard eyes fixed on Randallen.

"It all seems to be in order," Randallen said slowly. He scratched his name onto the second paper and placed the quill on the table. "But I can't very well sign my satisfaction without seeing the goods, can I?"

Maros unwrapped the cloth, and the material draped down his hand to reveal the Chiddari jewel in all its glistening glory.

Randallen's jaw dropped. His eyes widened, then narrowed to a frown as his mouth snapped shut. "It's..."

"Yes," Oriken said. "It really is, isn't it?"

Randallen glanced at him, then at Maros, then back to the jewel. "What's the black thing in the middle?"

"An imperfection, perhaps?" Oriken suggested, his tone a mixture of coldness and indifference. "Then again, maybe just grit. Or, and this is the most probable answer"—he uncrossed his arms and paced around the desk to stand over Randallen—"it *could* be a seed of the corruption that killed my friend."

Randallen stepped hastily backwards, both from Oriken and from the jewel. His fingers rose to cover his mouth and nose. "Corruption, you say?"

Oriken's smile did not touch his eyes. "That's right. A black little deadly piece of shit, full of fucking spores. And now it's yours. Congratulations."

As Maros covered the jewel over, Randallen puffed his cheeks. "Hm. Well. No matter. First thing tomorrow it'll be four feet under, right alongside my mother."

Oriken cast him a sharp look, then snorted. "should'a figured that was her plan all along."

Randallen glared at him. "*What* plan?"

"Forget it," Oriken muttered.

"Such practices might be irregular," Maros said in an attempt to diffuse the tension, "but they're not unlawful."

"Hmph." Randallen removed his cap and gripped it to his chest. "Don't start me on how distasteful I find the whole burial thing. It was mother's wish to be buried and to have that thing laid next to her, and it was *me* who had to dig the hole and heave her casket inside. And what do *I* get out of it?" He shook his head. "Nothing, of course. If you hadn't brought it back, at least I'd be getting ninety percent of her savings returned."

Oriken shook his head, narrowing his eyes contemptuously at the man. "The Chiddari line really did drop in quality, didn't it?"

"I beg your pardon?"

"Tell me, did your mother say *why* she wanted to be buried with the deadst— er, the jewel?"

Randallen barked a laugh. "Did she tell me why she preferred to rot rather than go to the Underland? Of course she didn't! I'd invite you to try getting a word out of the old hag, except for the fact that she's quite ripe at the moment."

Oriken tilted his eyes to the ceiling, drew a deep breath, then fixed a hard look on Randallen. "Now listen here, fellow. You don't seem too upset that you lost your mother. I lost mine when I was a boy, to a lyakyn, of all the bastards that roam this world. Not long before that, my father was murdered. Mother scarcely had chance to mourn. But, more than that"—he slapped a hand onto Maros's arm—"*we* lost a damned good friend out there while retrieving this rock for you."

"For my mother."

"To be honest, I've only been in your company for five minutes and I'm already sick of the sight of you. Carry on pushing me, and I'll personally throw you into your mother's fucking grave and bury you with her." Oriken glared at the plaid cap as Randallen clutched it nervously to his chest. "*And* your hat is stupid."

Randallen's jaw dropped.

"Please." Oriken took a step closer. "Say one word."

Maros held out the quill.

———. • .———

Jalis nodded as she listened to Maros finish reciting the altercation with Cela Chiddari's son. "Well," she sighed, folding a pair of leggings and glancing through the mirror at Oriken slouched against her wardrobe, "let's just hope he doesn't file a grievance against us. We don't want Headquarters' attention on this, no more than it needs to be." *There's no 'we' any more*, she told herself. *Not after tonight.*

Maros crossed his arms. "Oriken had the right of it though, lass. That Randallen is an unsightly stain, and, from what I've heard from some o' the lads around town, he's also a suspected degenerate. If he draws attention to us, he draws it to himself."

Jalis placed the leggings on the dresser and looked across at her bed, where Demelza lay with her knees tucked to her chest, quietly watching the exchange.

"I'm just glad we're rid of that deadstone," Jalis said.

Demelza nodded in agreement.

A thought came to Jalis. "Damn," she said. "I never did find out about the Drilos runes. And now Cela's dead…"

Maros looked at Oriken. "What's she talking about?"

Oriken shrugged. "Something about some god or other. Don't pay it any mind. You know how she gets." He looked at Jalis. "It's over. Let's just leave it behind us."

Jalis gave a dismissive grunt as she watched Maros regarding her stack of clothes upon the dresser. She'd lain the stiff corselette and puffy blouse – both of which once belonged to Gorven's long-dead wife – in a separate pile beside the others. Maros turned a shrewd eye on her, but said nothing.

I'm sorry, old friend, she thought. *I hate not being able to tell you.* In an attempt to make light of the moment, she quirked an eyebrow at him and said, "Didn't you notice the quality clothiers down by Dulèth? I could swear Orik pointed it out to you on the way home."

Maros snorted. "I never said nothing." Stabbing a finger at her, he added, "But I expect to hear it one day." He clasped his hands together. "Time to drink. Let's head down and join the others."

"One moment." Jalis crouched beside Demelza. "We'll be gone a while," she told her. "It could get noisy downstairs, but don't be scared. I'll come back later to see how you are. If you need anything, you might find one of the maids in the spare room at the end of the corridor. Alright?" Demelza nodded. Jalis touched the girl's shoulder as the men filed from the room, then she rose to join them.

As she clicked the door shut behind her, Maros said to Oriken, "What do you propose to do with Dagra's cut of the earnings?"

"They should go to his grandparents. Ilhdra and Gafrid watched over me during my last couple of years in Eyndal. They're almost family to me. I'll deliver the money to them personally."

"It'll take you the better part of a month to get up to the Kadelia Downs," Jalis said as they made their way to the stairs.

"I know."

"I told Demelza I'd take her to the port, organise an escort with the Ashcloaks."

"Then that's what you should do." Oriken paused at the top of the stairs and fixed her with a sombre look. "It's okay, Jalis. You go your way and I'll go mine. Besides, it's only right that I do this one alone."

"When will you leave?"

He shrugged.

The promises we make, she thought as she headed down to the common room. *The trials we go through. And yet, somehow, it all still falls apart...*

———— • ————

Maros perched upon the service counter and planted the boot of his good leg firmly upon a stool, letting his ruined leg dangle to the floor. For a disconcerting moment he felt like a cheap, ugly imitation of the enigmatic Taleweaver that had sat at the exact same place several years earlier, and he knew that while the Taleweaver had everyone enthralled with his wondrous stories, the speech Maros was about to make would not be met with the same spellbound expressions.

He roved his eyes across the freeblades that were gathered around the four largest tables set close together at the back of the room. All ranks were present, from novice to bladesmaster. *And bladesmistress* he thought as his gaze landed on Jalis. Thirty five had gathered to pay their respects – every freeblade who wasn't out on a contract, plus Luthan.

"Another of our number has taken the swan's path," Maros announced, his voice rumbling softly through the room. The chatter ceased and he glanced from one to the next until he'd made eye contact with everyone. "Losing a friend and a colleague is never easy, no matter your rank, no matter how many notches of losses you have on your blade or bow.

"I've been in this game for twenty years, the last four in Alder's Folly. I came here with three colleagues – one old friend and two fresh faces to the guild. Me and Jalis took Oriken and Dagra under our wings and watched them climb from novices to journeymen."

He paused to draw a breath and slowly release it. "The one truth we must all face as freeblades is that death is always somewhere around the corner, no matter how hard we train or how high we climb. For Dagra, as for many of those we knew and loved, it came too early. The how of it don't matter, and there's never a sense in asking why; it just is. Dagra's time came, as the gods willed it. Or as the stars willed it. Or as fuck all willed it. He's gone now. Maybe he'll be reborn in the Underland. Maybe he'll be taken into the Void to dwell with the Unbound. Maybe nothing. None of that's important to me; what is important is how our friend lived, and what he stood for.

"Not a day went by when I didn't admire that lad. He lived by his own code, as do we all, and he embraced the code of the guild, as have we all. Some of us hang our blades up." Maros raised a hand and flashed a congenial smile. "Aye, I'm one of 'em. But those who die never hang their blades on the wall, and Dagra's continues within the guild at Oriken's side. In that way, Dagra is still a freeblade." His gaze encompassed all four tables. "Once a freeblade…"

"Always a freeblade," came the combined response of all seated, spoken in reverent tones.

Maros caught Jalis's eye. She'd only muttered the words, but he understood. He gave her the briefest of nods, hoisted himself down from the bar and raised his tankard. "To Dagra!"

"To Dagra!" The staccato response hung in the air, like a wisp of fae-fire fading away.

CHAPTER FORTY ONE
THE SYMMETRY OF DISTANCE

The evening wore on and the drink flowed as the three serving girls glided from table to kitchen to bar and back again. No cups tonight but tankards, brought out for the special occasion, not that Oriken could see much special about it at all. He sat with his back to the wall, barely listening to the babble of conversation around him while his ale-fuelled brain wandered from moment to detached moment back in the furthest reaches of the Deadlands...

"Is life without purpose a life at all?" Gorven had mused. *"Or is it merely an existence?"*

He recalled Krea's face as she glistened in the steam, her blue eyes shining with experience and vitality. *"I'll forgive your ignorance,"* she'd told him sternly, *"and your bull-headed disinclination to open yourself to reason."* Laughing silently to himself, he stared into his ale as her parting words whispered in his ear. *"Well then, my outlander. If you ever decide to return, don't leave it too long."*

And then there was Sabrian, taking a long pull on the tobah. *"Immortality comes at a hefty price,"* he'd told Oriken. *"If I could trade my existence for yours, I might be sorely tempted to do so. And, with my few remaining decades, I would head out into Verragos and fill my life with meaning."*

Oriken's mind drifted forwards to the night when the proverbial black clouds twinkled briefly with a silver lining, as Jalis had placed her hand on his chest and whispered, *"I can feel your heart beating,"* and he'd paused as their bodies touched, her face a perfect vision in the moonlight. *"You do this, and you do it now."*

As he glanced to the next table, where Jalis sat beside Alari, nodding and listening to the seasoned freeblade's chatter, Dagra's voice came to him with sudden clarity: *"Are we tail-tuckers or are we freeblades?"*

"We're freeblades," Oriken said.

"Aye, that we are."

Oriken flicked his eyes to Henwyn.

The bowman raised a tankard to his lips and took a drink, then winced and glanced at his forearm. "Third glass of the strongest wine in the house, and the wound's still smarting." He looked at Oriken. "Copper for your thoughts?"

Oriken rested his head against the wall. "Just contemplating my place in the world."

Henwyn nodded. "As do we all, from time to time. Especially in moments like this."

Young Kirran was watching them from across the table. "Gods, man," he said to Oriken. "No offence, but you look like you stepped back in time to fight in the Uprising. Are you sure the Deadlands were as empty as they're meant to be?"

Oriken glanced down at his calloused, scabbed hands and visualised the numerous cuts and bruises his body had sustained over the last weeks from cravants, corpses, Mallak, the peasants, even the little critter that had tried to liquidise his innards as he slept. The wounds were all on the mend. The swelling around his eye had disappeared and the purple bruise was fading fast. They were all remnants, soon to be ghosts, though some would become permanent scars.

"There were a few monsters down in the sticks," he admitted to Kirran, with a nonchalant shrug. "But show me a place where there are no monsters, and I'll show you a place where there are no men."

The serving girl, Diela, glided across from the bar, an empty wooden tray in her hands. "Who's for a refill?"

Oriken drained the last of his ale. He summoned a weak smile as he passed her his tankard. As Diela wandered away, he took the case of tobah from his pocket and said to Henwyn, "Next drink's my last." He took a candle from the table and crossed to the saloon doors, stepped out into the night and set the candle into an empty sconce. He lit a roll of tobah and slowly exhaled a spume of smoke, watching it cascade over the flickering candle to dissipate into the darkness. As he eased himself onto the bench, an errant breeze caressed his face and guttered the flame. Taking another pull on the tobah, he slouched forward with his elbows on his knees and filtered out the chatter that drifted from the common room.

His reverie was stirred by the crunch of dirt under heels and the *swish-swish* of the saloon doors. Glancing across, he saw Luthan pause to straighten his shirt and vest. The chef inclined his head in greeting and the candlelight pitched his eyes into shadow before setting reflections into his pale irises.

"First time I've seen you out of your whites," Oriken said.

"It is a rarity," Luthan admitted with a smile. He paused a moment, then said, "You know, it wasn't easy for me to leave my home when Maros offered me the job of head chef here. As much as I loved my life in Aster and the surrounding dales, I had little to keep me there; no wife, no children, no regrets. The one thing that tugged at me, that tried to keep me there, was the land itself – the northern mountains, the golden-white sands, the magnificent dawn that sets the sea ablaze. These are the ties that bind us to one place or another. I'd be lying if I said I don't miss Asterdale; I do, but I'm glad I accepted Maros's offer to join him in the Peddler, and I'm glad to have met so many I can proudly name as friends. Dagra was one. You are, too."

Oriken rose from the bench. "I appreciate that. And I know what you're telling me."

"The pain will fade. The memories, too, but the most important of them will stay forever. That's the nature of pivotal moments in a person's life. It's all about the road we travel"—he tapped his fingers to his chest—"in here."

Oriken nodded and offered his hand to the chef. "Thank you, Luthan. And thank you for joining us tonight. It means a lot to me."

Luthan's hand clenched Oriken's, and his eyes shimmered with empathy. "It was an honour." He released Oriken's grip and walked away, the crunch of his footfalls fading into the night.

Oriken ran a hand through his hair, then took a final, long suck on the roll of tobah before stubbing it out and dropping it into a keg beside the bench.

I miss you, Dag, he thought. *I know I always will. But I damn well miss my hat, too.*

He returned to the common room and mingled with the remaining freeblades for the duration of his final drink, exchanging pleasantries, weathering condolences, and side-stepping questions. Draining the last mouthful of his ale, he set the tankard down and wandered over to stand behind Jalis. Placing his hands on her shoulders, he leaned down, his face close to hers. "I've had about as much as I can take for the night," he told her quietly. "I'm heading upstairs."

She half-turned, her lips close to his. Before she could answer, Alari leaned across with a conspiratorial wink. "I love you, girl," the veteran said. "You know that. But now you're hanging your blades up, I'm reckoning Oriken might be in sore need of some company." She smiled slyly up at him. "For the contracts, of course. What say you, feller?"

"Maybe, Alari," he said with a tired smile. "Maybe."

His hands slipped from Jalis's shoulders and he bid a hasty farewell. Striding to the stairs, he swayed and grasped the bannister to steady himself, glancing back to see Jalis looking at him. He held her gaze for a moment, then climbed the stairs and wandered along the corridor to step into his darkened room.

With the moon of Haleth hidden behind the clouds, only vague outlines guided his way as he crossed to stand beside the bed. He removed his boots and socks and tossed them into the corner where Dagra's gladius leaned alongside the blade Ammenfar. He stripped to his skin and slowly stretched his tired muscles. As he finished and sat upon the bed, he noticed Jalis stood poised within the open doorway, her curves cast in silhouette by the muted glow of the corridor.

"I didn't hear you," he said.

"I didn't want you to." She stepped into the room and closed the door. Kicking one shoe off, then the next, she released the bow of her chemise and drew it over her head, dropped the thin material to the boards without a sound. Then she pushed her leggings down and slipped them over her feet.

Oriken traced the shadows of her body as she glided across to stand before him and rest her warm hands on his shoulders. Gently, she forced him down until his back rested upon the sheets. The clouds broke and twin crescents shone in Jalis's eyes as her lips curled into the lopsided smile he'd seen so little of since they entered that far-away graveyard.

The memories will fade, he thought as he rose to kiss her. *But the most important ones will stay. Forever.*

In the hour before sun-up, the forest of Eihazwood was all streaks and swathes of black and grey as Ral glanced over his shoulder to the glow of lanterns from his cottage's rear window. Dropping the pack containing his mother's entire worth to the needle-strewn ground, he turned to regard the open grave before him.

He drew in a breath, eager to get the task over with but scarcely possessing the nerve to do so. "Hello, Mother," he sighed.

The headstone looked unimpressed, and the lid of the deeply-shadowed casket three feet below uttered no response. He gave a start as leaves shuffled nearby, and glanced along the ground to frown at a tiny rodent as it scuttled onto the second grave, paused, sniffed the air, then scurried behind the moss-strewn headstone. A fresh squirt of birdshit adorned the grave marker's front, partially concealing the name *Daneira* and the date *641* below.

"And hello, Grandmother," he said tiredly. He'd never met the woman, and all he knew of her was through his mother's oft-spoken fondness of her, showing that she cared more about the dead than the living. With a derisive sniff, he turned his attention back to the casket where his mother's body lay, weeks past fresh. The knowledge alone was almost enough to make him lose his nerve, not to mention the contents of his stomach, but he fought against them both.

"Some people think I never loved or respected you," he muttered. "I did. All I wanted was to provide security for my family, and for you to be at rest in the proper, gods-given way – *not* like this."

An acrid taste rose in his throat and he coughed; swallowing it down, he sank to his knees and rummaged into the backpack for the jewel. "You don't know how tempted I am to take you to the jewellers in Brancosi, or to the bank," he told it, shaking his head. "You could net me some serious dari. But then what?" Spitting upon the ground, he dropped to his belly and reached for the casket lid. As he eased it open, the stench of decay blasted into his face. His stomach heaved and he retched, raised the lid higher and tossed the jewel inside. It landed with a soft, wet *thunk*.

"Oh… Gods above and below…" He scrambled to the side and vomited loudly, while high above in the boughs of a maple, a nightingale trilled a liquid song as if cheering his display.

Rising to his feet, he regarded the pile of regurgitated food. "The job is done," he gasped, wiping a sleeve across his mouth. "Your final wish is granted. I hope you're happy." Snatching up a shovel, he plunged it into a soft mound of soil and glared down at the casket.

"Rest in peace, Mother, and may the Dyad guide your soul." He slung the dirt into the hole and watched it scatter across the lid. With a snort, he muttered, "Not fucking likely, in either case."

———— • ————

Oriken awoke alone, tired and tangled in the bedsheets. He cracked his eyes open and glanced through the window; the deep red of dawn hung behind the town's roofs and the forest beyond, painting the buildings in the deepest crimson. Kicking the sheets away, he sat up and ruffled his hands through his hair. With a groan, he slung himself from the bed and wrapped a towel around his waist, padded from the room and made his way down to the yard. After using the outhouse, he crossed to the washroom to brush his teeth, scrape the journey's growth from his face, and scrub himself down in the cool water left in the tub from the previous day. Drying himself off, he wandered back through the silent tavern and returned to his room.

From the wardrobe he took Gorven's freshly-washed breeches and pulled them on, followed by a tan drawstring shirt and his less-worn, hard-leather boots. As he fastened the straps, his gaze landed on a folded square of black material upon the dresser. Smiling to himself, he reached over and took the cloth, flicked it open and wrapped it around the top of the breeches; as he stood, the embroidered crossed-blades dropped to gather neatly at his thigh. The two gladiuses were still attached to his swordbelt as he clasped it around his hips; settling them into place, he selected his best coat of soft brown leather and pulled it on, the hem hanging just below the jewelled crossguard of Ammenfar.

He paused as the fringes of a memory rose from nowhere, his mood brightening as he reached his hand to the back of an otherwise empty shelf. His fingers found the object he'd stuffed there and forgotten about, an item acquired from a bandit leader during the golden days when he, Dagra, Jalis and Maros were an inseparable team. With a chuckle, he grasped the crown of the cow-hide hat and placed it on his head, pinched the lightly-curved brim and twisted it just-so.

"That's what I'm talking about," he said with a grin.

He turned to face the mirror, and nodded in approval. Everything had changed, and it was time to go it alone, whether he liked it or not. The long journey to Eyndal would give him enough time to sort through the tumult of emotions and questions he had about himself and his future. "Perhaps a spell of solitude will do me some good," he muttered to his reflection.

He gathered all the essentials he would need for the road, plus a few extras, and stashed them all into two packs. With a last, wistful glance around the room, he stepped out, locked the door and palmed the key. He walked quietly along to Maros's door and gave it a gentle knock. Within moments, Maros opened the door and peered out.

"You're up early," Maros said, eyeing Oriken's attire. "Going somewhere?"

"Yeah, I'm going somewhere," Oriken said, beginning to feel the weight of his decision. He passed the key to Maros. "Can you keep this in the safe for me?"

"What's going on, lad?" Maros poked his head around the door and glanced along the corridor.

"Dagra's family needs to know," Oriken said. "It's not just his grandparents, but his uncle and aunt, nieces and nephews, too. It's only right, and shouldn't be delayed. They have to hear it from me, not a nameless guild messenger."

Maros nodded. "You'll be wanting his savings then."

"And his wooden idols of the Dyad, if you'd get them from his room for me. I think Gafrid and Ilhdra would appreciate something to remember him by. It's scant comfort, but it's better than nothing."

Maros regarded him for a long moment, then said, "Give me a few minutes, lad."

"I'll be downstairs."

He made his way to the common room and climbed onto a barstool, rested an elbow on the counter and planted his freshly-shaved chin on his knuckled fist. A feeling of melancholy drifted over him, but with it came a sense of acceptance amid the hollowness that had dominated his heart since Dagra's death. His hand strayed to the pommel of Ammenfar, touching the oval of thunderglass, and he smiled to himself as he remembered the similarly-sized oval of bloodstone that was still within the side pocket of one of the packs.

I'll pay a visit to a smithy on the way to the Downs, he promised himself, then closed his thoughts and waited.

After a few minutes, Maros came creaking and grunting down the stairs, a sheen of sweat on his brow as he reached the bottom. He limped across to the bar and held his hand out to Oriken. Two small figurines nestled in his large palm, one of Aveia, one of Svey'Drommelach. "Here you go, lad," he said.

382

Oriken took the idols and stashed them inside a pack while Maros limped down to his office. When he returned, he dropped a heavy money pouch onto the counter. "One hundred and fifty silver dari pieces. Plus another thirty three which Dagra saved up." He fished in his pocket and took out three silvers, dropping them into Oriken's palm. "Figured you'll want to keep a little at close hand for the road. You sure you don't want any of your own coins?"

Oriken shook his head as he pushed the pouch deep within a backpack. "If I need any, I'll fill out a chit with the nearest branch."

"You might want to buy yourself a mule," Maros suggested. "Sure you could find a scrawny one for a few silvers. It's a long road, and a little company's better than none."

"I might just do that."

"Does Jalis know you're leaving already?"

Oriken sighed. "No. I didn't want to wake her. Besides, she's likely got her hands full with Dee."

Maros eyed him carefully. "I'm no fool, lad. Don't think I can't see the change that's come between the two of you. I care for you, Oriken, like a brother and a son all combined. But I love Jalis as much as you loved Dagra. Don't hurt her."

Oriken pressed his lips together. "It's been a trying time for all of us – including you, I know. I don't think Jalis or I know yet where we're going. We both need time to figure things out. I'd never hurt her, and I hope you know that. I hope she knows it, too."

Maros clasped his hands to Oriken's shoulders. "You do what you need to. See you in a couple of months?"

"Possibly." He pulled his eyes from Maros's scrutiny and glanced to the saloon doors, to the brightening sky beyond. "Possibly."

———— · ·————

As the first light of Banael burst over the woodland, Jalis stood at her window and looked down to the streets, watching as Oriken made his way through the town.

Goodbye, Orik. She allowed a tear to fall unchecked to her nightshirt. *I wish I could send you a thought as easily as they do down in Lachyla.*

Behind her, Demelza stirred in the bed they'd shared. The girl yawned and glanced over.

"Good morning," Jalis said, hiding her sadness with a smile. "Did you sleep well?"

"Better'n I 'ave in ages. It's nice to, er…" Demelza's brow furrowed as she searched for the right word.

"Snuggle?" Jalis stepped over and perched on the bed.

Demelza looked unsure.

Jalis laughed softly. "Yes, it *is* nice."

As Demelza sat up, Jalis's spare shift hung loose on her thin frame. "When do we go to the cosy, ah, I mean the Brancosi Bay?"

Jalis reached out and stroked Demelza's hair, clean from the previous day's hot bath. "We can leave whenever you feel ready. But remember, Dee, Brancosi Bay is only the first step in a long journey."

Demelza nodded. "I know."

Jalis placed her arm around the girl's shoulder and drew her closer. *Oh, you don't know, little siosi. You really don't know at all.*

Made in the USA
Las Vegas, NV
26 April 2025

21402674R00229